Daughter
of the
Yellow Dragon

Fractured Empire Book One

Starr Z. Davies

PANGEA
BOOKS

Starr Z. Davies/Pangea Books
www.starrzdavies.com
www.pangeabooks.online

Publisher's Note: While some of the events and characters are based on historical incidents and figures, this novel is entirely a work of fiction. Locales and public names are sometimes used for atmospheric purposes.

Book Layout ©2021 Pangea Books
Cover Design copyright ©2021 Pangea Books
Map copyrights ©2021 Starr Z. Davies
Icon illustration by Norovsambuughn Baatartsog

1] Historical Fiction 2] Asian History 3] Forbidden Romance 4] Historical Military Fiction 5] Women in History

Daughter of the Yellow Dragon/Starr Z. Davies – 1st ed.
ISBN 978-1-7363459-1-7

CHAPTERS

For Jack

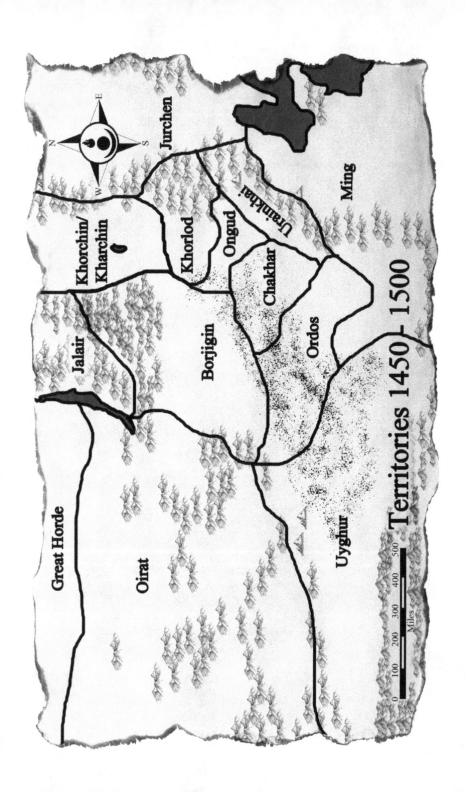

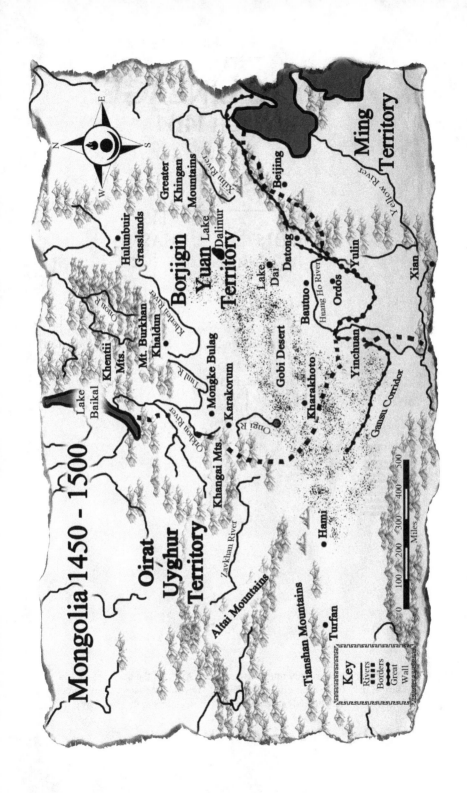

ROYAL LINEAGE
THROUGH 1464

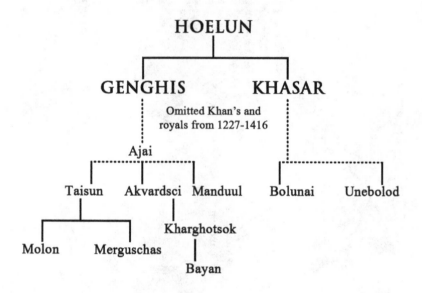

HOELUN

GENGHIS   KHASAR

Omitted Khan's and
royals from 1227-1416

Ajai

Taisun   Akvardsci   Manduul   Bolunai   Unebolod

Kharghotsok

Molon   Merguschas

Bayan

While there are certainly other royals before Ajai, for the purposes of this series, only those after him will be listed to avoid confusion. Esen is not listed on this chart because he does not descend from this royal tree.

Under the Eternal Blue Sky,
the Great Genghis Khan blessed our lands,
brought order to the disordered, and gave us heirs.

Along the White Road, His descendants walked,
expanding our empire until desire overcame pride.

And from this Black Road came the curse of the rabbit demon,
the desire to covert what was not ours, to draw blood for blood.

Soon after, all that remained of the once Great Khan's descendants
was bathed in blood and lost to time like sands in the Gobi.

As the age declined, we fell into disorder,
abandoned our cities and retreated to the north, licking our wounds.

BOY IN THE BASKET

EAST OF KHYARGAS LAKE – KHANGAI MOUNTAINS – SUMMER 1453

Thunder rumbled across the foothills of the Khangai Mountains, created by the hammer of hundreds of hooves pounding against the unforgiving rocky ground. Another volley of arrows whistled across the wide blue sky toward Lady Samur's hand-selected warriors. Unebolod didn't dare glance back as he heard a horse squeal and crash against the rocky earth, tumbling end over end and crushing the rider, or as dust coated his face and made his mouth dry. He didn't slow to assess the number of casualties this most recent volley claimed. Escape was paramount. He had given his word, and his word was iron. Being given such an important task at barely fifteen had made him determined to succeed and prove his worth.

It also offered him a chance to avenge his family by undermining Esen's reign.

Unebolod leaned closer to his own horse, urging it onward at breakneck speed. They passed spotty lines of fir trees in a blur of motion, their scent mingling with the smell of horse and body odor. The horse bobbed its head and huffed out quick breaths. It was a fine horse Lady Samur had given him, and one of the fastest, but it couldn't outrun arrows.

Esen's men outnumbered his own twenty to one. Unebolod and the rest of Lady Samur's warriors had attempted to make a stand, fighting Esen's own elite warrior, but they could not hold against superior fighters in superior numbers.

"Above all else, the Borjigin heir must survive," Samur had urged her men when she had set them upon this critical task. "Above me. Above your men. Above you. Bayan is the last blood and bone of the Great Khan, Genghis, the last true son of the Borjigin tribe and your future Great Khan. If he falls into the hands of Esen's men, he will not survive."

Unebolod vowed to escape Esen's grasp, along with the rest of the men riding with him, and deliver the three-year-old child to the safety of Lady Samur's allies in the east—Unebolod's own brother and Khorchin tribe. He knew that was the reason Lady Samur chose selected him, but it still filled him with self-importance.

A vow was a vow, and his word was iron.

Unebolod had tied the child in a basket for safety. He was youngest and lightest of all the men, so they had tasked him with care of the basket for a quicker ride. They had hidden the basket in a hole in the ground near the Khangai foothills before engaging Esen's men in battle. If none returned to Bayan, the child would die in that basket.

"Unebolod!" Altan called from beside him. Altan glanced over his shoulder and ducked low to his horse as an arrow narrowly missed the space his head had just occupied. "This will not work. The Oirat will overrun us or kill us with arrows in short time."

Unebolod risked a glance back, clutching the reins in tight fists. He swore a vow to Lady Samur that he would see this done and escort the boy to his own tribe where Bayan would be safe. His own brother had returned weeks ago to secure control over their Khorchin tribe.

My word is iron, he thought, remembering those same words from his own father. Oaths were unbreakable. Without honor, a man had nothing, and Unebolod was determined to prove himself a man.

"Let us circle around and engage the force to buy you time to make off with the child," Altan said.

Unebolod reached for his bow, but Altan shook his head.

"It has to be you. Go. Retrieve Bayan Mongke and take him to your brother as Lady Samur commanded."

Unebolod eased his grip on the bow and returned all his attention to the foothills where the basket waited.

Altan released a ferocious war cry, "For the Borjigin! For the Great Khan!"

The rest of Unebolod's companions broke off, circling their horses around to engage with Esen's men, bows drawn and arrows already returning fire.

The horse beneath Unebolod continued snorting as he veered away from battle toward the foothills, hooves beating the ground. But not loud enough to drown out the clash of battle he had left behind. Men shouted. Arrows whistled in the air. Swords clashed. Horses whinnied and shrieked.

The sounds soon receded and Unebolod fell into rhythm with his horse, leaning close to maintain full speed. His own body bobbed in tandem with the dip of the horse's head, taking short, even breaths with the beast. The Khangai Mountains rose higher as he neared them, their rocky majesty providing a promise of success—of escape.

Bayan Mongke was close. Unebolod would retrieve the basket, secure it to his horse, and escape into the mountains where Esen's men dared not go. Too many opposed Esen so far to the east after he had murdered so many of the Borjigin lords. Borjigin loyalists crawled the mountain passes waiting to pick off any who dared enter, but for one exception.

Bayan Mongke. The future of Mongolia. A true Borjigin prince.

The familiar sound of approaching horses echoed off the foothills. Unebolod hoped the men had succeeded in routing Esen's force. His horse was slowing and wouldn't be able to run much longer. Unebolod reduced the pace slightly, hoping to increase the distance they could travel before the horse gave out.

The hooves closed the distance with each passing breath. Unebolod glanced back, only to have his hopes dashed.

Esen's men approached. Only a handful remained, either successfully killing Lady Samur's men or breaking formation to pursue him while the others engaged in battle. At the rate they closed in, Unebolod could not afford to stop and pick up the basket. He could not afford to lose any speed before reaching the protection of the mountain pass.

The handle of the wicker basket peeked over the edge of the hole in the distance. Unebolod checked the progress of Esen's men. Fifty yards. At this pace, his horse might just barely make it into the pass before they closed in on him.

He could still outrun them. As long as he didn't slow his speed.

The basket was close now, and Unebolod didn't have the luxury of time to decide on a suitable course of action. Instead, he followed his instincts and let his father's training kick in.

Unebolod removed the string from his bow with a swipe of his hand, tucking the string in the belt of his deel. Without the string, the limbs of the bow curled outward into a hooked shape. Unebolod wrapped the reins around one hand, which he used to grasp the pommel of the saddle in a sturdy grip. In the other hand, he turned his bow to use as a hook. Applying his thighs for balance and strength, he shifted his body to the side to bend closer to the ground. With a mighty swoop, Unebolod hooked the basket handle with a limb of his bow and tossed it into the air ahead of him with a powerful thrust.

Esen's men persisted, but their focus shifted to the basket as it tumbled from the wide blue sky toward the earth. A few arrows zipped toward the basket, narrowly missing the wicker.

Unebolod held his breath as he righted himself in the saddle and released the death-grip on the reins. Knees guiding the horse forward and holding his balance, Unebolod stood and stretched toward the basket. It fell perfectly in his outstretched hands.

The men giving chase released a war cry.

Unebolod let out a whoop of victory and maintained his speed as he secured the basket to the horse.

Then the two of them raced into the mountain pass where other tribes were waiting to provide cover.

Esen's men did not stop. Not even as the arrows of the other tribes hiding in the upper passes of the mountains rained death down on them. Not until the very last of them died behind Unebolod.

CHAPTER ONE

SPIRIT OF KHUTULUN

ONGUD TERRITORY – EASTERN MONGOLIA – SPRING 1464

A warm breeze ruffled the hem of Mandukhai's riding *deel*—a simple tunic wrap worn by the Mongol people. The spring breeze carried with it the promise of a coming summer, and she closed her eyes, smelling the fresh grass in the air and savoring this moment of peace.

All around her, the Ongud tribe busied themselves loading carts with the promised bride-price. Women fussed over linens and chests of precious silver and jewels. Men checked the horses and oxen to ensure they were prepared for the journey ahead. Mandukhai did her best to ignore them all, to ignore her fate. The bones had been cast; the bargains struck.

Mandukhai would marry Manduul Khan, the ruler of the Mongol nation and a man she had never laid eyes on.

Ten steps away, her mother and step-father consulted with the soothsayer once more before her departure to be certain Mandukhai's journey would be without peril. She wished she could not hear their conversation, but the breeze also carried with it the hushed words.

"It is assured," Soothsayer Getei said confidently. He glanced her way. She pretended not to notice. "Your daughter will become the queen and bring honor to your family and her father's name."

5

Mandukhai had only just turned sixteen, and the last thing she dreamed of was becoming a queen. As a girl, her father had told her stories of Khutulun, the fierce warrior princess and daughter of Qaidu Khan of the Chagatai Khanate nearly two hundred years ago. Khutulun earned the respect of the men around her with her superb fighting skills. The tales Mandukhai's father had spun depicted Khutulun as superhuman, able to ride into enemy ranks and snatch captives as easily as a hawk could snatch a chicken. Mandukhai could also ride with proficiency, shoot with accuracy, and hunt with stealth. Her father instilled a deep desire to be strong and respected like Khutulun.

I do not want to be a queen, father, she thought, folding her hands into the sleeves of her *deel. I want to be a warrior, like Khutulun.*

But a bargain had been struck between Mandukhai's tribe and the Great Khan's advisors. The Oirat had a stranglehold on the Great Khan's trust, and after Mandukhai's father betrayed Esen, Lord of the Oirat, when she was only four, the Ongud had struggled to maintain peace between the opposing sides of a war. Mandukhai was the peace offering. Daughter of the Ongud and of the very man who betrayed Esen, she was the perfect choice. They had promised her to another Great Khan, years before, but he died before Mandukhai came of age. She had hoped that his death would bring about her freedom.

She never envisioned herself as a prize or a Khan's wife. The young dreamer in her had always fantasized about meeting a strong man able to best her in wrestling or archery, someone who understood how to read the Eternal Blue Sky and predict the weather. Someone who knew how to live the life of a nomad as she did. A man who could see her for who she was and not just as a potential womb for sons.

"It is time," her mother said, guiding Mandukhai's horse by the reigns.

Mandukhai shuddered.

Her mother's forehead creased in sympathy. "Any girl would be thrilled to make such a match. You have been gifted a great honor, Mandukhai. You will be respected and cared for. Your marriage brings us peace, and your children will inherit the Nation."

But Mandukhai didn't want to be cared for. She was perfectly capable of caring for herself—to ride with proficiency, shoot with accuracy, and hunt with stealth.

Knowing this was goodbye, and that she may never see her mother again, Mandukhai thrust her arms around her mother and hugged her tight.

Such displays were for children, but if these were her final days as a child, Mandukhai intended making the most of them.

Her mother hugged her back and whispered in her ear, "Remember what I told you about men. Be wary of who you trust. Keep Nergui close. He is sworn first to protect you above all others."

"I will," Mandukhai murmured back before letting go.

The withdraw of her mother's arms sharpened the cool spring air. Mandukhai wanted to retreat back into her embrace.

"Lady Mandukhai," Nergui said from several feet away, mounted and ready to ride.

Mandukhai spun around, scanning the carts and seeking any excuse to delay the inevitable.

They had packed her felts onto a cart—felts she had dedicated years to pressing from wool for the future structure her husband's family would provide. All was in order.

Once more, Mandukhai said goodbye to her mother, who sniffed one cheek. Mandukhai prayed her mother would not sniff the other. When she did, Mandukhai's heart fell into the pit of her stomach. Her mother did not expect to see her again.

Raising her chin proudly, afraid of showing any sign of weakness to her tribe, Mandukhai mounted her horse and started her journey away from the eastern steppes of her Ongud tribe to Mongke Bulag where Manduul Khan had established his capitol. She didn't look back as her mother made offerings of milk to the earth mother.

The saddle creaked as Mandukhai rode beside Nergui, surrounded by a distant guard of men. Only one servant accompanied Mandukhai. The rest would be supplied by the Great Khan once they married.

Two young girls from the tribe had come along, but one had died one week into the trip after drinking unboiled river water. The other girl had had a fever. Mandukhai had attempted mixing silver shavings into the girl's tea each night so the magical properties of the metal could heal her. The fever finally took the second girl as well. None of the silver could heal the girl's ailment. Mandukhai's one job was to protect them and keep them in the Great Khan's court until they found a suitable marriage match. She had failed before even arriving.

At night, she heard the men whisper when she was supposed to be sleeping. Such death proved an ill omen. Once she was delivered and they had attended the marriage festivities in honor of the Ongud, they would return home and leave her to her fate. Only Nergui and Tuya would remain behind to protect her. The men sounded eager to wash their hands of her.

The hushed conversations drove Mandukhai closer to Nergui's side on days such as today, where the men rode in a ring far enough that even their arrows would not reach her.

Nergui observed their surrounds as if expecting attacks to come from thin air. His vigilance was admirable, but she felt it a bit unnecessary with so many others around them.

Their group was set to arrive in Mongke Bulag before sundown. A rider had been sent ahead to alert the Great Khan's men of her arrival.

"What can you tell me of Lady Yeke?" Nergui asked for the hundredth time.

The politics of the court had been hammered into Mandukhai's memory for months, and Nergui tested her knowledge every day to be sure she retained the information.

"Lady Yeke is Manduul Khan's first wife, and daughter of the Great Khan's Vice Regent, Bigirsen of the Uyghur," Mandukhai recited, followed by a puff of irritation. "Her marriage to the Great Khan created an alliance between the southern tribes and the Yuan."

Nergui watched her, waiting. She knew what he waited for.

"Lord Bigirsen is a warlord and the Great Khan's senior military advisor. He also controls what remains of the Silke Route," Mandukhai spouted, allowing the boredom to bleed through her tone.

"And his allegiance?"

"To the Great Khan."

Nergui frowned at her in a way that narrowed his eyes.

"To the Uyghur and Oirat," she sighed.

The Oirat who murdered her father after he betrayed their leader, Esen, ten years ago. Mandukhai loathed the Oirat and was well aware that her new husband had an Oirat mother. Regardless of what she thought of her marriage to Manduul Khan, Mandukhai recognized the significance. Lady Yeke brought the southern tribes to the Great Khan's circle, and Manduul himself hailed from Oirat-Borjigin bloodlines, which left Mandukhai's tribe alliances in the east. This union would bring all corners of the Mongol Nation together for the first time in centuries. It offered her some solace.

As they crested a hilltop, a field of hundreds of domed *ger* homes covered the expanse of the valley along the edges of the Orkhon River. Even from a distance, Mandukhai could make out Manduul Khan's home among them, a larger, taller dome with blue banners fluttering on the gentle breeze.

A small party rode out to greet them as Mandukhai's own guards closed their circle and formed ranks around her.

"How do you address the Khan?" Nergui asked under his breath as they rode close.

"My old Lord Khan," Mandukhai said, smirking.

Nergui grunted. "Get it out of your system now, girl, because the moment we are within earshot you must show respect."

"My father taught me respect is earned," she said, sitting straighter in the saddle.

"Where did that get him?"

The words were as good as a blow and she flinched, sinking back. No amount of garnered respect had saved her father from Oirat arrows. They killed him just the same.

"What about wrinkled old Khan?" she asked, hoping to inject humor back into the tense moment.

"Joke all you want, but he will be your husband," Nergui responded. "Old, young, wrinkled, hairy, smooth, you will perform your duty regardless."

The food in her stomach churned at the thought. Her mother had instructed her on how to act and what to do when the time came to consummate the marriage. Mandukhai wanted no part in it. The entire act sounded horrific.

The capital nestled in the heart of the Orkhon Valley, along the eastern shores of Orkhon River that fed through all the surrounding land. Across the river, a birch forest encroached on the rocky banks. And at the forest's back, the looming Khangai Mountains. It was a beautiful, rich land for herding.

"Enough now," Nergui muttered as they drew close enough to be heard.

Mandukhai scanned the party that came to welcome her. Several men clad in black armor sat on horseback, alongside a woman in silk with a *boqta* headdress that marked her out as Lady Yeke and a young man with bushy eyebrows and a warm smile. Surely that was not Manduul Khan. He looked far too young, though she supposed she could consider him attractive.

"Welcome to Mongke Bulag, Lady Mandukhai," the young man said.

"Manduul is preparing for the ceremony. Lady Yeke and I have come to escort you to her *ger* as Manduul's men construct yours."

"Thank you, my Lord," Mandukhai said in an even voice she practiced for this day.

The corner of his mouth curled up in a crooked grin. "Please, call me Togochi. No lording necessary for you."

Mandukhai simply inclined her head and followed the welcome party, casting glances toward Lady Yeke. The woman was hardly a great beauty with her large, hooked nose, long face, and sharp features cast in perpetual anger. The way Lady Yeke rode in her saddle was stiff and straight, uncomfortable, unlike Mandukhai's own natural ease.

The swell of music and general merriment had begun already all throughout the maze of gers making up Mongke Bulag. Mandukhai had never loathed such sounds as much as she did this day.

And tonight, she would be a wife. Again, her stomach churned.

High Heavens, give me the courage and spirit of Lady Khutulun.

TWO QUEENS, ONE OMEN

MONGKE BULAG – ORKHON VALLEY – 1464

The inside of Yeke's ger offered protection from the spring breeze sweeping through Mongke Bulag. Mandukhai followed Manduul Khan's first wife—his only other wife—in silence, casting a terrified glance at Nergui as he posted himself outside the door to wait. She dared not speak, worried that her voice would crack or give away her fear. Could she not get settled first? Must they do this immediately?

As Manduul Khan's first wife, it became Yeke's responsibility to ensure servants properly prepared for the ceremony and that Mandukhai was also ready. Yeke had already dressed for the occasion before Mandukhai arrived in Mongke Bulag. Her blue silk deel bore the elaborate red stitchwork and silver fastenings Mandukhai would expect from the first wife of the Great Khan. Even the light yellow and red jacket pulled over her deel had detailed embroidery. It was a fine outfit, right down to the jingling jewels hanging from Yeke's headdress, neck, and belt.

The moment the door sealed the two women alone in the ger Yeke waved Mandukhai to a bench. "We have little time before sundown."

Mandukhai's stomach tumbled, but she nodded, then marched to the bench and sank down. There was no point in fighting the inevitable.

Yeke immediately pulled off Mandukhai's riding cap and produced a bone-white comb. The woman raked it through Mandukhai's hair as if attempting to rip it from her scalp! Mandukhai grimaced.

"We need to be sure it's secure," Yeke said, shoving another pin into Mandukhai's hair deep enough to press into her scalp.

Working up her courage, Mandukhai pinched her face and fought off the panic tensing up her muscles. "Manduul Khan is a good husband?" she asked, certain that she sounded far too timid.

Yeke huffed. "Would you expect less from the Great Khan?"

Mandukhai held her breath. It was hardly an answer to her question, and she simply wanted to engage her future sister-wife in conversation. They would be spending their lives together as much as they shared it Manduul. Surely they could strike a friendship.

"I was only making conversation," Mandukhai mumbled.

"We each have a duty to the future of this Nation," Yeke answered tersely, tugging at Mandukhai's hair as she fastened it on the top of her head. "Conversation is hardly required for the task."

Had the air just become thicker? Perhaps Yeke resented Mandukhai's presence. It was not a fate Mandukhai had asked for, and she disliked that Yeke could blame her. She must have faced the same fate when she married Manduul.

"Rise, Mandukhai," Yeke commanded after she finished fastening Mandukhai's hair on top of her head and placing the beaded *shanaavch* headdress in place.

The gems and bells on the headdress chimed as Mandukhai rose from the bench. The *boqta*—the tall column-like crown that marked her out as the Khan's wife—would come later, in front of everyone as a sign that Yeke had accepted her into the Khan's family. Not that Mandukhai felt any sort of welcome from this woman.

Yeke stripped off Mandukhai's dirty, coarse wool deel and used a cloth to wipe down her limbs. The water chilled Mandukhai's skin and made the flesh bump and rise. Once Mandukhai's body was scrubbed clean, Yeke slipped a golden silk deel over Mandukhai's out-stretched arms. It glided over her skin like water over stone, smooth and cool. Mandukhai had not grown up with such rich cloth. Her skin had become accustomed to the abrasive quality of the woolen clothing she wore on the Ongud steppe. She couldn't imagine she would ever grow used to such finery.

As Yeke fussed with the buttons on the left side of the deel, Mandukhai took a moment to examine the quality of Yeke's ger. Fine woven rugs of Muslim and Chinese design covered the floor—deep reds, bright yellows, flaming oranges, sky blues. The composition reminded Mandukhai of a sunset, just as the sun had set on her past life today. Soon, it would be darkness. Under different circumstances, Mandukhai might have complimented Yeke's rug arrangement. Yet the frosty way Yeke interacted with her kept Mandukhai silent.

Along the eastern wall, fine pots and silver cups and bowls rested on a shelf that collected dust—a sign this ger had not been moved in quite some time. The roof pole was thicker than her thighs, and someone had carved birds and flowers into the wood, then painted them in red and blue and yellow to make it more colorful. It was a monstrous pole that would be difficult to move in a hurry. Fine cloth from all around the world covered the lattice frame of the walls—likely gifts from her father, who controlled the flow of goods through Mongolia. The clothes shimmered in the light from the stove in the center of the ger as the flames made the embroidery come to life.

Yeke's clothing chest took up several feet of ger—much larger than anything Mandukhai had ever owned. The cherry-stained doors on the chest it were closed with a red ribbon tied around the golden handles. Not exactly a lock, but a clear warning to keep out. Mandukhai wondered what sort of treasures the queen kept within.

"It was a gift from Manduul when we married," Yeke said, catching Mandukhai staring at the chest. Her tone was not friendly.

Mandukhai said nothing back. Yeke didn't seem eager to talk and Mandukhai was not eager to say something wrong on her first day. Instead, she continued examining the ger as Yeke worked on the last ties of the deel.

The bedding rested on a slab of carved stone—another piece that would not easily be moved. While Yeke had made the bed nicely, months of slumber made the center of the bedding sag into the stone frame.

Yeke finished fastening the deel and adjusting the collar to cover Mandukhai modestly. She had brought little precious jewelry with her—a long pair of earrings made from pressed copper rings linked together, a thick matching necklace with a turquoise and pearl gem pendant, and an ornamented belt her mother had given her. It had been a gift from Esen when her mother had married her father, before Esen had turned to madness.

Yeke approached with another belt—a gaudy golden thing with more precious stones than Mandukhai had seen in her life. The light from the stove brought the metal and gems to life.

Mandukhai held up a hand and reached for the bundle she brought to prepare for the ceremony. "I brought my own. A gift from my mother."

"And I brought a new one," Yeke said tersely. "A gift from Manduul Khan. Would you refuse your Great Khan's gift on this day of all days?"

Mandukhai struggled to keep her disappointment from showing, shaking her head and making the gems and bells chime. "I would refuse my Great Khan nothing."

Yet she longed to refuse. That belt was one of the few pieces of her old life that remained, and she could not even honor her mother by wearing it.

A lump swelled in Mandukhai's throat and she swallowed it down as Yeke's lips thinned into a stiff line. She wrapped the belt around Mandukhai and tugged it tight, cinching her waist and pressing breath from her lungs.

Manduul's clothing chest was closed, but not secured. The space beside the door where weapons and saddle should be stored lay vacant. His side of the bed appeared untouched, lacking the depression similar to Yeke's.

Manduul Khan had his own ger, of course, and he could summon any of his wives or concubines to him. But it was the wife's job to seduce the husband in her own ger, according to her mother. *As I will soon have to do.* The thought made her skin crawl. She had no desire to lie with any man unless he proved himself worthy. Yet bearing Manduul's child would be her only way to secure her place with no other heirs. According to Nergui, Manduul had no children yet. She did not want to share a bed with him, but also knew she needed a child for the sake of the Nation ... and herself.

Yeke gave the belt one last tug, glanced at the Khan's bedding as if reading Mandukhai's mind, then turned and retrieved her own *boqta* from storage and secured it to her head. The narrow column matched her blue and red deel, rising two full hands into the air. This was the crown of queens, and the impressive height of Yeke's placed her importance on display.

As Yeke picked up the *boqta* for Mandukhai, she tried to catch a glimpse, praying it wasn't so ornamental even if it symbolized her importance.

"Come," Yeke said, striding toward the door and thrusting it open.

Mandukhai scrambled to follow Yeke out the door to the path leading toward the tallest ger—at least twice the size of all the others. The sides had been opened all around, and within the gathering space, nearly a hundred of the local Lords and Ladies had congregated to await her arrival.

This is it, she thought as she trailed beside Yeke along the path.

Yeke left Mandukhai near the entrance so she could join Manduul Khan at the head of the massive gathering tent. Mandukhai could not see him through the crowd, and her stomach churned. It was far too late to run away, but the temptation tugged at her sheepskin boots all the same.

The Borjigin shaman stepped before her, sprinkling milk in her direction as a symbol of purity and fertility. When he finished, the shaman spun on his heels and led her along the path that parted in the crowd of onlookers. He continued sprinkling the mare's milk before her. With each step behind him, her heart hammered harder and rose into her throat until all she could do was swallow reflexively. She folded her hands together in the sleeves of her deel, as her mother instructed. They shook against each other violently, coating in sweat.

I can't do this. I can't do this! She thought with each panicked step closer to her doom.

In the center of the gathering tent, two copper basins large enough to hold her entire body blazed with flaming life. Mandukhai followed the shaman between the two pots—a ritual of cleansing away her old life to start the new. Men and women nodded and murmured in approval, making Mandukhai overly aware of just how many eyes were on her now. She kept her chin high and gaze forward.

At the end of the path, Yeke stood beside a much older man atop a three-step high dais. The shaman joined them at the top of the dais, and Mandukhai prayed her knees would not give out as she climbed as well.

Manduul Khan bore no resemblance to what Mandukhai expected. Wrinkles creased his face from years in the sun, making him appear in his late forties. A black and red velvet and silk brocaded *toortsog* hat covered the bald spot atop the head popular among men. Thick, braided horns looped around his ears. The silken deel he wore was embroidered with a mesmerizing blue pattern that reminded Mandukhai of the sky. Around his waist, a rather large, golden-linked belt hung around his round belly. The slope of his broad shoulders made her swallow.

Manduul Khan was not an attractive man, by her estimation. The pounding in her chest intensified as she swallowed yet another lump in her throat. How could she lie with such a man when he stirred nothing in her?

I suppose I will find out soon enough. Suppressing a shudder, Mandukhai raised her chin proudly. There was no turning back.

15

Unebolod waited with Togochi inside the gathering tent. Togochi had teased Manduul when they entered the gathering tent, informing him that the bride he was about to receive would not disappoint him.

"Well, it can't be much worse," Manduul whispered to them before climbing the dais steps to wait for Mandukhai and the shaman. Excitement rolled off Manduul in waves, drawing a rare smile from Unebolod.

He had been happy for Manduul when he heard about the arrangement with the Ongud girl. Not only would the marriage help smooth ruffled feathers, but Manduul had been grossly unhappy with Yeke and he deserved a wife that made him happy.

Wanting to know more about this girl who would be joining the Great Khan's family, Unebolod had dug up all the information he could. His job was to protect Manduul and his interests. He had learned far more than he expected. Her father had been an advisor to Esen—a man Unebolod had loathed for over ten years. This had put him off toward her until discovering her father had been instrumental to the fall of Esen, a traitor to his own liege lord for the future of the Mongol Nation. In some circles, they considered her father a hero. In others, he would be a traitor.

He had also heard rumors that Mandukhai was a great beauty, but such talk from men occurred frequently and he dismissed it. Togochi's joking had felt more like a jest than him speaking the truth, so Unebolod was inclined to stick to his initial assessment.

Until he saw her with his own eyes. His heart seized the moment he laid eyes upon her entering the gathering tent.

Though Mandukhai moved somewhat stiffly, there was an air of grace around her that was admirable. She represented the very image of everything a true Mongolian man would want: face round, pale, and full as the moon, cheeks painted the color of a blazing sunset. Her back remained as firm as the mountains protecting their camp and as she approached the dais where Manduul waited, her movements were as fluid as the river waters that fed their herds.

Something deep within Unebolod stirred—a feeling he had not known since his own wife died; a dangerous sensation he would be forced to ignore. She belonged to Manduul. Nothing could ever happen so long as Manduul lived. Such an offense would cost Unebolod his life, and he had far more important things to concern himself with than giving in to the whims of the flesh. Such as protecting Manduul and the Mongol nation.

One day, Unebolod would need the favor of one of Manduul's wives if he wanted to become Great Khan after Manduul died. Yeke constantly gave him a cold shoulder and only spoke to Unebolod when she needed to. Mandukhai presented him with a chance to regain favor.

Yeke placed Mandukhai's *boqta* on her head. Mandukhai graciously accepted. Unebolod noticed the subtle difference in the headgear of the two women. Yeke was certain to make clear she was higher ranked than this new wife by giving her a shorter and less adorned *boqta*.

The crowd murmured in approval of the ceremony as the shaman blessed the marriage.

Togochi shifted as he watched from beside Unebolod. The two were not brothers, but Unebolod felt as close as brothers could be with the young Khorlod leader. The two of them had been tasked with watching over Manduul's nieces during the ceremony, and the two girls stood in front of Unebolod. Borogchin, fourteen and nearly of age to marry, watched with open awe and admiration. Esige, at only ten years old, appeared bored by all of it.

"Yeke is concerned about heirs," Borogchin whispered to her little sister. "She intends to see that hers are priority."

Unebolod frowned. They should keep such conversations private. There were too any ears around to hear such dangerous words.

Esige snickered behind her hand. "That would mean Uncle Manduul would have to sleep in the same ger with her."

Togochi gently thumped Esige on the shoulder to silence her, and Unebolod was thankful for his swift action. She shot a defiant glare at him, but fell silent.

Yeke had good reason to be concerned. Mandukhai came from Mongolian blood and bones; Yeke came from the blood of a Mongol mother, but the bones of a Uyghur father. This difference was imperative. The people would favor Mandukhai's children for succession. They would be pure Mongolians. To Yeke, this posed a very serious threat. She married Manduul to produce children her father could use to replace Manduul when they matured. If Manduul understood this, it might explain why he didn't enjoy sleeping with Yeke.

Mandukhai could ruin all of this.

Which was why Unebolod would dedicate his spare time to gaining Mandukhai's favor. When a Great Khan died, any man who had the favor of his wives could propose marriage. The marriage would put that man in a position to become the next Great Khan as long as no one from Genghis Khan's direct descendants remained. Unebolod did not descend from Genghis, but Genghis's younger brother, Khasar—a strong enough blood tie to put forward a reasonable claim to the title. Unebolod and his brother Bolunai were the only two with such clear claim, and Bolunai had no desire to rule the whole of Mongolia; only the tribe.

She is my chance, Unebolod thought.

"Yeke has been trying," Borogchin mumbled. Unebolod caught the glance she cast at him and Togochi. She dipped her head and flushed.

"Maybe if she didn't look like a dead horse," Esige said petulantly, not caring that anyone heard her.

"Silence," Togochi hissed.

So it begins already, Unebolod thought. Yeke's fears would bear fruit. She could not seduce Manduul into bed and people noticed.

It's likely that beak of a nose. Yeke's name meant "ugly nose," and was her name for good reason. Most women had perfectly rounded flat noses. Hers jutted out from her face and hooked down like the beak of a bird. It was a trait from her Uyghur father.

Unebolod loathed her father, Bigirsen. The man supported Manduul's rise to Great Khan to control Manduul, then married his only daughter off to further their alliance. But Unebolod could not forget the battle he fought against Bigirsen.

As Unebolod remembered this, it took some effort to keep from reaching up and touching the scar on his right cheek. A gift from Bigirsen in that battle.

Were Bigirsen from pure Mongol stock, he could have challenged Manduul for the title, but his father was not Mongol. He could never be Great Khan; not so long as the bones of Genghis's line survived. Why Bigirsen didn't just kill Manduul remained a mystery. Perhaps to keep the Mongolian people on his side. Perhaps hoping his daughter's children would one day take over.

We have had enough of this dissent, Unebolod thought with a hint of bitterness in his heart. Little true honor remained among tribes today. Just the remnants of a broken hierarchy that manipulated the system for death, glory, and power.

Manduul and Mandukhai walked together along the path between the copper basin fires. Unebolod stared at Mandukhai as she passed him.

Thankfully, he had mastered the cold face of a warrior years ago and none of the turmoil rolling through him reflected on the surface as the Khan and his young wife strode out of the gathering tent. Yeke followed close behind, along with Borogchin and Esige. Togochi nudged Unebolod's shoulder, and they joined the procession.

The crowd followed Manduul and Mandukhai to her new ger, where they would consummate their marriage before joining the festivities and feast.

High above, a falcon passed the camp. Its shadow rippled over the ceremony in a manner reminiscent of the *sulde* of Genghis Khan's banner. An omen of great strength. Unebolod nodded in approval. The sky father and earth mother gave their blessing to this day.

The corners of Unebolod's eyes creased as he turned them skyward. This marriage would change the fortunes of the Mongol nation. How it would happen, Unebolod was uncertain, yet there was a twisting in his gut spurred on by the omens. *It will happen.*

Mandukhai's slender, delicate hand pushed open the wooden door to her new ger and she disappeared inside. Manduul hesitated only a moment, glancing at Unebolod and Togochi with a smirk. Unebolod returned the smile, but he wanted more than anything to punch that smirk off Manduul's face.

The door closed behind Manduul, and Yeke was the first to dip her fingers in the mare's milk beside the door, then swipe it over the felt lining of the door. One by one, everyone stepped forward to do the same, a tradition to help with fertility.

Unebolod dipped his own fingers in the milk. His gut churned, and raw instincts made him yearn to deny Manduul this one thing. Manduul had already stolen so much from him.

Aware of Togochi lingering at his shoulder, Unebolod grunted and swiped his fingers across the felt before stalking away.

The current hierarchy was a joke—or insult depending on who was asked—and it needed to change. Manduul Khan was nothing more than a sheep herded where his master wanted. For now, that was the camp at Mongke Bulag, as it had been since his installation as Great Khan.

A title that will be mine eventually, Unebolod thought bitterly.

Unebolod turned his dark eyes to the sky once more, searching for answers. There were no more omens, no hints of to what lay ahead, yet he knew that everything would change.

CHAPTER THREE

THE FOX, THE WOLF, AND THE BUTTER

The cleansing fires at the ceremony had burned away Mandukhai's past and purified her for a future as part of this new tribe. Mandukhai's mother had told her she would feel different once she stepped over the threshold of her marital home, that it would give Mandukhai a sense of comfort and womanhood. But as she crossed the threshold, nothing changed. She still feared this change so much she worried she might be sick. She still yearned for a more suitable match with a handsome, strong man. Not a fat old Khan.

None of that would happen now.

Mandukhai didn't close the door behind her as she entered her new home. Manduul Khan would follow her across the threshold in mere moments. She suppressed a shudder, squared her shoulders, and examined the ger contents. It took but a few moments to take everything in.

The ger now belonged to her now. Not Yeke or Manduul, but Mandukhai. The prospect of living alone presented a certain appeal—even if the Khan could enter at his whim—yet also felt incredibly lonely. The expectation would be that she would fill this ger with children. But if the prospect of sharing a bed with Manduul Khan lacked appeal before laying eyes on him, it lost any potential charm after she saw him in the gathering tent.

The first thing she noticed upon entering her ger was the complete lack of adornment compared to what she'd seen in Yeke's. The poles holding up the lashings of the roof were simple and sturdy, making her home significantly easier to move, unlike Yeke's. The poles were smooth, but unpainted or uncarved, which was fine by Mandukhai. She would decorate it to her own taste.

The lattice wall remained visible. Simple rugs covered the floor—nothing nearly as stunning as those on Yeke's floor. The muted browns and worn whites had a mismatched pattern that reminded her of home.

In the center of the ger, a warming fire burned low with smoke rising up the narrow smokestack and billowing out the crown of the ger. The scent of burning wood served as another reminder of the life she left behind.

Mandukhai glanced at the bed, fresh and unused. Her stomach twisted in painful knots as she considered what would soon happen there. Her face heated.

On the north wall of the tent, a wooden altar held only the incense burner and a box containing the scented sticks to set aflame and cleanse the room. Beside the altar, a set of shelves held a meager supply of wooden bowls and porcelain teacups. Mandukhai picked up one of the cups and ran her finger along the blue flower painted into the white before setting it back down.

At the foot of the bed, the chest Mandukhai had brought along sat closed. She rushed over and kneeled in front of it, brushing a finger over the latch. Then she opened the lid as someone entered behind her.

Everything within the chest had been neatly folded and arranged. Someone had gone through her things. The contents of the chest were meager: fresh deels, a couple of belts, trousers, and a winter sheepskin coat lined with fur. Either Mandukhai or her mother had made everything in the chest. As she rummaged through the contents, her heart beat harder against her ribs. When she realized why, Mandukhai's heart leaped into her throat. Something was missing.

Sucking in panicked breaths that tasted like campfire, Mandukhai shoved around the contents of the chest, hoping to feel the smooth wood of her bow, or the horn handle of the hunting knife her father had given her. After a moment, she came up empty and sank further back on her heels. Tears stung her eyes as a presence loomed near the doorway. Mandukhai licked her lips, gazing past Manduul near the door to the hooks behind him, desperately praying someone had hung it for her. But the hooks were bare.

No rules existed stating that the Khan's wives couldn't have weapons or couldn't fight.

Manduul cleared his throat just inside the doorway. Mandukhai jumped to her feet, unable to suppress the concern pressing against her chest and the weight of what this night would bring.

Manduul Khan was older than her by at least twenty years, and while the age difference was nothing unusual and didn't matter to Mandukhai, the health in which he kept himself did. Sure, most men his age had weathered skin, but they also had the form and strength of men used to battle. The roundness of Manduul's belly revealed had made Mandukhai wonder, when was the last time Manduul had even ridden into battle?

"*Sain bainuul*, Lady Mandukhai," Manduul said, his voice a pitch higher than she had expected from a man of his size. *Hello, Lady Mandukhai*, he had said.

Mandukhai flipped the chest closed, adjusted the shifting *boqta*, and folded her hands together in the sleeves of her deel. Heat flooded her cheeks, and a bundle of nervous energy writhed in her stomach. *I'm going to be sick*, she thought miserably.

"*Sain bainuul*, Manduul Khan." Mandukhai hardly managed to get the words out.

A shadow fell across the doorway, and Mandukhai glanced over to find Yeke with her hands folded in the sleeves of her deel and her back straight, chin held high. Without a word, Yeke reached out and glared at Mandukhai as she pulled the door shut, leaving the two of them wholly and frighteningly alone.

Mandukhai knew what they expected of her, but she didn't have the courage to follow through. The idea of this man mating with her made Mandukhai's stomach twist with a fresh wave of nausea. How would she ever get through this?

Mandukhai immediately shuffled toward the shelves to retrieve a cup and offer Manduul a drink, then realized she had nothing. "I apologize, my lord Khan. It seems I have no food or drink to offer." Had Yeke intentionally left Mandukhai with nothing to offer? The admission filled Mandukhai with shame.

After placing his *toortsog* hat on the table beside the door, Manduul lumbered awkwardly around the ger toward her.

"You worry unduly," Manduul said.

He offered her a horse-hide container, which Mandukhai graciously accepted, giving a careful bow so her *boqta* didn't shift again. Up close, she could smell his sweat.

"You seem distressed," he said as she poured a cup of *airag* for each of them. "I would like to put you at ease."

Mandukhai offered Manduul the cup in her right palm, struggling to keep from shaking. He thanked her as he accepted the cup. At least he had manners. That had to be worth something.

"I seem to have lost my bow and hunting knife since arriving," said Mandukhai, retrieving her own cup. She was careful to choose her words so as not to accuse anyone of stealing her possessions. Such an offense could cost someone their life, and she had no proof of who may have done so.

Manduul watched her with curiosity, and it only took a moment for her to realize what he sought. Her throat clenched and she swallowed hard. *I have a duty to uphold, no matter how much I don't want to.*

"Please," she said, motioning him to sit on the only seat in the ger—the bed.

Would she ever be able to drink this *airag* without throwing up on him? Her stomach surely would hold nothing down the way it revolted against her. The first drink belonged to the hostess, and it would be rude of him to do so first. Mandukhai sank down—nearly collapsing as her legs betrayed her—and steeled herself as best she could, aware of the space she occupied, and kept her arms tucked close to her body. Once settled, Mandukhai took the tiniest of sips. The slightly sour taste quickly became overpowered by the bite of the alcohol.

Manduul grinned and sank down beside her. The bed shifted toward him under his weight, forcing Mandukhai to steady herself to keep from falling against him. He sipped his own drink.

For several long moments, neither of them spoke a word, making it difficult for Mandukhai to keep her mind from drifting to her duty. While she could choose the terms of their engagement, the expectation that she complete the act today weighed on her shoulders. Whether by her choice, it had to be done. And once it was, she could play the games of engagement to keep him from pressing further advances without her explicit permission. *It must be done.*

"Your bow. What need do you have for a bow now?" Manduul asked, breaking the silence, clearly seeking some sort of way to initiate a conversation with her. His weight made the bed sink deeper as he shifted closer to her, and Mandukhai had to adjust her own position again. "You are wife of the Khan."

"I am Mongol." Mandukhai set her cup on the table beside the stove.

"Wife of the Khan or not, what sort of Mongol would I be without a bow? I need it to protect our children."

Manduul laughed with hearty mirth, a sound that made the *airag* in her stomach curdle. "I like you," he declared.

Should I be relieved? she wondered.

"I will see what happened to your bow," Manduul said. "Later."

Later, but right now he had other ideas on what he would do. Mandukhai's entire body trembled and she could hear her own pulse thrashing in her ears. It took every ounce of strength she could muster to keep her back straight and lift the *boqta* off her head. *It must be done.*

Carefully, she set the headdress on the chest beside the foot of the bed. When she turned her attention back to Manduul, his hungry gaze devoured every inch of her, lingering on the exposed skin along her neck.

"I hear there is a feast in my honor today," said Mandukhai, attempting to delay the inevitable.

"Later," he said, then downed the rest of his *airag* and set the cup on the table. "Along with gifts to decorate our new home."

Our new home.

Manduul slid his hand along the nape of Mandukhai's neck. She gracefully pulled away to pick up his empty cup to refill it, heart thumping. He snatched her wrist, eased her back, and took the cup, returning it to the table. Mandukhai wanted to protest but could do little more than part her lips. Words failed her. What could she say?

Manduul pulled her into his lap. Surely he could feel how much she trembled.

"We can have our fill of food and drink later," said Manduul.

Later. She was beginning to loathe that word.

Manduul did not waste a moment more getting started. He unfastened her belt. The metal thumped against the brown rug in front of the bed. "Right now, I have other hungers."

Mandukhai grew certain her heart would explode. She was not ready for this. What would it feel like? Would it hurt? Would he be rough and insistent or gentle? No, she couldn't do this. There had to be a way out!

Mandukhai slid off his lap as his rough lips grazed the burning hot skin of her neck. "Race the horse across the steppe and the horse will have nothing more to offer," she said, the words coming out in a rush. "But keep the horse at a moderate pace, and the horse will go much farther."

He must know how difficult this is for me, she thought desperately.

Manduul frowned, holding Mandukhai's hand tight, until she reached up with her free hand and started unfastening her deel. Her fingers fumbled. Could he tell? Her mother had told her it was best to get the first time over with quickly, but she couldn't bring herself to begin. She needed to draw this out.

Again, he grinned at her, but this grin differed from the last. It reminded her of a wolf on the hunt, ready to spring into action against its prey. His hand slipped out of hers.

"Have you realized yet, my lord Khan, how similar our names are?" Mandukhai asked as she loosened her deel, careful to expose just a touch more skin without showing too much. Hopefully his anticipation would hold him off a bit longer. "Rising and Ascending."

"The spirit of Genghis Khan has brought us together," said Manduul, practically chomping at the bit for what was to come.

But Mandukhai took her time. *It must be done.*

"It was no mistake," she agreed, turning her back to him as she slipped the deel off, leaving her in just the robe beneath. "We were meant to meet in this place, my lord Khan."

The bed rustled behind her, and Mandukhai glanced over her shoulder as she let her hair fall down. Manduul now stood behind her, inching closer.

"You call me Manduul," he said, shifting her hair away from her exposed shoulders. "Unless we are in official meetings in the gathering tent."

His hot breath reeked of *airag*. The heat from his body radiated through her deel and seeped into Mandukhai's skin. His lips pressed hungry kisses against her neck and shoulder. Mandukhai's body tensed under his lips.

"Don't be shy," he murmured against her skin. "I won't hurt you."

Once he sees you as weak, it can never be undone, her mother had warned. But Mandukhai had never felt so weak. Her body trembled and she could not make it stop. Her stomach churned painfully. Every thought in her head betrayed her and insisted that she run—but that was out of the question. Running away could start a war. She was meant to bring peace. If Mandukhai was to get through this night, she would need to build a wall to protect herself. And for that she needed more time.

Mandukhai turned, taking a careful step back. "I'm not shy," she lied. "But should I be so exposed when you are not?"

Manduul chuckled deep in his throat and unfastened his own belt, tossing it onto the chest beside her *boqta*. Then he set to work on his own deel.

It must be done.

Men enjoyed playful games. Her mother had told her that as well. As long as they got what they wanted in the end. Mandukhai could use that to delay as well.

"Tell me, Manduul. Are you familiar with the tale of the Fox, the Wolf, and the Bag of Butter?" Mandukhai held her deel tight around her body. "A cunning fox and a fierce wolf. The two found a bag of butter they both hungered for."

Again, he grinned at her, and she knew she had him on the hook. "So which am I, wife? The Fox or the Wolf? The cunning trickster or the fierce hunter?"

Mandukhai did her best to play a teasing grin across her lips, letting the top of her deel slip down to expose her bare shoulder. "You are a Borjigin wolf. The fierce hunter, of course."

He advanced toward her as he finally loosened his deel, but she cleverly stepped just out of his reach.

"But if the Wolf wants the butter, it needs to outfox the Fox," said Mandukhai.

Manduul dropped his deel, exposing his round belly and leaving him in only his trousers. "And so the hunt begins."

Mandukhai knew this game would buy her precious little time before the inevitable, but at least she could establish her position in this ger. Outside, Manduul was Khan. In here, Mandukhai ruled. And just as the fox outsmarted the wolf, she would outsmart the Khan—even if he managed to get the butter in the end. He was Khan after all, and she could not refuse him for long.

It must be done, she reminded herself as the game began.

Mandukhai rose and pulled her robe tight around her body. Manduul reached for her but his fingers slipped over the cloth of the robe without grabbing hold. She had never felt so filthy in her life.

"Come, Mandukhai," Manduul said, patting the bed beside him. "The night is young, and this horse has much farther to travel."

The idea of lying beside him again made Mandukhai want to scrub every inch of her body raw. Manduul had been gentle enough with her, but she had no desire for him. In fact, her opinions bordered on repulsion. The feel of his hands and lips against her skin lingered, as did the weight of his body against hers. *My duty is done.*

"The feast in my honor awaits," said Mandukhai, thankful for the excuse more than she could ever express. "It would be rude of me to keep our people waiting."

"They will understand," said Manduul as he sat on the edge of the bed. "And when I have an heir, they will forgive."

An heir. She was little more than a prized brood mare for him now. Having his child wouldn't be the worst thing. It would offer her a position of power, and her son would be Great Khan when he came of age. Assuming it's a boy. Though the idea of thrusting a daughter into this sort of life didn't make her stomach settle easily. Centuries ago, during the time of truly great Khans like Genghis and Kublai, women had more power and control over their own lives. *Like Khutulun. If only we could return to those days.*

Striving for a child meant doing more of this with Manduul, and she was in no rush.

"The night is young, Manduul," she said, throwing his words back at him with a teasing that touched on unspoken promises. Though if he drank enough, she would not have to do this again tonight. *I will keep his cup full.*

An eager grin split his round face, making him appear little more than a boy. He could be a much worse man. Thus far, Manduul seemed to respect her and, judging by the way he gazed at her now, even adored her. She almost felt bad for him. If he knew the thoughts in her head …

Mandukhai moved to the bucket of water and dipped a cloth in. The water felt cool against her skin as she scrubbed at her neck and chest as if she could scrub away the feel of his lips.

"That it is." Manduul stood, seeking his clothes with no sense of modesty as he circled the ger in his bare skin.

Unlike Mandukhai, Manduul didn't bother washing up. *He probably wants everyone to smell the lingering scent of sex on him so they will all know it happened.*

By the time he finished dressing, Mandukhai had barely begun washing herself to her satisfaction. Her skin prickled as he stepped behind her and slipped his fat hand into her deel to press against her belly as if a child had already made its home there. Mandukhai battled to keep from stiffening at his touch.

"I am certain of it," he said, breathing rancid *airag* breath across her neck.

27

"You will give the Mongol Nation the heirs they seek."

This is a game. Keep him happy and close, but not so close that I can't insist on distance.

Mandukhai forced out an innocent laugh, praying she played the game well. "Go," she said, sliding his hand out of her deel. "I will be along shortly, but we shouldn't keep them waiting. I'm sure you can explain my delayed arrival."

Manduul's hand lingered on her hip. She wanted to pull away, but instead smiled as sweetly as she could. Before he protested further or touched her again, Mandukhai nudged him away to sweep her hair back up so it would hold in the *boqta*. Using her arms forced him to move out of the way or risk an elbow in the face.

He shuffled toward the door, slapped the *toortsog* hat back on his head, and stepped outside. A moment later, as the door closed behind him, he cheered victoriously and was met with equal enthusiasm from those who happened to be nearby. The sound made her stomach twist in knots, and she turned, downing the rest of her *airag* from earlier.

My duty is done for now. The real game between the fox and wolf begins.

CHAPTER FOUR

THE GREATEST GIFT

Torches lit every corner of the capital as people celebrated the Khan's marriage all around Mongke Bulag. Unebolod could hear the festive music and cheers for wrestling matches from where he groomed the pale white horse intended for the Khan's new wife. He had made several costly trades to acquire this horse, knowing that a horse as fine and fast as this would gain him Mandukhai's respect. A solid first step toward building his alliance.

Raucous cheering rose into the night sky, and Unebolod glanced over his shoulder to see Manduul strutting along the path in a manner that reminded Unebolod more of a waddle. Manduul raised his hands in the air and cheered again, and the men and women around him echoed the sound. Unebolod scowled and turned his attention back to the horse. He was happy for Manduul, but he could not help the jealousy that burned under his skin. He had no good reason to be jealous. Manduul was his sworn brother, and the two of them were as close as two men could be.

The pale white fur marked this stallion out as a rare beauty among horses, as exquisite as the new queen who was a rare beauty among women. The connection had merely been a coincidence, but the turn of events pleased him. All the easier to present her with this gift and gain her respect. It was grand, but he and Manduul were close enough that Unebolod could give her such a gift without arousing suspicion.

For the hundredth time tonight, he checked to make sure the saddle was securely in place. The saddle was just as fine as the horse. Smooth, padded, black-dyed leather with dragons pressed into the arching pommel and cantle, a small tribute to the great honor of her birth in the year of the yellow dragon. Yellow-gold ribbon trimmed the horn edge of the saddle and the saddle blanket. A deep purple saddle cushion was pinned with slick, golden ornaments so they didn't chafe while riding. The stirrups comprised sturdy steel that wouldn't bend or break under her weight, and a leather fender flap and saddle cashion covered the stirrup strap to protect from unexpected shifting and abrasion from heavy riding. Even the felt saddle blanket matched the brilliant yellow-gold of the ribbon. Unebolod swelled with pride, gazing at the horse and saddle.

Others wandered past, moving about their drunken joviality. A few offered admiration for the stallion, which he acknowledged before turning back to checking the stallion and saddle.

The price of this stallion will be worthwhile once she sees it, he thought.

Gossip rippled through the capital of Vice Regent Bigirsen's approach to Mongke Bulag. If there was one man Unebolod loathed above all others, it was Bigirsen and his arrogant assumption of power. Tonight, Unebolod would be certain to keep his sword close.

Another person approached to Unebolod's left, but he didn't look over until he heard the familiar voice.

"A stunning creature," Manduul said, cradling the horse's chin in one hand as he stroked the stallion's forehead. "Did you steal this horse, Unebolod?" Though he spoke in jest, Unebolod took offense to the suggestion.

"I think the horse has stolen me," Unebolod replied, forcing his grimace into a smile. "Or my heart, at least. He is a stunning creature."

"A gift fit for a queen," said Manduul, leveling his gaze at Unebolod.

Unspoken accusation hung in the air, and silence fell between the men. Had he misjudged Manduul's trust?

Manduul was not a complete fool. He knew it served Unebolod to strike up an alliance with Mandukhai or Yeke. Manduul knew that if he had no heirs, Unebolod would be next in line as the Great Khan. *Assuming the boy didn't survive his youth in my brother's care,* Unebolod thought, remembering the boy Bayan he placed in his brother Bolunai's care ten years ago, the last Borjigin prince. Had he known then where his fate would take him, Unebolod never would have sworn that oath to Lady Samur.

Choosing his next words cautiously, Unebolod said, "I would hate to insult your wife with an inadequate gift."

Manduul gripped the reins close to the bit in a fat, white-knuckled fist, and his eyes took on a dangerous edge. "But you would offer her a gift to dwarf my own? I thought we were sworn brothers, Unebolod."

Killing Manduul would be too easy. Most of the camp had already fallen into an intoxicated buzz, gleefully going about their own debauchery. He could slice Manduul belly to chin before Manduul's slow, fat hands could react. Then only Manduul's Vice Regent Bigirsen would stand in his way. But he couldn't kill Manduul. He swore an oath to serve the Great Khan when Manduul became the ruler. And they swore to protect each other long before that day had come. Unebolod's word was iron. It was his honor. Without that, what did he have?

Patience, Unebolod, he cautioned himself. He still needed the support of either Yeke or Mandukhai, and he had yet to speak to Mandukhai. Manduul would die soon enough, the way he cared for himself, and Unebolod would seize power and raise the black banner of war against any who opposed him. Men like Bigirsen. For now, his oath bound him to his honor and duty to the Great Khan.

Unebolod stepped closer to Manduul, dipping his chin in deference that made his skin burn in anger. "We are, Manduul. I didn't mean to dwarf your own gift. I simply wanted to show my respect for your new wife." The next words ground past his lips painfully. "We can exchange. Give her this horse and I will give her your gift. She never needs to know."

A victorious smile split Manduul's face in two and he clapped Unebolod's shoulder with his free hand. "Good man. I will have the gift brought to your ger."

Manduul gave the reins a gentle tug, forcing Unebolod to step back as the horse plodded forward, but the stallion's shoulder still brushed against him, nudging him out of the way.

Manduul stole his prize and undid all his hard work. *Just as he has always done,* Unebolod thought bitterly.

Unebolod did not fear Manduul, who hadn't fought in a battle in at least five years, before he even became Great Khan. Unebolod was younger, faster, and more skilled by the age of eighteen than Manduul had been in all his life. Yet Unebolod still had ten more years of battle experience after that. No, he didn't fear Manduul, but he cared for his sworn brother.

Bigirsen, however, posed a serious threat. Until Unebolod could neutralize that threat, he had to maintain his patience and bide his time. Patience was one of Unebolod's strongest qualities.

Patience and honor.

He turned to his own horse, a powerful beast with dark brown fur and a black mane. "You're ready though, aren't you, old friend?"

The mare snorted and bobbed her head.

More than anything, Mandukhai longed to bathe in a stream and soak in the cold water until her bones numbed, until she could not feel Manduul's lingering presence on her anymore. But it would be selfish, and she could not keep the people waiting. Important members of the Khan's court would be present. Nergui and her mother had advised her to find friends in order to survive the dangers of court life.

Mandukhai took as much time preparing as she dared, though Manduul had probably already made some crude joke about wearing her out. The very idea that others would laugh at her expense, that he would use such language to make a joke of her, encouraged Mandukhai to step a little more quickly toward the door.

Nergui waited outside, watching the surrounding landscape. His presence was strangely comforting. She knew he had been in that spot the whole time and probably heard everything. Her face flushed as she closed the door behind her and folded her hands in the sleeves of her deel.

Much to her relief, Nergui said nothing as they made their way through Mongke Bulag toward the heart of the celebration.

The darkness was too deep tonight—with no moon in the sky—to see more than the peaked shadows of the Khangai Mountains beyond the forest. In the morning, Mandukhai would take time to explore the capital to learn more about her new surroundings.

Despite the darkness beyond hundreds of blazing torches, Mandukhai admired the stars spotting the endless sky between clouds. She could discern enough from their locations to know it was only a couple hours shy of midnight.

As the two of them approached the circle in the center of the capital where most festivities raged, Mandukhai attempted to estimate the number of gers around them. The domed structures created a maze in uneven lines, clustered together in places where families all built their structures close to each other. Such organization was common among Mongol camps because enemies would find it harder to ride through the camp. It also made it harder to estimate how many lived in the area.

Nergui had informed her on the way to Mongke Bulag that only two hundred of the gers here belonged to Borjigin. Another four hundred belonged to the Khorchin and Khorlod, with a scattered few Uyghur.

Hovering around the main camp, other nearby tribes had set their own camps to join the festivities. Mandukhai couldn't discern how many there were. Two. Maybe three. That would account for most of the tribes in the north near Mongke Bulag. Her own Ongud—the few who came with her—constructed their gers on the eastern hills of the capital for easier leave-taking in the morning.

Mandukhai followed the path into the wide opening where more than a hundred people sang, drank, danced, and wrestled. Nergui shifted closer to her, his hand casually resting on his sword.

The Ongud men who accompanied her in the name of her tribe had clustered together at the edge of the ring, keeping a distance from everyone else.

On the other side of the open space, Manduul sat in a legless chair behind a long, low table. He laughed at something, a cup of *airag* in his hand. Spread out on the table, a feast of curds, mutton, boiled *buuz*—meat-stuffed dumplings—and fruits the likes of which Mandukhai had never seen before.

Beside Manduul, Yeke picked at her food, holding a cup of *boal*—honey wine—in her right hand, speaking to a girl beside her who couldn't have been older than ten or eleven. Yeke had no daughters of her own, which made Mandukhai wonder who the girl was.

Mandukhai approached the vacant seat on Manduul's other side, around the western edge of the circle. Manduul spotted her, rolled to the side and stood.

"My wife!" he called out, raising his cup of *airag* as he held out the other hand.

Thunderous cheers shook the earth.

A young woman roughly Mandukhai's age placed another cup in Manduul's outstretched hand with her head bowed. He didn't even glance at her as he presented the cup to Mandukhai. She slid her fingers around it and offered thanks.

Manduul slid his arm around Mandukhai's shoulders and crushed her against his side as he raised his glass. She plastered a warm smile on her face that didn't reach her eyes.

"Tengri and the Eternal Blue Sky smile upon this day, bringing us the bounty of health—" He grinned at this and then motioned to the feast on the table, "—wealth, and beauty." At the last, he released her. She breathed a short-lived sigh of relief before he grabbed her hand and raised it high in the air.

The crowd roared.

Mandukhai raised her cup of *boal*. The honey-sweetness rolled across her tongue and coated her throat. Maybe if she drank enough tonight, those unspoken promises wouldn't bother her as much. *Or I'll say or do something foolish and get into trouble.*

Lowering her cup, she spotted Yeke, still seated on her cushion, a bitterness in her tense lips and furrowed brow that made Mandukhai both sorry and envious. She hadn't meant to displace the other woman. Part of her had hoped they could become friends—sister-wives in this terrible tale. It became increasingly apparent that Manduul's interest in Yeke may only be slightly stronger than Mandukhai's interest in Manduul. If only she could find herself in Yeke's place.

By the end of dinner, Yeke rose abruptly and left the main circle of festivities. Esige—the young girl who sat beside Yeke—trailed along behind Yeke along with Borogchin. Mandukhai had learned their names over dinner and exchanged kindnesses with each. She had learned they were Manduul's nieces from his traitorous and long-dead older brother. Care of the girls had fallen into his lap when he became Great Khan. Mandukhai watched the three of them leave with envy. *If only I could go, too.*

Several other men and woman came and left over the course of the evening, offering her gifts in an endless stream. Togochi, she remembered from her arrival. He humbly offered her pearls "to match her beauty." While she knew he was a Khorlod Lord, she learned he also served as a general in Manduul's army. And he was so young! Only a few years older than Mandukhai.

One of the men spoke in hushed tones to Manduul, keeping his back to her. She could not see his face, only the slope of his broad, strong shoulders. When he finished, he strode away without looking back.

"Who is that one?" Mandukhai asked Manduul, watching the other man leave.

"Unebolod," Manduul replied. "He's *orlok* of my northern armies."

Mandukhai swallowed the lump that jumped into her throat. Nergui had told her only that he was a high lord of the Khorchin tribe and she should be wary of him.

As the night wore on, Mandukhai slowed her drinking of *boal*. Back in her old tribe, the girls had played a drinking game to see who could last the longest. The winner would dole out her morning chores to the losers. Mandukhai never had as strong a liking for *airag* as the other girls had, but she could often outlast them, even when they tried the game with black *airag*, which was much stronger and clear, despite what the name implied.

Tonight, Mandukhai could not drink herself into oblivion. She needed her wits to communicate with the endless stream of men and women offering gifts. Many of them offered simple, humble gifts that she graciously accepted and adored for their simplicity. A few of the Khan's higher-ranked officials brought porcelain or silk from China, stolen during raids, or precious gemstones. Two brought her rugs woven from Turkish fabric. The colors were strikingly bright and intricate, even in the torchlight.

Mandukhai watched her tribesmen throughout the night and noted how early they turned in. They planned to leave in the morning and would want rest, but she loathed to see them go. Only Nergui and Tuya would remain, her final ties to her tribe.

Manduul debated the merits of one particular wrestler in the capital over another, his attention turned away from Mandukhai completely as he boisterously made his arguments.

A man in his mid to late twenties skirted the edge of the circle, away from the two men wrestling in the center of the ring. A deep scar cut through his eyebrow and down his stone-like face. The muscles in his shoulder and arms strained the fabric of his deel. Clearly, this man was a fierce warrior. His dark eyes locked onto hers as he approached with a fur-wrapped bundle. Mandukhai's chest tightened. Her lips parted, but she couldn't find words.

Manduul's debate cut off as he turned his attention to the man before Mandukhai.

"Unebolod," Manduul said levelly.

Mandukhai's heart skipped. This was Unebolod?

Before Unebolod could speak, Manduul slid his arm around Mandukhai's shoulders, pulling her against his side once more, and raised his voice. "Bring my wife her gift from me!"

Unebolod retreated a step with his bundle, dropping his gaze. But

Mandukhai's stomach remained a torrent of butterflies that even Manduul's touch couldn't abate. She licked her suddenly dry lips, took a sip of the *boal*, and let the honeyed wine coat her constricting throat.

She found her voice at last, turning her gaze to her husband, "You have already given me a gift, Manduul." Her fingers played across her new belt, but he took her meaning very differently.

"I have." He pressed his lips to her neck repeatedly, and it occurred to her he was putting on a show. Was he threatened by Unebolod? Why?

Probably because he's far more handsome, she thought.

Mandukhai acted along in her own way—putting on her best smile and playing coy as she pulled away.

Manduul's words slurred together. "But a queen needs a gift fit for a queen. The greatest gift!" He waved his hand, sloshing *airag* over the edge of his cup.

"What greater gift could there possibly be?" she asked.

This question gave Manduul pause. Clearly he assumed she was talking about a child, and maybe she was. A child would secure her place at court.

"A gift fit for a Mongol," he corrected.

Mandukhai held her breath, hoping his gift would be returning her bow. But as her gaze turned to the center of the festivities and the crowd parted to make way, her breath caught in her throat. *A horse. He's giving me a horse.*

Mandukhai rose and rounded the long, low table, approaching the magnificent beast. The horse's coat was as white as the moon, and far more beautiful than the one she currently possessed. She ran her hand along the soft jaw, down the neck to just above the shoulder.

"He's a magnificent thing, isn't he?" Manduul said, his voice dripping with drunken pride.

A stallion! Mandukhai used her other hand to turn the horse's head toward her. He was strong, and the muscles along the chest and neck promised long and fast riding—a mount suitable for racing and for battle. Such a stallion should be beyond her, even as the Great Khan's wife. The stallion was too fine to waste in any camp.

The crowd murmured in appreciation of the fine horse, and she could hardly believe it belonged to her.

Mandukhai's gaze flicked over to Manduul. "He is magnificent," she agreed, nearly breathless and bubbling with appreciation.

As she returned her attention to the horse, her gaze caught Unebolod. He watched her from the edge of the ring with curious pride as she examined the horse.

Mandukhai struggled to keep a blush from her cheeks, distracting herself by assessing the horse's muscular legs. Then she noticed the saddle. The black leather contrasted against the stallion's white coat and yellow-gold accents of the gear. Shame washed over Mandukhai. If she accepted such a gift, what sort of debt would she owe? She was certain she could never pay it back.

Overcome, Mandukhai stepped back and shook her head. "I'm sorry, Manduul. I could never accept such a rich, noble, and valuable gift."

Manduul waved her protest off with a dismissive flick. "This gift is nothing near as valuable as you."

In his drunken state, Manduul would not have the presence of mind to offer any veiled comments. He truly meant what he said. *Maybe I was wrong to dismiss him so quickly.* For the first time since arriving in Mongke Bulag, Mandukhai felt genuine affection for Manduul to believe her worthy of such a gift. In a surge of heartfelt gratitude, she bounced toward him and leaned over the table to kiss his forehead.

"Can I take him for a ride?" she asked with childlike excitement.

Manduul's brows shot up his tall forehead. "In the dark?"

"I'm perfectly safe surrounded by so many of the Khan's men, and Nergui will accompany me," she said, this time smiling earnestly. "And I am a Mongol."

His apprehension faded as he chuckled. "Fine. Fine. Just don't wander too far. The night is young."

Mandukhai bit her lip as she tried to smother her glee. "Indeed."

As she stepped up to mount, two of the Khan's men strode forward to help, but she waved them off. "A woman who cannot mount a horse has no right to be the Great Khan's wife."

Again, Manduul barked out a laugh, as did a few of the men and women around the circle.

The saddle held her unlike any saddle she had ever sat in before. It cradled her hips in place as if made just for her. She took the reins and turned the horse, catching Unebolod's gaze again. He still clutched his gift against his wide chest, but he nodded. She wouldn't be offending him if she went for a quick ride. And as she rode away, Nergui striding along beside her, Unebolod watched her go.

CHAPTER FIVE

DUST AND ATTRITION

After seeing Mandukhai's reaction to the horse, Unebolod had no desire to give her the gift Manduul had intended for her. The way she lit up as she saw the horse, how she examined it with a gentle, expert hand, how her eyes shined—she loved the stallion. Manduul had been right. Unebolod's gift far overshadowed his own. Her face had transformed into such pure affection as she looked upon Manduul that it made Unebolod's blood boil with anger. Hopefully, no one had noticed the heat rising in his neck or the way his muscles had tensed. He'd gripped the bundle of silk so tightly his hands had turned white.

If she had given me that reaction, he may have had my head by the end of the night, he attempted reassuring himself.

Yet as she trotted out of the circle on the horse's back, Unebolod might have welcomed that death just to have had such affection bestowed on him.

These feelings aren't real, he thought. *She is a means to an end.* But he knew that was a lie. Somehow, without exchanging any words with him, Mandukhai had drawn feelings out of Unebolod he hadn't experienced since his wife had died in childbirth, along with their only son.

"I'm sure you can give her the gift another day," said Manduul, drawing Unebolod out of his thoughts. The comment was a clear slight, and he tried his best to brush it off.

"There is no rush," Unebolod agreed. "I'm pleased she liked your gift." *My gift.*

38

Manduul held out his empty cup. A serving girl came to refill it without hesitation. All of Manduul's words slurred together as he spoke, and Unebolod struggled to understanding him. "Me, too. I can't wait for her to show me just how pleased she is later."

Unebolod chuckled and hoped it didn't sound as forced as it felt. "No doubt it will be vigorous." *Unless you don't stop drinking.*

Unebolod sank into a seat at Manduul's table and accepted a cup of black *airag*. He would need it to get through the rest of this night. With great effort, Unebolod put on the mask he so often wore; that of a man grateful to be in his Khan's service.

Manduul took a generous drink, then slowly lowered his cup. Unebolod followed Manduul's stricken gaze across the ring as a crowd parted without a command for the man approaching. Unebolod's anger only intensified, and he placed his hand on his sword.

Bigirsen had arrived. His skin was darker than true Mongols, and gray had bled into his dark, braided hair since they last met. Trailing behind Bigirsen, four of his own Uyghur tribesmen carried gifts. A new lacky lingered at his shoulder with weaselly eyes that took in everything around him. Unebolod could not recall the man's name, but he didn't much care either.

"Where is she?" Bigirsen asked, not bothering to show Manduul any form of deference.

"Riding," Manduul said.

Unebolod acted relaxed, observing the interaction between Bigirsen and Manduul. An excuse to strike Bigirsen down would be acceptable. Any excuse that would not arouse suspicion or anger among Manduul or his men.

Manduul tensed under Bigirsen's penetrating gaze. "I gave her a horse and she couldn't resist riding it at once."

"A horse," Bigirsen said flatly. He towered over the table, somehow making Manduul appear small. "The gifts I sent for you to give her were not adequate?"

Unebolod glanced at the bundle on the cushion beside him. It shouldn't have surprised him that the gifts were from Bigirsen and not Manduul. All of Manduul's wealth came from Bigirsen.

"She will still receive them," said Manduul, offering reassurances, "but when you see the horse—"

"Where is my daughter?" Bigirsen interrupted, waving his men off. They melted into the crowd with the gifts as his lacky slithered away to direct them.

A hush fell over the crowd. Bigirsen pressed his luck with this rude behavior.

Manduul shrugged, listing slightly to the side. "Her ger, probably."

Bigirsen's sharp jaw twitched, and he gripped the sword on his hip in a fist.

Unebolod tightened his own grip on his sword under the table. *Just make one mistake*, he prayed, itching to draw his weapon and finally find out which of them was a stronger fighter, confident it was himself.

Both Bigirsen and Unebolod needed this drunken baboon as a buffer for their own goals. Bigirsen knew that just as well as Unebolod. But Unebolod did not doubt his own loyalty to the Khan.

"You will visit her tonight before your new wife," Bigirsen said, as if he could just command the Khan to do what he willed.

"On my wedding night?" Manduul scoffed. "I think not."

"You will not leave her feeling abandoned because you have a new toy to satisfy your drunken, primal urges," Bigirsen said, lowering his voice.

Unebolod rose from his seat, muscles tense for a fight and openly gripping his sword.

Manduul put his hand on Unebolod's arm and pulled him back. Then he rolled to the side and struggled to his feet, attempting to exude a commanding presence. Instead, it just reminded everyone of how drunk he was and how little power he held in this relationship. Unfortunately, in this drunken state, he only proved Bigirsen's point.

"I am your Khan, and you will not make commands of me," said Manduul, struggling to keep his words clear and even.

Bigirsen's expression hardened in an obvious challenge.

If he kills Manduul, I can raise the black banner and wipe out the Uyghur and their Oirat allies in retaliation, Unebolod thought, almost wishing for it to happen.

A battle of attrition waged silently between Bigirsen and Manduul as each waited for the other to back down first. Manduul only had such courage to stand against Bigirsen when he was too drunk to know better. But the men were at a stalemate. Manduul needed the riches Bigirsen sent his way to keep the tribes in the north happy—and to continue his lifestyle of slovenly wealth. Bigirsen couldn't kill Manduul outright without throwing all the Mongol tribes into war, and he was smart enough to know the tribes would never elect him at *kurultai*—where tribe leaders gathered to show support of the next Great Khan. Until Bigirsen's daughter had a son, he needed Manduul alive.

No one else dared move, as if the entire gathering feared they might be a casualty of this silent war.

Unebolod knew he should encourage Manduul to spend more time with Mandukhai to increase the odds that Yeke would never conceive, thus removing some of Bigirsen's power. But thinking of Manduul and Mandukhai together renewed his jealousy. Somehow, he would have to find a way past these feelings.

Manduul finally turned his gaze away from Bigirsen as he drank from his cup, a concession. Bigirsen strode forward and snatched the cup from Manduul's hand, slapping it down on the table. Clear black *airag* sloshed out.

Unebolod clenched his jaw.

"Neither of your wives will be satisfied if you continue drinking like this," said Bigirsen.

Manduul frowned at his empty hand, then fire burned in his eyes as his cheeks reddened. He glared at Bigirsen. "I know how to handle myself."

Bigirsen offered a mocking bow as he backed up. "Of course you do, my lord Khan."

Before Manduul could respond, Bigirsen turned and stormed off toward Yeke's ger. Unebolod seized the distraction as an opportunity to slip away from this evening as well. Before he managed two steps, Manduul called him to a stop.

"Where are you rushing off to, Unebolod?" Manduul said gruffly.

Unebolod paused, turning slowly. "To relieve myself." *And to find a better gift.* "Too much *airag*. I must put my gift aside for another day. Your wife is pleased enough with what she has received tonight."

Manduul nodded. "Go then. When you return, we will talk about finding you another wife. It's time."

"I agree," Unebolod lied.

As he slipped away, he knew that Manduul was playing another game with him. His glances at Mandukhai hadn't gone unnoticed.

The horse turned out just as fast as his physique promised. Mandukhai leaned close to the stallion's neck, clutching the reins as he thundered across the flat plains. Nergui struggled to keep up on his own mount.

At such speed, she was thankful she had left the *boqta* in her ger. Without it, her hair whipped free in the breeze. Cold night air kissed her face, and she relished the sensation.

They raced along the steppe together until the river began winding away, until the sounds of celebration melted into the night air, until the light from campfires and torches disappeared in the distance. Still, the horse didn't slow, didn't struggle for breath. For the first time since the arrangement of this marriage, Mandukhai felt free.

Not knowing the terrain, Mandukhai feared she might accidentally ride the stallion over a marmot hole and injure him, but this newfound sense of freedom drew her along. She couldn't halt herself even when Nergui called for her to stop.

Yet the reminder of Manduul's request to remain close, that he expected her to return soon, loomed over her shoulder as if calling her back to camp. She tugged the reins, and the stallion came to a swift halt. Mandukhai stared east—toward home. How easy it would be to keep riding; to race across the steppe and flee Manduul, never sharing a bed with him again. She could ride for another hour before Manduul would wonder about her absence, assuming he wasn't too deep into the drink. With this horse, she could run and make her own fate.

The stallion pranced beneath her, spinning in impatient circles. It wanted to run more. She wanted to ride further.

"Your duty is not done, Lady Mandukhai," Nergui said as his mount pulled up beside her.

She knew he was right. Leaving could start a war between tribes. Mandukhai couldn't live with herself knowing men would lose their lives and families would lose loved ones because of her petulance. She wanted to be like Khutulun, but that was little more than a childish dream.

The stallion whinnied, tugging west.

"Fine," she huffed. "You both win."

With a simple command, the stallion launched into a gallop, back toward Mongke Bulag. Nergui kicked his own mount to ride along with her.

The return journey felt so much shorter than the ride away. The two of them trotted back into camp, and she dismounted as they weaved their way through the mass of gers toward her own near the center of the capital.

As she passed Yeke's ger, heated voices rose from within in a vicious argument. One voice was Yeke for certain, but the other was a man who sounded nothing like Manduul. Mandukhai licked her lips, glanced at Nergui, and hesitated. Should they come to Yeke's aid?

"... make such demands of me!" Yeke said, her voice raised at a higher pitch than Mandukhai remembered.

Is she in trouble? What if another man forced his way in and demanded she pleasure him? The Khan would have his head!

Mandukhai cast a questioning glance at Nergui, who remained statue still, hand on his sword.

"It's your fault she's here in the first place," Yeke said.

Mandukhai placed a hand on Nergui's arm and shook her head. They were talking about her!

"If you were fulfilling your duties, he wouldn't have insisted on another wife in the first place," said the man, his tone sharp as a blade. "How hard could it possibly be to get him into your bed? All he does is eat, drink, and have sex."

"And now it will never be with me," said Yeke. "And I will never have his child."

Mandukhai tiptoed past the door, keeping her head down.

"Not with that attitude!" the man roared. "He will be here tonight. Make yourself suitably presentable so he doesn't want to leave."

Vice Regent Bigirsen. Mandukhai had heard he approached the capital. He must have arrived while she was riding. Who else would be in Yeke's ger?

Nergui apparently came to the same conclusion as he nudged Mandukhai along. She had no desire to meet Bigirsen yet, and her steps quickened.

"I gave him another wife to keep him placated," Bigirsen said, his voice muffled the further Mandukhai moved away from Yeke's ger. "Now it's your job to keep him in your bed as long as possible. As often as it takes. The more he is with you, the less he is with her."

Yeke's father sounded determined to be sure Mandukhai would not be the first to produce an heir. Without a son, Mandukhai could lose her position to Yeke. And Mandukhai was little more than a consolation prize to placate an unsatisfied man. She could not help resenting Yeke for not doing her own duty. If she had, perhaps Mandukhai would not have suffered this fate. *I cannot allow her to bear the first son,* Mandukhai thought. The idea of laying with Manduul again still did not settle well with her—she didn't find him terribly attractive—but he had been kind and tender. While she may not enjoy her fate, it certainly could have been worse.

Mandukhai reached her ger and began removing the saddle, leaving the blanket to help keep the horse warm during the chilly night. She stroked his nose. Manduul had given her this gift. She would give him an heir. Before Yeke.

"I will call you Dust," she whispered. "Because that is all anyone will ever see of us."

Dust bobbed his head and chuffed.

"I will retrieve your evening guards," Nergui said, holding the reins of his own mount.

Mandukhai would be perfectly safe here for now, so she simply nodded as he walked away.

Mandukhai stroked Dust's nose one more time before entering her ger to put the saddle away. As she placed it on the table beside the door, she noticed the detail pressed into the leather for the first time. Dancing dragons. She ran her finger along the smooth black leather, feeling the texture of the dragons. Mandukhai was born in the year of the Yellow Dragon, the strongest and most imperial of all zodiac symbols. Her mother insisted it meant she was destined for greatness. But what of all the other children born the same year? Were they not also destined for greatness? Regardless, Mandukhai appreciated this small symbol of recognition in a big way.

I have underestimated Manduul Khan.

Dust snorted outside, and Mandukhai glanced out the open door to see a wiry man in thick, fine furs petting her horse and admiring it with a critical eye. His dark hair was pulled back in a thick braid behind his back. Something about him remaindered her of a snake. Mandukhai stepped over the threshold.

"His name is Dust," she said, offering him a sweet smile. "And he's every bit as fast as he looks."

"What need does the Khan's second wife have for such a fine horse?" he asked

Who did this man think he was? He exuded a calm patience she found unnerving, yet could not place why.

"Excuse me?" she said, careful to keep her tone light and even. Why did Nergui have to leave? "Who are you?"

"Issama, my Lady. I am Bigirsen's advisor." Issama faced her, and Mandukhai took in the smooth edges of his narrow face. His gaze made her skin crawl. "I meant no offense, my Lady."

Bigirsen's advisor ... Mandukhai's eyes narrowed. "Regardless, Advisor Issama, this horse was a gift from my husband, and so I cherish it still."

Issama smiled politely and bowed in deference. "Of course, my Lady.

I wish you a happy marriage. Please, take this token of my respect for you and the Khan." He produced a pouch from within the folds of his deel and offered it to her. "It is a humble gift, but perhaps will assist in expediting the arrival of an heir."

Mandukhai accepted the pouch, frowning at it. When she looked back up, Issama had disappeared into the night as if he had never been there. She opened the pouch and sniffed the contents, making a sour face as the tart scent of herbs assaulted her senses.

Nergui approached with two guards following on his heels. "Is everything okay?"

Mandukhai handed him the pouch. "I was just given this as a gift."

Nergui took it and inspected the contents, sniffing, wincing, and closing the pouch. "It's too dangerous to take anything not approved by the shaman, my Lady." He pocketed the pouch. "I will see to it myself."

Mandukhai nodded and glanced at the new guards. The idea of sleeping without Nergui guarding her made Mandukhai uncomfortable, but even he needed rest sometime.

CHAPTER SIX

SPIES AND SILKS

Mandukhai finished wrapping the deel around her body and fastened the belt in place. Manduul snorted, flopping half-naked onto his round belly. Mandukhai froze, watching to see if he would wake. When his snoring resumed, she slipped on her boots and tiptoed to the door.

Late in the night, he had stumbled in from the festivities with his deel hanging open and hat in hand. Mandukhai had just climbed beneath her blankets, and she barely escaped them before he had tumbled onto the bed, slapping a fat hand around her waist before promptly passing out. His skin had been slick with sweat. With any luck, he wouldn't remember that nothing had happened between them. While she knew now that she needed a son before Yeke, it felt too soon to allow him to use her in such a way again.

Mandukhai opened the door just enough to slip out, closing it quietly behind her. Let him sleep it off.

Crisp, cool morning air caressed her skin. She drew in a deep breath until the stink of Manduul was completely expunged from her lungs. Dust snorted near the door, tethered to a post. Mandukhai retrieved the saddle from its place beside the doorway, then stepped up to his side to slip the saddle on his back. In less than a minute, she had it secured in place and was ready to ride.

"Let's explore the camp and find you something to eat," she said, settling into the saddle.

Nergui approached, guiding his own mount as if he knew precisely what she would do so early. He said nothing, riding along beside her with ever-vigilant eyes.

After the indulgence of the late evening, an eerie hush had settled over the capital. Most residents still slumbered, but Mandukhai long ago learned that sunrise was the best time to read the clouds and predict whether rain would come or if the camp needed to move to better grazing pastures for the animals. Even if she had drowned herself in *airag* the night before, she'd still have been up. Those morning rituals would make life with Manduul somewhat more bearable.

Manduul's camp never seemed to move. No grass remained between gers, worn away by months of foot traffic and grazed away by herds. Pedestrians and animals dirtied the bottom edges of the felt lining the outside of the gers all along the thoroughfare with splashed-up soil. Even through downpours, the gers remained as if taking root.

Adjusting to this life might be even harder than Mandukhai thought. Her tribe constantly moved around the eastern steppe in favor of better water and grazing, avoiding the harsh winters as much as possible. Mandukhai had learned to deconstruct and reconstruct a ger in about an hour. Taking root had never been an option. Could Manduul truly be so careless to remain in one place? Mandukhai could not help wondering if this put him at a tactical disadvantage. How did the massive herds graze over barren, worn-out land? *Mongols were not known for their farming, though back in the days of Kublai, they had tried. And the Ming swept in easily to destroy them*, she thought as she rode through the capital.

Mandukhai spent the better part of the morning riding around capital. It turned out larger than she had anticipated. Hundreds of gers indicated thousands in the area. Such living could not be sustainable for long. Those with chores that couldn't wait or children who wouldn't sleep were up and moving about their daily tasks as well. Mandukhai bid all of them a good day as she rode along. One woman, overcome to meet her in person, had given Mandukhai a generous portion of sweet curds—a treat she doled out to the children as she passed, offering kind smiles and sweets to the children. They would run away with their prizes, squealing in delight as mothers chased after them, ordering them to hush.

Mandukhai wound her way along the organized chaos of the ger clusters, headed toward the river where there would hopefully be grass for grazing and water for Dust to drink. She noted several potters and leatherworkers, and very few armorers. Various herbalists and herder homes were apparent by strips of meat drying in the sun or herbs hanging to dry. Those smells of the capital were familiar, yet stronger. Excrement piled outside the camps to dry caught on a change of breeze and blew their stink through the camp, mingling with the burning scent of ger fires warding off the cool spring air.

Dust circled the entire capital as Mandukhai assessed the sheer size of it. At least two other tribes had joined the capital last night after she had first examined their numbers, adding up to more than ten thousand men, women, and children. Such a large gathering was rare and could not be sustained for long.

Mandukhai led Dust to the eastern bank of the Orkhon River and gave him a chance to graze and drink. As the horse wandered around her, Mandukhai sat under the shade of a birch tree, staring into the forest on the other side and at the white-capped Khangai Mountains beyond. Perhaps she could adjust to this life.

Nergui dismounted, watching over the horses and searching for signs of danger. He left Mandukhai in silence as if she were alone, and she privately thanked him for understanding.

The sooner she could produce a son for Manduul, the better. A son would secure her place. And once she had a son, she would feel more comfortable distancing herself from him. But a son with Manduul presented a different concern as well. Would that son turn out like his father—slovenly and willing allow others to do his work for him? *I will teach him to be better*, she thought confidently.

"A queen with a passion for riding," said Bigirsen, stepping up beside her on the riverbank. "I trust she knows that riding too far could cause the Khan serious concern."

Mandukhai jumped to her feet and immediately hated herself for showing him such a reaction. How had she not heard his approach? And why had Nergui, who observed Bigirsen from a distance, not whistled a warning to her?

Attempting to recover, she huffed and brushed the dirt from her deel. "And sneaking up to give his wife such a fright would worry him as well."

"Apologies, my Lady." Bigirsen bowed in a way that felt more mocking than deferential. "I assumed you heard me coming. My steps are not exactly quiet."

Mandukhai mistrusted Bigirsen on a deep level. He was leader of the Uyghur—a tribe with allegiance to the Oirat responsible for supporting tyrants like Esen, and the death of her father. Bigirsen may not have struck any killing blows, but the affiliation was enough to arouse her suspicion.

"Did you need something, or have you simply come to cause me alarm?" Mandukhai adjusted her *boqta* then leveled her gaze on him.

"Your husband is, in fact, worried. He woke and you were gone. Thankfully, some people reported seeing you riding this way, so he sent me to retrieve you."

Did Manduul fear she had run? Mandukhai would be lying to herself if she did not admit considering it.

"Surely a task below your station, Vice Regent," she said, her words sickly sweet.

Bigirsen didn't take the bait as he turned a pensive gaze toward the mountains. "I helped him become Great Khan. I live to serve him and respect him as a brother should."

Mandukhai turned from him, taking Dust's reins and mounting. "I will be sure to let him know. Where might I find him?"

"In the gathering tent," he said.

Before Bigirsen could say another word, Mandukhai urged her horse away at a trot, fast enough to put distance between them but not so fast that it appeared she was fleeing.

Most of the capital had come alive as Mandukhai returned to the heart of Mongke Bulag. Men stumbled from their gers and rubbed sleep from their eyes or devoured breakfast in the open air. Women gathered to exchange threads for embroidering or clothing. Despite being absorbed in their daily routines, most still bid her a good morning as she trotted past, showing due deference to the Khan's new wife.

Manduul Khan's gathering tent was not like other ger. The round structure was twice the size of the Khan's personal ger, with a roof that reached higher than any other in camp. Since Manduul entertained or conducted business in the gathering tent, extra space was necessary to accommodate diplomats, scribes, or nobles. Mandukhai had not taken in the space the previous night, preoccupied with what was about the happen. Now, she took her time to absorb all the details.

White felt covered the outside, embroidered in blue along the door, and all around the roof. Unlike most of the gers in the capital, which had wooden doors, the gathering tent had a set of curtained felt flaps in colorful layers. The opening was wide enough to fit three men abreast and tall enough for her to enter with the extra height of the *boqta*. Someone had tied the flaps open this morning.

Mandukhai entered, taking in the riches with a shock she couldn't mask. A dozen red columns lined either side of the main gathering space. They held up the tall canopy of the ger, which currently opened in the center to the sky beyond; golden gilt-work of twisting birds wrapped around each of the massive columns. Red silks with colorful embroidery bowed out from each of the slender *uni* poles supporting the roof. Silks tied around the top of the lattice walls, then draped down over the felt and fur insulation.

At the head of the round space, a golden-gilded throne with a high back rested on the dais high enough that anyone wishing to approach Manduul Khan would have to climb three levels of steps first. A matching cushion offered comfort for long days of sitting. The dais was fashioned from the wood of the northern lands, and the engravings were intricate, dyed red and blue.

Thanks to the generosity of Bigirsen, the gathering tent was filled with luxuries rarely found in Mongolia: silks that cascaded over the skin like freshly falling snow, textiles embroidered with flowers and birds prepared to take flight, and beads of colored glass shined an array of brilliant hues of light as they hung from the ceiling. Persian rugs with geometric patterns and rich colors covered the rough floor. It was a space fit for a Great Khan at the height of Mongolian power, even if that power had become significantly diminished over the years.

Manduul Khan perched atop his golden throne, leaning back in a lazy, casual demeanor. On one side sat Yeke, turned sideways in her own chair to face Manduul. Beside her, a vacant chair awaited Mandukhai. Yeke cast a glance at Mandukhai that only lasted a moment, but the hate in her eyes burned deep just the same. Mandukhai made her way toward the chair along the edge of the gathering space.

Unebolod stood at the bottom of the dais, hands folded behind his back as he met Manduul's gaze unflinchingly. Mandukhai's heart leaped into her throat. They had not gotten a chance to speak the night before. Was it too late now?

Mandukhai silently joined Yeke. Manduul glanced at Mandukhai briefly from the corner of his eyes in a way that made her worry she had raised his ire by riding this morning.

"You are telling me this boy has been with your own brother this whole time, and you have said nothing to me? Why am I learning of this from my Vice Regent and his advisor instead?"

"My brother and I swore and oath to Lady Samur ten years ago," Unebolod said calmly. "We would do nothing to endanger his life before he came of age. We would protect him. My word is iron, my lord Khan."

Manduul's face wrinkled into a scowl. "And what of your vow to me? Does that mean nothing to you?"

Unebolod didn't flinch as Mandukhai would have. Instead, he raised his chin proudly. "I swore to protect you and ride for you as my Khan. I have made no such promise to him. Protecting him until he comes of age is not the same as an oath to my lord Khan."

"He is my kin," Manduul growled. "And a danger to me, the very Khan you have sworn your life to protect."

"He poses no danger to you under my brother's watchful eye," Unebolod replied.

Mandukhai admired Unebolod's courage and conviction when Manduul so clearly shared his anger openly.

"You will retrieve him, then, and bring him to me," Manduul said. "And I will determine what sort of danger he poses."

Unebolod inclined his head in agreement. "That would be within the boundary of my oath, since I swore to return him to his place, which would be at your side, my lord Khan."

"Even if I kill him?" Manduul asked.

Mandukhai had no idea what these two men were talking about, but it piqued her interest. Who was this boy Manduul sounded so afraid of?

Unebolod tensed so subtly Mandukhai would have missed it were she not already openly gaping at him. "I have promised you horses, gers, salt, and blood. My duty is first to the Great Khan."

"Go, Unebolod," Manduul commanded. "Use that silver tongue of yours to convince your brother to hand over the boy to me. If he needs convincing, let him know I can send Bigirsen to aid in negotiations, if need be."

"Threats are unnecessary," Unebolod said. "Bolunai will listen. I will see to it."

"I want to be sure I'm clear, Unebolod," Manduul said. "If he doesn't agree to his Great Khan's terms, I will be left with no alternative. He may be khan of his tribe, but I am Khan of khans. Go now, while the sun still rises."

Unebolod bowed. "As my lord Khan commands. I should return with news in ten days." As he stood upright, Unebolod's gaze flicked to Mandukhai long enough to make her chest tighten. Then he turned and marched out with a small contingent of men on his heels.

Manduul raised a hand toward Mandukhai, holding it upright as if waiting for something. Everyone watched. A dozen sets of eyes, all staring at her. Mandukhai licked her lips then rose, gliding toward him and slipping her hand into his with a bow.

"My lord Khan," she said, remembering what he had said about deference in his court.

Only the two of them remained with Yeke and her two wards, Borogchin and Esige—each wearing beaded silver *shanaavch* that hung low at the temples. Bigirsen slipped in as the last of the Lords left.

"I hope I didn't worry you, my lord Khan," Mandukhai said, hoping to cover any tracks that could lead Manduul to anger or distrust. "I woke early and was so excited about your gift so I went for another short ride, just to the river so he could graze and drink."

Manduul raised her hand to his lips, pressing a dry kiss against it. "I was more disappointed than worried. But that is not why I summoned you." He snapped his fingers.

Borogchin and Esige approached the dais, drawing Mandukhai's attention. "Your tribe sent generous gifts and dowry, but only one servant and no girls to join your court."

Mandukhai's heart seized, and tears welled in her eyes. "There were two girls, but they both died on the way here." Grief tightened her throat.

"A pity," Manduul said. "I hope it was not your neglect that caused their demise."

Mandukhai's eyes widened at the implication. "On the contrary. I did everything within my power to save them once they took ill." It took everything in Mandukhai not to show how the comment hurt. "Have I disappointed you, my lord Khan?"

Manduul grinned wolfishly. "Hardly. But this is a problem we must remedy. Yeke has kindly agreed to allow these two girls into your care. I hope this is not a mistake."

Mandukhai didn't believe for a second Yeke did this out of kindness, even if Manduul had pressed her on the matter. *Unless the girls served a different purpose. They are probably spying for her.* But Mandukhai had nothing to hide.

"A generous offer," Mandukhai said, smiling sweetly at Yeke. "I am honored."

"These girls could use both of our guiding hands," Yeke said, smiling back just as sweetly, with a telling fire that burned in her eyes. "It is the least I could do."

"Borogchin and Esige are not simply any pair of girls," Manduul said. "They are my nieces and princesses of the Mongol Nation. You will raise these girls as your own daughters and teach them how to fulfill their expectations to the people."

Bigirsen stood beside the girls, looking them over. "Yes. And when the time comes, we will find them a suitable marriage to strengthen the Great Khan's rule."

Sadness for these girls pierced Mandukhai's heart. Particularly Borogchin, who appeared close to marital age already. They were nothing more than pawns in a political game—pieces for the men to push around into a beneficial position.

Mandukhai floated down the dais toward them. Esige couldn't be much older than ten, but her eyes exhibited intelligence beyond her years. Mandukhai held out her arms, and Esige embraced her.

Mandukhai leaned forward and sniffed her cheek in greeting. "Esige, daughter of my heart, I'm pleased to welcome you."

She moved to Borogchin, who took her arms in an embrace as well. She was a pretty girl approaching maturity, which didn't give Mandukhai much time to find a suitable match, and she knew so little about the young men of the tribes to make an educated decision. Was this Bigirsen's doing? Did he seek to prove her incapable of her position? Or perhaps this was a distraction from bearing her own son, giving Yeke more time to seduce Manduul.

As Mandukhai sniffed Borogchin's cheeks in greeting, Borogchin glanced over Mandukhai's shoulder. Her body turned rigid at whatever she saw. *What is she afraid of?*

Mandukhai released her. "Borogchin, daughter of my heart, I'm pleased to welcome you, too."

"These girls are now part of your home, Mandukhai," Manduul said, drawing Mandukhai's attention back to him. "Our home. Make them comfortable."

"Of course." Mandukhai bowed, and as she did her gaze fell on Issama, who watched everything like a curious bird. Bigirsen openly stared at Borogchin, his gaze prowling the girl in a way that even made Mandukhai's skin crawl. She placed a hand on each girl and turned them away.

Borogchin and Esige already had a ger beside Mandukhai, so there had been no need to settle in. By dinner, they had both entered Mandukhai's home with marriage gifts. Custom allowed eight days of gifts for a new couple, and more would surely pour in for the Khan and his new bride before those eight days expired. Borogchin dipped her head as she held out the bundle to Mandukhai. The silver bells on her headdress chimed. Esige beamed, bouncing on her toes with excitement.

Mandukhai immediately recognized the fur bundle in Esige's arms from the night before. It was the same one Unebolod clutched as he watched Manduul gift her the horse. *Why are they giving his gift as their own, and how did they come about it?*

After setting down her teacup, she sank down onto her bed. Borogchin gracefully placed the bundle at Mandukhai's feet as Esige struggle to contain her excitement—a sentiment Mandukhai shared. What would he have gotten for her? And why did these girls have it now?

Both girls sat on the floor, watching Mandukhai closely; Borogchin with passive curiosity and Esige with pride. The fur wasn't bound closed, and Mandukhai flipped it open as the girls watched.

A stack of silks shifted, sliding loose from the fur that bundled them together: reds, blues, yellows, golds, and whites for her use, as well as several embroidered silk deels fit or a queen. Mandukhai gasped. Last night, such a gift would have seemed extravagant, but after appearing in the gathering tent today in such simple clothing, Mandukhai knew she needed to dress as a queen or risk her authority being questioned.

Such wealth of extravagant silk here, she thought, plucking a jade deel from the stack and holding it up to examine.

"It's so lovely," she said. "I have to wonder, though, how you came about it when I saw it in Unebolod's arms last night."

Borogchin sat back on her heels, brushing an admiring hand over a bolt of white silk. "He gave it to us last night. We had gifts prepared, but this is far richer than what we had to offer. He told us it seemed too personal a gift to give you without upsetting Uncle Manduul, so he gave it to us to give to you." Her face adopted a distant, dreamy glaze.

Last night he had seemed eager to present his gift. Why change his mind? Sadly, Mandukhai would have to wait until his return to ask.

Mandukhai looped the jade deel over her arm and held up the white silk to Borogchin. "Please take this. I can teach you how to make your own marriage deel with it."

Borogchin hesitated, leaning away as if waiting for a condition, but Mandukhai offered none. If Yeke intended this girl as a spy, perhaps with enough kindness, Mandukhai could shift Borogchin's loyalties.

Finally, Borogchin slipped her hands around the fabric and murmured her gratitude. Mandukhai offered the yellow to Esige, who blinked as if unsure what was happening. Her gaze darted to Borogchin, who cradled her white silk affectionately, then Esige accepted the yellow with childlike eagerness.

"Good." Mandukhai smiled brightly at both girls. "Now that's settled, let's discuss how to gather supplies for this ger. It's grossly understocked."

CHAPTER SEVEN

VIPER IN THE TEACUP

As the wolf dawn broke across the sky, casting the world in lighter hues of blue that chased away the darkness of night, Mandukhai sent the girls to make trades with families around the capital for food and other various supplies for her ger. Her servant, Tuya, accompanied the girls to carry the goods back, as well as Nergui for protection.

While they were out, Mandukhai set to decorating her new home. The rick shades of red silk the girls gave her were just enough to cover the lattice walls. She then precisely arranged the rugs people had given her as wedding gifts on the floor to display a rainbow of colors circling south to north and back again so that the brightest shades of yellow and orange covered her side of the space. For now, she placed the gifts of jewels in a leather pouch and buried them in her chest along with the new deels—except for the jade one she wore today.

By the time the girls returned with the resources Mandukhai had requested, the interior of the ger had been transformed from a simple, ordinary dwelling into a home fit for a queen. The water on the stovetop began boiling, and she set Esige to work preparing the tea and setting out the breakfast meat-stuffed dumplings they had acquired from another family. Ideally, the girls or Tuya would have made the dumplings, but there hadn't been time this morning without the supplies.

Mandukhai handed a horse brush to Borogchin and nudged her toward the open door where streams of warm light from the sunrise bathed the area in golden light. "I need you to watch for Lady Yeke. Be certain to invite her in for tea and breakfast dumplings."

If Mandukhai had to be sister-wives with the woman, she would at least try to get to know her a little better. Yeke could not refuse or risked insulting Mandukhai—and possibly Manduul by extension.

As Mandukhai and Esige were about to sit for tea, Yeke stepped inside. Mandukhai smiled brightly at her guest as Yeke's gaze swept the interior of Mandukhai's ger with uninhibited shock.

"Good morning, Yeke," Mandukhai said, her voice honey-sweet. "We were just sitting for tea and breakfast. Please, join us." She motioned to the bench on the other side of the ger.

Yeke appeared ready to refuse, but to do so would be an insult, and Mandukhai could report her to Manduul. Not that she would, but Yeke didn't need to know that. This was a game, and Mandukhai had spent enough time around politics and women during her childhood to know how to play.

Finally, Yeke bowed her head ever so slightly in gratitude as Esige poured a cup of tea. The gems on Yeke's *boqta* chimed with the motion. By the time she sat on the bench, the tea was in her hand and Esige offered a small plate of dumplings to Yeke.

"We have had little chance to talk since my arrival," Mandukhai said, opening the conversation as Yeke cautiously sipped her tea, watching Mandukhai over her cup. "I hope we can take this time to get to know each other more intimately. We are sister-wives, after all."

Yeke slowly lowered her cup, her eyes examining Mandukhai as she attempted to decipher the hidden meaning. "I suppose we are. I'm afraid there isn't much to know about me, though. You already know who my father is."

Borogchin buried her face in her teacup at the mention of Bigirsen. Mandukhai hadn't asked the girl yet, but she could guess well enough that Borogchin had no desire to be an object of his interest. *I will remedy that soon enough. She will not end up in a marriage where she fears her own husband.*

"I do," Mandukhai replied evenly. "We spoke yesterday."

"And I know who your father was as well," Yeke said innocently. "A traitor, I've been told. He betrayed Esen Khan and led the revolt against him." She took a sip.

Mandukhai fought off a grimace. Only those who supported Esen's madness would believe such a thing. Did that mean Yeke's father supported Esen? It made sense, she supposed. Bigirsen had alliances with Oirat leaders, as far as Nergui had told her. But Esen was not blood or bone of Genghis.

"Esen butchered the Borjigin royals—our husband's family," Mandukhai replied, grateful that her anger did not reveal itself in her tone. "It's a miracle Manduul survived."

"And Unebolod," said Yeke.

The revelation took Mandukhai by surprise, and just hearing his name made heat rise in her cheeks. *I thought he was Khorchin. Was he part of the Borjigin butchering?* She took a drink of her tea, hoping it covered her reaction well enough. Yeke was testing her. She wanted to gauge how Mandukhai reacted, which meant Yeke believed there was a reason to probe in the first place. Did she notice Mandukhai's lingering gaze on him yesterday? *It was nothing more.*

"I was not aware he is Borjigin," Mandukhai said casually, reaching for a dumpling. Borogchin held the plate closer to her from where she seated herself on the pillow on the floor beside Mandukhai. "I hardly even know his name."

"He is not Borjigin," Yeke clarified sharply, "but descends from Khasar, the blood brother of Genghis, which still made his family a danger to Esen."

That makes more sense, Mandukhai thought. Khasar had been one of Genghis's younger brothers, and loyal to his end even after all of his brothers died. Unebolod came from high noble stock, and without a Borjigin heir, Unebolod's family had the strongest claim to the khanship. If Esen wanted to ensure no one could change his right to the title, destroying Unebolod's family would have been necessary as well.

Yeke raised a skeptical eyebrow at this. "Lord Unebolod has quite a reputation. I find what you say hard to believe."

Mandukhai's mind churned as she slowly chewed her dumpling. The longer she considered it, the more certain she became that she had, in fact, heard of Unebolod before. A seasoned warrior. Brutal and brilliant in battle. Mandukhai took her time chewing her food to buy a moment to collect her thoughts.

"I have heard stories about the Steel Soldier," said Mandukhai, hoping she sounded naïve. "Is this him? His name means steel, after all."

"You are very curious about a man who isn't your husband," Yeke said pointedly, perching her dumpling between her fingers.

"You brought him up," Mandukhai pointed out. "I'm merely making conversation. And such a warrior would be a fine addition to the Great Khan's court."

"He is *orlok* of Manduul's northern *tumens*," Yeke said, as if it were a boring matter of fact to be so highly ranked among the Great Khan's men. "Just as my father is *orlok* of the southern *tumens*."

So Unebolod is a field commander over thousands of Manduul's men, and a potential heir to the title should Yeke and I have no children. Mandukhai found this fascinating, and a bit terrifying. Unebolod had every reason to dislike her. Perhaps that was why he stared at her as he so often did. He was assessing the new threat.

Mandukhai grew more fascinated by Unebolod. He was the Steel Soldier she had heard stories of. The same man who defeated an entire *mingghan* of a thousand men with only three of his own warriors, ending an invasion from a nearby hostile tribe, when he was only eighteen years old? The same Steel Soldier who would have defeated Bigirsen in battle had Bigirsen not insisted on meeting with Manduul, who acted as the Borjigin tribe leader, before he became Great Khan?

Mandukhai's skin prickled beneath her deel, and she was thankful for the long sleeves covering her skin. "How is Manduul? Have you seen him this morning?" she asked, changing the subject while also implying that Manduul had not spend the evening in Mandukhai's ger.

"Yes," Yeke replied, but she couldn't meet Mandukhai's gaze. Had she lied? "He headed to speak with my father about matters that are none of our business. I'm sure we will see Manduul soon enough, if you are missing him."

Was Yeke mocking her? Missing Manduul was the furthest thought from Mandukhai's mind, but as long as Yeke didn't know that, Mandukhai still had the upper hand. *Let her think she is withholding something I want.*

"Maybe a little," she admitted with feigned sheepishness, smiling shyly before taking another sip of tea. "And your father? How long will he be staying with us? I owe him thanks for arranging this marriage."

Yeke set down her half-eaten dumpling and wiped her hands together. "Two days, I believe." Though she spoke sweetly enough about her father, just mentioning his delayed departure seemed to stiffen Yeke's back. "He brought gifts for the three of us in celebration. Silver and rare trinkets from the west, as I understand. I expect he will deliver them tonight."

Mandukhai noticed Borogchin listened intently to Yeke's response, though she pitifully pretended otherwise as she gathered the dishes and brought them to Tuya to clean. Mandukhai smothered a smirk. Borogchin did not like Bigirsen, and that worked in Mandukhai's favor.

"Is your father riding off to battle from here?" Mandukhai asked.

Yeke folded her hands into her sleeves. "How should I know? Matters of war are not my business." She stood suddenly, seeming anxious about something, though she tried to hide it. "I should go. Thank you for inviting me. We will do this again."

"Can you not stay for a second cup?" Mandukhai asked innocently, though secretly she wanted Yeke to leave as well.

"I'm afraid not. The day's tasks wait whether or not I delay them."

Mandukhai stood and bowed to Yeke. "Until next time, then."

The moment Yeke stepped out, Mandukhai relaxed a little more. Somehow, she needed to pry information from Esige and Borogchin, both of whom already cleaned up breakfast.

"Esige, please fetch some fresh water from the river," Mandukhai said, motioning to an empty bucket near the door. "Tuya, accompany her."

"Yes, Mother." Esige swiftly moved to comply with Tuya on her heels, leaving Mandukhai alone with Borogchin.

"Borogchin," Mandukhai said, joining Borogchin at the butcher slab where a basin of water waited for the dishes. Mandukhai took her empty cup to the small basin. "I am about to ask you a question, and I need you to vow absolute honesty in your answer."

Borogchin froze, glancing at Mandukhai. "I always will speak honestly with you, Lady Mandukhai."

"I need you to promise me."

The girl cocked her head slightly to the side, and she seemed both curious and cautious. "I promise."

"I noticed how Bigirsen looked at you, and how you reacted," said Mandukhai, setting her cup on the table beside the bowl.

"I don't know—"

"You promised."

Borogchin lowered her gaze to the washing and fell silent, her hands slowing their task as if to draw it out.

Mandukhai swept Borogchin's hair over her shoulder the way her mother used to do to her. "Poor, sweet child. I understand. You are afraid of being married off to him, aren't you?"

Borogchin scrubbed harder at the plate until Mandukhai placed her own hands over them.

"He ... he would be an excellent match, and an honorable one," Borogchin said. Mandukhai heard the strain in her voice as she fought off tears.

"But not a necessary one," Mandukhai reassured her, taking Borogchin's hands in her own and forcing the girl to face her. Tears rolled down Borogchin's face. "We will find you someone more suitable and it will help strengthen your uncle's hold on the nation." She tilted Borogchin's face up. "Someone more desirable."

Borogchin's body quivered, and inner war waged in her eyes. For a moment Mandukhai thought she would refuse, that she would insist on it being a suitable match. Finally, she swallowed a lump in her throat and spoke. "Lady Yeke told me he was a good man. That he would be a suitable match for a strong Borjigin princess like me, and that I should be lucky."

Mandukhai tensed, grasping Borogchin's hand urgently. "Did she already make the arrangements?"

Borogchin shook her head.

Of course, Yeke couldn't have or Manduul would not have accepted shifting Borogchin to my care. Come to think about it, the change was an insult to Yeke. Mandukhai's heart hammered against her ribs. No wonder Yeke despised her.

Still, Mandukhai beamed. She no longer could do anything about her own situation, but she would do everything in her power to ensure Borogchin and Esige did not suffer the same fate. "Then let me worry about the details. I promise you, I will not send you into a marriage with a man you clearly fear."

For a moment, Borogchin studied Mandukhai as if wondering if the offer was a ploy. Tears continued flowing down her cheeks. Suddenly, in a very unexpected display of affection and gratitude, Borogchin collapsed into Mandukhai's arms, weeping and clinging to her. *What has this poor girl been through already?*

And with that promise, Mandukhai knew any loyalty Borogchin had for Yeke had dissolved away with her sudden outpouring of emotion. There would be no spying for Yeke. But Yeke didn't need to know that.

CHAPTER EIGHT

SWEETROOT

As the days of gifting passed, more gifts arrived less frequently. Bigirsen made a dramatic show of giving his gifts in front of Manduul's entire court before he and his men departed—offering to each Mandukhai and Manduul a small chest filled with precious gems and various items from the Persian countries to the west. Mandukhai had opened hers out of courtesy toward Bigirsen, but hadn't thoroughly inspected the contents beyond the jade necklace at the top. She had no intention of using these items. She feared it would give him some unspoken power over her, and Mandukhai had no desire to give another man any such power.

Mandukhai spent her days with the girls, teaching them to make their own clothing and how to prepare meals. Borogchin displayed a natural adeptness for stitching cloth, whereas Esige struggled. However, Esige could butcher meat with smooth, skilled cuts. Mandukhai swelled with pride the more she spent time with each girl. They were delightful and helped her days pass with ease. Every other day, she would take the girls out riding, and Nergui would dutifully follow at a close yet respectful distance. Mandukhai often lamented that she no longer had a bow during those rides. The girls should know how to shoot, and she could attempt teaching them as her father taught her.

For the first few of days after the marriage, Mandukhai sidestepped Manduul's advances without raising his ire. Her heart may have softened to him a little, but she found her lack of desire toward him had not changed. Until she knew she was within the window of conception, she had no wish to lie with him. After a week of this, Manduul summoned her to the gathering tent. She stepped in, thankful to discover it empty.

"Why do you avoid me, wife?" he asked once she stopped at the foot of the dais.

"Avoid you?" Mandukhai knew they played a game. She would bear his child to secure her place, but she would do so wisely.

"For a week now you have refused to share my bed. I'm inclined to believe you are doing so on purpose." His thick eyebrows narrowed as he challenged her.

Mandukhai swallowed the lump in her throat, thankful that this, at least, she could answer truthfully. "My monthly blood has come. I did not want to bother you with it."

Manduul's face drooped, mirroring his shoulders. "Ah. Disheartening news. You seemed certain you were with child before."

"Sadly, time is the only accurate way to know." Mandukhai did her best to appear ashamed. "I am sorry to have disappointed you, Manduul."

"We will just have to try harder next time," he said.

Mandukhai suppressed a shudder, yet understood he was correct. She needed a child before Yeke, and right now she had his full attention. How long would that last?

To Manduul's credit, he waited two more days before pressing the issue again. And the excuse wouldn't hold up any longer. As he stood just inside the ger door to inquire, Mandukhai responded swiftly and confidently.

"Mother advised me that the best way to conceive is to wait for two weeks after the bleeding ends. She advised that doing so enhances the chances of conception. I would hate to fail. I don't think I can bear the disappointment on your face again. I would like to try waiting."

"Nonsense," Manduul said, stepping further inside. "We can still practice."

Mandukhai dipped her head and shook it slightly. "She insisted that I not fail in this, and I don't want to fail you. Mother said doing so before my body is prepared to accept a child reduces the chances. I believe we should reserve ourselves each month for that opportunity. I want nothing more than to bear you a son."

Mandukhai suspected Manduul would inquire about this himself, perhaps by asking other women or a shaman, and if he did, they would not be able to disprove anything she said. And she did want a son, even if she didn't want Manduul.

Manduul grumbled under his breath, but agreed to give her space. As he headed back out the door, Manduul paused. "You will not ride Dust after we do have sex until we can verify you either are with child or are not. I won't have you risking a premature loss because of it."

Mandukhai dug her nails into her palms to keep her anger at bay. Agreeing would mean she could not ride for weeks—perhaps longer if she ended up with child and he insisted she carry on not riding. But this would be the only way to minimize their encounters. She could either refuse and suffer at his will, or accept and be unable to ride. The choice was terrible.

"Agreed," she whispered.

The weeks passed, and Mandukhai knew that her own argument would give her little choice but to give in to him. Hopefully one night would do. After the first night, Mandukhai could not bear the idea of another, so she used the only option that remained.

Mandukhai ingested a safe amount of sweetroot in her tea. Not enough to harm seriously her, but just enough that she spent the next two nights in her ger sick while her servant Tuya, and the girls all took care of her while Nergui kept unwanted visitors away. When Manduul arrived that night, Borogchin tried to encourage him to leave lest he risk catching the illness. He insisted on seeing Mandukhai for himself before eventually leaving in a huff of anger.

The next morning, Yeke pushed past Nergui with a few tart words, then entered with an herbal tea mix, insisting on nursing Mandukhai back to health. Mandukhai tried to excuse her, asserting that the girls had it under control, but Yeke refused.

"Manduul asked me last night to see to you," she said tersely, wrapping a cool, damp cloth around Mandukhai's head then retrieving the silver bowl she had brought along. "He believes the girls are improperly educated to deal with this and wants to be sure you are on your feet swiftly."

Thus the silver, Mandukhai thought, watching as Yeke soaked another strip of cloth in the silver bowl. Silver retained healing properties. Though no one could say for sure how it worked so effectively, everyone agreed it was a gift from the earth mother. Silver could purify water, and when held against the skin, it would slowly heal most ailments. The worse the ailment, the more silver required. Everyone heard the tale of the khan who had been poisoned and pierced by an arrow, and suffered a broken leg. They wore out two silver bowls to heal him. But it worked.

"The girls..." Mandukhai's throat tightened as her stomach threatened to let loose.

"I have sent them away for the day," Yeke replied tersely. "I have no desire to do your job for you."

Mandukhai squeezed her eyes closed at the barbed comment. It was her job, after all, to be sure Borogchin and Esige knew how to deal with such illness.

For the rest of the day, Yeke stayed with Mandukhai, replacing the cloth wraps, washing the sheen of sweat from Mandukhai's face and limbs, feeding her soup and water from silver dishes. When Mandukhai vomited, Yeke cleaned up the mess herself, mumbling the entire time. Neither woman spoke much to the other for most of the day. Tuya appeared occasionally, bringing fresh buckets of water or removing Mandukhai's vomit bucket.

Mandukhai focused on resting while Yeke focused on healing. The shaman appeared at one point, but Mandukhai was too exhausted to hear more than fragments of the conversation.

For the first time, Mandukhai actually felt a kinship, a bond growing between them—even if that bond was strained.

By dinner, Mandukhai's stomach clenched constantly, but she no longer felt the urge to vomit. The two women sat together—Mandukhai on her bed and Yeke on the bench across the ger.

"Did Manduul stay with you last night?" Mandukhai asked. She felt much better than she had in the morning and sat up in her bed with a cup of tea between her fingers.

"Yes." Yeke's shoulders tensed as she stoked the fire to make sure the flames continued to burn high. "Apparently he had been prepared for an evening with you and, since he couldn't have it, he wanted to satiate his needs."

"A hardship, I'm sure," Mandukhai said with a teasing roll of her eyes. *High Heaven's don't conceive a child with her!* Had her willfulness just cost her dearly?

Yeke flashed a disapproving glare at her. "He is my husband. It isn't a hardship."

"That isn't what I—" Mandukhai faltered. "I only meant it as a joke. A reverse of how you would actually feel about it. In jest."

Yeke studied Mandukhai as if probing for something more. For the first time, Mandukhai saw how young Yeke was. The smoothness of her face. The hope in her eyes. *She can't be much older than I am.*

"I'm afraid I don't find humor in it," Yeke said at last.

"What do you find humor in, then?" Mandukhai asked, exasperated and too exhausted to think before she spoke. "Because you always seem so serious and stern. Surely something amuses you."

Yeke seemed to consider this, adopting a far-off expression as she fell into contemplation. Mandukhai held her breath, hopeful that she would actually crack into the barricaded exterior of her sister-wife. But the hope was dashed quickly as Yeke suddenly appeared deeply saddened and turned her back to Mandukhai as she collected her things.

Before heading to the door, Yeke moved to the alter at the back of the ger and lit incense, fanning her hand over it before turning away.

"I hope I haven't upset you," Mandukhai said. She wanted to follow Yeke, but her limbs were still too weak to hold her weight.

"Get rest," Yeke said as she opened the door with her hip. "I'm sure Manduul will expect to visit you soon."

Before Mandukhai could protest, Yeke slipped out, ordered Nergui to ensure she rested and that the girls spend the evening watching over Mandukhai, then closed the door.

Mandukhai slid back against the wall, utterly confused.

CHAPTER NINE

WHAT THE FUTURE HOLDS

Unebolod knew the moment he left Khorchin territory that his return to Mongke Bulag would not be met with happiness. His brother's failure would now be his own to bear. Manduul now sat before him on his throne, practically quivering with rage.

"Three weeks!" Manduul bellowed. His thunderous voice rolled across the ceiling and down the walls of the gathering tent, making Unebolod's ears ache. "Three weeks when you promised half that, and still you come back with nothing! Should I wonder if your vow to this boy is stronger than your oath to me?"

Unebolod stiffened his back. What did Manduul expect of him? Manduul sent him to retrieve the boy before he was ready, and Bolunai had sworn the same oath as Unebolod to Lady Samur. Convincing him to give up the boy had been an impossible problem to start. Not that Unebolod had any interest in following through. It didn't benefit him in any way to bring Bayan to Manduul alive. The boy would take Unebolod's place as next in line to be Great Khan.

But matters turned out much worse than Unebolod had anticipated. He arrived in Hulunbuir to speak to his brother Bolunai, only to discover Bayan had run off more than a year ago and Bolunai's men had been unable to track him down. *The boy is turning into a dangerous loose end.*

"Bolunai said Bayan went on a hunting trip with his son, Tengghar," Unebolod explained. "In the middle of the night, the boy rode off on one of

Bolunai's horses. He fled south."

"Across the Gobi?" Manduul gripped the arms of his throne tight enough to make the leather squeak in protest.

"We believe so, my lord Khan," Unebolod said evenly.

"At least bring me a body or bones!" Manduul roared.

If only I could have uncovered a body, Unebolod thought, but he held an even, undaunted expression.

Unebolod's three men—Yungei, Soke, and Berkedai—shriveled back, but he didn't. Manduul posed no serious threat to him.

Manduul's voice lowered to a dangerous pitch. "And it took you three weeks to return to me with this news?"

"I had no desire to return to you with nothing, so we attempted tracking him south," Unebolod explained.

"And?"

Unebolod raised his chin, preparing for the next wave of anger. "And his trail went cold near the desert. There is good reason to believe he wouldn't have survived crossing the desert alone. Bolunai insisted the boy lacked certain survival skills."

"Reason to … Don't feed me sheep dung like it's mutton." Manduul rose, stalking toward Unebolod as he gingerly descended the three steps. "You toy with me, Une. Me, your sworn brother. You tell me the story of a man—a *boy!*—who escaped his grandfather Esen's wrath. A secret you have kept from me for years. A boy you escorted across the steppe for his own safety eleven years ago. A boy you handed over to your brother and your tribe. A boy who can stake his claim on *my* title as soon as next year! And then, I ask one thing of you, to bring that boy to me, and you fail me?"

Unebolod's men stepped back and bowed as Manduul approached. Unebolod did not. He stared Manduul down, unafraid. He loved Manduul … and hated him.

"Would you rather I continued tracking him down, across the Gobi, unprepared without first giving you word?"

Manduul leaned close, angry lips peeling back from his vicious teeth. The sour scent of *airag* rolled off his breath. "To the ends of the earth," he growled.

Unebolod took a stiff step back and bowed to Manduul. "Then I will do as my lord Khan commands." He turned to leave, but before he could take more than a step, Manduul's fat hand pinched his arm tight, stopping him in his tracks.

"No. Not you."

Those three words turned Unebolod's blood cold. Manduul posed no serious threat to his body. Unebolod knew how much stronger he was. However, his position among the tribes hung precariously at Manduul's whims. Denying Unebolod the opportunity to correct his error gave Manduul something to hang over his head later. The last thing Unebolod wanted was Manduul using this failure as a weapon. Staying in Mongke Bulag also kept Unebolod from ensuring that Bayan never survived to claim his place.

"If I have wronged you..." Unebolod began.

Manduul released Unebolod's arm, then gathered himself as tall as he could. "I want to be sure this boy is brought to me alive, no matter the cost. It will be up to me to determine his fate. Send no less than a full *arban* of ten men, with one of the Borjigin loyalists at the head, to ensure the boy doesn't run away again. And if he tries, they are to isolate him ... and kill his horse." Manduul started back toward his throne. "He can't run far without a horse."

Unebolod heard Soke suck in a breath at the command. Killing a horse could incur the wrath of the sky father. Unebolod couldn't argue with the logic, but more than anything, he wanted to go along to be certain this threat to his own position wouldn't make it back to Mongke Bulag. Without giving himself away, there was nothing Unebolod could do, though. "I will choose my best men," Unebolod said. "It will be weeks before they can catch his trail around the desert."

"I want them on their way tonight."

That left little time for his men to gather supplies and prepare to leave. *At least I get to stay in camp to deliver my gift, assuming he still allows me to.* If nothing else, the trip had not been a total waste. Unebolod had acquired a new gift for Mandukhai. One he was certain she would appreciate. The period of gift-giving had passed, and if Unebolod gave a gift to Mandukhai without permission, Manduul would be within his rights to punish him.

"I have a small request," Unebolod said, hoping he appeared more deferential than he felt. "Since I missed the eight days of gifts before leaving, would you be kind enough to allow me to still give your new wife a gift?"

Manduul stopped at the top of the dais and turned slowly, his head cocked curiously to the side. "If you didn't give your gift, why has she been wearing the silks?"

Unebolod had weeks to think of an excuse for this question. "I felt the gift was still too fine for me to give, and it felt deeply personal. I didn't want to give her the wrong idea, so I gave them to your nieces to give her instead. It seemed more appropriate. I acquired a new gift for her instead. Something not nearly as grandiose."

Manduul studied him as if weighing the honesty in his words. Just when Unebolod was about to give up hope, Manduul waved a careless hand and returned to the throne. "At this point, it doesn't matter. Give her whatever you wish."

What does that mean? Unebolod wondered as he bowed and left the gathering tent.

Unebolod found Mandukhai sitting on a blanket at the edge of the river, with her *boqta* beside her. Her long, black hair rippled across her back in the breeze. Borogchin and Esige sat with her, absorbed in conversation. A gentle breeze carried their words away from him. The easy manner with which they sat together, the way they chatted and smiled, struck him hard in the chest as he remembered his long-dead wife, Odsar. Unebolod froze at least fifty paces away, watching them with the new gift tucked under one arm.

Only Mandukhai's guard noted his approach. Not fifteen steps away, the guard eyed Unebolod critically, weighing him, assessing the sort of threat he might pose. Unebolod gave a small inclination of his head as a show of respect, and the guard turned his attention back to the girls.

Mandukhai raised her hands in the air, making a grand, exaggerated gesture as she spoke, and the girls struggled to contain their laughter.

She's telling them stories, he realized. He took a steadying breath, hoping she would see his gift as a simple one and not anything too extravagant. Though it was finer than it should be.

Borogchin noticed him first, and a rosy blush flooded her cheeks before she looked away and whispered to Mandukhai.

Unebolod broke from his trance and approached, stopping several feet away and bowing to Mandukhai. Her gaze flicked to the leather-wrapped bundle under his arm, then she turned her attention to the girls.

"Esige, gather the rest of our food and take it to Halan," she said. "Her family has been struggling the last few days and we don't have need of it. Borogchin, see to the horses."

Both girls scrambled to obey. Esige offered Unebolod a bright smile as she passed with a wicker basket of food. Borogchin shyly averted her gaze, something she had never really done to him before. *I wonder what brought that on.*

Mandukhai remained on the blanket, and as soon as the girls set off, she motioned to their vacant spaces. "Join me, Lord Unebolod."

He swallowed the lump that lodged in his throat. Sitting on a blanket with her beside the river alone—well, alone aside from the guard pretending not to watch. Being alone like this could be enough to push Manduul over the edge. "I won't be long."

Her brows shot up, and a small smile danced across her lips, lighting up her round face. "You would deny me such a simple request?"

Unebolod hesitated. *Will her guard report this back to Manduul?*

If Mandukhai told Manduul that he refused to sit with her at her insistence, it would be considered rude, perhaps even a slight against the queen. However, if Manduul found out that he sat with her in private like this, it could be considered a personal move against the Khan's wife. Either way, he could end up in trouble. Only one of those options put him in a better position for his own personal gains. *I just need to be cautious about keeping distance and show no moves that could be construed as anything other than respectful.*

He let out a sigh, hoping he sounded more put out than he felt, then settled on the far side of the blanket, as far as he could without being seen as rude.

Mandukhai kept her hands folded in her lap, patient and far more like a queen than he would have expected from her so soon.

"As I said, I won't be long," he said, shifting the leather bundle under his arm to offer it to her. "I am sorry I missed the opportunity to present your gift, but Manduul Khan permitted me to give this to you still."

Mandukhai didn't glance at the gift, nor did she make a move to accept. Her dark eyes fixed on him, pulling him in. "I already received your gift. From the girls."

Unebolod lowered the bundle, setting it in the space between them. Her comment caught him unprepared, and for a moment he fumbled to pull the right words together. "After reflecting on the choice, I didn't feel it right to give the gift to you. It just seemed—"

"Why would you go to such trouble to get me these silks only to change your mind at the last moment? It's a rich, fine gift, to be sure, which makes your decision all the more curious." Her hands smoothed over the red silk skirt of the deel, which he noticed complimented the color of her cheekbones.

Unebolod slid his hand off the leather wrapping around his new gift, unable to turn his gaze away from her. "Have I offended you?"

She considered this, which deflated his hopes of establishing a friendship with the queen. "Perhaps. Should I be offended you gave the gift to the girls instead of me? What does that say about your opinion of me?"

"That's not—"

She held up a hand, cutting him off. "Do you now offer me a lesser gift?"

Was it a lesser gift? Is that what he was doing to avoid raising too many alarms in Manduul's mind? *I'm not afraid of him.* But as he thought it, he wondered if he was just trying to convince himself.

"Can I speak frankly, my Lady?"

"Only if you call me by my name," she said sharply. "I may be a Lady, but I have a name and identity all my own."

A fierce and stubborn will burned in her expression, and he found it just as illuminating as her smile had been. This simple quest to solidify his position quickly had become a dangerous battleground.

"Mandukhai," he said, and realized it was the first time he had said her name aloud. It poured from his mouth like honey, and he wanted to taste it again.

She gazed away from him, toward the river. *Is she blushing?* The idea of her blushing just because he said her name humored him, but he contained his amusement.

Unebolod sat up straighter and stared at his gift. What he wanted to tell her was how he had bought that horse for her, that he had put a lot of effort into making sure all the details were perfect, right down to learning her size for a proper saddle fit. He wanted to tell her that Manduul had taken it away in jealousy and thrust those silks on him. The memory of her abject adoration for the horse had traveled with him these last weeks, filling him with an interchangeable mixture of pride and anger. But speaking those truths would cost both of them dearly once Manduul found out.

Race a horse across the steppe and the horse will have nothing more to offer, he thought. *But keep the horse at a moderate pace, and the horse will go much farther.* He needed to be patient. The truth would come out eventually, and when it did, he needed to be sure it played in his favor.

"The night of your wedding, Manduul told me about the items missing from your possessions," Unebolod said, deciding to take a different course of action. "A hunting knife and a bow. I attempted recovering them."

Mandukhai turned a curious eye to the leather bundle between them, but she didn't interrupt.

"I decided that, even if the silks were a fine gift for a queen, they weren't the gift I was prepared to give. I wanted to return what you lost. I had hoped to give you a gift that fit better with you, Mandukhai, and not just Lady Mandukhai." Her name gave him goosebumps, and he was glad for the long sleeves covering his arms.

Her fingers brushed across the edge of the leather, but she still didn't open it. Unebolod waited patiently, studying her smooth, round face and full lips, the arch of her thin eyebrows as they drew together. He shoved the desirous thoughts out of his head and forced himself to look at the bundle, but could not redirect his attention from her slender fingers as they gently grazed the leather.

Unable to wait any longer, needing to get this over with and get away before he said or did something foolish, Unebolod cleared his throat. "Allow me," he said, peeling back the leather unceremoniously.

Mandukhai gasped and pulled her hand back sharply as if the bow and quiver of arrows had bitten her. "This isn't my bow."

"I know. I couldn't find yours, but Manduul mentioned you were concerned about not having one. How you felt like less of a Mongol without it." Though Unebolod imagined that, beside her, all other women were lesser. "You deserve a bow fit for a queen."

She appeared hesitant to pick it up. "You said the silk was a fine gift, but this…"

"It is well-crafted," Unebolod said. *Is this too much or not enough?* he wondered. Either way, he wasn't sure he wanted the answer. "The balance is perfect, and the pull should be just right for you. Try it." He picked up the weapon, holding it out to her.

Mandukhai's lips parted as if about to say something, but nothing came. She slid her fingers around the black leather handle and brushed his hand as she did. It was an accidental touch, but the effect was greater than if she'd done so on purpose. A surge of energy rushed through him, and he nearly recoiled, only holding still out of fear of dropping the bow or showing her too much too soon. Once she had a good hold of the bow, he retreated.

The wood was reinforced with a pearl-white horn glued to the limbs with sturdy fish glue, and the handle was padded with soft leather for a better grip. Along the limb, Unebolod requested dragons be etched into the wood. Mandukhai didn't seem to notice the etchings, instead focusing on hooking her thumb around the string to pull it back, testing the strength of the bow. She did it with such practiced ease, becoming an extension of her arm, a part of her. Unebolod no longer questioned the value of the gift.

She eased the string and slid on the protective leather ring. He had been prepared to go, but froze, curious as she pulled an arrow from the quiver. He pressed his hands against the blanket beneath them, wondering if she could properly shoot.

Unebolod glanced at her guard, but the man remained as still as a statue, watching Mandukhai.

The loud whoosh of the bowstring snapping was followed a breath later by the whistle of her arrow. Unebolod snapped to attention as the arrow soared across the river and stuck in a birch tree.

Mandukhai sagged in disappointment.

"An excellent shot," he said.

Mandukhai's lips thinned, clearly annoyed with herself. "I was aiming for the knot. I missed by several inches."

"You're sitting on the ground," he said, amused by her disappointment.

She glared at him, and he flinched. "Instead of on a horse? What difference should that make?"

"It could be all the difference," he said, shrugging. "You are lower to the ground. Your hips aren't in the right position, and your shoulders aren't prepared for the release as they would be while riding or on foot."

Mandukhai studied him. Though Unebolod knew he should leave before someone thought he had lingered too long, he wanted to stay right where he was, even if it meant she would pick him apart. As long as she continued studying at him.

"I should go," he said at last. "Manduul is sending some men out, and I need to help them prepare." He stood, straightening his clothes, then bowed. "I hope you enjoy my gift."

Mandukhai stood abruptly, taking a swift strides toward him as he started toward Mongke Bulag at their backs. "Wait!"

He paused, both pleased and afraid of staying any longer. And very aware of her guard watching them closely. She followed his gaze and waved off Unebolod's concern. "Nergui is my protector."

Nergui—Nameless. Either his parents or her tribe had given him a name that would disguise him from enemies. *All the better to protect her.* Nergui clearly wore the Ongud deel.

"I could use proper training with my new bow," she said, gliding over the sparse grass to approach him. "You will teach me."

A jolt rocked through him. His lips parted to speak. He wanted to agree, but Manduul knew he had shown too much interest already. Spending so much time with her would be dangerous. As much as he wanted to say yes, the refusal was so much easier. "I don't think Manduul would approve. There are others who focus on training."

"Others with experience like yours?" She cocked her head, and a breeze picked up, blowing wisps of hair across her face. Mandukhai pulled them back with the tip of her finger, never looking away from him.

"Do you expect to ride into many battles, Lady Mandukhai?" Unebolod asked, fighting off a smirk.

"Who knows what the future holds?" She said it so innocently, he almost believed her. But something about the way she stood with a hand on her hip made him wonder if she was playing a game with him. "Would you have me ill-prepared for the worst? Let me handle my husband."

Unebolod didn't believe for a moment that Manduul would ever give her so much one-on-one time with him. Not unless Unebolod could avoid staring at her, to avoid giving her any sort of special attention at all. *That won't be a simple task.*

"If you get the Khan to agree, I will train you," he said, because there wasn't another answer. "But I would like to hear it from him myself."

"You don't trust me?"

"Did your father trust Esen?"

She flinched, dropping her hand at her side and stiffening her back. "What is your point?" she asked sharply.

I've said the wrong thing. Unebolod attempted recovering before it was too late. "Only that trust is a dangerous thing to give. Your father offered Esen his trust, and Esen used that trust to butcher hundreds. Everyone wants something for themselves, Lady Mandukhai, and you may not be prepared to pay the price."

Mandukhai raised an eyebrow at him. "And what do you want?"

To be Great Khan. To serve and protect the Nation. You. The last was most dangerous of all. "To have lived two hundred years ago." Which appeared to be a good answer, judging by the way Mandukhai smiled.

"I will speak to my husband about the training," she said, as if it were already settled. She walked back to her blanket to gather the rest of her things, clearly dismissing him.

Unebolod lingered only a moment longer before heading back into camp.

That conversation had taken an unexpected turn, and more than once he had feared his emotions or desires would get away from him. Spending time around her would continue to be treacherous unless he could find a more effective way to control himself.

As he strode along the thoroughfare between gers, he wondered if she actually could convince Manduul to let him train her—and if he truly wanted the opportunity.

Mandukhai returned to her ger, her steps lighter than they had been this morning. She placed her new bow and quiver of arrows on pegs beside the door. While she busied herself with dinner, her gaze continuously drifted to the weapon—and the encounter with Unebolod.

The conversation had been innocent enough, but unless she mistook him, his actions had not always agreed with his words. The way his body would stiffen when she moved too close. The way his gaze lingered on her. Something unspoken in his eyes. Asking him to train her and insisting she would convince Manduul to allow it had been foolish. Such a request was for lovesick girls, not for married women.

Mandukhai sat beside the stove, trying to distract herself, but unable to take her eyes from the bow. Up until now, Mandukhai had assumed Manduul somehow was responsible for her missing weapons, that he did not believe she would need such things anymore and so he took them. But Unebolod mentioned Manduul's concern about them. If not him, then who took them?

After several long minutes chewing her lip while studying the shape of the bow, the elegant curve and recurve, she noticed something about it she'd missed before. The etched details.

Mandukhai rounded the fire and picked up the bow, running her finger along the etchings. A dragon, long and thin, carved its way up the limb of the bow. The same dragon that was pressed into the leather of the quiver. She stepped out the door and crouched beside Dust's saddle, currently on the ground beside her door.

The same dragon were pressed into the leather on her saddle.

How can they be the same? Mandukhai inspected the saddle for the tribe marking and found the Khorchin craftsman seal pressed into the leather in front of the pommel. It must be coincidence. She rose and entered the ger once more, inspecting the bow only to find another Khorchin craftsman seal near the horn.

Mandukhai's heart hammered against her ribs. Unebolod was Khorchin. He had given her the bow, which only reasoned that he could have retrieved it from his own tribe. But the saddle as well? Plenty of Khorchin camped around Mongke Bulag. Manduul could have just as easily commissioned it from anyone around them. But the dragons ... it had to be coincidence.

She licked her lips. What did this mean? Did it mean anything at all?

CHAPTER TEN

ELEPHANT'S GAMBIT

Mandukhai's mother had taught her that a happy, satisfied husband was far more likely to be pliant than a dissatisfied one. Though it pained her, if what Unebolod said was true, and Manduul would not approve of Unebolod teaching her to use her bow, Mandukhai would have to use her mother's method.

It had been challenging at first, to act eager as Manduul pressed his sweaty body against her, but she closed her eyes and let her mind wander, imagining him as someone else. Only one person came into her mind. At first, imagining Unebolod's hands on her instead of Manduul's made her body tense up, petrified, but soon enough her body shuddered with delight and she stopped trying to push his face out of her mind. When she and Manduul were both spent, Manduul relaxed against the bed, clinging to her.

"I don't remember it being quite like that last time," he said. She couldn't change his voice into anyone else's in her mind, even if she could block out the rest of him.

"Perhaps it's the waiting that makes it better," she lied. Yearning for a man she could never have was a sure path to destruction.

More than anything, Mandukhai wanted to slither away from him, but exhaustion kept her unmoving as his hand settled on the small of her back, hugging her body against his.

"I see you found your bow after all," he said, staring at the weapon still hanging on the wall.

Mandukhai didn't correct him, nor did she agree with him. Did he not know that would be the gift from Unebolod? Did he not notice the dragons? Instead of questioning him, she hummed against his chest. "I'm a bit out of practice though."

"A problem I'm sure you can remedy," he said, his fingers moving in small circles on her back.

This was her chance to ask, but she knew he wasn't pliable enough. Not if her mother had taught her anything. The bigger the request, the more pleased he would need to be, and she would not take the risk. *If you want something from a man,* her mother had told her as they prepared for her journey to Mongke Bulag, *you must please him in every way you can. Do this, and he will give you anything for a chance to do it again.*

The coincidence between the saddle and bow continued to press on her mind. Perhaps she could get him to admit something that would reveal an answer. Not that she was certain what sort of answer she sought.

"I noticed the detail on Dust's saddle," she said, tracing circles on his chest with her own hand. "It must have been quite a task to get a hold of."

"Not really," he said. His breath hitched as she kissed his chest. "But the trade had been quite expensive."

"What made you choose dragons?" she asked, inching her hand lower.

Manduul tensed at her touch before sliding his fingers into her loose hair. "What dragons?"

Mandukhai's heart thumped. *What dragons?* "On the saddle."

"Oh yes," Manduul said, clearly attempting to recover for his own ignorance. "Fierce creatures, much like you, it turns out."

Mandukhai leaned her body over his, trailing kisses along his sweaty chest, struggling not to recoil while sliding her hands down to stroke the semi-flaccid erection. He groaned. "Someone is hungry tonight," he teased.

"Fiercely," she teased back, playing his game, then closed her eyes and allowed her mind to wander away from him to the man she truly yearned for. It was a precarious place to be.

Mandukhai rose long before Manduul had even stirred the next morning. She gathered fuel for the stove and stoked it to warm the ger. As she used a poker to shift the lumps of fuel, Manduul finally woke, grinning at her like a love-struck boy.

"Good morning, my dragon," he said.

She shuddered, and then rubbed her arm as if it were just a chill in the air. She didn't want him calling her dragon. He hadn't even been aware of them, which made her wonder where the details on the saddle came from, hoping her suspicions were wrong even if the Khorchin mark should have confirmed it. Even if Manduul purchase the horse for her, Mandukhai grew more certain now that Manduul had not been the one to choose the saddle.

An opportunity to ask about the training hadn't presented itself last night, and she needed to ask before he left for the day. *I only need to delay him slightly.*

Mandukhai set down the poker and climbed on top of him, her knees straddling his body. He grinned at her, sliding his hands up her robe and across her bare skin. His grip on her hips pulled her insistently down against him.

"I have been thinking about what you said last night," she said, pressing her hands into his shoulders to hold him back. "About the bow. And I think I need training. My skills are adequate, but not good enough."

"Why do you need better skills?" he asked, pressing his desire against her body.

Mandukhai shifted her hips just enough to give in. "Because there could be a day when I might need to defend our sons, and if my skills are bested by my foe, it won't end well."

He pressed against her repeatedly, but she pulled away just enough to slow him down and take away the control. "Manduul, I want a trainer," she said more resolutely.

"Fine. I'll gather my best." The tone made it clear he was agreeing just to get what he wanted right now. Judging by the way he lifted his own hips while pressing hers down against him, he assumed that was the end.

Mandukhai relented, just a little, but it was enough for him to increase his enthusiasm. She beamed down at him and said, "I've already found one."

"Who?" The question came out with a groan of pleasure.

"Your *orlok*, Lord Unebolod."

Manduul's nails suddenly dug into her hips, and his rhythm slowed. Uncertainty warred with pleasure in his face. "Why him?"

"Because he is the best," Mandukhai pulled away, just enough to make him think she would stop. "And I want to be trained by the best to protect our children."

"We don't have any children," he snapped, stopping altogether.

Mandukhai flinched at his tone, so full of anger, and for a moment she wondered if she had made a terrible mistake. He appeared ready to throw her off and storm out. *Why is he angry? Is it because I'm not pregnant yet?* Mandukhai had expected hesitation. But this anger took her by surprise.

"We will," she said, adopting a confident smile. She leaned toward him, kissing his jaw.

Manduul didn't react. His entire body tensed under her. Mandukhai twisted her hips just enough to show she hadn't lost the urge to continue, to entice him along. Then again. And again.

Manduul suddenly snatched her hair, pulling her head back as his lips roved her neck, collarbone, chest. All of the passion and tenderness he had shown her in their previous encounters vanished, replaced by the hunger of a predator staking his claim. No passion and all possession.

And it hurt far more than she wanted to admit.

The encounter with Manduul left Mandukhai weak and trembling—and not in any way that accompanied pleasure. When he finished—on his terms and not hers—he cast her off like a common whore and dressed. As he stomped into his boots, he agreed to let her learn from whoever she wanted.

"Just remember who your husband is," he warned, then stormed out the door, slamming it hard enough to make the entire ger quake.

Mandukhai was too proud to cry. Instead, she huddled on her bed, telling herself it could have been worse, that she asked for this by pressing the issue, by encouraging him along. She remained in her bed as Borogchin entered with breakfast, but Mandukhai refused to eat. When Tuya and Esige offered to help Mandukhai prepare for the day, Mandukhai withdrew from their touch.

By mid-morning when she had not shown her face outside, Nergui stuck his head in to check on her, but Mandukhai threw a cup at his head and shouted for him to get out. He did as she commanded. Borogchin and Esige kept their distance from Mandukhai, but didn't dare leave her alone for more than a few minutes as they fetched fresh water. They returned shortly before lunch with Yeke in tow. Yeke entered, uninvited and unannounced, taking in Mandukhai still lying in bed, trembling naked under her blankets. She hissed and order the two girls to leave, and they swiftly obeyed.

For a moment, Yeke gazed at her as if she understood, but the moment quickly passed. She marched over to the bed and threw a deel at Mandukhai.

"Every woman suffers this," Yeke said, yanking back the blanket. "But you are a queen. Get up."

Mandukhai shivered at the sudden cold, but she didn't obey. Yeke made a noise of disgust in her throat, then turned and tossed more fuel on the fire.

"Has—has he done this to you?" Mandukhai asked timidly.

"It doesn't matter."

"It does matter." Mandukhai sat up, pulling the deel Yeke had thrown at her over her legs.

Yeke spun around at the stove, where she soaked a sponge in the warming water bowl. "No. It doesn't. Because you aren't a girl. You aren't a helpless woman. You are a queen, and you will act like one."

Mandukhai hated how she shriveled away from Yeke's anger, how she knew that Yeke's lack of answer was only confirmation of her fears, how Manduul had taken the one piece of control Mandukhai had and ripped it right out of her.

Yeke huffed and grabbed the bowl of water and sponge, then climbed onto the bed behind Mandukhai to bathe her.

"We share a husband," Mandukhai said, trying to stop her limbs from quivering. "We can share the truth, even if only with each other."

Yeke didn't respond, sliding the sponge along Mandukhai's shoulders with a tenderness that was at odds with her armored exterior. The cool water only enhanced the chills Mandukhai felt deep in her bones.

"You don't want the truth," Yeke said after several long, silent minutes. "You want confirmation that this isn't your fault and that you aren't alone. None of that will help you. If you want to be coddled, you won't find companionship from me."

Was she right? Mandukhai didn't want to hear about what Manduul may or may not have done to Yeke. It only stripped him of any remaining shreds of potential affection she might cling to—if it wasn't already too late. But Mandukhai also didn't want to feel so terribly alone. And she didn't want to feel like what happened was her fault, even if it was. *I pushed him. I did not know he would react so strongly.*

Yeke finished with the bathing and began combing and fixing up Mandukhai's hair. Maybe Yeke had said she didn't want companionship, but she had come to Mandukhai's ger uninvited. She'd set to work cleaning and caring for Mandukhai without prompting.

"Why did you come if you don't care?" Mandukhai asked.

"Borogchin came to me crying," Yeke said. "Such a weak girl. She said she didn't know what was wrong with you. That you might be sick again. That you hadn't moved all day. And your watch dog has been guarding that door all morning like he will attack any who tries to enter." She finished pinning Mandukhai's hair up and reached for the *boqta*.

Nergui. What did he overhear? Does he know? Humiliation rushed through Mandukhai's body.

Mandukhai held up a hand, pushing the crown away. "I don't want to wear that." It reminded her of him and reminded everyone else of whom she belonged to.

Yeke grumbled something under her breath, but she didn't set the crown down. "You will wear it. If you want to take his power away, then stop wallowing and walk out of here like what he's done has not affected you. Don't let him have that piece of you."

Mandukhai dropped her hand into her lap, allowing Yeke to strap on the *boqta*. When she finished, Yeke fished out a jade necklace from among the gifts in Bigirsen's chest, then draped it around Mandukhai's neck. Mandukhai wanted to rip it off and toss it into the stove, along with the *boqta*. Bigirsen was just another man trying to gain control of her. *And what of Unebolod? Is he the same?* Mandukhai knew he had every reason to dislike her. If she had Manduul's son, that boy would be next in line, before Unebolod.

"You are a queen," Yeke said as she headed for the door. "Never let him forget it."

With that said, Yeke left Mandukhai alone again.

Angry, full of vengeful hate, Mandukhai crouched in front of her chest and rummaged through it until she found what she desired. A pouch of herbs she had hidden in there before leaving the Ongud.

Before Mandukhai stepped outside, she ingested enough mugwort to ensure Manduul couldn't have the one thing he wanted more than anything else.

A child.

The encounter with Mandukhai had stuck with Unebolod all the previous day and bled into his dreams until he woke in a sweat, holding his knife, certain Manduul loomed over him with a knife of his own. When he had entered the gathering tent, Unebolod had almost expected Manduul to punish him, though there had been nothing condemning enough to deserve punishment. It hadn't been until the meetings of the Khan's council began with no comment or hints of suspicion that Unebolod had finally relaxed.

As the meeting ended and the council filtered toward the door, Manduul called to him. "Stay, brother."

Unebolod turned to face Manduul, concerned that the Khan had waited until after the meeting to call him out. "Do you need something of me, my lord Khan?"

Manduul motioned to the chess board then stalked toward it. The two of them often held private conversations over a game of chess or knucklebones to sort out any doubts lingering in Manduul's mind. Most of the time, Unebolod felt those doubts were trivial, but he humored Manduul just the same.

Today felt different.

Unebolod crossed the gathering tent to join Manduul. A serving girl approached with drinks as Manduul and Unebolod settled into their normal seats and began their game of chess.

"Do you think your men will track down this boy, Bayan?" Manduul asked, pushing his first pawn into position.

Unebolod rubbed his chin as he studied the board. The early game moves often revealed the tactics Manduul would use against him. If Unebolod paid close enough attention, he could spot the strategy after only two or three moves, even before Manduul realized it himself.

"Boys are often reckless when they are seeking adventure," Unebolod said, shifting his own pawn forward.

Manduul gazed over the board at Unebolod, his finger on his knight. "Or women."

Unebolod's chest tightened. The comment sounded a lot like a warning. *I've done nothing wrong.* He forced out a bark of a laugh. "Especially women, at his age."

Silence settled as each carefully chose their next few moves. Manduul's strategy revealed itself swiftly, preparing Unebolod for his next few moves. Elephant's Gambit always proved a challenge for black, but he knew he could manage.

"How old is the boy now?" Manduul asked after several long minutes of silence.

"Fourteen. Maybe fifteen." Unebolod moved his bishop into defense against his own pawn, in case Manduul thought to capture it with the knight.

"Old enough to challenge me." Manduul leaned back, staring at the black bishop and falling into studious silence before making his move with his own bishop.

"Yes, but he's still too young."

Manduul frowned. "Molon Khan was younger."

"True, but Bayan doesn't have support. Molon Khan did." Unebolod's finger lingered over his pawn. Taking the bishop would be easy. Obvious. But this game felt much different from others. Unebolod leaned back in his chair, hands in his lap, studying his options.

"He is Taisun Khan's grandson, and Esen's, which makes Bayan an undisputed direct descendant of the line of Genghis Khan." Manduul swirled his drink in his cup, watching Unebolod. "Do you not think he would easily gather support around him?"

"No," Unebolod said, glancing up at Manduul. "He hasn't fought in battle. The only advantage this boy has is his lineage." Unebolod prayed that was true. If the boy lived, perhaps Unebolod could turn the tribes against him before he became a real danger.

He studied the chessboard. *Manduul's trying to pin me in, keep my important pieces stuck in defense.* But one opportunity presented itself, as long as Manduul didn't notice how obvious it was. Unebolod moved his queen between his king and bishop.

Manduul harrumphed, then gulped his drink down and held the cup out to the serving girl, who promptly refilled it.

"Mandukhai wants to improve her archery skills," Manduul said gruffly.

Unebolod tore his eyes away from the game and found Manduul's gaze boring into him. His chest tightened. *And here it comes…*

"She wants a trainer," Manduul said. His voice took on a dangerous edge. "What do you know of this?"

Hiding the truth will cost me in the long run. "She asked me, but I refused."

Manduul's jaw clenched so tight the muscles twitched. His nostrils flared. Had that response really angered him so much? Finally, Manduul wrenched his mouth open and said, "You refused your queen?"

"I hope that doesn't offend you, Manduul," Unebolod said evenly, as if it were nothing at all, when in fact it had been everything to him. "I thought she would be better taught by one of your trainers, and I told her as much." Now he was so glad he'd had the presence of mind to tell her that, in case Manduul asked her about it.

Manduul watched Unebolod as if expecting him to squirm or shy away under his penetrating glare. Unebolod didn't give in. *He has nothing on me.*

Finally, Manduul reached out and moved his knight to take Unebolod's pawn, a reckless move. "Well, she was quite persistent," he said. "You will train her, and my nieces. Someday, they will have just as much reason to know the skill as she claims to need."

Esige and Borogchin. No doubt a few spies would report to Manduul about exactly what happened in those sessions. Anything to keep the two of them from being alone together. Not that they would ever be alone together with Nergui always lurking about.

Both of them fell into silence, staring at the board, and Manduul saw his mistake, grimacing. His queen was wide open.

"Would you steal my queen away?" Manduul asked.

Unebolod met Manduul's gaze and immediately knew his answer was a double-edged sword. He could throw the game now, let Manduul have it by taking his knight instead, at which point Manduul would take his queen and lock his king into check. But then Manduul would know that he had let him win after calling attention to the most obvious move. The best move. He either gave up the game or seized the queen which still felt a lot like losing.

The elephant had won this round.

CRESCENT MOON'S RED KISS

raining with the new bow began the next morning, to Mandukhai's
surprise. Part of her had secretly suspected Manduul would back out
on his word and refuse to allow it. The mere fact that she feared him at all
made her furious. Yeke had been right. The one power Mandukhai knew she
had left was not showing him that what happened bothered her—and not
showing the people in Mongke Bulag that anything had changed.

But how had that worked out for Yeke? Mandukhai wondered as she led the
girls to where they would being their training. Nergui trailed behind like
her shadow. *How many times has Manduul done something like this to Yeke?* The
other woman refused to acknowledge that it happened at all, but the way she
refused told Mandukhai enough. Mandukhai did not want it to happen again.
She wanted him to respect her.

Esige had been over the moon with excitement when Manduul announced
they would train with Mandukhai. Borogchin had been excited as well, but
Mandukhai could tell the girl cared little about the actual archery.

Having the girls come along to learn from Unebolod hadn't bothered
Mandukhai. It showed Manduul that this was just as she said—an opportunity
to learn from the best man he had. If she had insisted on doing this alone,
it would have certainly raised unnecessary suspicion. Or outright refusal. *Or
worse.*

When they arrived at the training ground—an open space near the edge
of camp—Unebolod waited, checking the fletching on the pots of arrows.

He greeted the three of them with a respectful nod. His gaze flicked to the bow he had given Mandukhai, which she carried at her side. Then he frowned at the girls.

"Where are their bows?" he asked.

"They don't have bows," Mandukhai said. Learning this had caused her some distress the previous night. Yeke had never seen a reason to give either of them a bow, which naturally meant they would need to at the beginning with the basics of archery.

Unebolod grimaced, and then turned to the bows on the rack beside him, testing the pull of each before settling on one and offering it to Borogchin. She accepted the weapon, and her fingers brushed his hand as she did. Mandukhai noticed the touch and felt a flash of jealousy in her chest, along with understanding. That was the reason Borogchin had been excited about these lessons. Unebolod certainly was handsome. Why wouldn't Borogchin be interested?

Unebolod's jaw tightened, but he didn't acknowledge the touch.

Borogchin knew how to hold the bow, but she did not know how to draw it properly. When she struggled to pull it back, Unebolod stepped around her and he adjusted her grip. Irritated, Mandukhai wondered if Borogchin faked her inability just so he would have to touch her. Borogchin lowered her elbow as she drew back, and he sharply grabbed it, lifting until her elbow was level with her shoulder.

"Again," he said.

Borogchin nodded and relaxed her arm, then repeated the process.

Esige watched with child-like excitement, bouncing ever so slightly on the balls of her feet as she waited for her turn. Mandukhai noticed the younger girl studied how Unebolod instructed Borogchin, absorbing the information like a pen absorbs ink from a jar.

"Better," he said.

Borogchin lowered the bow, beaming and blushing bright red as he walked back to the table to select a new bow for Esige.

Attempting to seem supporting despite the jealousy burning in her, Mandukhai raised a teasing brow at Borogchin, who only flushed more as she averted her gaze.

Esige accepted the bow offered to her, and the ease with which she drew the string back in proper form made Mandukhai even more suspicious that Borogchin had been faking her inability. How could one sister be so proficient and the other so inept?

Once both girls had their bows, Mandukhai moved to join them where he lined them up across from the wooden targets. Every time he stepped closer, Mandukhai's pulse quickened and she yearned for him to move toward her and guide her arms as he did with the girls. Every time she felt the bitter sting of disappointment as he instructed Esige instead.

Most of the lesson passed with Unebolod paying more attention to the girls than to Mandukhai. It grated on her nerves. She was the one who had requested these lessons. But he went where he was needed, and her skills were more advanced than those of Esige and Borogchin. Unebolod focused on making sure they knew how to draw properly on their feet, which required a different set of skills than on horseback.

By the end of the lesson, the girls had enough and were eager to go. Mandukhai hesitated. Unebolod hadn't taught her anything she didn't already know. The girls each took a drink of water from the bucket beside the table, chattering with excitement as they wiped sweat from their brows. Unebolod turned his back on them, putting the bows the girls had used away after inspecting each string.

Mandukhai strode up to him, clutching her bow tight against her side.

As she opened her mouth to speak, he spoke first, keeping his back to her, "I can train them for weeks, but they need their own bows. It will feel different in their hands than these. I recommend finding each of them one before tomorrow's lesson."

Mandukhai faltered, unsure how to respond. Of course, she would get them their own bows! Before she could put words together, Unebolod turned to her and bowed.

"Same time tomorrow, Lady Mandukhai." Then he strode away.

He had ignored her for most of the lesson, had hardly spoken more than a few words at a time, had never touched her to adjust her aim or grip as he had with the girls, and then had brushed her off. Mandukhai bristled, her grip on the bow tightening as her anger came toward the surface.

Don't show your emotions, Mandukhai, she admonished herself. Maybe there was another reason he had distanced himself. If Manduul had reacted so strongly toward her, what had he said or done to Unebolod?

After dinner, Mandukhai and Nergui set off to find the craftsman who created her bow so she could acquire two more for the girls. They entered the Khorchin area of Mongke Bulag and approached the most well-known fletcher—according to one of Manduul's men.

The fletcher's face sagged around his eyes, and his long mustache twitched as he examined her bow. "A fine piece, my Lady, but I did not make this. I don't know another Khorchin fletcher in the capital capable of making such a piece."

"But it bears a Khorchin mark," Mandukhai protested, showing the marking to him.

The fletcher nodded. "I saw."

"Well if not here, where would he have found such a piece?"

The fletcher smoothed his beard to a point. "Hulunbuir, I would assume. The grasslands of the Khorchin tribe."

Mandukhai thanked him, the pieces in her head spinning like knucklebones prepared to determine her fate. Nergui offered coins for two bows and as they started away, Mandukhai froze, then turned to face the fletcher. "Tell me, who of your tribe makes the best saddles?"

"Samut, my Lady. Right down that way." The fletcher pointed along a narrow path between gers.

Mandukhai thanked him again and guided Nergui back to her ger. He matched her stride, asking no questions though she could almost smell the smoke as he burned for answers.

"Saddle him," she ordered Tuya as she entered the ger to deposit the bows for the girls.

By the time she exited, Nergui was double-checking the harness holding the saddle on Dust's back. His own mount waited nearby.

"Manduul doesn't want you riding," he warned.

"I am approaching my bleed, which means I am free to ride at my will," she replied tersely, climbing onto Dust's back. "You can come along or go tell him. Either way, I'm riding."

Nergui grumbled under his breath and jumped on his own mount to follow her. "You play a dangerous game."

"This is no game," she replied, smiling at a family as they waved at her. "This is my life."

Nergui fell into sullen silence. He knew how headstrong she could be. Long before coming to Mongke Bulag, Mandukhai had a reputation among her own tribe for digging in her heels. Even if it ended with her in trouble. Her mother had beaten her with a ladle more than once, and Mandukhai always knew it would change nothing.

"We are headed back to the Khorchin district," Nergui said at last, breaking the silence.

"We are."

"What are you up to, my Lady?" Nergui's tone sounded anxious.

Mandukhai had some sympathy for Nergui's plight. He was her guard and would defend her from anyone. However, that also meant any trouble she stirred up would be his to bear as well. Mandukhai knowingly dragged Nergui into a dangerous game of mouse and elephant.

As they approached Samut's ger, the leatherworker looked up and his brows shot up his wide forehead. He stumbled forward and bowed deeply.

"My Lady Mandukhai, you honor me with your presence," Samut said.

"I may owe you thanks instead, Samut," Mandukhai replied, jumping down from the saddle.

"I humbly disagree." Samut's gaze flicked past her to Nergui and he stiffened.

Mandukhai motioned toward her saddle. "I received this as a gift, and may wish to commission a few more like it. It's a fine saddle. Do you know who created it?"

Samut crossed his arms and did little more than glance at the saddle before nodding. "I remember this piece quite well. Lots of detail requested, and at a hefty price, too. I made this for Lord Unebolod."

Mandukhai's heart jumped into her throat. Her breaths quickened.

"Are you okay, Lady Mandukhai?" Samut asked.

Mandukhai forced a smile that battled the nerves writhing in her stomach. "Of course."

Nergui edged his mount closer, as if he suddenly understood what Mandukhai sought. "Time to go, my Lady," he said firmly.

"Thank you, Samut," Mandukhai said, inclining her head toward him politely. "I will consider coming to you when I am ready to commission a few more saddles."

"I would be honored, my Lady."

Mandukhai swung her leg over Dust's back, following Nergui toward home. He increased their pace to a quick trot, and Mandukhai noticed how his gaze darted around them anxiously: at a man watching them with a frown from the doorway of his ger, to a group of young men playing knucklebones in an open space, to women who fell into silent whispers as they passed. He said nothing until they returned to her ger.

Mandukhai entered, and Nergui ducked in after her, waving Tuya out the door and closing it firmly behind the servant.

"What are you doing?" Nergui hissed, spinning on his heel to confront her.

"Manduul lied to me. He told me he traded for that saddle."

"Maybe he did. How would we know?" Nergui glanced at the door.

"Unebolod commissioned it for me." Mandukhai bit her lip, wondering if she said too much. Surely she could trust Nergui. He was sworn to protect her, even above Manduul.

Nergui stiffened, staring at her. Silence settled between them, long and dreadful.

Nergui broke the silence first, his voice low and dangerous. "Lord Korgiz swore me to protect you and advise you, as did your mother, so listen to me very closely, my Lady."

Korgiz, the Ongud leader. Mandukhai wanted to spit in Korgiz's face for bartering her off to this fate.

"I know what you seek, but it is forbidden," Nergui continued. "He is the Khan's *orlok*, a sworn brother to Manduul Khan. He will not break that vow. Not for you. Not for anything. You must cast aside any hopes you might hold in your heart."

Everything inside of Mandukhai sank, and she could feel the tears threatening her. A lump swelled in her throat and she could not swallow it down no matter how hard she tried.

"For all we know, Manduul Khan traded Lord Unebolod for that saddle," Nergui continued. "Or perhaps he had it commission for Manduul Khan. Either way, that does not make Manduul guilty for giving you such a fine gift."

Mandukhai glanced at her bow, but said nothing. She simply dipped her head and nodded.

Satisfied that he had ended the issue, Nergui left her alone in the ger. And the moment the door closed, Mandukhai stiffened her back and swiped a tear from her cheek. Nergui was wrong though, she was certain of it. Why would Unebolod commission the saddle and the bow if he did not want her to find out?

The days fell into a routine. Mandukhai and the girls rose early for breakfast and then met Unebolod on the training ground. Nergui stood off to the side, watching without a word. Mandukhai became acutely aware of how closely Nergui observed her behavior around Unebolod. She said nothing to either of the men about what she knew in her heart to be true. Not yet.

After two days of practicing their drawing skills—using the bows Mandukhai had acquired for the girls—Unebolod taught them how to hold the arrows steady for the shot. Mandukhai was past all of this and had been for years. Even if the girls needed to start with the basics, couldn't he at least offer Mandukhai something more? But what more did she want from him?

He still paid little attention to her in each lesson, and after the fourth day of training, Mandukhai summoned the courage to confront him about it.

"Why do you teach me nothing?" she asked, trying to sound demanding when inside she trembled with fear that he might spurn her again.

"You don't need me yet," he said. "They do."

Mandukhai hated the answer. And she hated even more that he was right.

After the first week, Unebolod began paying more attention to Mandukhai, though only a little. She yearned to ask him about the saddle, to discover the truth, or trap him into it at the very least.

The girls weren't great at their aim, but Mandukhai's own aim had been off enough for him to notice as the days passed.

Unebolod stepped up behind her, so close she could feel the heat radiating from his skin, and told her to aim. Mandukhai raised the bow, pulled back the arrow, and took careful aim, struggling to keep her breaths steady. Unebolod leaned closer, nearly touching her shoulder as he peered down the arrow.

"The bow is too low," he said. His voice rumbled in her ear and his breath heated her neck. It took everything in Mandukhai to raise the bow higher, hold steady, and not react. He reached out and put his hand over hers, adjusting the aim, and her heart jumped into her throat. "Release," he said, his hand still over hers.

"But—"

"Do it."

Mandukhai released the string, and his grip guided her hand to relax on the release. The arrow shot straight and true, striking the center of the target. Unebolod pulled away from her. The absence of his heat made her suddenly

93

cold.

"Again," he said, crossing his arms and standing several feet away.

Mandukhai glanced at him, trying to read him, but his expression remained as stony as any of the Khan's men. Completely unreadable. Just past him, she noticed Nergui scowling. Mandukhai took a breath to steady her racing heart, grabbed another arrow, and did as he ordered. After that, he didn't touch her again for the rest of the lesson.

The mugwort Mandukhai took after sustaining Manduul's anger did its job effectively. Two days after she took the herb, she bled, confirming that she once again wasn't pregnant. However, the early arrival of her monthly blood drew Manduul's attention. At first, Manduul had refused to believe her, and she had to prove it to him, which humiliated her terribly. However, it meant he wouldn't come into her bed again while she was sleeping and insistently press his advances until she had no choice but to give in.

Mugwort also made her bleeding last longer than normal, and halfway through the second week, Manduul's patience had run out. He argued outside with Nergui.

"I'll be here tonight," Manduul said. "You can go. She has no need of you."

"I am sworn to remain," Nergui said.

"And I am your Khan. Go."

Mandukhai caught Nergui's gaze with a subtle gesture when Manduul was not looking, waving her guard off for the night. Manduul's men would watch over her through the night regardless. It would be better for Nergui to leave before confrontation with Manduul begins—a confrontation Nergui would certainly lose.

As Nergui frowned and abandoned is post, Manduul stormed into her ger. Borogchin and Esige froze with dishes in their hands, staring at their uncle. The set of Manduul's jaw sent a shock of dread down Mandukhai's spine. The slight squint of his angry gaze hinted at too much *airag*. Mandukhai's chest rose and fell with rapid breaths.

"It's been long enough," he said, his words slurring together.

"Girls, you can go. I'll finish this up myself," Mandukhai said, eager to get the two of them away from him before either he lost control, or they realized that something unsavory was happening between her and Manduul.

To their credit, both girls understood when they weren't wanted. The girls quickly scrambled to the door, giving Manduul extra space as they squeezed past. They clung to their boots, not bothering to slip them on in their haste.

As Manduul shuffled forward, Mandukhai slipped her paring knife into the sleeve of her deel. Mandukhai inched toward her side of the ger.

"What has been long enough?" she asked, hoping to buy a few more seconds of time. Maybe she could circle around and slip out the door before he reached to her.

"A woman can't possibly bleed for two weeks, not so long after she already bled," he said. "Which means you are either broken or deceiving me."

Mandukhai's heart jumped in her throat. Neither of those choices would bode well for her. If she was broken, she was of little use to him. If he caught her deceiving him, the punishment could be painful—or deadly.

"Perhaps it has something to do with the rough treatment you have given me lately," she said. Her words came out biting, and she gripped the handle of the hidden knife tight as his face turned red.

"You've hardly been willing to perform your duties," Manduul growled. He lurched across the ger toward her.

Mandukhai's eyes widened and she shifted closer to the door on her side. "I was until you forced yourself on me that morning."

"Oh, you were more than eager, climbing on me like a dog in heat." He cocked his head, and the way he studied her made Mandukhai's already-pounding heart hammer so loudly she was certain he could hear it. "Or you were using me to get what you wanted."

"You're drunk," Mandukhai spat. "You wouldn't say such a thing if you were sober."

"Wouldn't I?" Manduul shrugged off his fur-lined cloak, letting it fall carelessly to the floor. The muscles in his shoulders and arms coiled like a predator about to strike. He was hardly a strong man compared to others, but his mass more than made up for it.

Mandukhai rushed toward the door, but Manduul moved faster than she expected for one his size. Manduul sprang forward, seizing the back of her deel and tossing her away from the door and onto the bed with far more strength than she thought he had. The force knocked the air from her lungs, and she dropped the knife somewhere on the bed.

As she sucked a breath to refill her lungs, Manduul loomed over her. He yanked the belt around her waist hard enough to make the links snap, then he tossed it aside.

"Don't." It was the only word Mandukhai could think of as pain shot up her back. "I'm still bleeding."

"I don't care."

Mandukhai scrambled up the bed, attempting to slip out from under him as he climbed onto the bed over her.

"I'm not a common whore!" Mandukhai snapped, and her hand closed around the handle of the paring knife on the blanket. "I'm a queen, and I will be treated like one."

Manduul grabbed Mandukhai's ankle and yanked her back. She lifted the knife under his chin. Everything froze. Neither of them dared to move. If she moved, he would wrench the knife from her hand. If he moved, she would slice him open. Each held their breath, waiting for the other to break first. All it would take was a slice, and she could kill him. She could run away and leave here.

And then what? she thought. If she killed the Khan, her life would be forfeit, and she could very well take her former tribe down with her. *I can't kill him. I can't even hurt him or he will send men to wipe out my tribe while he abuses me further.*

Hopelessness gripped her chest. Tears leaked from her eyes and rolled down her temples.

Manduul seemed to understand the same thing. He grabbed her wrist and wrenched it away with so much force that she had to let go. The knife thumped against the rug. A backhanded slap sent a jolt of pain through Mandukhai's cheek and made her vision momentarily darken. She choked out a sob, unable to control her terror.

"You don't have to look at me as you look at him," Manduul said. "But you will remember that you are my wife."

He adjusted a ring on his hand. A golden ring with the crescent moon of the Yuan—with her blood on the moon.

Mandukhai squeezed her eyes shut. Pain from the cut in her face pulsed like fire, and she could feel it swelling. "If you do this, I will never be yours."

Manduul sneered. "You will always be mine."

CHAPTER TWELVE

THE MOUSE WHO BATTLED THE ELEPHANT

Nightmares made Unebolod's sleep restless. When at last he woke, sweat drenched his skin and clothes. He couldn't recall what any of the nightmares had been about. Eager to wash away all traces of the nightmare, he threw off the blanket and stretched to ease the pressing pain between his shoulders. Kilgor, his *Bankhar* dog, sat on up her hind quarters and bobbed her head hoping to join him. Even seated, she came to his hip. Unebolod scratched behind her dark fluffy ear. "Come, Kilgor."

She jumped to her feet and rushed to join him.

The two trotted through the capital toward the river. The wolf dawn had yet to break the horizon, giving Unebolod at least two hours before sunrise. The silence of Mongke Bulag broke with the occasional bleat of sheep or cluck of hens. In some gers, rumbling snores shattered Unebolod's momentary peace. Even though he couldn't remember the dreams, he still felt phantom pains as he walked to the river. Grinding, burning pain in his feet slowed his progression, as if all the skin had been peeled away. Stabbing pain in his chest made him double over and gasp for breath as Kilgor cocked her head and panted curiously, then she nuzzled his hand. The pain quickly passed, and he scratched her snout.

The wolf dawn brought memories of Odsar to the surface. She had loved this time of day. She would wake him with strong salted tea and they would sit together at the edge of camp, watching the stars disappear into the sunrise. Sometimes he missed Odsar so much it made his chest ache as though an arrow had pierced his heart. Odsar was the only woman he had ever loved, and until meeting Mandukhai, he never imagined he could ever care so deeply for another woman. Losing his wife had torn him apart.

Unebolod shook off the memory of Odsar's smiling face as he slipped into the river. The cold water sent a momentary shock through his limbs, but the sensation quickly passed. Spring had given way to summer, and the winter cold that had clung to the river all spring switched to warmer temperatures. Within weeks, the midday heat would reach its peak.

Unebolod enjoyed summer. The riding and hunting offered relief from the monotony of everyday life—not to mention the opportunity to submerge fully into the river instead of using cloths in a bowl of water. He took his time as his dog kept watch on the riverbank. Unebolod enjoyed the swim, the river, and the chance to let the current seep into his skin until it pruned. Only then did he emerge and dress.

The sun had yet to make an appearance as he entered Mongke Bulag, though the blue haze of the wolf dawn had begun. Unebolod headed home with Kilgor trotting alongside. The pads of her paws clicked on the packed dirt paths. All remained blissfully quiet until he neared home.

The soft clink of metal against metal and the creak of leather caught Unebolod's attention. He silently slipped into his ger to retrieve his bow and quiver. Kilgor sat at attention near the door, then whimpered slightly when commanded to stay. Such sounds were not uncommon, but at this time of morning, Unebolod worried how the men on watch had not taken notice. Was it an intruder?

He followed the soft sounds, creeping around the outer walls of his ger, keeping his steps silent. Manduul's ger rested behind his own by about twenty paces, with the wives on either side. Whoever created the sounds was close. Too close.

Keeping in the dark to avoid detection, Unebolod silently slipped an arrow onto the string of his bow and held it in place. The clink of metal accompanied another soft thump. A horse huffed, and its hooves thumped impatiently against the dirt-packed ground. Whoever lurked in the darkness of the wolf dawn was near Manduul's door, or Mandukhai's. From where he pressed against the wall of his ger, Unebolod could see Yeke's door.

Unebolod slipped out and raised his bow to fire, then froze when he recognized Mandukhai fastening a felt bundle behind her horse's saddle. Nergui was nowhere to be seen. *Where does she think she's going?*

Unebolod lowered the bow and stepped out of the shadows. "Going somewhere, Lady Mandukhai?"

Mandukhai squeaked and jumped high as she spun around, a knife sliding into her hand. The side of Mandukhai's face was swollen. Unebolod's heart leaped into his throat. When she saw him, her shoulders relaxed only a fraction, still holding the knife high between them. Her fierce gaze studied him, as if trying to decide whether she should trust him or stab him.

Unebolod slipped the arrow back into his quiver on his hip and closed the gap, reaching for her chin. Mandukhai flinched back.

"Who—?" The shape of the crescent moon ring was unmistakable. Only one man had a ring with that shape.

Mandukhai slapped his hand away. "Don't touch me."

"Mandukhai—"

"You've caused quite enough grief." She turned her back to him and tucked her knife into her belt.

Me? What had he done? Red fiery anger burned in Unebolod's veins. Manduul had done this to her. But why? Unebolod had been so careful, keeping a respectful distance, never approaching her without being prompted by Manduul himself. Suddenly the elephant's gambit had become a very real, very treacherous game. Unebolod had underestimated the Khan. Manduul had always been so pleasant and pliable. So easy to sway. But this…

The bundle on her saddle could only mean one thing. Mandukhai intended running from Mongke Bulag. His heart seized. *Where is her guard?*

Unebolod placed a hand on her saddle, keeping Mandukhai from making a huge mistake. He didn't want her to stay with Manduul, but he feared what her leaving could mean. To the Khan. To the tribes. To him.

"You can't run away," he said.

Mandukhai's lips thinned. She didn't avert her gaze from the bundle. "Remove your hand."

"If you run, he will chase you." Unebolod knew this much for certain. Manduul would never let her go. Not like this. "And if he doesn't find you, if you escape him, your tribe won't. He will send his best men to destroy the Ongud."

Mandukhai snorted. "I'd like to see him try."

Unebolod set down his bow and turned her to face him. Black hair hung down her shoulders, framing her face and partially obscuring it. She seemed to be using her hair as a shield so she wouldn't have to look at him directly.

He wanted to tell her that Manduul would send him, and Unebolod knew he would have no choice by to obey. With the Khan's best men at his side, there was little chance he wouldn't win. But he couldn't find the right words.

Mandukhai seemed to understand. Realization sparked in her dark eyes and her entire body quivered. "I can't stay."

"You are a queen now, and your people are counting on their queen for protection. The girls are depending on you. If you escape him, who do you think he will punish? Who do you think he will blame?"

Mandukhai's eyes widened, and she shook her head vehemently. "Esige and Borogchin have nothing to do with any of this."

"It won't matter." Unebolod glanced around them, but even though the sky had shifted to lighter hues of blue, no one else stirred. For now. "Do you know the story of the mouse who battled the elephant?"

Mandukhai hesitated, her hand frozen on the bundle, clinging to the rope. He couldn't read her expression, so he pressed on.

"The mouse lived in a hole beside a pond. The elephant came every day at the same time to drink and wash, then would fill the mouse's hole with water to amuse himself. It made the elephant feel bigger and stronger to assert himself this way." Unebolod studied Mandukhai's reaction, but as understanding sparked in her eyes, she ducked her head. Waves of black hair fell around her shoulders. His hand itched to touch the silky locks.

He continued, "One day, the mouse had enough. It warned the elephant that if it didn't stop, the mouse would declare war on the elephant, which only amused the elephant more. After all, it had all the power and strength, and the mouse had none.

"The next day, the elephant returned, but this time, the mouse was ready. When the elephant placed its fat trunk in the water, the mouse climbed in and destroyed the elephant from the inside out. The elephant tried to dislodge the mouse, raging and stomping, but in the end all that remained was the dead elephant and a battlefield of destruction."

Silence settled over them. Unebolod understood what he was asking of her, and he didn't doubt for a moment that she grasped the meaning. If she wanted Manduul to understand that she was strong and capable, she would have to make him see it, just as the mouse had done to the elephant.

At last, she lifted her face to meet his gaze again. Her dark eyes drew him in. Tears shimmered in them, making her eyes sparkle in the slowly growing light of dawn. It reminded him of the stars chased away by the sunrise, and his heart lurched.

"Why should I trust you?" Mandukhai asked, the sharpness in her tone mismatched with the light in her eyes. "By your own lips, trust is a dangerous thing to give. Everyone wants something for themselves. What is it you want? And don't feed me another line to mollify me. I want the truth."

Unebolod's nerves clenched tight, a sensation he hadn't felt in a long time. Even charging into battle outnumbered didn't make him this nervous. He wanted to tell her the truth, but the truth was far too perilous to speak.

"Trust and truth are two edges of the same sword," Unebolod said, drawing back. "And both can cut just as deep."

"That isn't an answer."

"It's the only answer I can give."

Elsewhere in camp, he could hear people stirring. Mandukhai indicated that Manduul already suspected Unebolod of something, and she had suffered the punishment. He could not bear her suffering again because of him. And if anyone discovered them speaking together like this, alone, it would only make matters worse.

Mandukhai's expression turned into a thunder cloud. *Let her be angry with me. It's better than the alternative.*

"I won't stop you," he said, picking up his bow. "Just know this. There are four kinds of queens in this world. The cowardly and cowed, the ruthless and greedy, the careless and complacent, or the strong and wise. You get to choose, right now, which to be. If you choose to stay, I will see you on the training grounds. If you choose to leave, I will see the Ongud on the battlefield."

Afraid of seeing her reaction, afraid he couldn't bear it, he turned and slipped away to his ger. Once he was inside, Unebolod walked to the north wall, holding his breath, ignoring the eager pants of his dog, and listening for the sound of hooves against the ground on the other side of the wall.

Fear froze Mandukhai in place, one of her hands gripping the reins and the other on the saddle to hoist herself up. As much as she tried, as much as she willed herself to slip her foot into the stirrup and climb on Dust's back, she couldn't move. *You get to choose, right now, which to be.* Unebolod's words had sliced right into her heart.

Running wouldn't solve the problem. It would only make matters worse for everyone she cared about. But Mandukhai knew she couldn't stay and allow Manduul to use her like that again. She couldn't fight back, either. Who would dare call the Khan out on the way he treated his wife? Worse, what if he blamed someone else to save face? *What if he blames Unebolod?*

Mandukhai still didn't know if she could trust Unebolod. The man remained shrouded in mystery. She knew little more about him than fragmented pieces of his past, and tales of the Steel Soldier. Manduul would send Unebolod to fight the Ongud if she fled. And if his reputation bore any truth, her people would put up a fight but ultimately lose.

Not to mention how he made her feel every time he touched her. No one had ever caused such a spark in her before. Could she run away from that? *I am a married woman. I cannot run away, but I also cannot run toward him.* Perhaps, once she had a son, she could find a way to kill Manduul and free herself to choose whoever she wished.

Mandukhai removed the ropes holding her felt-wrapped possessions with resolve. All of her frustration and anger came out on the ropes as she yanked them loose to remove her felt bundle. Manduul still slept in her ger. After their encounter, she had offered him tea, shaking so violently she had nearly spilled it on the rug. But she had slipped an herbal mixture into his tea that would keep him asleep for hours. Regardless, she didn't want to risk him waking to find her sneaking back in with a bundle. She picked up the felt wrapping and turned away from her ger, storming in to wake the girls in the ger next door.

"The day is wasting," Mandukhai said loudly, dropping her things just inside the door.

Both girls woke slowly, rubbing sleep from their eyes as they sat up in their beds. Mandukhai placed her fists on her hips. "I need to know everything you know about Lord Unebolod."

Mandukhai had implied she inquired about Unebolod for Borogchin's benefit. Borogchin had been more than willing to share everything she knew, likely assuming Mandukhai considered a match between her and the Khorchin lord. The chance to be matched to a man like Unebolod had kindled a fire in Borogchin's eyes. Not that Mandukhai had promised any such thing.

What Mandukhai had learned about Unebolod had been filtered through the eyes of a girl with a crush—all glowing praise and heroics. It had taken a fair bit of reflection for Mandukhai to sift out fact from fiction. Even then, she wasn't confident she was correct.

The most shocking piece of his story was that he had a wife, Odsar. Borogchin explained how he had doted on Odsar, how she'd died within a day after giving birth to a stillborn boy. According to Borogchin, his wife had given up her will to live, but Mandukhai found that hard to believe. Death was an ordinary risk with having children. More than likely, the truth had been that she had bled out. Regardless of the circumstances, it was certainly something Mandukhai could never ask Unebolod about.

The war stories were nothing Mandukhai had not heard before, with a few key political implications. Unebolod had fought off Bigirsen in an attack against the Borjigin tribe with only a handful of men, which meant he would have no loyalty to Bigirsen or the Uyghur tribe outside of what Manduul required. Borogchin explained that, at some point before that battle against Bigirsen, Unebolod, Manduul, and Togochi—who led the Khorlod tribe— swore themselves brothers by bond, but not by tribe or blood.

"They are as close as real brothers could be," Borogchin explained. "Always protecting each other above all others. I even heard a rumor that Uncle Manduul wept for Unebolod's loss when Odsar died."

Sworn brothers. It was not uncommon among men who served together to become like brothers, yet somehow she sensed this bond went even deeper, which made her wonder if his loyalty to Manduul would outweigh his desire to keep her attempt at escape secret. *He warned me about trust. Can I trust him at all?*

After their archery lesson today, she would attempt uncovering the truth.

But first, she had to cover another truth. With Borogchin and Tuya's help, Mandukhai use powders to cover the mark Manduul left on her face. They had asked, but she and refused them answers. No one needed to know what Manduul had done. She would not be seen as weak.

Mandukhai and the two girls met Unebolod on the training grounds, as they had every day. Their approach drew his attention, and his expression shifted ever so subtly to surprise. *He expected me to flee*, she thought. Mandukhai was pleased to prove him wrong.

Mandukhai gave no indication they had spoken earlier. She carried on with business as usual. Picking up on her cue, he began the lesson without comment. Relief flooded through her. It had terrified some part of her that he might bring it up again or ask how she was—anything to give away what happened.

Halfway through the lesson, Manduul strode past the training grounds with his guards, pausing to watch with his arms over his chest. A flash of anger pulsed through Mandukhai, and she funneled all of it into her aim, imagining Manduul as the target. Each of her arrows struck true, which drew praise from the girls and Manduul. Praise she didn't want. Then a pulse of fear rushed through her. What if he thought she didn't need the training any longer?

The fear made her aim waiver. Manduul grumbled something about women and fighting to his men, who laughed as they all walked away. Mandukhai gripped the bow in a fist with an arrow on the string, glaring at his back.

Unebolod stepped between her and Manduul, shooting a warning glance at her bow. *He thinks I will shoot Manduul here, in the open, after everything.*

"A queen should choose her targets carefully," he said.

For a moment, their gazes locked on each other, then Mandukhai huffed and turned her attention back to the target, drawing and releasing swiftly.

The arrow struck the center.

"Nice shot," he said moving behind her.

"It's a fine bow," Mandukhai said, turning to face him. "A lot of detail. Tell me, Lord Unebolod, why did you choose dragons?"

He shifted subtly away from her, watching the girls. "Esige, we talked about your shoulders," he called, then fell silent as he watched her adjust. Mandukhai was about to give up hope that he would answer her when he finally replied. "You are a daughter of the yellow dragon. A sign of power. It seems a queen should put something like that on display."

A sign of power. Manduul had not asked Unebolod to commission that saddle for him. He did not know what it meant to her, which proved to Mandukhai absolutely that the saddle had been Unebolod's idea from the start.

Nergui had warned Mandukhai to be cautious and drop this issue altogether, but Mandukhai's anger and hate toward Manduul burned in her heart. Perhaps Nergui was right, and Unebolod had traded that saddle to Manduul, but she had to be certain. It was a fine saddle to trade willingly. If Unebolod's loyal truly lay so firmly with her husband, she would be in serious trouble. The only evidence in her favor was the inclusion of the dragons on the bow as well. Why would he include them on the bow if he did not want her putting these pieces together?

"Is that why you also requested the yellow ribbons and dragons on the saddle?" she asked, keeping her tone light and conversational.

Every muscle in his body stiffened. Neither spoke as they watched Borogchin and Esige, but his lack of answer encouraged Mandukhai, as did his reaction. "How did Manduul end up with the saddle you commissioned?"

"I see you've been investigating," Unebolod said evenly. "He is Great Khan. What is mine is his."

Mandukhai narrowed her eyes at him, but Unebolod remained focused on the girls. The way his arms crossed over his chest and his shoulders lifted tensely gave him away. "Did he take it?"

"He is the Great Khan. He cannot take what—"

"Stop defending him," she said. "He took the horse from you and pretended it was from him."

"Did you not like my gift?" he asked, glancing at the bow in her hand.

Mandukhai's heart sank. He hadn't denied it. "You gave me this bow on purpose."

"Of course I did," he said plainly. "I have already explained. You wanted a bow. I got you one."

Mandukhai squared off in front of him. He'd given her that bow to get her attention. It had worked—not that he hadn't captured her attention long before that. "You knew I would put these pieces together."

Unebolod's gaze pierced into her, hard and unrelenting—and slightly amused. "You make bold assumptions, my Lady. Dangerous assumptions."

"You asked to speak freely with me before," Mandukhai said, glancing over at Nergui whose scowl alone could have sliced Unebolod to shreds. "I demand you do so now. You wanted me to learn the truth of the saddle, which is why you gave me the bow with the dragons. Otherwise, what was to stop you from simply giving me a bow like any other?"

Unebolod stared at her, and the amusement slipped from his face. Instead, he studied her as if attempting to pick her apart. "If I am to speak freely, Manduul is my Khan and my brother. I would deny him nothing. Infer from that whatever you wish, but do so cautiously. I warned you about truth."

Why can he never just answer me? Unebolod had not denied or confirmed anything, but his body language and warning made the answer clear enough. Whether innocently or by devious design, Manduul had taken that saddle and claimed it as his own. *And I rewarded him for it.* More than ever, she loathed her husband. Had everything been a lie?

Manduul would pay.

Mandukhai knew what she had to do next, and it would be utterly humiliating, but it certainly would leave a lasting impression. "By the end of this day, everyone will know what sort of queen I will be."

"What will you do?" Unebolod asked. Mandukhai thought she heard a hint of fear in his voice.

"Give warning to the elephant." Mandukhai turned away from him and marched toward Nergui.

"Mandukhai—"

"Girls!" Mandukhai called out. "Gather your things. We are done with lessons for today."

Both girls voiced their dismay. Borogchin sighed and quietly lamented their early departure. Esige simply grumbled loudly as she kicked up dust with her shoes.

Mandukhai had spent months bound to Manduul's will—much like the mouse in its hole. She had spent weeks afraid of him, of what he might do next. Or what he might make her do.

It was time to show the elephant that even the small can be mighty.

CHAPTER THIRTEEN

SHEDDING SIN

Mandukhai created a new *boqta* out of the yellow silk, increasing the height. She had been careful to ensure it wasn't higher than Yeke's, but it would come terribly close. Esige slipped out to check the height and be certain. She returned thirty minutes later, slipping in and closing the door quietly behind her.

"Within a hair, but not too tall," Esige confirmed.

Borogchin sat on the bench with pearls, coral, and gemstones Mandukhai had received as wedding gifts. She worked diligently, inspecting each and arranging them in order before stringing them together.

Mandukhai sat patiently in the only chair as Tuya braided and bound her hair. Once finished, Tuya accepted the new *boqta* and fastened it in place. The result of their labor was a stunning piece that sang with even a breath of air or the slightest breeze.

"You look beautiful!" Esige gasped as Mandukhai stood.

"If I am to be queen, I will make a show of it," Mandukhai said as she retrieved a skin of *airag*. She handed it to Borogchin. "Give this to Nergui with my blessing. He deserves a night off."

Borogchin accepted the skin and cocked her head. "And if he won't leave?"

"Convince him." Mandukhai waved off further protest as she moved toward her chest of clothing.

Manduul's council would still be gathered until dinner, which gave Mandukhai little time to spare. She slipped on layer after layer of silk, every one of the deels the girls had given her—that Manduul had given her. She wrapped the damaged belt around her waist, tying the broken ends together with a strip of silk she ripped off one bolt.

"He accepted the gift," Borogchin reported as she slipped back inside and closed the door, "though not without protests." She smiled innocently. "I swayed him."

Mandukhai nodded in thanks. Her stomach was twisted in impossible knots. "I still insist the two of you go to your ger and stay there for the night," she said as she adjusted the bulky layers. "This will be dangerous."

"Are you joking?" Esige asked, her youthful eyes doubling in size. "This is the most exciting thing ever to happen. I won't miss it."

Borogchin's mouth twitched into a fake smile. "Our place is at your side."

Mandukhai's stomach sank. Hopefully Manduul would not punish his nieces for Mandukhai's indiscretions. Their insistence filled Mandukhai with a sense of pride.

And dread.

What she was about to do would either force Manduul to reconsider how he treated her ... or he would just kill her. On one hand, she would receive the respect she deserved, and if she couldn't get it, death would be preferable to living under his thumb another moment longer.

Unebolod had been locked in meetings with Manduul and his advisors since lunch. Lanterns hung from the support posts and copper pots of fire near the dais lit the gathering tent, reflecting light off the gemstones having from the silk. More than a dozen of the lords and commanders in Mongke Bulag sat on benches assigned by rank to either side of the path through the center of the tent. For hours, they had bickered over various matters of state. Now, only a handful dared to offer advice on the current matter at hand.

News from the Great Horde in the far northwest had arrived. Lord Mahmed was losing control, and the Great Horde was on the brink of an internal war. Mahmed had sent word to Manduul, asking for the Great Khan's help.

The meeting also kept Unebolod from seeking Mandukhai to find out what she planned. He couldn't shake the sense of anxiety worming into his mind.

"If we do nothing and Mahmed stamps out this uprising before it comes to fruition, he will come at us next," Lord Unige said. His tribe was small, hardly worth more than a footnote, but his loyalty to Manduul was unwavering since the early days. Unebolod did not exactly despise Unige—they two of them got along—but Unige had a weak will and even weaker constitution. It befitted a small man from a small tribe to respond with fear.

Unebolod grew weary.

"If you have nothing useful to add to the conversation, keep your mouth closed, Unige," Manduul growled. "I am aware of how few men we have. But if Mahmed is so pitiful as ruler of the Great Horde, maybe he deserves to be overthrown."

"We could still use reinforcements if he wins," Togochi added. "Send word to Bigirsen so if we need reinforcements, they will already be on the way."

Unebolod snorted, keeping his arms crossed as he leaned back on his bench.

"Do you have something to add, Lord Unebolod?" Manduul asked, glaring at him. "You are *orlok*, after all."

A lot. Though little of what he had to say to Manduul had anything to do with the current conversation. He considered the question seriously, though. What could be done? "The best course of action is to do nothing."

This comment drew a flurry of protests from everyone. Unebolod locked his gaze on Manduul as the Khan studied him, contemplating his words while ignoring the others as they bickered. At last, Manduul held up a hand. The council fell silent. Unebolod's eyes latched onto the golden crescent moon ring of the Yuan, polished and gleaming. His jaw twitched.

"Explain yourself, brother," Manduul said.

Unebolod didn't flinch. "Bigirsen is busy fighting for control of what remains of the Moghul Khanate. His remaining forces are tied up on the western China front, holding back another Ming army in the Gansu Corridor. He won't have men to spare to protect our pride. Nor should he. Mahmed would be foolish to ride against the Great Khan's horde after quelling an uprising. Not only would he lose his position while he was away, but it would deplete his forces. Too depleted to put a dent in our own." *If I were in Manduul's place, this would be done already.*

Manduul sank back in his throne, rubbing his chin as he considered this answer. The seat creaked as it strained under his weight.

"You can't simply do nothing, Great Khan," Unige insisted.

Manduul waved his protests off. Over the years, Unebolod had proven himself adept at strategy; he had won many battles, which was the entire reason Manduul appointed him *orlok* of the northern armies. Manduul would not dismiss his advice easily. He knew better. As Manduul flicked his gaze up to Unebolod, he knew what the Khan would suggest before it even slipped past his lips. If Manduul decided against his advice, Unebolod would be the one to lead. He braced himself for the inevitable.

As Manduul's mouth opened, the doors to the closed session swung open to firm and wild protests from the guards stationed outside. All eyes turned to see who would dare enter, or who may be missing from the council to arrive so late. Collectively, several of the men gasped. Unebolod's mouth went dry.

One of the guards attempted explaining the disturbance. "My lord Khan, we tried to stop her, but she would not—"

Manduul raised a hand to silence the guard. Fury creased his face as it turned redder by the moment.

Mandukhai strode into the tent as if invited, followed by much more timid versions of Esige and Borogchin than Unebolod had seen before. Mandukhai's body puffed out with layers of clothing, and the *boqta* on her head was not the same as she usually wore. This one was taller, more ornate. *And yellow, like the dragon of her birth*, he thought. *What is she doing?* Fear leaped into his throat and he glanced sidelong at Manduul.

"This is a closed session," Manduul growled. "No place for women."

The girls stopped on either side of the exit, and Unebolod wondered if they were skilled with knives. Mandukhai could bring the girls in here and kill everyone while the girls stopped any who fled. Then she could seize control of Yeke to pinch Bigirsen. *Please don't let that be her plan.* It was a terrible plan. A smart plan. A stupid plan.

Yet, as he considered this, it sounded less stupid with each hammer of his heart. Manduul would be out of his way, and for all the love he bore for the Khan, he also hated him. Bigirsen would be forced to submit or march all of his armies against Mongke Bulag to retrieve his daughter—which would then cause further division, and many of the northern and eastern tribes would shift alliance to Unebolod. Then he could stake his claim on the title, and nothing would stand between himself and Mandukhai.

"I thought I was your queen," Mandukhai said, not slowing her step. "If I'm not a queen, I'm little more than one of your whores."

Everything about her was fearless. The set of her jaw, the way she held her chin high and proud. The crescent mark Manduul left on her face—which she had covered with powders earlier in the day—Mandukhai now wore like a badge of honor for all the men present to see. Every time Unebolod thought he understood her, she surprised him again, revealing a new side to her complexity. Right now, despite the layers of clothing and the mark on her face, Mandukhai was more fearsome and radiant than she had ever been before. Did anyone else notice, or was it just him?

"You don't know how to battle," Manduul said, sitting up straighter. Anger burned in his voice. "Your kind only knows rebellion."

"Are you calling me rebellious?" Mandukhai asked, amusement in her light tone. She climbed the steps without hesitation.

She's goading him. Drawing him out in front of everyone. He will kill her. Unebolod tensed, casually sliding his hand over the knife tucked in his belt. *Woman, don't make me do it.*

Do what, though? His job, his purpose, was to protect the Khan and his family. That included her, but he was duty-bound to protect Manduul even from her. His honor demanded it. Part of Unebolod wanted to believe he would do his duty above all else and protect Manduul from any danger. But another, deeper part knew that he would likely do something foolish to protect her. Even from Manduul. Especially if it gave him an opportunity to become the next Great Khan.

Manduul's voice lowered to dangerous levels, causing Unebolod to tighten his grip on the knife. "Go, woman," Manduul said. "We will talk about this later."

Mandukhai bowed her head, the gems attached to the *boqta* singing a sad song. The movement was more out of sorrow than deference. Unebolod's breath turned ragged.

"As my Great Khan wishes." Mandukhai untied the belt around her waist. As she held it to the side and dropped it to the ground—making a show of the motion—Unebolod noticed the broken links. His throat constricted. Yet another sign of the struggle she faced at Manduul's hand. "But as a simple woman, I should return the gifts meant for your queen, such as this fine belt."

"Don't make a show of this," Manduul said, wrinkling his nose in disgust.

Unebolod glanced at the other men gathered only long enough to see how they reacted. None of them appeared disgusted. Each of the men watched with curious fascination. Manduul's guards remained just inside the doorway by the girls, their hands on their swords and prepared to jump into action.

Mandukhai stripped off the first layer, a blue deel that covered the rest. Manduul protested, but she simply dropped the silk on the ground at his feet, then began with the next layer.

"Your behavior is childish," Manduul said, gripping the arms of the throne so tightly his knuckles turned white.

She dropped two more layers.

"I don't deserve the silks you've given me," she said, shedding the jade one on the pile.

"The girls gave them to you," Manduul roared, "and your lack of respect for their offering is a disgrace."

Unebolod wanted her to stop before Manduul lost control, but he knew that if Manduul struck out in front of everyone, it would make him look weak. Did she know that?

"And I have been disgraced," she said sadly. She dropped another, leaving her in the last layer. The red silk spilled around her body like the blood of sacrifice.

Manduul surged to his feet. Unebolod shifted, preparing to strike out in her defense. But Manduul didn't approach her. Not even as she removed the *boqta* and placed it on the ground gently beside him. Not even as she shed the final layer, leaving her covered by nothing more than white bands of cotton around her chest and private areas. Not even as she crawled to him and kissed the ground at his feet, then pressed her forehead to the wooden floor and awaited his judgment.

As much as he wanted to look away, Unebolod couldn't. Not at first. His face flushed with embarrassment for her laid so bare, and a glance revealed a mixture of embarrassment and horror from the other men gathered. In a matter of minutes, she had gone from a queen in all her power to a common groveling whore. *And she's done this on purpose*, he realized.

It was a bold move, a risky move. Manduul would either have to pass off her behavior and accept her position at court—and later explain his own behavior, which may disgrace him—or he would have to kill her for such humiliation. Which could spark war with the Ongud. She's turned his power to her benefit. Like the mouse against the elephant. Her tribe would hear about this. All Mandukhai would have to do is send word, and they would ride to her side.

Suddenly, Unebolod realized Nergui was not present. If she knew what she was doing right now—and he didn't doubt for a second she did—Nergui would be waiting near the edge of Mongke Bulag to hear word of her murder, then he would ride immediately to the Ongud, who would rally all the southeastern tribes to their aid. Manduul would be disgraced.

Unebolod's heart raced. His breath quickened. The seconds seemed to pass forever as he waited to see what Manduul would do.

No one dared move. It seemed like no one else even breathed. Unebolod heard nothing but the pounding of his own heart in his ears and Manduul's labored breathing. His gaze locked on Manduul.

At last, Manduul bent over, and for a moment Unebolod feared the worst. Instead, he stroked her hair tenderly and picked up the *boqta*. "Rise, Lady Mandukhai. A woman such as yourself—a queen and a Mongol—shouldn't humiliate herself in such a way."

Unebolod released a breath he hadn't realized he had been holding, watching as she lifted her head, gazing up at Manduul, then accepted her *boqta* back.

"Girls, take her home." Manduul ordered them forward with a flick of his fingers as Mandukhai rose.

Borogchin and Esige rushed forward, and Borogchin draped the red deel around Mandukhai's body like one of those royal robes rulers in the far west seemed to prefer. Esige scooped up the rest of the discarded clothing. Unebolod watched them go, and for a moment he feared his gaze lingered. Thankfully, his wasn't the only one.

As Mandukhai passed him, Unebolod was certain he saw a ghost of a smile on her face. *Manduul has no idea what sort of woman he has wed.*

CHAPTER FOURTEEN

MIDNIGHT RIDER

Upon returning home, Mandukhai moved straight to the altar along the northern wall and lit incense, then kneeled and pleaded to Tengri and the High Heavens to protect her from Manduul's wrath. "I meant no ill will or disrespect toward the noble line of Khans." For nearly an hour, she kneeled at the altar, praying as the incense slowly burned away.

Mandukhai then paced her floor as she waited for Manduul to arrive and punish her in private. What she had done was humiliating not just to her, but to him as well. She expected him to be furious, that the men in his council now doubted his ability to lead. She could already hear his voice: *A man who cannot control his house cannot control a Nation.*

Knots twisted in her gut like endlessly spinning silk, bunching tighter and tighter, coiled around her pit of despair in an iron fist. When at last she heard his voice outside, Mandukhai raised a trembling hand to her mouth, then forced herself to sit on the bed and continue a stitching project. When he entered, she wanted him to see her acting normal and unafraid.

His boots crunched against the dry ground outside. She held her breath as they drew closer. He wouldn't kill her now that he accepted her in front of his men, but she knew very well there were many ways to punish her without leaving a trace.

Mandukhai held her breath as she waited for him to open the door.

Then his steps moved past, toward his own ger.

He's not coming. The realization flooded her with relief.

For the next few hours, she listened to the laughter of multiple women and sounds of pleasure coming from his ger. *At least it isn't me,* she thought. The relief washed through her, cleansing the horror of the past few weeks, offering a refreshing sense of freedom. But she wasn't foolish enough to think this was over.

Mandukhai waited until long after his ger fell silent, confident he wouldn't rouse in the middle of the night and come to her.

After opening the door a crack, she peered out into the torch-lit darkness. Four of Manduul's guards watched over his ger at night, as well as Mandukhai, Yeke, and the girls. She had grown used to their presence and occasionally convinced them she would ride the winding thoroughfares of Mongke Bulag without leaving. Every time, she slipped out after offering the man on watch on the eastern edge of the capital a skin of *airag* to keep warm in exchange for a brief ride out to her favorite tree. They were often eager to comply.

With Nergui off duty and the guards and watchmen easy to assuage, Mandukhai easily slipped away from Mongke Bulag.

Dust grazed at the dirt beside Mandukhai's ger, still saddled from the morning. Mandukhai hadn't wanted to remove the saddle in case the worst happened, and she did in fact have to flee. Not that she was sure she would. She climbed onto Dust's back, riding along the thoroughfare at a careful, rhythmic trot. Her purpose was clear in her mind, but she couldn't be sure it would work.

Crouching in front of Manduul wearing nothing but her cotton undergarments had been far more humiliating than she had expected. Part of her had hoped Manduul would stop her before it went that far. All his loyal Lords had been there, and all men at that. Including Unebolod. But when she left the tent, she saw the way they gazed at her. Not leering or covetously, but with wonder.

Mandukhai had carefully inquired earlier where she might find Unebolod tonight in a way that would arouse no suspicion. He was on watch this night, and she intended to catch his attention as she rode out of camp. She needed to speak with him without Nergui or Manduul's men looming over their shoulders.

When she reached the edge of Mongke Bulag, Dust broke into a gallop. Wind whipped Mandukhai's hair in streaming ribbons behind her. She rode far enough from Mongke Bulag to see the remaining torches, but not close enough to be spotted by anyone easily.

Except for the man on watch. *Hopefully, he follows.*

Over the last few weeks, Mandukhai's riding had been restricted, but not to enough to prevent her from becoming acclimated to the surrounding land. She knew where the hills crested and fell, where marmot holes might pose a danger, where the streams were, and which areas might prove dangerous for Dust to ride over at night. Tonight, a crescent moon and a smattering of stars cast the only dim illumination. It allowed her to see well enough for safe riding.

Her favorite place to visit had become a large, lonely, misshapen birch tree just over a low eastern hill a mile from the edge of the capital. Nothing else came close to the tree for hundreds of paces, if not more.

Tonight, she raced toward it, jumping off Dust's back and tethering the reins to a low branch where he could graze as she waited. The limbs of the tree twisted in odd directions, as if each battled the next for more exposure to the sun. Animals had chewed away at the strips of bark or made ruts with their horns near the base of the tree. The tree was beaten, used, and discarded, yet it still sought favor from the Eternal Blue Sky, and its roots still carved deep into the soil, seeking nourishment from earth mother.

Mandukhai stepped up to the tree's thick trunk, tracing her finger along the grooves, the scars left behind. The mark Manduul had left on her cheek throbbed with pain, and she understood the agony of this poor tree. Dust stamped a hoof and danced to the side just moments before Mandukhai heard the thump of hooves approaching. She could feel them in the ground. When the rider drew closer, the horse slowed to a canter, then a slow trot. She smiled at the tree. He came.

"Do you follow everyone who rides out of camp at night?" she asked Unebolod, pressing her palm to the tree.

"Only those important to the Great Khan," Unebolod said. His boots thumped against the hard grass as he dismounted.

"Am I important only to the Khan?" Mandukhai turned, surprised to find him standing so close.

Only a step separated the two. For a moment, her breaths came in uneven, rapid succession. Mandukhai took a minute to collect herself, raising her chin and staring at him proudly.

Unebolod's arms remained fixed at his sides, staring so intensely at her she feared he might do something foolish. *Would I care if he did?* His Adam's apple bobbed, and his jaw remained clenched tight.

"Why did you lure me out here in the middle of the night?" he asked at last.

She feigned intrigue. "Lure?"

"I've seen enough not to underestimate you," he said.

Mandukhai could almost see him building up a wall around himself. *Don't! Let me in!*

"You wanted me to follow you out here. I just haven't figured out why."

"I'm certain you have." Mandukhai folded her hands into the sleeves of her deel. "Just as you knew I would figure out it was you who arranged for the saddle. Just as you knew that with the right words, I would choose not to flee this morning. Don't pretend you have pieced none of this together. I know who you are. I know where you come from." Mandukhai stepped closer, daring him to disagree with her as her gaze bore down on him. "I know what you stand to gain."

Unebolod's expression soured, and he took a step back. He turned to check his horse's reins, tethered to the tree beside her own. They remained secure. "What do you want from me?"

Mandukhai took a careful, steady breath. If she was wrong about Unebolod, this would end poorly for her. He would take her to Manduul and confess everything. Manduul would then have no choice but to kill her. *Please don't let me be wrong*, she prayed to the sky father.

"You know who my father was," Mandukhai said.

His frown deepened. "Everyone knows who your father was."

"My father did not choose to be Esen's advisor," Mandukhai said, choosing her words carefully. "He was chosen by Esen and he was powerless to refuse. Everyone remembers Esen the Tyrant. But I have memories of his kindness, his loyalty to Taisun Khan. Until Taisun Khan betrayed him. He refused to uphold his promise."

"Taisun Khan did not betray Esen," Unebolod snapped. "He made no promise."

"Perhaps," Mandukhai replied evenly, shrugging her shoulders. "I was a child and my memories are unreliable. I do remember my father supporting Esen right until Taisun Khan's death. Until Esen unlawfully seized control—"

"Without *kurultai*," Unebolod interrupted. His jaw twitched.

She struck a nerve. *Good.*

"Yes, without being selected by a gathering of tribe leaders. Still, my father supported him. What choice did he have?" Mandukhai closed her eyes for a moment, and saw her father's face, wrinkled in concern. It was the only expression she could ever remember. "Then Esen began butchering any man with links to the Borjigin royal line."

"I remember," he said darkly, grasping his sword. "He intended to exterminate us."

"My father organized the revolt against Esen," Mandukhai continued. She needed Unebolod to understand her own motives, her own desires. "To protect Mongolia. To protect the royal line. He knew Esen would kill him, yet he knew, deep down, it was right. It was the only way to save Mongolia from total ruin."

"And you think Manduul is no better a Great Khan," Unebolod said.

Mandukhai hadn't said it. She hadn't even hinted it. Hearing it from Unebolod made her wonder if he felt that way. "I am saying that even the strongest oaths must be broken for the good of the Nation. Complacency can be just as dangerous. Mongols need a wise, fierce, and fair hand to guide them."

Unebolod's shoulders sagged, and he turned his gaze toward Mongke Bulag. "I know all about Esen's despicable treachery. I was there. He deceived my father and brothers, lured them into his tent under the guise of Guest Rights with the promise of celebration and drinks, of brotherhood. Then his men sang songs and made noise while he killed them. Their screams were drowned out by the music."

Mandukhai's heart clenched in her chest. Had he seen this for himself or only heard others tell of it? When Unebolod turned his attention on her again, hatred burned in his eyes. Breaking Guest Rights constituted a serious breach of etiquette—and could end in a call to war.

"My brother Bolunai and I escaped. We ran like cowards back to our homeland. I warned my tribesmen, the other noble lords, not to join Esen, but by then it was too late. Most of the men in my tribe had already gone, riding to their death or dead already." Unebolod's shoulders were so tense they quivered with rage.

It occurred to Mandukhai that he directed the hatred in his eyes inward. *He blames himself for not doing more, but he couldn't have been older than twelve or thirteen.*

"Manduul's nephew, Mergus, had been named heir, but he was young. His mother tried taking him to war against the Oirat for Esen's betrayal, but he died. That left only Manduul and his last nephew, Molon." Unebolod shifted uncomfortably. "Molon became the next Great Khan shortly after Esen died, but he was just a boy, barely old enough to rule. I swore to protect him and Manduul. I was young and foolish. It was not the first oath I made without understanding the implications, but it was the last. It wasn't long before Molon Khan's own advisor, an Uyghur, tricked him into the battle that took his life." Unebolod dropped his gaze to the ground as if ashamed.

Mandukhai listened in rapt silence. She had been so young at the time herself, barely six years old. Most of what she remembered had become a hazy, distant dream. She remembered the stories, amplified over time, and the mysterious tribesmen who secretly visited her father. Unebolod couldn't have been over sixteen at the time of the revolt against Esen. Had he been in the battle that claimed Molon Khan's life?

"And that's when the tribes fell into Uyghur and Oirat hands," Mandukhai breathed as the pieces slid into place. "So how did Bigirsen end up in his position?"

Unebolod's cheek twitched, amplifying the scar. "He attempted forcing the eastern tribes into submission, but we would not go quietly," he continued, his voice as sharp as an arrowhead, and just as deadly. "I think he assumed if he could take control of our tribe, he would increase his claim on the title of Great Khan. I nearly had him routed. We clashed on the battlefield and … let's just say we exchanged gifts. I gave him a deep scar in his left side. He gave me this." He motioned to the scar on his face.

"Rumors of discord stole in among the men on both sides," he said. "Bigirsen was losing support. The Khorlod were the first to defect. Togochi led the tribe into Manduul's arms. He fought beside me against Bigirsen's Uyghur-Oirat army. Then, one day, Bigirsen requested Guest Rights with Manduul. He swore to support Manduul's claim on the title and bring his forces into Manduul's leadership. It left Manduul with more than enough tribes to sweep the meeting of *kurultai*. Bigirsen offered Yeke as a wife, as a show of faith."

Mandukhai suddenly understood so much more. Unebolod had no love for Bigirsen. He hated Manduul's southern *orlok* for what he did to the Borjigin tribe.

For the first time since first meeting Unebolod, Mandukhai felt like she knew him, understood where he came from. A gentle summer evening breeze blew between them, accentuating the intimate moment. Mandukhai edged closer and reached toward his scar. Unebolod flinched back, and for a moment the two of them just stared at each other. Her hand lingered in the air until she gathered the courage to trace the long scar that cut through his eyebrow down to his jaw. Her hand trembled. He didn't pull away, and as her fingertips brushed along his cheekbone, she swore he leaned into the touch. The idea that he might crave her touch made her heart skip.

"Why tell me all of this?" she asked, allowing her fingers to linger as long as he permitted it.

"Because I need you to understand," he said, and desperation crept into his voice. "Manduul may not be my blood brother, but he and Togochi are my sworn brothers. We have been through so much together. I know Manduul is not the Great Khan we need, but he is the one we have."

Mandukhai pulled her hand back and folded it into her sleeve. Had she misunderstood him before? Perhaps he didn't want to be Great Khan. Perhaps he didn't desire ruling as most men did, which made what she was about to say a gamble. "You are a powerful warrior," she said. "And from what I've seen, you are wise, fierce, and fair. The men respect you. The women admire you." Mandukhai paused at the last, staring into his eyes, praying he would understand who she meant.

Unebolod's jaw twitched, and he folded his arms over his chest. His stoic nature pulled Mandukhai in. This was the sort of man she had dreamed about as a young girl. A fierce warrior. A compassionate man. The very image of long-lost Mongol men of the great empire she remembered from stories. Sadly, she had met him too late.

"And you?" he asked.

Mandukhai's heart jumped into her throat. Her feelings went much deeper than mere admiration. But she couldn't bring herself to say it aloud. "Truth and trust are a double-edged sword. Both cut just as deeply."

Shock flickered on his face, but he quickly masked it with that steadfast, stoic expression and said, "And without either, we have nothing more to discuss." Unebolod turned away, removing his reins from the tree branch.

Mandukhai rushed between him and his horse, her chin raised stubbornly. "Don't you dare."

He didn't even glance at her. Unebolod's demeanor shifted suddenly cold as swiftly as if she had plunged into a winter river, and it left Mandukhai well aware of the chill in the night air.

"Without truth, we cannot have trust," he said. "And without trust, we have nothing."

"You were the one who warned me to be wary of trust," she said, reaching for the reins in his hand.

He pulled them out of her reach. "I needed to be sure."

"And now?"

Unebolod squared off in front of her, leaning close. "Now you can't even admit to me what you really want. And I'm not about to risk everything and break my oaths for the good of the Nation without hearing the words from your own lips."

Anger burned in Mandukhai's chest, making her heart ache. Did he really expect her to tell him how she felt? It could ruin her if Manduul found out. And it would ruin Unebolod. Besides, even if she wanted him, she wasn't about to let Unebolod possess her like some crowning jewel like Manduul did.

"Yet without either my support or Yeke's, where will you be if Manduul dies without an heir?"

"You are jumping headfirst into the most dangerous game of all." His warm breath rolled off her face, contrasting with the crisp summer air. "Be sure you have your wits about you."

"I know what sort of game I've fallen into," Mandukhai said, her words a whisper with him so close. "I understand the risks ... and the rewards. It's too late to turn back now. The mouse has already declared war on the elephant."

Unebolod's eyes bore into her very soul, making it impossible to breathe. His face crept closer—or maybe it was her imagination. The movement was so subtle she could hardly notice.

A stick snapped nearby. Unebolod swept her behind him as he retrieved his bow and strung an arrow in the blink of an eye. Mandukhai hardly had time to register that someone had found them before he prepared to fire. Darkness masked their spy in shadows.

"Who goes there?" Unebolod's voice was ice cold.

Mandukhai arched her neck to gaze over his broad shoulders at the intruder. Was he an unfortunate soul out for a midnight ride when he just happened to stumble upon them? Or had he been sent to follow?

"Nergui," the intruder announced. "I heard what happened in the gathering tent and tracked Lady Mandukhai's hoofprints this way to ensure her safety."

Unebolod eased the tension on his string but didn't remove the arrow. Did he suspect Nergui would turn against them? Mandukhai put a hand on his arm and stepped around him.

"I'm fine," she reassured Nergui. "Just out for a midnight ride."

Nergui's gaze turned on her sharply, and the disappointment burning in his eyes made her want to flinch.

"Did anyone else see you leave camp?" Unebolod asked, scanning the horizon, though it was impossible to see so far in the pitch black of night.

Nergui stepped closer. "No." His accusing gaze pierced Mandukhai. "You had the girl reassure me you would stay in your ger tonight. Then I hear you laid yourself bare at the Khan's feet."

Mandukhai's chest clenched. "Nergui, I—"

"I have one job to do," Nergui said in a tight voice. "If you lie to me and keep me in darkness, I cannot do that job. He could have killed you, and he would have been within his right to do so!"

"He would not have killed her in front of the council," Unebolod said with certainty.

Nergui inched closer to Unebolod, and she worried the two would draw swords on each other here and now. "The Khan is already suspicious of your solicitous behavior. I doubt he is the only one. You put her in danger by meeting in secret like this."

Unebolod met Nergui's glare with a cold one of his own. "Go back to Mongke Bulag," Unebolod ordered. "Tell no one of this. Not even the girls."

Mandukhai swallowed. Would Nergui listen to him? Unebolod turned to her, and the way his stern gaze narrowed at her, she realized he wasn't just talking to Nergui. He was ordering her to return as well.

"The girls know I come out for rides," Mandukhai said. She wanted to keep the girls out of this.

"Will they speak of it?" Unebolod asked.

Mandukhai bit her lower lip. Esige wouldn't. She adored Mandukhai and had little love for Yeke. She also distrusted Bigirsen. But Borogchin ... if she thought Mandukhai was a threat to her chance at pairing with Unebolod, she would. "Esige won't. I'm certain of that. And there is a way to keep Borogchin from telling." *But I don't want to imagine it.* "And it could remove Manduul's suspicion for a time."

"Then do it." Unebolod nodded as if that decided it.

Mandukhai couldn't believe he would just agree without knowing what he had agreed to. *Because he trusts me.* The realization cut her deeply. He hadn't said as much, hadn't acted like the trusted her either, not fully, yet she could not deny there would be no other reason he would simply agree without asking which strings she would tether to him. He trusted her, and she hadn't been willing to trust him. She stepped aside and stood beside Nergui as Unebolod climbed onto his horse.

"I will speak to Manduul over breakfast," Mandukhai said, but her voice sounded distant, detached.

He gathered the reins and turned his horse to face her. "What is it?"

"You—" Mandukhai struggled to bring the rest of her words to the surface.

His frown deepened.

Mandukhai took a deep breath. "You will marry Borogchin."

Unebolod's face fell. "I have no desire to marry her."

"It will keep her appeased and distract Manduul from suspecting anything, especially if I make the offer to him." The words cut sliced into her heart and it required all of her strength to remain upright and outwardly confident in the face of such devastation.

Unebolod stared at her, the pain in his eyes mirroring her own. Desperation clung to the air like humidity. Then Unebolod's face turned to stone. "Is that really what you want?"

"It's what we need."

Unebolod nodded stiffly. "If it is what my queen commands, who am I to disobey?"

The words slammed against her, knocking the air from her lungs. *Is he distancing himself from me now?* Mandukhai opened her mouth to respond, but words evaded her. Before she could find them again, he rode away.

Nergui stood at her shoulder as they watched him disappear into the darkness. "I warned you."

"Not now." Mandukhai could hardly speak the words as her throat constricted.

Nergui shifted to stand in front of her and Mandukhai yearned to push him away, to hop on Dust's back and flee before she had to watch Unebolod marry Borogchin. She wanted to race after him, throw caution into the wind, and confess her true feelings.

"What happened before I arrived?" Nergui asked.

"Nothing," Mandukhai croaked.

"It did not look like nothing," Nergui said firmly. "I am sworn to protect you. That includes guarding you from the games of these men. If he can steal you away from Manduul..."

"Nothing happened! And he wouldn't."

Nergui marched around her, unwrapping Dust's reins from the branch. "He already has."

Has he? Mandukhai's feet rooted to the ground, her knees weak. A single movement could press her into the earth forever. Her desire for Unebolod went far beyond physical. She felt connected to him, as if they were two sides of the same coin, always together. Tears rolled down her cheeks, and she briskly swiped them away as Nergui approached with Dust.

He has. How did Nergui see that before she did?

"No more lies," Nergui barked, thrusting the reins at her.

"I was only trying to protect you," Mandukhai whispered as she mounted.

"Wrong. That is my job." Nergui strode toward his own mount and hopped into the saddle. "Your job is to produce an heir. If you survive beyond his years, you can fall into the arms of any man you deem worthy. And if you want to live so long, then stop deceiving me."

Mandukhai fell silent as she rode alongside Nergui back toward the capital. He was correct, yet also wrong.

Because when Manduul died, any man who could capture her could lay claim on the khanship. *And how long before he dies?*

CHAPTER FIFTEEN

THE BEST OF MEN

Mandukhai hadn't been able to fall asleep once she returned to Mongke Bulag. Fear that someone would storm in and drag her before Manduul, accusing her of cavorting with Unebolod or conspiring against the Khan kept her from even closing her eyes. Before sunrise, she prepared herself to approach Manduul on her own, and offer the proposal.

With rational purpose, Mandukhai selected her yellow silk deel—a color considered soft, gentle. Mandukhai brushed her hair with great care, making sure no sticks or dirt or evidence of any kind might give away where she had been in the middle of the night. Tuya joined Mandukhai as she finished combing her hair, and her servant set to work pinning up Mandukhai's hair with precision. Tuya draped pearl strands at Mandukhai's temples before placing the new yellow *boqta* on her head. The strap rubbed at Mandukhai's chin, but she did her best to ignore it.

Tuya and Mandukhai worked in perfect rhythm together preparing breakfast. Mandukhai set everything on a tray precisely.

"Shall I join you, Lady Mandukhai?" Tuya asked.

"No, Tuya," Mandukhai said, hefting the tray. "I can handle him. Get the door for me, will you?"

Tuya bowed and moved to obey.

Sunrise burned at the horizon, casting long shadows from her ger over Unebolod's in front of hers. She paused outside the door, examining the white walls of his ger, before turning to her task.

Nergui stood alert as Mandukhai exited, and he glanced at the food in her hands. She offered him one of the dumplings. He accepted the food without comment, following her toward Manduul's door so close she worried he might step on her heels.

Two of Manduul's guards stood outside the door, and neither of them moved to stop her. Both of Manduul's dogs lay beside one guard, furry heads resting on massive paws as they watched her. Nergui gave her a concerned glance as one of the guards opened the door for her. He said nothing as he took up his position outside to await her exit.

Balancing the tray carefully, she slipped inside. The stench of sweat slammed into her the moment she stepped over the threshold. It stuck in her throat, and she gagged as she shuffled toward the table in the center of the ger, setting the tray down before she dropped it.

Manduul's ger was set up much like her own, with a table in the center beside the stove and alter along the back wall. On the west wall, Manduul's old armor collected dust; on the east wall, a wide bed.

Manduul snored on his back, blankets kicked off his bare body. Instead, a blanket of two women covered him, draped over his stomach with limbs twisted in a mass. Mandukhai recognized both of them as servants who worked in the gathering tent for him. Both women were just as bare as him, slumbering soundly. Mandukhai couldn't have cared less. Let him cavort with all the women he chose. The more he did it with them, the less he did it with her. Any accidental pregnancies would not take precedence over her own son, assuming she ever had one.

Mandukhai could not help a flash of jealousy. Not for these two women, but for his ability to do what he wished with whomever he wished. She yearned for the same freedom.

Embers from the stove glowed, and Mandukhai stoked them to life with ease. But the ger needed light and air to diffuse the smell. She pulled the rooftop flap fully open, which caused the women draped over Manduul to stir awake and over their eyes as they blinked at the sudden light. Mandukhai then marched to the door without giving them a second glance and swung it wide open. The guards outside would see everything if they checked, but she didn't care.

She turned to the bed as the women sat up, squinting at her. Mandukhai kept her face calm, gathering up her full height as she folded her hands into the sleeves of her yellow deel. "I believe the Khan is satisfied enough,"

Mandukhai said.

The two of them didn't have to be told twice, and they rushed to slip on their clothes. Each of them bowed to her as they scurried out the door, mumbling "my Lady" as they passed.

Manduul grunted but didn't wake.

As she waited, Mandukhai carefully arranged breakfast dumplings on a plate for each of them. Her hands shook as she lifted the teapot, and Mandukhai focused on calming them before he could notice. The teapot rattled for a moment, then settled as she poured out the steaming tea.

In the wee hours of the morning, Mandukhai understood something she hadn't fully grasped before. Manduul was weak. His physical strength was greater than her own, for certain. But his confidence and will were easily swayed. The relationship he had with Bigirsen made that clear enough—if Unebolod's story proved truthful; and she had no reason to doubt him. Manduul held a position that should belong to a better man. If she played their game, bided her time, and planned carefully, Mandukhai knew she could have what she wanted—who she wanted. *And if not, perhaps I will run away still.*

Playing the game meant she would have to confront Manduul about what had happened between them. She would have to gain his trust. *Trust is a dangerous thing to give,* she thought. If he was as pliable to manipulation as she suspected, it should be easy—as long as she was careful. Before, Mandukhai had stretched too far too fast. This sort of planning would take time, patience, finesse.

"It's too early," Manduul grumbled, slapping an arm over his eyes.

"It's my understanding that you have urgent business to attend today," Mandukhai said, pleased with herself for keeping her tone light and steady. "A substantial breakfast will set you on the right path."

He grunted.

Mandukhai set down the teapot and turned to him, keeping her hands visible so he didn't suspect her of holding a knife again. Not that he could see her hands while covering his eyes.

"At least dress yourself before someone walks past and sees you in this state," Mandukhai said.

Manduul pulled his hand away and glanced down at his large body, then barked out a laugh. "We need to talk about your little act last night," he said, sitting up.

Mandukhai tensed, wondering if he knew about her meeting with

Unebolod before realizing he meant her act at the meeting. Hoping to appear nonchalant, Mandukhai went to the chest of clothes and pulled out a deel of brown silk with white accents along the edges and over the shoulders. It was a perfect complement to the yellow one she wore. Manduul struggled to roll his body out of bed, grunting and groaning. By the time he was on his feet and in fresh trousers, she had the deel in hand, and he held out his arms.

Mandukhai slipped it over his arms and stepped around in front of him to fasten it under his arm. Manduul studied her as she kept her gaze on the task. She couldn't see his face, but she could feel his eyes digging into her, trying to break her down like pieces of a puzzle. When she finished, Mandukhai stepped back and smoothed out the silk, giving a sharp nod.

"Mandukhai, look at me," he said, lowering the pitch of his voice.

She did as he ordered, raising her brows at him. "I thought we were past this. Or shall I grovel again?"

Manduul's large forehead creased downward. "You debased yourself in front of all my council. And you made a fool of me."

"No more than you did to me," Mandukhai said calmly.

The anger rose in him, turning his neck red, and she feared he would lash out again. But she didn't back down. She wouldn't back down again.

"I am Great Khan—"

"And I am your queen! Unless something has changed between last night and this morning." Mandukhai raised her chin, holding her breath, praying he hadn't changed his mind. Praying he wouldn't punish her for speaking out like this in private. When he said nothing, she carried on. "If you mistreat me or disrespect me, it tarnishes you just as much as me. It weakens you. They knew my shame. Now they know yours. And that makes this a thing of the past."

Her comment left him dumbstruck, and she took the opportunity to return to breakfast, picking up his cup before turning to offer it to him.

"Now, can we enjoy breakfast?" she asked. "I have more to discuss with you."

Almost absently, he reached out and accepted the cup, staring at her like some strange apparition he had never seen before. Mandukhai paid it no mind, settling herself on a cushion beside the table. Manduul shuffled uncertainly to the table and settled across from her.

"I won't apologize for those women," he said, as if he expected her to be waiting for the apology.

Mandukhai rolled her eyes and sipped her tea. "I didn't ask. I don't care.

Do whatever you like with whoever you like, as long as you don't mistake *me* for a common whore again."

He grumbled, stuffing a dumpling into his mouth.

"I'm not sure how you have treated Lady Yeke, but I expect respect from my husband. If you want to be remembered as a powerful Great Khan, you might do well to remember that men like Genghis and Kublai respected their wives and took advice from them. I don't expect to run the tribes with you, but I expect you to respect me enough to listen to me. My family has a history of helping Great Khans."

"And killing them," Manduul said, glaring at his plate.

"And killing the Oirat fraud who butchered your tribesmen and killed your brothers," she corrected. "I would think you, of all people, would keep that in mind."

"And not a moment before my family was nearly wiped out." Manduul set down his cup and leveled his gaze at her. "He could have acted sooner. Why didn't he?"

Mandukhai faltered. She was too young to remember. "I don't know. I was only six. But I'm sure my father had good reason to wait. He was not a hasty or impulsive man." She reached across the table, placing her hand over his. Touching him made her stomach tie up in knots and she wanted to pull it back. It was important he felt she was on his side now. "But you are here now. And so am I. That can't be coincidence."

Manduul chewed thoughtfully, and Mandukhai kept herself as calm and composed as she could. In reality, she wanted to slap him in the head, beat some sense into him. After her conversation with Unebolod last night, she knew he wouldn't kill Manduul. Not without good reason.

"The child," Manduul muttered to himself, then leaned back to shift his weight. "What do you remember of a boy-child?"

Mandukhai wiped her fingers on a cloth and shook her head. "Nothing. Mother never spoke of Father much after his death, and certainly never about what he did in those last days. Aside from saving the Borjigin and rescuing Mongolia from Esen's path of destruction."

He crossed his thick arms over his massive chest. "Unebolod says there was a boy, my brother's only remaining grandson. That he secreted the boy away from Esen to save him. I think the boy still lives."

Mandukhai froze, holding her teacup in midair. A grandson to Manduul's older brother? Which one? Either way, that boy would have a strong enough claim on the khanship to challenge Manduul. And if he won, she would lose everything. *He must be close to my age by now,* she realized. "What if he survived?"

"He is a challenger to my title," Manduul said, confirming her worst fear. "You want to advise me? Tell me, Mandukhai, what do I do with this boy who can steal my title from me?"

Mandukhai's pulse quickened. If this was true, in another year or two, if the boy rallied enough support behind him, he could contest Manduul's title as Great Khan, an undisputed direct descendant of Genghis Khan. Manduul's connection was tenuous. He shared a father with his brothers, but Manduul's mother was not a noblewoman. From what she gathered, his mother was a concubine and not a wife. No one outside of the Borjigin could confirm this for certain. As the son of a concubine, Manduul would be considered less worthy in the eyes of the tribes. Had she been forced into a marriage to a Khan only to have everything taken from her?

If he is no longer khan, I can leave, she thought. *I can run away and choose my own fate. I could choose Unebolod.* The very idea made her pulse quicken. This boy could be her key to freedom! But if Manduul killed him first, Mandukhai would be forever trapped.

Suddenly, she worried that it was already too late. Had Manduul ordered the boy's death? *If he does, and the tribes learn who the boy was, Manduul would be condemning himself. But then Unebolod would fight to defend Manduul ... to his own death. I have to stop this.*

"What have you done?" she asked, her chest heaving.

"Nothing yet. I sent some men to track him down a few weeks past." Manduul reached for his boots. "If he lives, they will find him, and then they will return to camp with him."

"You know you can't kill him," Mandukhai blurted.

His dark eyes bore into her. She needed this boy alive, to save Unebolod. To save herself from this marriage.

"If you kill him, your own tribe will turn against you. Manduul, you will lose everything."

"I have Bigirsen's support." He thrust his foot into one boot.

"That won't matter." Mandukhai shifted around the table, kneeling beside him. She placed a hand on his arm. "Manduul, please consider my warning. Bigirsen is one man. He may be powerful now, but that's because he has your support. If you lose your power, he faces losing his power, which might motivate him to turn against you to preserve his own position."

Manduul's expression darkened, making her flinch back. "I trust Bigirsen."

Don't! she thought desperately. "All I ask is that you consider what I've said. If you bring this boy into your court, support him and teach him. He is young still, and if you show him kindness, he will treat you like a father instead of an enemy. And your people will support your decision as well."

Perhaps that would allow her a chance to convince this boy to turn against Manduul, thus freeing her to make her own choice. She could prepare Unebolod for the transition to save him from rash acts that may cost him his life. And if her luck held out long enough, perhaps Manduul and the boy would kill each other and she would have no one to stop her from running off with Unebolod.

Manduul jerked the other boot on and stood.

The proposal! With news of the boy, Mandukhai had nearly forgotten the sole purpose for her visit. She rose, trying to calm the unsteady beating of her heart. Instead of rushing after him, Mandukhai began gathering the dishes into a pile.

"I have one more request, before you go," she said.

Manduul stopped near the door, holding his *toortsog* hat in his hands as he waited.

"Borogchin will soon be of age to marry," she said, busying herself at the table. "A year. Maybe less. But she does not yet have a husband arranged."

"And you have a suggestion?" he asked.

"Yes. And she is certainly interested in him as well."

"Out with it. I have business to conduct."

Mandukhai nodded, and the gems on her *boqta* sang. She straightened, meeting his eyes. "Your *orlok*, Lord Unebolod." The words tasted like ash in her mouth.

Manduul couldn't hide his surprise. His brows shot up. His arms went slack at his sides. "That is who you choose for her?"

Mandukhai nodded. Her mouth felt unnaturally dry. "He is an excellent match. You must know that." Mandukhai hoped she sounded more confident than she felt, because at the moment her stomach tumbled. Pain clenched her chest, making it hard to breathe. "She is from your family, and he is your sworn brother. What better way to further bond your brotherhood then by joining your families?"

"But..." Manduul's protest faded on his tongue.

But what? Maybe Manduul assumed Mandukhai had been holding back

Unebolod for herself. She knew he suspected the two of them were up to something. *This is my chance to steer his suspicion away.*

"I wanted those lessons so I could see how the two of them interacted. I had planned to bring the girls along before you insisted on it. Borogchin lit up when she spoke of him the day before I asked. I figured if I could spend time around him, I could judge him for myself. You know, to decide if he would be good enough for her."

Manduul scoffed. "He's one of the best men I know. But not without fault."

"Who isn't?"

He rubbed his chin, as if considering the lies she just spilled, weighing them against the truth. Finally, he nodded. "I can't say I haven't also noticed her interest. I wish you would have told me sooner."

Mandukhai dropped her gaze, pretending to be a foolish girl. Hopefully he bought it. "You terrified me after I asked and…"

Manduul's shoulder slumped, and he pulled her into a gentle embrace, kissing her cheek. Mandukhai stiffened, and this time she didn't pretend something else had caused it. More than anything, she wanted to withdraw. She didn't want his hands on her ever again.

"I'm sorry I doubted," he said. "You are so proud and beautiful. I let my fear and jealousy get the better of me. I promise you I won't let it happen again."

Mandukhai didn't know that she believed him. *Let him feel the guilt. Let it weigh him down. Let him understand he created the tension between us with his own jealousy.*

Manduul pulled back, slapping the hat on his head. "I will speak to him and make arrangements. It's high time he married again, anyway."

As Manduul turned for the door, Mandukhai struggled to keep her weakened knees straight. She wanted to stop him, to tell him he was right. That she wanted someone else. That she didn't want Borogchin to marry Unebolod because she wanted him for herself. But none of that could happen, and it would only end in misery or death. *Be the mouse*, she thought. Besides, if she had to be a sister wife with another woman, Borogchin was a good enough match.

He stepped outside and closed the door. Mandukhai let her knees give out and kneeled on the rugs of Manduul's ger, crying for the man she'd lost. The man she could not have.

CHAPTER SIXTEEN

SACRIFICES AND AGONY

Unebolod saw no indication Manduul knew what happened in the dead of night as the morning council passed. Later in the afternoon, Unebolod, Togochi, and Manduul intervened in a fight between two families. Manduul simply called it to a stop. He didn't ask what happened. He told them he didn't care what happened. They could either stop or deal with the wrath of his own men. At that, the fighting men all gave Unebolod shifty, anxious glances, possibly wondering if it was worth the risk. Most men in camp respected—or feared—Unebolod too much to gamble their fates. Men needed fierce, strong leadership to keep them in line.

Mandukhai's words resurfaced. *You are wise, fierce, and fair. The men respect you.* She was right. He knew she was right. The way the men looked at him, he knew he had their respect, and if he pushed for it, he might even have their support. But he could never overthrow Manduul. He gave his word to serve and protect Manduul, and his word was iron.

Manduul, Togochi, and Unebolod returned to the gathering tent once the dispute was settled and everyone had dispersed. They passed a group of young women gambling away a small fortune in semi-precious stones over a game of knucklebones. The girls paused their game, watching him as they passed. Or maybe they were looking at Manduul. Unebolod averted his gaze and the girls giggled.

"Can I ask, Manduul, about Mandukhai's display last night?" Togochi asked, drawing Unebolod's attention sharply back to the conversation.

Manduul grunted. "What about it?"

Togochi glanced at the two of them. "You've heard, right? Word has spread through all of Mongke Bulag."

Unebolod knew what Togochi referred to. Word of her display in front of the Khan and his men had spread quickly. And when that happened, the people increased the scale of the event in question.

"Let them talk!" Manduul barked out a laugh. "You were there. There was little to be respected in her display."

Unebolod shook his head. "I disagree. She is a queen. You agreed as much last night when you gave her that *boqta*. She offered you the choice and you chose to lift her—a wise decision, I should add. She showed a level of fearlessness we haven't seen in many queens these past few generations."

Manduul grumbled under his breath. Unebolod couldn't hear exactly what he said, but it sounded something like "not fearless." It made Unebolod's skin prickle. What did that mean?

"Either way, she has gained the respect of the people," Togochi said.

"She shed her skin like a snake, not a wolf," Manduul said gruffly.

Unebolod stiffened in shock and was relieved to see Togochi have a similar reaction.

"Togochi, go see what you can learn about how the dispute this afternoon began," Manduul said as they reached the door into the gathering tent.

Unebolod knew when a subject was being changed and he understood his sworn brother well. Mandukhai's act last night hadn't settled as well with Manduul as she might have thought.

I must keep a closer eye on him, he thought as Togochi broke off.

Manduul led Unebolod into the gathering tent. A serving girl jumped to her feet the moment they stepped inside, and she bowed deeply to Manduul before rushing off to retrieve their drinks. Manduul led the way to the chess board where their last game remained as they had left it—with Manduul winning the elephant's gambit. Manduul made no sign he was interested in the game, though.

The girl came back, offering them both a cup of *airag*. Manduul accepted his, drinking it while his eyes roved over her. Unebolod wished he could smack the stupidity out of Manduul. He didn't appreciate what he had. Instead, he abused it and turned his attention elsewhere. Unebolod's disgust filled him to the brim, and he struggled to keep it from showing, downing the whole cup of *airag*. A poor decision, since the girl rushed back over to refill him, giving

Manduul another chance to leer at her with those hungry eyes.

"What did you want to discuss, brother?" he asked, hoping to distract Manduul's attention from where it didn't need to be.

"Marriage." Manduul took a long drink but didn't down it.

Unebolod knew this was a possibility—Mandukhai had brought it up last night—but he hadn't expected it so soon. Certainly not under the circumstances. "Again?"

"Odsar has been gone a few years now, brother," Manduul said. "If you ever want sons, you need to take a new wife. Mandukhai spoke with me about the same thing just this morning, over breakfast. She believes it's time, as well."

No, she doesn't. She doesn't want this any more than I do, Unebolod thought, wishing he could put a stop to all of this. But Mandukhai had insisted, and Manduul would as well. Unebolod had no escape.

"And?" Unebolod asked, staring into his cup at the milky liquid within.

"Borogchin will be of age soon, and she has a quite sizable dowry, as you know," Manduul said, leaning back in his chair. "And from what I've gathered, she is very interested in you."

Unebolod's gut churned, and he set the cup on the edge of the table. He should play along, make this sound like an agreeable arrangement, but he just couldn't fake it. In the end, it would be better to lean into his reaction than to force out an obvious lie. "I'm not sure I share the interest."

"Why not?" Manduul chortled. "She's a beautiful young woman and well-positioned. Trust me, it's much easier to have a wife who is interested in you from the start than one who has to grow into it."

He's talking about Mandukhai, Unebolod thought. "It feels like cheating Odsar's memory."

"Most men have multiple wives, Unebolod," Manduul said, amusement curling up the corners of his mouth. "And you can't even deal with one who is gone."

Unebolod recoiled as if slapped. "You know how I felt about her." Odsar had been his world.

Manduul adopted a sympathetic expression and sighed. "I know. But I don't think you will get a better proposal than this, no matter how many girls in Mongke Bulag offer."

Unebolod heaved a sigh, drained his cup again, and waved the servant girl off. "If this is what my Khan wants, I would be a fool to refuse. But not until

Borogchin bleeds. What do I owe you for bride-service?"

Manduul waved the suggestion away. "You have already paid the debt several times, brother. Just keep your faith in me."

"Always." A bold lie. Unebolod had little faith in Manduul. But he had given an oath to follow Manduul, thus he would continue faking his faith. Even if it tore him apart inside.

After the meeting, Manduul had encouraged Unebolod to speak with Mandukhai about the arrangement. The suggestion to visit her ger unattended shocked Unebolod, but he could never refuse.

Nergui held his typical daytime vigil at Mandukhai's door, scowling openly at Unebolod whose boots rooted into the earth.

Everything about Mandukhai made Unebolod's blood warm with excitement and terror. Being alone with her inside her ger presented him with a particular set of challenges he wasn't sure he had the strength to ignore. He had almost kissed her last night. He would have, he knew, if Nergui hadn't interrupted. For that, he was grateful. All of this would have been so much harder to face if he had given in to that moment. That moment would have pushed him over the edge.

She had felt it. She must have. The way she had looked at him. The way she had breathed when he stood so close to her. Mandukhai wouldn't admit it, and he supposed he understood why, but she felt something for him as well.

Now he would have to marry this girl, and Mandukhai would become his mother by marriage since Borogchin was her daughter-ward. It almost made him laugh.

He edged closer to the door, removing his *toortsog* hat and clenching it in anxious fists. He cleared his throat, but before he could speak, Esige's short frame bounced up and down in front of him from inside.

"Unebolod!" she shrieked with happiness.

Mandukhai appeared behind Esige, and the questioning gaze she gave him as she wiped her hands on a cloth said more than anyone else could know. He shook his head, ever so slightly, indicating Manduul had no idea. Mandukhai relaxed, offering a kind smile. "Well, come in."

Esige took his hand and pulled him through the door. Nergui's eyes narrowed suspiciously.

"If you would, please remove your boots," Mandukhai said, returning to Borogchin's side.

Borogchin froze in place, staring at Unebolod with wide, terrified eyes.

Mandukhai picked up the knife on the butcher's block and continued her work. "The dirt seems to track terribly today."

Unebolod glanced behind him at the path and noticed she was right. He nervously slipped his boots off but remained near the door. Borogchin continued staring at him, and when he stared back, her face turned a brilliant shade of red. She spun around, putting her back to him. He supposed she was an attractive girl, and he could certainly do much worse.

"You have spoken with Manduul?" Mandukhai asked as she continued preparing the meat for the stew.

"I have."

"And I assume your appearance here means you agree," she said, glancing at Borogchin with a grin. How could she so convincingly act like this was good news? The other girl couldn't contain her smile. Even angled away from him, he could tell it split her face in two.

"I have."

"Then you will stay for dinner," Mandukhai said, turning to drop the chopped bits of meat in the stew pot. "Girls, we will need more water. Take the bucket and fetch some from the river to boil for dinner."

Esige rushed to the bucket and snatched it up, nearly tripping over Unebolod in her haste. Borogchin hustled to follow her sister but came to an abrupt halt in front of him. Unebolod attempted meeting her gaze with an encouraging smile, but he wasn't sure it offered any real encouragement. Borogchin bit her lip and slipped past him with a shy smile on her face.

Once the girls were gone, leaving him blissfully, terribly alone with Mandukhai, Unebolod huffed out a breath. Except for Nergui's endless presence lingering outside the door. He glanced toward the exit and saw the guard staring at him.

Unebolod straightened his back and returned his attention to Mandukhai. "I assume being in the Khan's care, and yours, that she's never been with a man," he said. He hated the idea of being the one to steal that away from Borogchin.

"Not to my knowledge." Mandukhai stepped around to the west side of the ger, knowing full well he would never cross the line to the east. Guests could not cross over to the eastern side of the ger without direct invitation. It was a bold move for her to approach him alone, especially with the door wide open. "Does he suspect anything?" she asked, lowering her voice.

"No, he doesn't seem to. Your stunt last night has left him a little flustered, though." Unebolod took a reflexive step back, maintaining distance between them, aware of how close she stood.

"Manduul seems to be put off enough, for now," he said, trying to change the subject. "But that will only last for so long if…" He couldn't finish the sentence. More than anything else, he didn't want to picture her with Manduul.

"If what?"

"If you want to avert his suspicion, you will need to be a happier, more pliable wife. Make him think this new accord between you has changed something. That you—"

"That I love him?" Mandukhai wrinkled her nose. "No. That's the one thing I have control over. I get to choose whom I love. That isn't chosen for me."

"You don't have to love him," Unebolod said. "You just need to make him believe you do. We are all making sacrifices."

Mandukhai spun away from him, her shoulders rising and falling with angry breaths. "I know. And I'll try. At least your sacrifice is an excited, pretty young girl. Mine is a sweaty, fat old man."

Unebolod smothered the laughter rising in his throat. He took a hesitant step toward her, placing a hand on her shoulder. She shrugged it off.

"What are we sacrificing for, anyway?" she asked, going back to her side of the ger where he couldn't follow without raising serious questions. Questions they didn't need. And what did she mean by that? He knew exactly what he was sacrificing for. Her safety. A still-lingering chance to be the next Great Khan.

"He doesn't care well for himself," Unebolod said. "We are making this sacrifice now so that, when the time comes, we are prepared."

Mandukhai's shoulders rose and fell, and he could see the anger building within her. "I don't need you to be prepared." Her tone cut sharply into his heart. Why was she angry with him? She was the one who asked for this! *Burn you, woman, this was your idea.*

She didn't need him? Her words carved into his chest, and he wasn't sure he could ever remove them. They rooted themselves deep. And he knew that for the foreseeable future, those words would cause him unending agony.

Mandukhai had spoken out of turn, said something she hadn't meant to say, and nothing could take it back. *I didn't mean it,* she thought pitifully. *I do need you. More than anyone can ever know.*

Mandukhai had been frustrated with the situation, and so angry that when he even hinted at her needing him to prepare, as if she could not take care of herself, she had resented the remark. But the damage had been done. She yearned to apologize, but Unebolod had drawn away, dropped his gaze away from her.

Unebolod didn't speak another word until the girls returned and Esige bombarded him with questions about archery and riding and battle. She reminded Mandukhai so much of herself; no doubt her fate would end up much the same.

Manduul and Yeke joined them for dinner, and Yeke hardly spoke once she learned about the arrangement. She sat on a cushion, her expression unreadable. But her eyes told a different story. It made Mandukhai certain she had missed some critical detail in this arrangement. Or, perhaps, Yeke had attempted to make this arrangement before and had failed.

Unebolod engaged in easy conversation with Esige and Manduul, but everything he said to Mandukhai and Borogchin was rigid, distant. Yeke never once spoke to him, despite his heroic efforts to involve her.

As dinner ended, Mandukhai, Yeke, and Manduul walked Unebolod out. Yeke said a very polite goodnight and disappeared back to her own ger.

"Well, Borogchin will warm up," Manduul said. "She seemed stiff tonight, but she is happy about this. I am certain of that." Manduul shook Unebolod's arm.

"We all make sacrifices," Unebolod said, but his tone was far more good-natured than it had been with Mandukhai earlier. They both laughed. As Manduul laughed, Unebolod shot a quick glance at Mandukhai. *Be the wife he needs you to be,* his gaze said.

"Have a good night, brother," Manduul said.

"You, too," Unebolod said.

Manduul stepped back to give Mandukhai space to say farewell, but she didn't reach out. Her hands remained tucked in her deel in front of her. Instead, she smiled sweetly at Unebolod.

"Rest well, Unebolod," she said, keeping her goodbye simple.

"Thank you." He bowed to both of them and turned toward the path beside his ger in front of her own.

Mandukhai took Manduul's arm, faking happiness, faking love. Faking anything remotely close to affection toward Manduul would be the hardest thing she ever did. *But I have to do this to get what I want.* "I think the girls and Tuya can handle cleaning up. Would you walk with me? I could use some fresh air."

Manduul looked surprised, but he nodded.

Mandukhai wouldn't be the woman Manduul needed—nor the woman any other man needed, for that matter. She would be the woman she needed to be. For the girls. For herself.

CHAPTER SEVENTEEN

RED SANDS AND SUMMONS

CHAKHAR CAMP – SOUTHEASTERN GOBI EDGE – FALL 1464

Despite the early fall, the infernal heat of the sun burned through Bayan's deel as he marched back to camp from the small lake created by an underwater spring nearby. Degghar had sent him early to retrieve water for the day. Now that the unpredictable rains of summer had passed, this region of the Eastern Gobi offered just enough vegetation and water to prepare for the harsh winter. Bayan had spent two winters traveling with the Chakhar tribe already, and he had no desire to experience another.

But I have nowhere else to go, he thought, wiping sweat from his brow as he stomped onward. Despite his endless desire to move on, he felt safe with the Chakhar—a sensation he still had not grown wholly accustomed to even after two years with the tribe.

Once the heat finally broke, temperatures would plummet. Today, he wore light clothes to avoid overheating. In a few short weeks, he would need layers to protect against the freezing cold.

Initially, Bayan had joined the Chakhar Mongols to protect himself. His youth had not been like that of any other Mongol boy. While he had learned how to ride a horse and fire a bow as effectively as most soldiers, he was also educated in strategy and politics. Lord Bolunai, the Khorchin khan who had raised him from the age of four, had reminded him constantly of who he was

141

and what that meant to his future. *You will be Great Khan one day, as the last true heir of the Yuan Dynasty, and others will hunt you for it.*

Lord Bolunai had used force by way of brutal beatings when he felt it necessary to teach Bayan how to be a stronger Great Khan, and how not to be a stupid boy. By the time Bayan turned ten, he had wondered if the real danger had been the man raising him. By age thirteen, he had been ready to fight back, but he had no experience or understanding of how to fight back against a superior Lord. Not long after, as soon as the opportunity to run away had arisen, he had seized it.

The Chakhar were far enough from Bolunai's reach to keep Bayan safe. No one knew who Bayan was. To them, he was just another boy. Had he known at the time that Degghar would force him into bride-service with his daughter, a girl he had only a passing interest in, Bayan would have continued riding. Two years was a long time to serve in bride-service. Now, barely sixteen, Bayan feared that if he lingered with this family for too much longer Degghar would force him into the marriage.

There must be a better place to make my home, he thought—not for the first time and probably not the last—as he wove his way between rows of gers to Degghar's home.

Bayan had made no promises to wed Degghar's daughter, Siker. Marriage remained far from his mind, a distant future. The nights he spent with Siker had little to do with love and more to do with satisfying his own urges.

As he drew closer to the ger, Bayan's steps slowed.

Degghar stood outside the entrance to the home. The door was closed tight behind him. Degghar's back stiffened straight as an arrow as he stared down the men outside. A group of six well-armored soldiers crowded around the entrance. Guden, the Chakhar khan, stood among them.

Bayan did not need to hear a word to know exactly why the soldiers had come. He knew deep in his bones that they had discovered him. Had Lord Bolunai come to collect him? Sudden fear froze Bayan's boots to the ground as if winter had already come and wrapped its icy grasp around him.

"We had an understanding!" Degghar argued, challenging Lord Guden. "He is performing bride-service and is promised to my daughter."

"He has been summoned by the Great Khan," one of the soldiers said. "We didn't come to make a request. We came with orders."

The Great Khan... Bayan stumbled back a step, bumping into the ger behind him and sloshing water on the ground. The soldiers turned. In a moment of panic, Bayan dropped the bucket and sprinted away, dodging and weaving between ger in what he knew deep down was a feeble attempt to escape. Having the Great Khan's men after him was worse than Lord Bolunai. So much worse.

If they find you before you are of age to take your rightful place, they will kill you. Lord Bolunai's warning rang in Bayan's mind as the pounding of boots and shouted orders pursued him. Their numbers swelled.

I'm not ready. I'm not ready! Desperation clenched Bayan's heart as he darted away. At sixteen, he was old enough to claim the title, but he didn't want it. He didn't want any of this!

Bayan had one advantage over the Great Khan's men. He knew this camp. As they stumbled over chicken coops, he easily hurdled them without slowing his speed. As he juked at the last second through narrow passages between gers, they skidded past and were forced to backtrack to follow. Bayan bumped shoulders, knocking people over, sometimes hurling them in the path of men on horseback to slow his pursuers. They shouted protests and insults, but he didn't care about insulting them. If these men caught him, he was as good as dead.

When he reached the edge of camp, Bayan didn't hesitate to jump on the back of the first horse he found, gripping the mane and kicking it into a gallop away from camp.

But where could he go? Traveling south would put him in Chinese territory. The Gobi barricaded north and west—a path he had not desire again. Bayan had barely survived the last time. As he raced across the chalky red rocks, Bayan dared to look east, hoping beyond hope there would be somewhere to flee.

Red dust kicked up in massive clouds behind a wave of men charging toward him on horseback. Dozens of them, all chasing him. Some were the men who had been outside Degghar's home, but the rest belonged to Lord Guden. A single arrow shot past Bayan's knee, narrowly missing him. Before he could thank Tengri and the High Heavens for his fortune, his horse squealed, then tumbled toward the ground. Bayan threw himself off the horse's back to avoid being crushed under its weight. Hooves shook the ground as his pursuers thundered closer, and the rhythm matched his racing heartbeat.

Bayan scrambled to his feet, prepared to flee on foot. Before he could regain steady footing, the horses circled him. The chalky stones kicked up into his mouth. Bayan covered his mouth with his sleeve, coughing it up and spitting the red sand on the ground. When the dust settled, one of the Great

Khan's men stood five feet from him. The man was a hulking mass that would have intimidated even Lord Bolunai.

"Bayan Mongke," the warrior said, resting a hand on the sword at his hip. The threat was clear.

Bayan spun in a slow circle, probing for a gap somewhere, anywhere, that he might slip through. None of these men had weapons drawn on him. Why weren't they drawing their weapons?

"Bayan, son of Tsetseg, bone of Genghis," the warrior said. "We aren't here to kill you. The Great Khan Manduul, your uncle, summons you to join him in his court."

Bayan's mouth was already dry, and the heat of the day began reaching a peak. Sweat rolled between his shoulder blades and down his forehead. *Join him? This must be a trick.* He tried to come up with something clever to say, but nothing came to mind. Instead, he coughed up more red sand and spit it out.

The warrior pulled a waterskin off his horse and held it out to Bayan.

Poison? Bayan thought as he reached a tentative hand toward the offered water. He uncapped it and sniffed, but if there was poison in the water, he couldn't smell it. Another fit of coughs ripped his throat. Bayan rinsed and spit the sand on the ground. Then he took a long, greedy drink. The cool water soothed his throat and coated his insides, momentarily chasing away the heat.

Say something clever, he thought as he lowered the waterskin. "My uncle? I was told he wanted me dead." *Not clever enough!*

The Khan's man reached for the waterskin, but Bayan didn't move to give it back. After a moment, the warrior dropped his hand.

"He has been working to rebuild what your grandfather, Esen, nearly destroyed," the warrior said. "We would prefer if you came willingly, but if we must use force, we have authorization."

Bayan swallowed the lump that swelled in his throat. Authorized for what sort of force? He didn't think he wanted to find out. Part of Bayan resisted and wanted to argue. He wanted to tell them he was promised into marriage here so he couldn't just leave, but that wouldn't stop them ... and he didn't want to say that out loud. Siker could stay here if he said nothing about it, and he would never have to marry her. He could still argue his way out of the agreement, insist that he never made such an arrangement. But if he uttered the unspoken agreement aloud, they would likely force her to come along, and he would have no choice any longer. Going with these men could riding to his death. *Better than staying and condemning myself to an eternity married to Siker.* He didn't want a wife. He didn't need a wife. Not yet.

Bayan took another long drink of the water, then wiped the sweat from his brow. "I need to gather my things. And I need a horse." He had been considering leaving before winter, anyway. This gave him a place to go.

One that hopefully wouldn't cost him his head.

The Great Khan's men kept watch outside the ger as Bayan packed. He owned little. Only a few remnants of his life with Lord Bolunai—namely his sword—and a few trinkets he had bartered for among the Chakhar remained. When he fled, most of his valuables had been traded in exchange for help or food. Even his chestnut stallion had been traded for water—and silence—in desperation. He had lost the bow when he scaled the red cliff faces in the desert. The new bow he made was not as fine a piece as the one Lord Bolunai had given him, but it worked.

Bayan slipped his sword into his belt, then packed what little clothing he had into a cotton sack.

Siker entered her family ger, her hands dirty from a day of hard work. Her hair had been tangled by wind despite the feeble attempt at tying it back. She made no move toward him, but simply stood and watched silently.

"I don't suppose you are bringing me along," she said, disdain dripping from her words when she finally broke the tense silence.

"No." He shoved his last deel into the bag and fastened it closed.

She nodded as if she had expected the answer.

Outside, Degghar's voice rose in anger as the Khan's men blocked the door. "It's my ger! You have no right to keep me out!"

"He won't understand," Siker said, glancing toward the doorway. "He will hate you for this."

"I don't care. You knew this day would come." Though Bayan had hoped this day would be much further in the future—and he had dreamed it wouldn't come at all. *I can't run from this forever.*

Siker was the only one who had known Bayan's true lineage, to his knowledge. She had surmised it on her own one day not long after his arrival. "It's your eyes," she had told him. "They give away the truth." Bayan hated his golden eyes—the eyes of Genghis's descendants.

"He made a promise!" Degghar roared.

Bayan strode toward the door, stopping in front of Siker. He supposed if he squinted hard enough or drank enough, she would be pretty. At the moment, he found her charmless. Simple and plain. If the Great Khan truly wanted him to join the court, Bayan would have much better options than her. If this was a trick to kill him, all the better that she not come along to her own death. "You won't make a scene like him."

"Would there be a point?" Siker shrugged, as if she really didn't care about what was happening. They had based their relationship on sex and nothing more. They shared nothing in common. Their relationship hadn't even been about companionship—she was terribly dull. He had urges, as did she. Once those were satisfied, they went about their day on their own.

Degghar, on the other hand, had assumed their relationship went much deeper.

"Bayan, you coward!" Degghar shouted. "Siker, pack your things!"

Bayan threw the door open and ducked out, slinging the bag over his shoulder. "Get a hold of yourself. You look like a fool. I never promised you anything. I stayed to work off my debts. Those debts have been paid."

"Take that abomination you made with you," Degghar growled.

Bayan sighed, hoping he appeared casual in front of the Khan's men. "Degghar, why don't you ask your daughter how she feels about our arrangement?"

Degghar lunged at Bayan, but two of the Khan's men seized his arms and shoved him to his knees. Degghar spit at Bayan's feet. The hulking mass of a warrior pulled his sword, ready to strike, then offered it to Bayan.

What does he want me to do with that? he thought. But Bayan knew the answer. They expected him to kill Degghar. Spitting at Bayan was as good as spitting at the Great Khan himself. If Bayan didn't kill him, they would see Bayan as weak and probably kill Degghar anyway. If Bayan did it himself, Siker's family would likely hold it against him forever. Lesser of two evils.

Bayan held out his bag to the massive warrior, then took the sword. He crouched in front of Degghar, placing the edge of the curved blade under Degghar's chin. "For the sake of your family, I would suggest apologizing. I would hate to see Siker lose me and her father in the same day."

"You have ruined her," Degghar sneered. He leaned into the blade until it cut just enough to draw a few drops of blood. A clear challenge, as if Degghar didn't think he would kill him.

"One day," Degghar said, "they will all learn what sort of man you really

146

are. And when that day comes, may the sky father strike you down."

The words burned into Bayan's flesh. As much as he wanted to deny it, somewhere deep down he knew Degghar was right. Assuming Bayan lived long enough, how long before the Khan or his men learned that he hated killing? Bayan clenched his jaw to keep from showing his fear as it reached for his bones. Degghar had left him with no choice.

Bayan stepped back, slicing the blade across Degghar's throat, praying no one could see him trembling. Blood sprayed out for a moment, and Degghar's hands came to his throat even as his body collapsed to the ground. Siker shrieked, rushing forward and falling over her father's body. Degghar's blood spilled out onto the ground, mixing with the packed red sand, coating it in darker shades.

Siker turned angry eyes on the Khan's men as grief creased her face. But she didn't cry. Instead, she wailed hatefully. *Why is she not casting angry looks my way?* he wondered.

Bayan exchanged the sword for his bag. He had to leave before his own grief and disgust swallowed him whole. Eager to get moving, Bayan turned and walked away as if none of this mattered to him. The Khan's men followed.

The blood on his hands made them shake, and he struggled to get control of himself. *Can they see me shaking?* he wondered, casting a glance at the hulking soldier. Degghar certainly wasn't his first kill, but it was the first time it had been so close, calm, and personal. Forcing himself to maintain steady breathing, Bayan pulled a cloth from his bag as casually as he could and wiped the blood away.

The blood on his knuckles reminded him of Lord Bolunai's beatings. Memories flooded back. Memories of Lord Bolunai looming over him. Of Bayan trembling on the tiled floor of the sparring chamber, his body bruised and his face swollen. Of his own fingertips bleeding as he dug his nails into the tiled floor of Lord Bolunai's palace. For a moment, Siker's shrieks matched his own from those memories—a painful reminder of Lord Bolunai's brutal lessons.

Adding insult to his own inner turmoil, the Khan's men appeared satisfied with Bayan's nonchalant murder of the man who saved him from death. Even Lord Guden, who strolled alongside them, nodded in appreciation of Bayan's show of strength. *But I am not strong.*

Bayan swallowed repeatedly until his throat was raw, fighting the urge to vomit all over the ground. One prayer repeated over and over in his mind. *Tengri, please let this Khan be different.*

CHAPTER EIGHTEEN

A Spy, A Weapon, and Broken Promises

Mongke Bulag – Fall 1464

Summer passed much more quickly than Mandukhai would have liked, and before she knew it Mongke Bulag prepared to hunker down for the long, harsh winter months. Fall settled over the mountains in the distance. Golden, orange, and red leaves of the birch trees colored the opposite edge of the Orkhon River, creating a stunning array of colors.

As Unebolod had urged, Mandukhai dedicated every moment she could to pretending to be a loving, attentive wife. Unebolod reminded her she didn't have to forgive Manduul for what he did; she only needed to pretend she had. But pretending hadn't been a simple task. Some days, she was sure Manduul could see through her act.

For the first couple of weeks, he remained skeptical of her intentions, as he should have been, but eventually he accepted that their dispute had become a thing of the past and now they moved forward together with a new understanding. Mandukhai had not forgotten her need to produce an heir before Yeke either, and continued trying every month when the time was right. Mandukhai frequently caught herself daydreaming about running off with Unebolod, a distant and impossible dream.

The routine swiftly had become second nature: bring Manduul breakfast, sit with him quietly in meetings, studying carefully as information passed between him and his men. She offered advice when she felt it necessary, but only in private. Every piece of advice she gave him, Manduul followed more and more willingly as the weeks passed. His growing trust and respect did nothing to quench her burning need to escape this marriage. Memories of what he had done to her plagued her sleep and often made it hard to meet his gaze without willful determination.

Yeke had joined the meetings once she learned he had permitted Mandukhai. At first, Mandukhai feared Yeke would sway Manduul contrary to Mandukhai's plans. However, after the first few private conversations with Manduul, it became apparent Yeke had nothing to offer him. She lacked the intelligence and finesse required for large-scale politics, lessons Mandukhai had been surprised to learn Bigirsen had not given his daughter. Before long, Manduul avoided notifying Yeke of their meetings. Her resentment toward Mandukhai developed into a cold-faced hatred that she hid in front of Manduul but shared openly when he was not present.

Mandukhai and the girls spent mornings in archery lessons with Unebolod, now mounted on horseback as they progressed. Borogchin warmed up to him, often touching his arm or flirting openly now that she knew they would be married. Watching Borogchin fawn over him filled Mandukhai with rage she could never satiate. At dinner, he would join them more often than not, sitting beside Borogchin, across from Mandukhai, and they had perfected a dance of gazing at each other while the other wasn't looking in a way that had caught no unwanted attention.

Borogchin perked up significantly since the arrangement, bringing Mandukhai bits of information about Yeke, such as Yeke's quest to delegitimize Mandukhai in the event of Manduul's death.

"She is consumed with jealousy," Borogchin had said. "I almost feel sorry for her, to be trapped in a marriage to a man who does not desire her."

This had broken Mandukhai's heart. Not for Yeke, but for Borogchin. Unebolod had expressed his lack of interest in the girl. Surely he would not treat her as Manduul treated Yeke. Mandukhai knew she would have to speak to Unebolod about this before he married Borogchin.

As the weeks passed, Mandukhai more desperately wanted to be with Unebolod, even if it meant being a second wife again. In public, he kept a respectful distance from her. With the arranged marriage, the two often spoke with each other in the open and even Manduul had ignored their new friendship. Neither she nor Unebolod let down those walls they built around themselves, but their alliance took careful, slow shape. If something happened to Manduul, they both wanted to be prepared. Though he never said as much aloud, Mandukhai knew Unebolod aspired to be the next Great Khan. And they both knew that her favor would solidify his claim if—or when—the time came.

She and Unebolod never discussed overthrowing Manduul. Mandukhai could not do it without armies, which came from proper support from someone like Unebolod, but after what he told her about his oath to serve Manduul, she could never ask. A few times, she did joke about running off, testing the waters to see how he would react.

"I've told you before, if you run, he will catch you," Unebolod had said.

"Even if I have someone strong to protect me?" she had asked, smirking playfully at him.

The way Unebolod had clenched his jaw and refuse to respond had been like a knife in her heart. Yet it was no less than she had expected. Unebolod might desire her. He might covet Manduul's title, and sometimes loathe Manduul or think him incompetent, but he bore a deeper love for Manduul that would prevent him from acting against his sworn brother. Mandukhai respected it. She never once proposed the idea of overthrowing Manduul aloud, no matter how much her heart yearned for freedom. Instead, they prepared for the possibility of Manduul's untimely death. After all, he was several years older than both of them.

More than once, Manduul had offered Unebolod time to spend alone with Borogchin. Though he never stated the purpose of that offer, the implication was clear enough. Every time Manduul offered, Mandukhai felt everything inside of her shrivel up and die all over again. And every time, Unebolod found another reasonable excuse to refuse. But she knew it only postponed the inevitable. Was that what he felt like when she shared a bed with Manduul?

One cold, early fall evening, Mandukhai enjoyed a cold ride with Dust as she delivered a few tokens for sheep to struggling families whose own herds had either thinned or died out. Nergui, as he always did, followed behind her without a word, ever watchful. As she finished and rode toward home, she noticed the engorgement of the camp on the southern edge of the capital.

"Those are Uyghur banners," Nergui noted when he saw her straining in her saddle for a better view. "Vice Regent Bigirsen is in Mongke Bulag."

Mandukhai huffed in dismay, sinking into her saddle. *Just what we need*, she thought bitterly as she dismounted and approached Manduul's ger. *What is he even doing here?*

Mandukhai stepped toward Manduul's door and reached out to open it. Two of the guards blocked her path, and Nergui's hand fell to his sword, watching both guards.

"You would refuse your queen the right into her husband's home?" she asked, glaring at the pair of them.

"The Khan and his Vice Regent, Lord Bigirsen, have ordered privacy," one guard said. "We are only following their orders, Lady Mandukhai."

Resentment burned in Mandukhai's skin, but she remained calm as she stalked away. Nergui waited until she had passed him before he followed, giving the guards another warning glare as if he expected them to attack Mandukhai with her back turned.

It only took a few steps before he realized she was not headed home. "Where are you going?"

Mandukhai clenched her jaw as she stepped around the front of Unebolod's ger. "For answers," she snapped, then called toward Unebolod's open door. "Hold your dog!"

Unebolod stepped up to the door after giving Kilgor a sharp whistle that had her settling back on her haunches. Unebolod frowned, glancing over her shoulder, first at Nergui, then at the people who walked up and down the thoroughfare. Mandukhai could not have cared less who saw her standing there. They spoke openly often. Who would even worry at this point if she stood at his door?

"You shouldn't be here," he said, frowning.

"Do you know why Manduul is having a secret meeting with Bigirsen as we speak?" Mandukhai asked.

He stepped outside and closed the door behind him, crossing his arms over his broad chest. "No."

"They won't let me in."

"Not everything the Khan does is your business," he said, sounding slightly amused with himself.

Mandukhai bristled. "I'm the queen."

"Have you no secrets?" Unebolod asked.

He knew damned well she had secrets. She opened her mouth to protest, but snapped it shut again and tried to calm herself before speaking. "It doesn't worry you, then?"

Unebolod shook his head. "Should it? They meet like this every time the

Vice Regent visits."

Mandukhai couldn't believe he was so calm about this. Something about this meeting crawled under her skin. Manduul never excluded her anymore.

"Fine," she said sharply. "Goodnight, Unebolod."

As she and Nergui walked away, Mandukhai felt Unebolod's eyes on her, watching as she slipped through the space between gers and returned home. He could act as calmly as he wanted, but she knew, deep down, something was wrong.

Cold fall air bit through Mandukhai's fur-lined cloak the next morning, and she tugged it tighter as she marched to Manduul's gathering tent. With chills settling in during the mornings, Unebolod had put a hold on archery lessons with the girls. Borogchin had lost interest as soon as her fingers started to numb, and Esige spent a fair amount of time complaining about it.

Last night still rankled at Mandukhai's mind, and Manduul had been missing from his ger this morning when she arrived with breakfast. He never rose before her. From there, she had gone to see the girls, and Esige said they had called Borogchin in front of the Khan last night. She hadn't returned. Mandukhai couldn't for the life of her imagine why. Unless Yeke had caught Borogchin in a lie. Mandukhai's stomach churned at the thought of the girl being punished for doing Mandukhai's bidding. Though Borogchin was a princess and Manduul's niece. He wouldn't punish her on Yeke's word, would he? What had Manduul done to her, then?

When Mandukhai entered the tent, drawing the flap closed to keep out the morning chill, she nearly drew up short.

Manduul sat in his usual place with a massive dog laid at each of his sides. Two massive, copper pots burned with fire on either side of the dais, warding off the cold. Yeke sat on her chair atop the dais, appearing triumphant. Mandukhai's stomach twisted.

In front of Manduul, Borogchin hugged herself tightly and trembled violently. Bigirsen stood beside her, hands folded behind his straight back.

What is going on? Mandukhai rushed to Borogchin.

"My girl, are you hurt?" Mandukhai asked, sweeping a gaze over Borogchin, but she saw no apparent signs of injury. "What is the meaning of this?"

Borogchin's face was paler than usual, and her eyes were reddened from weeping. To her credit, Borogchin sucked in deep breaths and controlled the sound of her crying. But it didn't stop the tears or the obvious emotional agony she suffered. Bigirsen, however, appeared very satisfied beside the girl, and he turned his narrow face turned toward Mandukhai, victorious in a way that rested uneasily in Mandukhai's stomach.

"Should I ask again?" Mandukhai asked more firmly, holding Borogchin's hand. She tried to offer as much reassurance as she could with a simple look or touch, but somehow it didn't feel like nearly enough. "This girl is in my care, and she is in obvious distress."

"We were just finishing up here," Manduul said. "She is no longer your concern."

The words knocked the air from Mandukhai's lungs. She whipped her head toward Manduul, making the *boqta* chime. She opened her mouth to ask why, even to protest, but the truth was too horrible to consider. *No. No, I promised her. I made other arrangements!* Manduul had gone back on his agreement with Unebolod.

The meeting last night. They barred her from entering because they knew she would never agree to this, that she would fight every one of them to her last breath to stop it. Instead, the men had decided without her. Mandukhai didn't want Borogchin to marry Unebolod. She didn't want anyone to marry him. But she also couldn't allow a man like Bigirsen, someone who clearly terrified Borogchin, to marry her, either. *She will be no better off than me!*

Mandukhai took a slow breath, attempting to center herself and suppress her boiling anger. "Have you spoken to Unebolod? You already formed an agreement with him."

Yeke clucked softly in disapproval of Mandukhai's confrontational behavior.

"I am Great Khan, and she is my family," Manduul said. The sharpness in his tone held no real threat toward her and seemed more for show than any genuine anger. "He will understand."

"You put her in my care and put me in charge of these decisions on her behalf. On your behalf. She has not even bled yet," Mandukhai argued, squeezing Borogchin's hand. She would fight this. What they had done was beyond inexcusable, dishonorable. How dare they change the marriage arrangements and go back on their word!

"She has," Yeke said. "As of yesterday."

Once again, Mandukhai had been left to catch up. Her gaze locked onto

Borogchin's. How had Yeke found out first? *The rations and tokens.* Mandukhai had gone to the northern edge of Mongke Bulag yesterday with Nergui and a few baskets of spare food to distribute for the winter months. She had been gone, and Yeke had been there. *This is my fault.*

So much desperation and pleading poured out of Borogchin and bore into Mandukhai's very soul that she couldn't hold the girl's gaze for long. *There must be something I can do; something that will stop this.*

"Manduul, my love, please." Mandukhai grudgingly released Borogchin's hand and stepped in front of Manduul, kneeling and taking his hands in hers. The dogs watched her with wary interest. "Unebolod is your brother. If you go back on your word to him, you are breaking a sacred trust, a bond. He follows you faithfully. What do you think he will make this?"

Manduul leaned forward, cupping her cheek in his fat hand and offering a sickeningly sweet smile that only fueled Mandukhai's anger. These were not circumstances for sweet smiles.

"You worry too much about the feelings of another man," he said, and though his tone matched his smile, a warning hid beneath the surface.

"I worry how that broken bond will affect you," Mandukhai corrected, placing her hand over his.

"It is too late," Manduul said, drawing back sharply.

Mandukhai's heart felt as if someone had plunged it into a frozen river. She sank back on her heels. "No."

"It is already done," Bigirsen said behind her. Borogchin choked off a sob. "We were simply here this morning to complete the transaction."

Transaction! He spoke of Borogchin as if she were a mare for sale. Esige's response clicked into place. *She didn't return home last night.*

Mandukhai's chest heaved with angry breaths. Bigirsen did this. He leered openly, covetously at Borogchin months ago. Now that she had become a woman, he used that strange power he had over Manduul to get what he wanted. And Manduul had given in, even though it had caused his niece, his own flesh and blood, grief; even if it would turned his own sworn brother against him. Mandukhai wanted to show Bigirsen exactly what she thought of his power. She wanted to plunge a knife into his cold, greedy heart and smile over him as he died. The knife she kept tucked in her belt would do just fine.

Mandukhai shifted her feet under her to rise. Manduul placed a firm hand on her shoulder. "Do nothing rash," he said under his breath. "You're smarter than that."

154

But she needed to. No matter the price. Even if it cost her everything. She wanted to kill Bigirsen and rid Borogchin, Manduul, Yeke, and Unebolod of his lecherous grasp. She wanted to free them from the invisible chains he yoked them all with.

"Come, wife," Bigirsen said. "Let's gather your things to settle into your new home."

Wife? Bigirsen did not simply consummate the marriage with Borogchin, but Manduul had performed the blessing himself last night. Mandukhai's muscles tensed, yearning to lash out, to make someone pay for this horrendous betrayal.

Manduul's hand remained steadfast on Mandukhai's shoulder. He wasn't forcing her to remain; it felt more like a warning, like if she acted out against Bigirsen it would cost them all. And it would. Mandukhai knew that. But the agony of Borogchin crying for Mandukhai's help as Bigirsen pulled her from the tent spread numbness through Mandukhai's body. She buried her face in her hands, unable to keep from crying in front of Manduul and Yeke. *I promised to protect her from this fate.*

Yeke left Mandukhai and Manduul alone not long after Bigirsen had dragged Borogchin away. Manduul said nothing and offered no reassurances. What was there to reassure? Mandukhai had promised Borogchin this wouldn't happen. He had promised her that Unebolod would be Borogchin's husband. Now this betrayal. This broken promise. This abominable action.

After some time, Manduul shifted closer, taking Mandukhai's arms and pulling her up to her feet. She wanted to shove him away, drive a dagger through his heart as he had done to her so many times. What sort of Khan had no control over his own men?

"He reminded me that Yeke had already promised Borogchin to him," Manduul said at last. "I must have forgotten."

"Forgotten?" Mandukhai stepped back. "I don't believe either of them, and I can't believe you do, either." She wanted to put as much distance between herself and Manduul as possible, stepping cautiously backward, almost afraid to turn away.

"What choice did I have?" he asked, desperation creasing his face. *He actually thinks I love him! He thinks he can redeem himself!* Mandukhai wanted to spit at his feet.

Fire sparked deep inside of her, burning in her voice. "You are Khan of khans! He bows to you, not the other way around."

"It's not so simple." Manduul had the decency to appear ashamed, but his humiliation wasn't enough. Not by a long shot. He edged closer, reaching for her as if he understood he was losing her in this moment. *He is. I've had enough.* Mandukhai jerked her arm away from his grasp.

"You have listened to my council these last months, have you not? I have not steered you wrong before, so listen to me closely now." Mandukhai stood straighter, raising her chin and glaring at him, hoping that her fury burned into his skin, forever marking him as the coward he was. "You have insulted your niece. You have insulted me ... again."

"How could you possibly understand what is at stake?" Manduul replied, his voice strained.

"How can you not?" Mandukhai quivered with indignation. "Bigirsen is not your ally. He makes a mockery of you. While lesser khans live in cities and palaces and grow in strength, he has you, the Great Khan, sequestered into this corner of the empire, living the life of a nomad without the benefit of moving across the steppe. And as soon as you question him, he gives you everything you want, showers you with riches and women, and you forget. As if you had never questioned him in the first place. If you don't put him in his place, he will ruin you and your legacy."

Manduul's face turned redder the more she spoke, and his shoulders sloped as they often did when he was angry, about to strike. But Mandukhai didn't care what he did now. If he did nothing, she won. If he struck out at her, she would bring the Ongud, Unebolod, and his loyal men down on Manduul with enough force to rend mountains to dust. Mandukhai knew, in that moment, that she had far more power and courage in her small toe than Manduul possessed in his worthless, shriveled cock.

Manduul didn't move. He remained stiff, his muscles taut enough to snap, but despite his simmering anger, he didn't so much as flinch.

Mandukhai snorted in disgust. "Esige's future is mine to decide. I will not allow you to turn her into a slave to a pitiful, unworthy man. You no longer have a say." Mandukhai turned her back on him and marched toward the door. "Borogchin is your blood. You have just condemned her. I hope you can live with that."

The flap slapped shut behind her as cold air bit into her face, but Mandukhai welcomed it. The cold helped soothe the heat burning her skin and boiling in her heart. Manduul was limp and useless. He held no power. Even the power he thought he grasped in Mongke Bulag belonged to another, to someone stronger and more deserving to wield that power. To Unebolod.

It took some effort to hunt down Unebolod. He worked with a small crew of men to construct extra shelters for the coming winter.

As she stormed into the midst of working men, most of the men stopped working, bowing to her. Mandukhai ignored them all.

Unebolod slipped one of the willow roof lathes into place, not sparing a glance at her. "You reek of rage," he said.

"As should you," Mandukhai said, her tone biting.

He dusted dirt from his hands as he turned to face her. "Why?"

The men who had stopped to show her deference resumed assembling the shelter.

Mandukhai kept her voice lowered. "Manduul broke his promise to you."

"What promise was that?"

"The arrangement." Mandukhai couldn't believe he hadn't heard about it already. Rumors spread like fire in this forsaken place. "With Borogchin."

A few of the men working with Unebolod glanced toward the two of them at mention of the princess, but no one wanted to appear as if they were eavesdropping.

When Unebolod didn't give any indication he knew what she spoke of, Mandukhai threw her hands up in the air. "He married her to Bigirsen last night, without my permission, against the agreement he made with you."

Unebolod's jaw twitched, then he turned and picked up another of the long lathes to slide it into place.

Has he nothing to say at all? Maybe he was just choosing his words carefully. Unebolod had a habit of falling silent just before finding the right words. His ability to think before he reacted, to see all sides of the problem before choosing a course, was one of the things Mandukhai found endearing. But right now, she wanted him angry. She needed him upset. She wanted him to feel all the anguish burning in her chest. Mandukhai gave him a moment of peace to think and find the right words.

Unebolod picked up another lathe and began sliding it into place, giving her no sign he would say anything at all.

"Nothing?" she snapped. Her patience evaporated. "That's what your reaction is? Nothing?"

"We both know I had no genuine interest in her," he said. "What would you have me say?"

"He broke his word!"

"He is Great Khan," Unebolod said without missing a beat. "He does what he must."

Mandukhai opened her mouth to yell at him for defending a man who didn't deserve to be defended—a man who didn't deserve to be Great Khan—but too many others worked around them. No one veiled their attempts to listen in any longer. Two of them men stared openly at her from the other side of the structure. Someone would tell Manduul. A queen must choose her targets wisely.

"I gave her my word that this wouldn't happen," Mandukhai said. She glanced around. Her outburst had gathered attention from more than just a few of the men working with Unebolod. Some of the women passing by paused, staring at the exchange between her and Unebolod. Mandukhai's jaw twitched and she lowered her voice. "She trusted me. She trusted us."

Unebolod shrugged as yet another lathe slid into place, and his gaze fell on her, impenetrable, unreadable. "Trust is a dangerous thing to give."

"Don't start." Mandukhai gathered all the regal bearing she could muster and stormed away. Someone besides her must care what happened to Borogchin.

Mandukhai spent the remainder of the day seething alone in her ger. On her orders, Nergui kept everyone out, Manduul and Esige included. Shortly before dinner, she pulled herself together, prepared a meager offering of food, and collected a rather large bundle of gifts—leathers coated with fat to ward off the bitter cold, fur for warmth, a full quiver of arrows, a hunting knife, and some dried cheese and meat for a long journey. Mandukhai then put on her best winter clothes and marched to the south side of camp where Bigirsen's men had set up.

"Should I expect trouble?" Nergui asked as he followed Mandukhai closely.

"I'm just delivering gifts," she said with a shrug. "If that causes trouble, Bigirsen will have bigger issues to deal with." She glanced at the sword hanging on his hip, then met his eyes. "But it never hurts to be prepared."

Nergui nodded stiffly as they entered the Uyghur encampment. Bigirsen had brough a full *tumen* of ten thousand with him, and the gers spotted far across the horizon.

Mandukhai heard Nergui's leather glove creak as he tightened his grip on his sword. He wisely knew not to trust any of Bigirsen's Uyghur warriors. His dedication was appreciated, but unnecessary. Bigirsen may be a vile, disgusting excuse for a human, but he certainly wasn't foolish. If anything happened to Mandukhai in this camp, the Borjigin would turn against the Uyghur even if Manduul was too spineless to do it himself. Except Bigirsen had a full *tumen* of ten thousand men at his command—men used to regular battle, unlike Manduul's own men. Would Unebolod's battle prowess be enough to win if a fight broke out?

Two guards blocked the door to Bigirsen's ger, which was easy enough to find with its richly swathed cotton over layers of fur and felt.

"I was led to believe Lady Borogchin is his wife, not his prisoner," Mandukhai said, allowing some anger that simmered in her all day to boil over.

"Lord Bigirsen's orders were explicit," one guard said, and his Uyghur accent made her stomach sick with hate.

"I am your queen, and I will enter to offer gifts to my recently wed daughter. I would dare you to stop me and try to explain yourselves to Manduul Khan. How long do you suppose he will wait before wrapping you in blankets and trampling your bodies?"

The question made each of them shift in their lacquered armor and exchange glances, then they cast an uneasy glance at Nergui. Her declaration had been a gamble. If they were bright enough to know their *tumen* was stronger, they may not care. But the hesitation played into her hand, and she seized it before they could puzzle the truth out. Mandukhai nodded as if that had settled matters and pushed through the door, spotting Issama watching several paces away in front of his own ger.

Despite the rich appearance of the outside of the ger, the inside was remarkably simple for a man with access to all the wealth the Mongolian empire had at its fingertips. Mandukhai took little time examining the furs or rugs or wools. Her mission had one face.

Borogchin kneeled at the table, pouring soup into bowls with shaking hands. Her alarm at Mandukhai's appearance wasn't particularly well-hidden. She dropped the ladle in the pot. Mandukhai's gaze swept the ger for Bigirsen, but he was blissfully absent, though his dogs bared their teeth at her.

The guards must have come to their senses, because they opened the tent flap, making Borogchin's back stiffen. "I have offered Lady Mandukhai Guest Rights," she said, her voice trembling. "Leave us."

Both men hesitated. Guest Rights protected Mandukhai from harm, and if they acted aggressively toward her, Nergui would be within his right to defend her at any cost. And Bigirsen would have declared war on Manduul. It was a bold move, and Mandukhai was pleased that Borogchin had thought so quickly. In moments, the two of them were alone inside the ger.

Borogchin's outer strength dissolved before Mandukhai. Fresh tears brimmed in Borogchin's eyes. Mandukhai didn't know why she thought this was a good idea, coming to see this heartache all over again.

"I'm so sorry," Mandukhai blurted, dropping her gifts on the bed and pulling Borogchin into a fierce hug. One dog growled. "I did not know. They excluded me from their agreement. But all isn't lost. I bring you gifts, and a chance to escape."

Borogchin pulled back sharply, shaking her head. "No. I can't run away."

"But—"

"*You* didn't."

Mandukhai wished Borogchin wouldn't use that argument. "I want you to be happy. Leave tonight. I've given you a mixture of herbs you can put in his drink to keep him asleep all night, and you can slip out unnoticed. If you take the northern pass through the mountains, you will find allies to my tribe. They will help you."

"You have put some thought into escape," Borogchin noted.

Mandukhai swallowed. She had considered following that same path more than once. More times than she could count, actually.

"No," Borogchin said, shaking her head more firmly this time, gripping Mandukhai's arms. "If I stay, I can help you, guide him as you've done to Manduul. And when you are ready, I will bring his entire world crashing down."

So Borogchin had noticed how Mandukhai had guided Manduul along. The girl was more observant than Mandukhai had given her credit for. Mandukhai knew it was a good plan, but it put Borogchin in serious danger. Toying with Yeke was one thing. Toying with Bigirsen was another altogether.

"He will kill you if he learns anything."

"I can be strong like you," Borogchin insisted. "Let me prove it." The stubborn set of her chin and confidence in her tone, despite the unshed tears, gave Mandukhai little to argue. This was a matter of pride for Borogchin. She offered herself as a spy and a weapon. And a valuable one, at that.

"You have nothing to prove." Mandukhai had no better offering to give

Borogchin, for in this moment Borogchin indeed had nothing to prove to anyone. She was a woman with powerful bloodlines and allies. She was a daughter of Genghis.

Borogchin seemed to understand, forcing a smile and nodding as if everything had been settled.

Whether or not she liked it, Mandukhai could not undo what Manduul and Bigirsen had already done. Instead, she would honor the only choice Borogchin had to make for herself. Her own purpose.

And Borogchin chose to fight.

CHAPTER NINETEEN

TALL TALES

ROAD TO MONGKE BULAG – LATE FALL – 1464

The first two nights of the journey were the hardest for Bayan. Not because he couldn't ride—he was a skilled rider—but because he couldn't sleep at night. When they stopped to rest, they slept under the stars, out in the open and unprotected from the increasingly harsh winds.

Every night, the snores and twitches of his guards kept him alert, ready for a sudden assassination attempt. People died in the desert all the time. The Great Khan could have him killed and leave his body to rot where no one would be the wiser. Bayan had been certain one of the Khan's men would kill him in his sleep. By the third night, he was too exhausted to stay awake.

Then the sun rose again.

They traveled into Uyghur territory near the southwestern edge of the desert—and dangerously close to Oirat territory. Bayan knew all about the Oirat and the man—his own grandfather—who had tried to kill him as a boy. Bolunai had told him the story so many times Bayan knew it by heart. Since the Khorchin spirited him away to safety as a little boy, Bayan had not been so close to their land.

With each passing day, Bayan relaxed a bit more. Perhaps the Great Khan really wanted him to come join him. Maybe Bolunai was wrong and Manduul Khan would welcome him with open arms. Maybe, just maybe, he could find safe refuge in the capital of the very man he spent years avoiding. It was a desperate and dangerous hope to cling to, but the longer they traveled, the more confident Bayan became he was truly safe for the first time in his life. At least, that was what he told himself.

Manduul Khan's men had other orders, aside from simply retrieving him. The most significant stop had been in an Uyghur encampment thirty miles from Hami. The Uyghur leader had a cart of supplies waiting for the Great Khan—tithes and resources sent from Turfan to help stave off the harsh winter as its icy grasp closed on the world.

Impressive snow-capped Altai Mountains to the northwest and the Singing Sands of the Gobi to the southeast made the area a uniquely fortified location in the empire. Hami proper was under Ming control, but Uyghur families passed in the shadows of the city with little notice.

Hami had a reputation for constant warfare as Ming and Mongol fought for control of the oasis. At the moment, peace was tenuous in the city, and Bayan could sense the tension as he rode through the packed-dirt paths of the Uyghur camp nearby. The people were weathered and worn, their skin leathered from the recent summer sun and their narrow eyes suspicious of the newcomers among their gers. Bayan didn't like the attention.

Winter had already bitten into the southern steppe with crisp winds that ripped through Bayan's clothes.

Bayan used his newfound authority as the Great Khan's nephew to acquire a new deel lined with thick fur, and a matching cloak to wrap him in warmth. He took the clothes to a seamstress and waited rather impatiently as she added golden accents to the trim and clasps. It took the better part of the day, and within an hour he lost interest and began flirting with a girl close to his age in the neighboring ger.

The girl had eyebrows that reminded him of a woman in constant anger, and the way her lips perpetually puckered hadn't given him much motivation to kiss. Still, boredom won out. Her conversation proved to incredibly dull, and he kissed her just to shut her up. Bayan was always quite proud of the fact that he could ignore the faults in a woman once he'd made his first move, and in no time the two of them found ways to keep warm and occupied as he waited. After all, what girl could say no to the Great Khan's nephew?

By the time he tired of her, his new clothes were done.

"Will I see you again?" the girl asked, clinging to a fur blanket.

Bayan didn't answer. She was asking a question she really didn't want the answer for, anyway. Besides, he couldn't even recall her name—not that it mattered. He left rather unceremoniously wearing the new robes and cloak as he stepped outside. He couldn't wait to get back on the road.

Their horses were replaced with fresh mounts, and Bayan admired the chestnut stallion given to him—a gift to honor the Great Khan's blood, he was told. The stallion reminded him of the one he traded in exchange for food and water years ago. This one was almost as impressive, with muscular shoulders and neck to promise good stamina. Between the girl, the gifts, and the fine clothing, for the first time in his life, Bayan actually felt like the Great Khan's nephew.

The cart of supplies slowed them down as they continued north through the winding passes of the Altai Mountains. On the way to Hami, they had traveled at great speed, nearly eighty miles a day, making it to the camp near Hami in just over a week. From there, it should have only taken a few days to reach Mongke Bulag, but the weight of the cart slowed them to less than half that. At night, they would make camp in trees or in the cover of a valley to avoid Oirat raiding parties.

At the slower pace, Bayan had time to get to know the ten men escorting him. It surprised him to learn that most of the men were from the Khorchin tribe, selected by Lord Unebolod to serve the Great Khan. The same tribe that had turned a blind eye as their own khan beat Bayan, a young boy, senseless repeatedly. Bayan had resented these men at first, but he learned that none of them were in Lord Bolunai's court by the time Bayan was seven. They had followed Unebolod into battle to protect their tribe from raids and outside invasion, and to defend the remains of the Borjigin line.

"Have you ever ridden with Manduul Khan?" Bayan asked one night as they huddled under the makeshift canopy around a fire.

"We ride for him all the time, beside *Orlok* Unebolod," said Berkedai, puffing out his chest proudly. He was a stout man with bowman's muscles Bayan could easily see even through his layers of clothing, and the commanding officer of the men.

"But what about with the Great Khan?" Bayan asked. "I'm sure he led you in terrific victories."

"He guides our hand through his Generals and commanders," Berkedai said. "We avenged the death of our Borjigin princes with him, but now that he has subjugated the tribes, the Great Khan needs no further glory. Instead, he offers us, his skilled warriors, a chance to prove our value."

Bayan turned his gaze to the firelight. Manduul Khan never fought in battle anymore? Was this the way of all Great Khans? Bayan wanted to prove himself a capable fighter—or at least he felt like he had to so he could gain their respect—but the idea of sending others to do his work for him certainly wasn't without its merits. *Can I do this one day?* he wondered.

The ride north continued, and he listened to stories of battle shared among the men. Over and over, the same name cropped up in stories. *Orlok* Lord Unebolod. Whoever he was, the guards certainly respected him. Quite a bit, actually. They spoke more about their *orlok* than they did about their Khan.

Bayan shared his own sort of battles. He wove tall tales of his encounters with women and death-defying escapes from enraged families. He shared the story of how he took on three wolves with nothing but his sword, flashing the scars on his arms as proof of his success, omitting the part Lord Bolunai's son Tengghar played in rescuing him. If Tengghar could keep the wolves and the glory for himself, Bayan felt he had every right to remove the lordling from the story altogether.

Bayan wove a tale of his harrowing journey across the Gobi Desert, on the brink of death and without a horse, when he was saved by the touch of the sky itself. The water had not been rain, as he led the men to believe, but an old woman who nursed him back to health before Tengghar's men killed them all. Again, Bayan left out his pursuer from the tale.

He told the men about how he climbed the desert's red rock bluffs with no food or water to reach the safety of the other side; and how, upon reaching the other side, he nearly died of starvation until the touch of a young woman—Siker—nursed him back to health and her family had welcomed him into their ger. It amused the men as Bayan entertained them with the story of how Siker's father assumed Bayan performed bride-service, though no agreement had actually been made and both he and Siker had no interest in marriage. Berkedai chortled as he labeled Degghar a fool. Most of the stories had some kernels of truth imbedded within, though he kept out the details that touched too close to his fears—and the men who had chased him down.

By the last night of the journey, they listened to his stories more than he listened to theirs, and all the men showed him far more admiration and deference than they had when they first chased him down. Even without actual battle experience, Bayan quickly learned that his stories could earn him respect.

Bayan hadn't known what to expect in Mongke Bulag. Grand palaces of chiseled stone and golden gilt? Tiles that shone in the torchlight? Walls reaching into the sky, protecting the Great Khan and his people from outsiders? Great wooden pillars engraved and painted? The luxuries afforded the Great Khan must have been far richer than those of Lord Bolunai's small palace. After years of nomadic life among the Chakhar, and years of brutal abuse, the promise of wealth and comfort helped chase away the exhaustion of weeks of riding.

Berkedai rode at the head of the group with Bayan as two of the other men scouted in each direction to prevent raids. The rest of the *arban* of ten men remained a mile or so behind to escort the carts of goods sent from Hami. As Bayan and Berkedai crested a rolling hill, hooves crunching the brown grass, Bayan stood in his saddle, squinting into the distance. Row upon row of gers faced their approach from the south. Hundreds of them. Bayan had seen such encampments before. They weren't uncommon among larger tribes.

"Who is that?" Bayan asked. He thought they were close to Mongke Bulag, having passed Karakorum a day ago. *What other tribe would camp so close to the Khan's capital? Maybe we aren't as close as I thought.*

"That is the Great Khan's capital," Berkedai said.

Bayan sank into the saddle and gazed at Berkedai, dumbfounded. *That was the Great Khan's camp? Where were the walls, the palaces? Where was the wealth?*

Berkedai barked out a laugh when he saw Bayan's expression.

"You look like a pony shit in your ger," Berkedai said.

"I just ... I guess this isn't what I expected." Bayan let his stallion slow his step, suddenly not so eager to spend the winter in yet another ger.

"Spoiled little *hudin khankhuu*," Berkedai teased.

Bayan straightened his spine and glared at Berkedai. *Princeling? Did he just call me a princeling?* "I am not a spoiled *hudin khankhuu*. You don't know the half of what I've suffered."

Berkedai grinned. "You've certainly shared a fair few stories. You aren't old enough to have much more to tell."

"I could curl even your calloused toes."

Berkedai nearly fell out of his saddle laughing. Bayan hoped his expression didn't appear as if he were a pouting child. That certainly would not improve matters. Though he could not help the way his mouth down-turned at

166

Berkedai's amusement. Just because he was half Berkedai's age didn't mean he hadn't suffered his share of misery. How many of them had suffered brutal abuse as a child? Had they fled in fear for their lives and risked death in the desert to escape? What did they know?

A scout from their group raced across the dead grass toward them from Mongke Bulag. Bayan took a moment to recall his name. Yungei. He was one of the two among the Khan's men Bayan had remained most wary of. Yungei never laughed or even cracked a smile at any of Bayan's stories. The way Yungei glared at Bayan made him wonder just how long it would be before he found an arrow in his back.

Yungei jerked his pony to a halt, then matched pace with the two of them. "We are to escort him to the gathering tent where Manduul Khan waits to welcome him."

Berkedai reined in his amusement suddenly, giving Yungei a grunt of acknowledgement.

The weight of Bayan's situation created tension in his shoulders as if the Khangai Mountains to the west expected him to bear some of their burden. Bayan struggled to take slow, steady breaths, to keep his expression neutral. Despite the act of nonchalance, the reality of his potential impending death pressed down on him. What if Manduul Khan wanted to kill Bayan himself? He could be walking straight into his own death. All the certainty that he might have found his place of safety washed away in a moment. Instinct kicked in, and he glanced around them for an escape route. But where could he go so close to the Khan's capital? The best riders would easily catch him.

There would be no escape. Not this time.

The three of them rode into Mongke Bulag, though Bayan felt more and more like a prisoner under armed escort the deeper they rode. Mongke Bulag reminded Bayan of any other camp, and it fell far short of what a Great Khan's capital city should be. Could it be called a city without walls or stone structures?

The people seemed comfortable enough, at least on first appearance. Not overtly wealthy, but from what he could see, they didn't struggle much either. They huddled close to their homes in layers of fur and leather, prepared for the coming winter. Conversations hummed along the thoroughfares, broken by the occasional shouts of men or women calling out to friends or neighbors or hawking their wares. Children squealed and challenged each other as they raced, weaving deftly between and around the legs of adults or jumping over chickens. It was all so very typical.

As the three of them rode past, people bowed out of the way, opening the path for them to pass through the crowds easily. Bayan could ignore most of them easily enough—it wasn't like most of these people were worth making note of—but for one exception. The vast number of girls. So many of them, and many a far throw more attractive than Siker. Leaving her behind had been a wise choice.

Bayan spotted a group of four girls about his age staring at him as he passed. He flashed his best smile at them. All four of the girls blushed a brilliant shade of red. *I'm going to like it here*, he thought.

CHAPTER TWENTY

CHARMS OF THE RUNT

MONGKE BULAG – FALL 1464

Picking out the gathering tent had been simple. Bayan easily spotted the large round structure towering over the rest of the gers in the capital. His escorts did not slow until they reached the door. Berkedai dismounted and gazed up at Bayan as he hesitated in his saddle.

"Come," Berkedai said. "Let's not keep the Khan waiting."

Bayan licked his lips and followed Berkedai's lead, dismounting as he fought to smother his fear. Would this be his death?

Berkedai stood at Bayan's shoulder as Yungei opened the door into the gathering tent. Bayan's heart thudded against his ribs.

Grinning at him, Berkedai nudged Bayan's shoulder playfully. "Let's go, *hudin khankhuu.*"

Bayan shot him a scowl before straightening his back, taking a breath, and crossing the threshold.

The gathering tent was bigger on the inside than it appeared. Along the outer walls, rows of benches sat empty. Silks and sheer cloth looped along the ceiling lathes and around the lattice walls. Gems shimmered in the light of the copper pots burning brightly.

At the head of the room, Manduul Khan sat atop his throne, examining Bayan in a way that made Bayan's skin crawl. Two other men sat on the steps of the dais near Manduul. They wore black lacquer armor and heavy, rich furs. Manduul wore some of the richest white furs Bayan had ever seen, and he was happy he had taken time to acquire new clothing. His old clothes would have been rags compared to the striking hues of white fur, black dyed leather, and golden accents each of these men wore.

Bayan struggled not to trip over his own feet as he approached his uncle with Berkedai and Yungei at each of Bayan's shoulders.

Manduul was older than Bayan had expected, but the two men with him were younger, perhaps in their twenties or early thirties. One of them had big eyes only dwarfed by the bushy eyebrows that hung over them, but his face bore a welcome, jovial smile that Bayan couldn't help but return. The other had a jaw that looked chiseled from stone, and a scar from his eyebrow to his cheek that reminded Bayan more of a fissure in a mountain than an actual scar. Unlike the first man, this one didn't smile. He watched Bayan with a critical yet impassive eye.

Berkedai and Yungei were all business now, standing at Bayan's sides like they were his personal guards and not the Khan's men. Bayan's gaze flicked momentarily to the two men sitting on the dais. They were clearly guards of some sort. Or Lords.

Two women were present as well—the Khan's wives, most likely—and a young girl of about ten. Both of the women studied him in very different ways. The woman with the hooked nose appeared curious by his presence, though a bit cold. The woman with the heart-shaped face examined him just as critically as Manduul Khan's two guards. Though she smiled warmly at him, her eyes seemed uncertain of him. A feeling he shared.

"My boy," Manduul Khan said. "You look well."

Bayan swallowed the lump that had lodged in his throat and stepped toward Manduul. "Manduul Khan. I feel well." *Sort of*, he thought.

"Glad we could finally bring you back where you belong," Manduul said.

This place? Bayan didn't want to spend the winter here. He wanted to go somewhere with stone walls.

Manduul rose, drawing up everyone else in the gathering tent as well. He approached, offering Bayan a shake. For a moment, Bayan examined the offered arm, then glanced anxiously at Stoneface. "An honor to be welcomed."

"Don't let him bother you," Manduul said with a conspiratorial smirk. "Lord Unebolod is all bark and no bite."

Bayan couldn't help looking at Stoneface again—Lord Unebolod. This was the man the guards talked about? "That's not what I've heard."

"Perhaps we can find out?" Lord Unebolod said. Despite the jest in his tone, his face remained a mask.

"No hurry," Bayan said with an uncomfortable smile.

Manduul laughed and patted Lord Unebolod on the shoulder. The gesture of brotherhood brought out a trace of emotion to Lord Unebolod's face. For just a fraction of a moment, his lips thinned, and his gaze turned dangerously sharp. It passed so quickly Bayan wasn't sure if he had actually seen it. *Keep an eye on that one*, he thought.

"This is Togochi," Manduul said, patting the man with the bushy brows on the shoulder as well. "They are my sworn brothers. You and I are the last of the Borjigin wolves, and Togochi and Unebolod are honorary wolves. Without children, we Borjigin have to stick together or there won't be any more of us in the future."

Stick together. Something told Bayan that these were wolves hungry to be the alpha. Each of them probably had some sort of claim on the Great Khan's title. *Myself included*, he realized. *I'm like a runt amongst a litter of strong wolves.* Maybe Manduul Khan wanted Bayan alive, but these other two men had invisible arrows—hard to see, but just as deadly.

Unebolod winced at this, and Bayan wondered why. Something else Manduul said clicked into place. The Great Khan has no heirs. Manduul had to be in his forties, which meant he wouldn't have much longer to produce heirs. Without them, Bayan was next in line whether he wanted to be or not.

While they had waited for Bayan's escort to bring him into the gathering tent, Mandukhai observed those assembled from her usual seat beside Yeke and Manduul. Esige sat at her feet. Ever since Borogchin's marriage, Esige had been more distant. The loss of her older sister had broken something in the girl that Mandukhai couldn't figure out how to fix.

Today, Esige sat in her silk deel, back straight and chin raised high. Mandukhai had braided her hair back before securing her *shanaavch* on the crown of her head. Now, the small silver bells dangling from the headpiece fell silent. Esige didn't move.

Mandukhai had caught Yeke examining the yellow *boqta* on her head as they waited. Yeke's disapproval had been palpable the first time she had seen

Mandukhai wearing it. Since then, she examined it as if wondering whether a knife was hidden within. The two women hardly exchanged more than a handful of terse words since Borogchin was stolen away. Mandukhai resented Yeke for the betrayal in a way that burrowed deep into her bones.

When at last the door opened, a cold breeze blew in with the three men. Bells chimed as the women all turned their attention on the newcomers. Manduul sat up a little straighter as the boy—or young man, apparently— entered with two guards.

Unebolod's expression was as unreadable as ever as he studied the boy, but Mandukhai had learned a lot about his eyes in the past few weeks. No matter how hard he worked at keeping his expression neutral, she could see the frustration burning in his dark eyes.

Manduul rose to welcome Bayan to Mongke Bulag, and she was careful as she rose to her feet as well, not wanting to seem eager. As Manduul introduced Bayan to Unebolod and Togochin, she bristled. Would they not be introduced as well?

At last, Manduul waved the three ladies toward Bayan. Mandukhai moved at a deliberate pace, unlike Yeke, whose steps almost seemed eager to reach this newcomer.

"Ladies," Manduul said. "This is Bayan, blood of Tsetseg and bone of a Borjigin prince, my brother's grandson."

Bayan examined each of the women with a gaze that felt far more appreciative than was proper. Bayan was scrawny, despite the thick layers of fine clothing. Yet despite his wiry form, Bayan's smooth, young face bore a charm that made even her own heart momentarily flutter. Bayan was certainly handsome, even if he was smaller than the others by head and shoulders.

"He is as much blood as Esige and you will treat him as if he were my own son," Manduul proclaimed.

Son? Mandukhai suppressed a gasp at this. She had advised Manduul to welcome Bayan, but she needed to be careful about the bond these two formed. Bayan would be her key to escaping this marriage, if she chose the right moves at the right time.

Esige mumbled something under her breath and Mandukhai suppressed the urge to thump the girl. Now was not the time for her derision.

Yeke smiled warmly at Bayan, seemingly unbothered by the news.

Mandukhai glanced at Unebolod from the corner of her eye, but his frustrated gaze remained rigidly fixed on Bayan. His jaw twitched so slightly it would have been easy to miss unless one knew what to look for. And she did. Manduul's proclamation instantly put Bayan in a higher position than Unebolod. Unebolod would have to fight Bayan for control of the tribes. *And I told Manduul to bring the boy here*, she thought.

It had been the right call. She knew that. If Manduul killed Bayan and other tribes—including his own—found out, he would have a revolt on his hands. That could end in her death as well. *Or worse*, she thought. Another man could just sweep in and claim her. Though she could attempt fleeing. Maybe Unebolod would protect her. Bringing Bayan here was a sure way to ensure her freedom and the boy's downfall. Still, she felt overwhelming guilt, as if she had stolen something away from Unebolod herself.

As Mandukhai contemplated this, Yeke seized the opportunity to be the first to welcome Bayan, stepping forward and offering her arms. Bayan accepted them, and the two leaned close to sniff the other. As Yeke stepped back, Bayan failed to smother his grin—or perhaps he didn't try at all—and Yeke smiled, her cheeks a slightly brighter shade of red. *No. I can't let her control him.* The entire reason for brining Bayan here had been to find a way to use him for her own freedom.

Mandukhai offered the same greeting. Bayan's touch whispered over her sleeves, almost like a lover's caress. It sent a shiver down Mandukhai's spine that she only just managed to control. She leaned close, as Yeke had, and was surprised that he didn't reek of sweat as she took a slow sniff. Instead, he smelled of fresh water and leather. His breath rolled down her neck just a moment before he sniffed her. As he pulled back, his hands slid along her sleeves ever so slightly, fingertips brushing her palms before stepping fully away. Mandukhai swallowed but didn't blush as Yeke had. His touch was far too intimate. A glance at Manduul revealed he had noticed none of it.

As Esige stepped forward, Mandukhai straightened, glaring at Bayan. Perhaps he felt her eyes boring into him, because a moment before he greeted Esige, he stiffened and offered a less intimate greeting to the girl. *He's a scoundrel*, Mandukhai thought as she folded her hands in to her sleeves. The feel of his fingertips still lingered on her palms and arms, and more than anything, she desired expelling that sensation.

Manduul clapped Bayan's back hard enough to make Bayan stumble a half step forward. "Excellent!" Manduul rubbed his hands together. "Tonight, we feast, for a wolf of the Borjigin has returned to his pack. Come, Bayan. My wives and their daughters have prepared a ger for you."

As the evening feast began, Mandukhai sat primly in her place at the low table, picking through a meal of *buuz*, mutton, and curds. Though it wasn't a grand feast, with no proper time to prepare it, everyone enjoyed themselves. People gathered to meet the Great Khan's nephew, passing Bayan in waves. Bayan greeted each with a charming smile, clasping hands with the men and lingering a touch longer on the women. Wrestlers fought in the large open square in the center of the gathering space, showing off their skills to Bayan. The best wrestlers could be selected as honor guards, if Bayan so chose.

Near the end of the feast, the wrestlers cleared out and musicians set up along the sides of the square as a group of female dancers glided into the center. As the lively strokes of the horse fiddle began the *biyelgee*—the traditional dance of celebration and community—the ladies crouched, moving their shoulders first, then adding in motions of the wrist, beckoning. Their arms began the sharp motion as if pushing away invisible hordes of men while simultaneously encouraging them to advance. As the music rose, so did the ladies.

Bayan watched the dancers with uninhibited interest, leaning toward Manduul and cracking jokes Mandukhai couldn't quite hear. Manduul sometimes grinned, sometimes snickered, and sometimes roared with laughter. The rapport was instant between them, and Mandukhai's stomach churned. *Have I made a terrible mistake?*

Manduul poured his attention over Bayan as the night wore on. Mandukhai had advised him to keep the boy close. Now, as she studied the way Bayan interacted with everyone tonight, she prodded for weakness. Where Manduul mixed gravity with his own sort of grim amusement and Unebolod remained ever stoic and steadfast, Bayan waved his hands and flashed his smile in a way that made more and more people gravitate toward his flamboyant charm. The men who had returned with Bayan already acted familiar and friendly with him, and the Khan's nephew drank it in, using it to pull in more and more people to him.

Bayan posed a new sort of danger. One Mandukhai had not anticipated. His energy and charisma were like dancing, enchanting flames of a bonfire drawing all the moths closer. And like the flames of the bonfire, Mandukhai somehow knew his touch would be dangerous. *And like a raging bonfire, I must contain him before he burns out of control*, she thought, rising from her chair.

Manduul didn't notice as Mandukhai slipped away. Some time ago, Unebolod had excused himself to check in with the scouts around the camp. Manduul had waved him off carelessly, yet Mandukhai knew Unebolod had only sought a means to escape. Now, as Manduul preoccupied himself with *airag* and his new pet, Mandukhai removed her *boqta* and left in search of Unebolod, tucking the crown under her arm until she could return it home.

As she passed, people stepped aside and offered her pleasantries. Mandukhai greeted each warmly, as she always did.

The sound of steel on stone caught Mandukhai's attention as she drew closer to Unebolod's ger. The door stood open, allowing the cold night air inside. Mandukhai stepped up to the threshold, and Unebolod's dog, Kilgor, rose from lying on the floor to sitting at attention, ears perked toward her. The dog bared her massive, sharp teeth and emitted a low growl, drawing Unebolod's attention away from sharpening his sword. For a moment, he just stared at her, then finally whistled briefly. The dog settled back down on the floor.

"A cloud hangs over you, my friend," Mandukhai said, ducking inside.

Unebolod tensed as she entered, setting his sword on the bed at his side. "A sign to the storm raging inside," he said.

Mandukhai glanced over her shoulder, then edged deeper inside. Entering his home could have serious repercussions, but somehow she doubted anyone would miss the two of them tonight. Everyone was far too enchanted by Bayan.

"This changes nothing," she said, wondering if she should sit or remain standing.

"It changes everything, Mandukhai. I haven't spent years obeying Manduul like a whipped dog, only to have everything stripped away from me."

"Keep your enemies close, Unebolod." Mandukhai bit her lip, clutching the *boqta* in her hands. "Better that he is here where we can watch him than out there where we cannot."

"Better he dies in the desert alone, as he should have." His hand fell on the sword and she scowled.

"What will you do with that?" she admonished him, swatting his hand away from the weapon. "If you kill him, you kill yourself. Bayan's undoing won't be at your sword or arrows. It will be of his own making."

Unebolod quivered with rage, and Mandukhai placed a hand on his shoulder. She could feel how tight his muscles were, the intense pressure straining at him.

"How do you mean?" he asked at last, lifting his gaze to hers. For the first time, she saw uncertainty in his eyes.

"The brighter a flame burns, the faster it burns out," Mandukhai said. "And right now, he is blazing like a wildfire. He will make a mistake, and it will cost him his life. Don't add fuel to his fire."

Unebolod lifted his hand, hesitated, then set it over her own, still resting on his shoulder. "You are different, you know. A true daughter of the yellow dragon."

His fingers slipped around hers, and Mandukhai felt everything inside of her slide toward him. She took a step closer, but before she could move another inch, Kilgor rose again, growling toward the doorway. Both of them swiftly withdrew from each other. Unebolod grasped his sword and edged toward the door, relaxing a moment later.

"Nergui," he said, blocking the doorway with his wide frame—and thus blocking her from sight.

Mandukhai let out the breath she had been holding.

"She is here?" Nergui asked from outside the door.

Unebolod didn't relax until Mandukhai stepped closer and urged him back. "It's alright. I trust Nergui more than anyone in this camp."

Unebolod flinched as if her admission had slapped him in the face, but it was true. Mandukhai trusted Nergui more than even this man who stirred something deep inside of her.

"You shouldn't be here," Nergui said, stepping closer. Kilgor snipped at his feet.

"No one will miss me," Mandukhai said.

"I did."

Unebolod sighed and stepped out of the way, kicking the dog back. "Go. Make friends with the Khan's new pup."

Mandukhai wanted to protest. She wanted to stay. She wanted to hold his hand again. Instead, she nodded and slipped out the door, refusing to give him a backward glance as she left with Nergui.

"Manduul may be distracted tonight, but if anyone else saw you in Lord Unebolod's ger and reported to him, tomorrow you would face his wrath and you know it," Nergui said sternly, keeping his voice low so no one else would hear him.

Mandukhai wanted to tell him to mind his own business, but it was hardly a fair judgment. Nergui's life was tethered to her own. His concern was reasonable.

Bayan did not know how late it was, and he didn't really care. For the first time in his life, he dared to feel safe and wanted. Manduul had not killed him, but indeed welcomed him and gave the appearance of respect toward him. These people seemed to adore him. Letting his guard down could be dangerous, he knew that, but he drank too much *airag* and exchanged flirtatious words with too many of the women to care. Manduul grinned just as devilishly at the girls hanging around Bayan, and it gave him a false sense of security.

With a handful of young women draped over his legs, listening intently, Bayan finished one of his stories—a great tale about climbing to the peak of a tall rocky ledge in search of an eagle's nest only to find the nest abandoned. Berkedai chortled at parts, but the listening women murmured appropriately. Most of them were dancers. Earlier, during their performance, Manduul had asserted their pleasurable movements were not limited to dancing. Each of them had quite a lovely face. Deciding to test his luck, he coaxed the ladies off his legs and shifted to stand.

"I should find my way home," Bayan admitted, his voice dripping with regret and disappointment. "The night is late and the fires burn low."

"No, don't go yet," one girl begged, taking his arm and holding him close to them. "The night is still young."

"And so are we," another girl added.

Bayan sighed regretfully, placing his hand over hers. "I have a busy day ahead tomorrow." *Or I won't wake up at all,* he thought bitterly.

All the girls groaned and asked him to wait a little longer. Bayan stumbled a step to the side. The *airag* had gone to his head, though he did emphasize his unsteady feet more than necessary. Two of the girls shot to their feet to help stabilize him, each looping one of his arms over her shoulder.

"You need an extra set of limbs tonight," one girl said, grinning.

"Oh, I have enough limbs," he teased back.

"Try to get some rest, Lord Bayan," Berkedai said teasingly.

Bayan couldn't help the wolfish grin that spread across his face as the girls helped him walk away from the circle beside the fire toward his ger. Maybe he would be dead by morning. He should at least enjoy his last night. *Or maybe these two women will deter any would-be assassins in the night,* he thought with a smirk.

Along the way, they passed a startled Mandukhai. Her stunning eyes flashed wide with disapproval upon seeing the state he was in, and the two girls he hung himself upon. She muttered something under her breath that sounded like swearing, though he had a hard time imagining her doing any such thing. A voice he tried to bury into the far recesses of his mind told him he should be careful to make friends with her, but with two girls fawning over him, he couldn't bring himself to care right now.

After all, the night was young.

CHAPTER TWENTY-ONE

RETURN OF THE WOLVES

Only three incentives brought Bayan out of his ger in the first weeks of winter: women, piss, and drinks with Manduul. Endless *airag* had helped warm his insides significantly in the dead of winter, just as a female body warmed his outsides. He and Manduul would meet in the gathering tent for a game of knucklebones. Manduul taught him everything. The ongoing struggle with the Oirat who sought control. The way the Jalair tribe tested their boundaries to the north against those of the Great Khan. Why certain tribes considered the remaining Borjigin wolves a threat. The benefits and pitfalls of women. Manduul certainly loved to share his wisdom.

As they sat in the gathering tent drinking and joking, Manduul went into great detail about his wives—well, one wife in particular. Mandukhai was a strong, proud Mongolian woman with a big heart. In the council meetings she was intelligent and as sharp as a herding whip, and just as quick to keep order, but in bed she was as wild as a mare in heat, often fighting him for control. Bayan found her quite intimidating already, but Manduul's praises only made Bayan more wary of the woman.

Manduul rarely mentioned Yeke. "She has no head for politics, and she's as alluring as a yak and bleats like a sheep," Manduul said one day over a game of knucklebones, as if his comment explained everything.

Bayan found Yeke intriguing. Her father was Manduul's Vice Regent and *orlok* of the territories in the southwest. This meant Yeke had powerful allies, despite how little Manduul cared for her. He made a few passing jokes about his wife's long face or her beak of a nose. Bayan didn't see those as faults. Aside from her long face and big nose, she was a pretty young woman.

Bayan also longed for Manduul's approval. The more frequently the two of them spoke, the stronger that drive to prove himself became. He suggested that he and Manduul take a few men and secure their norther territory if for no other reason than to show Manduul that he might be worthy of the Khan's affection and trust. At first, Manduul had seemed intrigued, but after a night to think—keeping himself warm in Mandukhai's bed—Manduul returned to the idea with more hesitation. Somehow, she had created a wave of doubt in Manduul. The woman had a hold over Manduul that only solidified Bayan's certainty that he was in no rush to marry.

Bayan turned to Berkedai for consolation. The warrior had become his only friend in Mongke Bulag—aside from Manduul.

"What man wouldn't fall under her spell?" Berkedai asked, grinning at Bayan as they sat in Berkedai's ger. "Women have two weapons. Their whip and their trap. Fall into the trap and a woman will whip you into shape."

"Sounds like a good reason to never marry," Bayan snorted, taking a drink of his *airag*.

Berkedai shrugged. "Maybe. But it certainly is fun falling into the trap." Berkedai refilled Bayan's cup. "You have to understand your uncle. He may just be afraid of losing you as he lost his other nephews."

"What do you mean?"

Berkedai wove a story of Molon Khan, a boy only a year older than Bayan himself when he became Great Khan. Molon had suffered enslavement at the hands of the Khorlod—a plight Bayan could sympathize with—before he was released. The Khorlod swore to serve the Borjigin from that moment on. "That's how Togochi and Manduul became like brothers," Berkedai explained. "Togochi swore to forever serve that oath with honor and pride in the name of his tribe."

"So what happened to Molon Khan?" Bayan asked, leaning his back against the wall of the ger as he sat on the bed.

"He was betrayed by his own advisor," Berkedai said. "An Uyghur who whispered lies into Molon's ear. Those lies started a war. Molon died in the battle, and after he died the truth came out. To restore balance, Molikhai, the man who killed Molon, killed the Uyghur traitor who had deceived Molon in an act of good will toward the Borjigin." Berkedai leaned closer as if sharing a dangerous secret. "But listen to this. The traitor was Bigirsen's half-brother."

Bayan's chest clenched. *Bigirsen? The very man who put Manduul in charge after Molon Khan's death? That can't be a coincidence,* Bayan thought. Would Bigirsen do the same to him the moment he had a chance?

Berkedai grinned as he understood Bayan's thoughts and found them amusing. "It gets better. After Molon Khan died, the Oirat-Uyghur alliance solidified and they took control for years. Whenever tribes attempted fighting back, Bigirsen's Uyghur-led forces would ride against them and smother the revolution."

"Then how did Manduul end up Khan?" Bayan asked.

Berkedai glanced toward the door and lowered his voice. "Lord Unebolod stopped Bigirsen when he attempted riding against the Khorlod and Manduul. We were outnumbered ten to one, but his strategy was brilliant. We swept across the Uyghur flanks like ghosts. While we did, Lord Unebolod took a *jagan* of a hundred men and plunged them right into the heart of the Uyghur forces. He and Bigirsen clashed on the battlefield. Bigirsen left a nasty gash on Unebolod's face. Unebolod nearly killed Bigirsen with a wound in the side that sliced straight through his padded leather armor." Berkedai swept his hand across his own side as if mimicking the sword. "The Uyghurs retreated. What choice did they have?"

Bayan heard this story. Some of the Chakhar warriors told the tale shortly after Bayan had arrived in their camp. The battle had been fresh and news spread fast. But the Chakhar men had called Unebolod the Steel Soldier like he was a god who brought the Uyghur and Oirat to their knees. If Bayan had been apprehensive about Unebolod before, it was nothing compared to the fear that now chilled him. He downed his *airag* and held out the cup for Berkedai to refill it.

"Not long after that battle, Bigirsen returned, asking Manduul for Guest Rights. Bigirsen claimed his brother had been framed and he deserved justice," Berkedai continued as he poured the drink. "I don't know what exchanged between the two when they met, but next thing we knew, Manduul called for *kurultai* so all the tribe leaders could support him as Great Khan. And Bigirsen's tribes threw their support behind him. Right after the tribes gave Manduul their oaths, Bigirsen's daughter married Manduul."

The story stuck with Bayan for days, burrowing under his skin. Each time he turned the details over in his mind, the more certain he became Bigirsen had somehow orchestrated the whole thing. The Uyghur were notorious for their allegiance with the Oirat, and the Oirat had no love for the Borjigin. The mere fact that Bigirsen's half-brother had been the advisor who deceived Molon Khan only solidified Bayan's suspicion. Bigirsen had always intended to destroy Molon, and possibly hoped to do the same to Manduul until Unebolod came to Manduul's rescue. If Bigirsen could hatch such deception so easily against a Great Khan, would he do the same to Bayan? Perhaps, if Bayan made friends with Yeke, it could save him.

A few days after the conversation with Berkedai, Bayan met Manduul for drinks in the gathering tent. They played a game of chess as they drank, and Manduul continually kept his pieces a step ahead of Bayan's own. Steeling himself for the conversation, Bayan took a long drink of *airag*.

"Have you ever considered it may have been Bigirsen who set up Molon Khan?" Bayan asked, gazing into his cup of *airag*, afraid of seeing Manduul's face wrinkle downward in anger.

"Bigirsen has been good to our tribe," Manduul said evenly, crossing his arms as he leaned back in his seat to observe the board. "He has brought us much wealth."

"Spoils of his conquests," Bayan said. "I know he supported you, but why?"

Manduul shifted, drawing Bayan's attention up to him. To Bayan's alarm, Manduul appeared more confused than angry.

"Because I was next in line," Manduul replied.

"But why did he support you? Oirat have no love for the Borjigin, and the Uyghur have always been allied with the Oirat." Bayan shifted uncomfortably, his muscles ready to recoil if Manduul lashed out. It was a lesson Lord Bolunai had taught him well. Always be ready for the other hand. "I'm not saying you didn't have a right to the title. The other Lords supported you, and that's not nothing. But he attacked the Borjigin, nearly suffered defeat, then retreated. Not long after, he returns to support you? It seems suspicious. Plus there's the fact that it was his brother who betrayed Molon Khan."

Manduul's thick brows knitted into one massive curve over his eyes as he considered Bayan's implication. Several excruciatingly long minutes passed as Bayan tried not to consider what Manduul might do to him if he had stepped too far. At long last, Manduul drained his cup in one massive gulp and held it out for the serving girl to refill.

182

"You aren't the first to wonder this," Manduul finally said, breaking the tense silence. "But he has been good to us, and the wolves are growing strong again. The men respect him. Bigirsen's influence has grown strong. What can be done?"

Though Manduul hadn't meant it as a serious question, Bayan had waited for this opportunity and he closed in on it like a hungry wolf. Eager to prove himself to Manduul, to solidify his place beside the Khan, Bayan leaned forward, resting his elbows on his knees. "Take that influence back."

Manduul frowned, rubbing his chin, then shook his head and drank more *airag*. "Bigirsen has treated me with respect for years. He gave me his only daughter. He fights for me."

"No," Bayan could almost smell the uncertainty boiling in Manduul. "Every battle he wins, all the riches he gives his men, takes more power away from you. Let me ride out with you against the tribes who abandoned the wolves when we needed them most. Let's show your men and the men of the other tribes that you are Great Khan and not to be taken lightly. Manduul, uncle, let me help you take back what belongs to you."

Manduul's lips thinned and he glowered into his cup between drinks. Bayan struggled to wait patiently for him to decide. More than anything, Bayan wanted to ride with Manduul, to prove the strength of the Borjigin wolves to the other tribes once more—to prove his worth to Manduul. Bayan had been in fights before; one-on-one bouts between himself and Lord Bolunai or his men. But battle—true and fierce battle—was one beast that continually eluded him, mostly because he had always tried to avoid it.

Right now, all Bayan had were stories woven from half-truths. The men saw him as a child still. He needed their respect. Great Khans were forged in the fires of battle. While he didn't want to die as Molon had, Bayan knew that if the tribes forced him to be Great Khan in Manduul's stead—and without an heir, Bayan would be pushed into that position—he had to be battle-ready to defend himself.

"I am Great Khan," Manduul said at last. "And we do no need to ride into battle to prove our right to anyone. The men respect me."

"And what of the Jalair?" Bayan asked. "You said yourself they have no respect for your borders and infringe on your herds and territory. Show the men in Mongke Bulag your strength and punish those who disrespect your lands."

Manduul turned his cup in his thick fingers, studying the contents as his moustache twitched. "In spring, when the thaw comes. We will ride north to the Jalair tribes who have raided our herders and infringed on my lands this past summer."

"Why wait until spring? They may be on higher alert by spring and more prepared for attack. If we ride now, in winter, we can take them unaware and chase them further north." Bayan grinned so widely it split his face in two. "Let's show the Jalair that we are strong when they believe we are weaker. In the heart of winter."

Manduul tipped his head back, staring at the ceiling, then dropped his chin and nodded. "Once the storm has passed."

Bayan raised his cup to Manduul. "To the return of the wolves."

"May the sky father bless our path," Manduul agreed, holding up his own cup for a moment before each took a long drink.

The warmth of the drink paled compared to the excited fire burning in Bayan's skin. At last, he would prove himself.

Mongke Bulag buzzed with excitement as Manduul and Bayan prepared to lead a full five-thousand-man assault against the Jalair to the north. Mandukhai had heard as everyone else had, through word of mouth spreading like wildfire among the people. Disbelieving Manduul would dare to prepare such a campaign without talking to her first, she had gone in search of her husband.

Her boots crunched the snow-packed ground as she stopped outside the gathering tent where Manduul and Bayan prepared to ride. Unebolod and Togochi hovered nearby. Neither were dressed for the fight.

Mandukhai's breath quickened and she rushed inside. "What are you doing, Manduul?" she demanded.

He struggled to fasten the padded leather around his belly. Clearly he had not worn the armor in some time and it strained to fit around his girth. "We are going to show the Jalair dogs that we are wolves still."

She cast a glance at Unebolod, whose face was cold and impassive. "Why are Togochi and Unebolod not preparing to ride with you?" she asked.

Manduul growled in frustration as the strap popped loose again. "What do you want, woman?"

Bayan grinned with all the wide-eyed innocence of someone who did not know what he prepared to embark upon. "Don't worry, Lady Mandukhai, he will remain safe."

"He's not bringing us along," Unebolod added, and the coldness in his tone matched his face. "We are to stay behind and to protect those who remain here. And again, as your *orlok*, I must object. My duty is to marshal your forces."

Mandukhai could hardly believe it to be true. Who rode toward battle without their best weapons at their disposal? "Manduul, is this true? Are you leaving your brothers here, your best fighters? Your *orlok*?"

"I have Bayan," Manduul said confidently as Mandukhai stepped closer to help fasten the padded leather as best she could, tugging a bit too harshly at the leather strap to force it tight around him. "And we have five thousand men. I'm hardly worried about a few Jalair."

"A few." Unebolod snorted, then crossed his arms as he squared off in front of Manduul. "The Jalair have more than twice your number. Even if they are spread out for the winter, it will be no easy task. You will have to take each camp by surprise, move in and out before they realize you are there. Once they sound the horn a rider will race out to warn the rest of the tribe. You need speed and stealth. Does he know how to handle that?" Unebolod shot a deadly glare at Bayan.

Mandukhai knew Bayan had never fought in battle. If Bayan served as Manduul's guard—or worse, his General—they would both be dead before the fight ended.

"At least take one of them along," she pleaded, stunned to find she truly was worried about whether they would return. "You will need them more than we will."

Bayan laughed. "Do you doubt the Khan's abilities?"

"I doubt yours," she snapped, firing a hard glare in Bayan's direction. "Your stories will protect no one."

Berkedai entered, offering Bayan's sword to him, then said, "The Khan and his nephew will be safe, my Lady. I swear this on my own life."

The words hardly offered reassurance. Berkedai had been one of Manduul's guards and now acted as Bayan's. Mandukhai heard Berkedai was an adept fighter, but he was not nearly as skilled as Unebolod.

Manduul tilted Mandukhai's face up and stared into her eyes. "My sweet wife, are you worried you will become a widow? I am as strong as ever, and when I return, you will see that at last. While I am gone, Unebolod will watch over the tribes. I trust you will advise him as wisely as you have me."

He placed a kiss on her lips and she wanted to pull away from him. What *was* she so afraid of? For months, Mandukhai had prayed to the sky father and the earth mother to free her from her marriage. Now Manduul rode into battle without the two men best equipped to protect him and she worried about his return? If Manduul didn't return, she would be free. How had she not considered this before? This could be everything she had prayed for.

But it could also be the end of the royal Borjigin line. Neither man had a son to carry on the title. The line of Genghis would end, and it would be all-out war. *I will be free to be with Unebolod though*, she thought. *And with my support, he will become the next Great Khan.*

Mandukhai met Unebolod's gaze, and he stared at her as if he understood precisely what she was thinking.

She could not stop this, nor did she want to any longer. But her position required her to put on a show, so as Mandukhai headed toward the door she paused beside Bayan and placed a hand on his lean shoulder. "If you come back without him," she whispered. "I will cut your throat myself." Then she kissed his cheek and left the men to prepare.

The last thing Mandukhai saw as she slipped out the door was the dumbfounded look on Bayan's face as he stared after her.

Unebolod shouldn't have been so angry to be left out of a battle forged for no other purpose than Manduul's personal vanity. He had everything to gain from both men not returning. If Bayan fell in the fray, Unebolod would once again be second in line without contest. If Manduul fell, Unebolod would gather enough support to become the next Great Khan. The boy would die either way—whether at the hands of the Jalair, or at Unebolod's. And if Manduul died, Unebolod could finally approach Mandukhai without fear of consequences. He could take everything he wanted in one glorious moment. Yet the yearning to fight in battle when he had spent so long doing little more than holding off raiders and skirmishes packed him with envy and anger. How could Manduul leave him, his best soldier, his *orlok*, behind?

Togochi hadn't complained about being left behind, and he maintained his usual jovial demeanor, but the slight obviously chaffed him as well. The manner of his jokes made that clear to Unebolod.

The two of them stood aside with Yeke, Nergui, and Mandukhai, as the shaman performed a blessing for the Khan and his men. The ceremony ended quickly, leaving their small group to watch as five thousand men rode off with the Khan and his nephew. No one spoke as they watched the flurry of snow the horses kicked up. No one moved as the thunder of hooves against the packed snow dulled in the distance. They stood in sullen silence, bracing against the bitter wind.

Yeke was the first to leave once the army disappeared. She didn't utter a word, but simply turned on her heel and marched toward home.

"This is an unnecessary risk," Mandukhai muttered beside Unebolod once Yeke had disappeared. "They could both die." She turned away from the northern horizon to face him, hoping to see in his eyes the same wish she held in her own heart—that they would die and the two of them could be together at last. "And then what?"

"Then we have Bigirsen to contend with," Unebolod said, but his eyes did not match his words. He understood. He shared her hopes.

"How long?" Togochi asked, crossing his arms tightly over his chest and folding his hands into his furs.

"By spring, maybe," Unebolod said. "He won't wait long to strike."

"No." Togochi cast a disapproving glare at each of them. "I don't care about Bigirsen. He's a dog who thinks he's a wolf. How long have the two of you been keeping each other's beds warm?"

Unebolod's heart stopped, too stunned to speak the truth, that they had done nothing. They had barely even touched each other. He struggled to come up with words, but Mandukhai's reaction was instant. She moved with lightning-fast speed, striking Togochi hard across the face. A red welt sprang to life on his cheek. It was over before either of the men knew what had happened. Nergui tensed, hand on his sword as he stood a few paces behind Mandukhai. Togochi's eyes flared in anger and Unebolod reacted quickly, before Togochi could do anything foolish.

"Nothing is happening between us," he reassured Togochi, resting a hand on the other man's arm to keep him from reacting impulsively toward Mandukhai. "I give you my word on that."

Togochi glanced at Nergui as if suspicious of her guard's intentions as well, then spit blood on the ground. "I know that you two have been meeting in secret, and I don't know if it's anything more than what it seems on the surface. But it's easy enough to surmise why. Don't lie to me, brother."

Unebolod flinched. He had given Togochi his word, yet his brother still accused him of deception. A great pain swelled inside. How could Togochi doubt his word after everything they had been through? A breeze ripped through them as if mocking the suddenly frigid air between the three of them.

Mandukhai's hand shook as she smoothed it over her stomach. "I have been faithful to my husband and resent your allegation. I should cut out your tongue just for implying as much."

Togochi stiffened, suddenly appearing uncertain. "I've watched you these last few weeks. I've seen what passes between the two of you. I'm surprised Manduul hasn't."

Unebolod caught movement from the corner of his eye as Nergui inched closer to Togochi, hand wrapped around his sword.

Mandukhai must have noticed the same, because she brushed past Togochi, her chin raised high, and started back toward her ger. "Come, Nergui. I have no time for children."

As Togochi spun to watch her go, Nergui subtly slipped his hand off the sword and glared at the two of them before following her.

"You're a fool," Unebolod said to Togochi, shaking his head. "Nothing has happened between us. Believe me, she has suffered enough."

Unebolod started toward his ger.

Togochi kept stride beside him. "I was so sure," he said as his shoulders drooped.

Togochi's accusation only meant Unebolod had to be more careful about how he approached Mandukhai. Especially with Manduul away.

"She is a dangerous woman, brother," Unebolod said, clapping Togochi on the shoulder affectionately. "A dragon in women's clothing. Be careful how you tread around that one or she will burn you alive."

Togochi sighed. "I've noticed. Do you think Manduul has any idea how exceptional she is?"

Unebolod shook his head. He doubted as much. In fact, he wasn't sure he understood her at all, either. Just when he thought he had figured her out, Mandukhai would throw another surprise his way. There were moments when cracks appeared in her demeanor, and in those moments Unebolod felt like he was tumbling into the depths of her gaze. But just as quickly, those cracks would close. One of these days, if he wasn't careful, the cracks would close with him trapped inside. By then, it would be too late to save himself.

BONES OF WINTER

JALAIR-BORJIGIN DISPUTED TERRITORY – SOUTH OF LAKE BAIKAL
LATE-WINTER 1465

After five attacks in three weeks, the Jalair were significantly weakened by Manduul's forces. Bayan was no idiot. When Unebolod had laid out the best strategy for attack, Bayan had listened. Each time he and Manduul strategized for the next attack, Bayan used Unebolod's wisdom. Manduul had been too pleased with each victory to realize Bayan just spouted Unebolod's plan back at Manduul. As Bayan suggested, they moved too quickly from one encampment to the next for the Jalair to prepare. Yungei suggested planting a handful of men around the Jalair camps to cut off any riders attempting to send word to the other Jalair encampments.

With each victory, Bayan basked in the praise Manduul offered, though that praise rarely came with words. In front of the other men, Manduul simply nodded with a cold warrior's face. When the two of them drank alone, Manduul would sometimes propose a toast to another of Bayan's successful strategies, or he offered a pat on the back as they shared the story of the most recent battle.

They sent those who submitted to the Khan to Mongke Bulag with an escort of a *jagan* of a hundred men and the spoils of war. Those who did not submit were killed as their homes burned away the bones of winter that remained on the ground. Manduul and Bayan continued onward without returning to their people. Manduul had refused to turn back until they brought the Jalair to heel. Bayan refused to disappoint Manduul by suggesting anything else; especially when his strategies were working against the Jalair.

Bayan also learned the benefit of being in command alongside the Khan. While the men rode into battle, he would watch the fight and rarely had to engage. On the rare occasion that he did, Berkedai remained at his side like an impenetrable shield.

With each victory, the bond between Bayan and Manduul strengthened. Any fear Bayan had that Manduul would take his life had long ago vanished, replaced by a mutual respect that could only be born from fighting side by side. Bayan loved Manduul, a feeling he had never experienced with anyone else before; and Manduul seemed to return that feeling.

Snow had stopped falling an hour before dawn as the mounts crested the yellow, rocky outcropping overlooking the next Jalair encampment. This encampment was the home of the Jalair khan. Manduul had gazed at the mass of ger against the snow with a fevered determination Bayan admired. Bayan had suggested they attack before the sun fully rose in the sky so their men could catch the Jalair sleeping, and Manduul had agreed without hesitation.

Now, Bayan watched from atop his chestnut stallion on the outcrop as their wolf pack surrounded the camp, closing in on all sides. The Jalair men on watch were among the first to die, but not before sounding the horns to warn the rest of their tribe. The Jalair were not without bravery as the wolves closed in around them, raising swords and firing arrows, but their accuracy could not match that of Manduul's men. Arrows rained down on the camp with deadly precision, killing men and setting gers ablaze. The fires created a wave of chaos as women and children ran in the way of the warriors.

Bayan's stallion whinnied and stamped his foot, impatient to run. He knew the feeling. They watched the battle from afar. Screams of death and roars of bravery filled the air. Bayan patted his stallion's neck, itching to ride out and join the fight.

The itch intensified, impossible to ignore between Bayan's shoulders and he glanced sideways at Manduul, who watched the entire battle with resentment wrinkling his flat nose. Manduul had not spoken about his reasons for choosing this group of Jalair as their next victims, but their scouts had confirmed in the night that the Jalair khan was among the gers.

A dozen of Manduul's guards sat atop their mounts behind him, watching everything, seeking challenges against their Khan. The excited tension among the men grew so thick even the icy breeze could not slice through it.

"We should ride in and force their Lord to kneel," Bayan said. His voice dulled as a gust of wind whipped past them.

Manduul snarled but said nothing for several long minutes. Finally, he broke the silence. "Go. Show him the strength of the Borjigin he has abandoned."

Excitement pulsed through Bayan as he heeled the stallion into action. He sprang down the path leading to the plains below. At last, another chance to show Manduul his loyalty. Berkedai whooped as he joined Bayan, along with the rest of Bayan's guards, leaving Manduul atop the outcropping with only his own guards to protect him.

The horses galloped at a careful pace, guided by the knees of their riders who stood with bows ready to fire. Bayan's pulse hammered in his ears, matching the rhythm of the hooves pounding the frozen grass and snow. His unit reached the edge of camp, crashing through the line of Jalair attempting to halt the Khan's warriors. Bayan took a careful breath and released as his mount's hooves left the earth. The Jalair whose sword was raised to slice into the leg of Bayan's mount spun as the arrow lodged in the warrior's eye. He fell dead on the spot.

Bayan whooped, blood thumping through his veins, the thrill of the battle warming him against the bitterness of winter. His vision momentarily swam as he raced past a headless body in a pool of blood. Bayan focused on his task, attempting to ignore the blood and death around him. As long as he focused on reaching the Jalair Lord, Bayan could overlook the horrors of the fight around him.

As more Jalair fell, and others replaced their fallen comrades, Bayan raced deeper into the camp, trampling men who dared step in his path, firing at others. Fires burned into the sky and smoke clogged his throat, but he pressed on. His men followed in tight formation, protecting him from stray arrows or unexpected swords like a layer of padded leather around him. He appreciated the safety his men offered him.

A tight knot of mounted men near the center of camp caught Bayan's attention, and he used his knees to guide his mount toward it. Thousands of Manduul's men closed in on all sides, raiding ger and killing any stray men who did not surrender immediately. The wails of widowed women mingled with the screams of death. It curdled Bayan's blood, but he had one target.

In the center of the knot of men, an older man in full padded armor and a protective iron helmet sat atop his own mount. The sword in his hand arced with practiced ease, but Bayan knew it could strike like a viper. The man, the Jalair Lord by his best guess, bore no fear in his eyes, nor despair. His confidence seeped into the surrounding men. When his gaze fell on Bayan, he pulled back his lips in a vicious sneer of pleasure.

Bayan's men fired arrow after arrow into the handful of the Lord's men. One Jalair warrior punched an arrow into Berkedai padded armor. Bayan glanced at Berkedai, momentarily worried. But Berkedai grinned and shot the man through the throat. The Jalair warrior grabbed the shaft. As the bloodied hand gripped the wood, Bayan held his breath. Then the warrior slumped against his startled mount. As his body slid off to the ground, Bayan returned his attention to the Lord and his sole remaining guard. Berkedai yanked out the arrow lodged in his armor.

Bayan reined in only a few paces from the older man, not bothering to glance at the only remaining guard. Berkedai halted beside Bayan, an arrow ready to let loose.

"What is your name, pup?" the older man asked, lowering his sword.

Bayan's jaw twitched. He was not a child any longer and resented being called such. "I am Bayan, wolf of the Borjigin, nephew of Manduul Khan."

The din of battle dulled around them. The fight was over. This man just had to realize that himself.

Bayan leaped off his stallion, standing with all the confident pride victory offered. "You have forgotten your place, raiding the Great Khan's herds, abandoning your blood oath to the Borjigin." He crossed the narrow gap between himself and the Jalair Lord, then stroked the man's mount on the neck. It was another beautiful and strong chestnut mount like his own. "This is a fine stallion. I think I'll keep him."

The Lord's last guard tensed his hands around his own reins, edging a touch closer to Bayan in an obvious threat. Bayan ignored him.

"I am Hulun, khan of the Jalair." Hulun dismounted, placing him within reach of Bayan. Hulun's hand rested casually on his sword. "And I have abandoned nothing. I answered the call of the Great Khan's Vice Regent. I have fought alongside Bigirsen. You abandon your honor by killing my people."

Berkedai shifted atop his mount, ready to strike, but Bayan wouldn't give him this moment. It belonged to Bayan alone.

"You do not serve Bigirsen. You serve Manduul Khan." Bayan unsheathed his sword. "Your Jalair women are ours. We will remind your Jalair sons who rules these lands. Manduul Khan's men will take what they want from your camp, and we will burn the rest."

Hulun raised his sword slowly. "It's you and me, boy."

Bayan's chest tightened at the challenge. He heard the creak of Berkedai's saddle behind him, but Bayan could not back down from the challenge. Not in front of his own men. Bayan's stomach twisted and he fought to keep a cold warrior's face. He had to show these men he could be just as hard in battle as any of them. This was not a time for weakness.

Bayan took a step back, wishing he had paid more attention to the sword fighting lessons. He assumed a defensive position, praying Hulun would not be fast enough to gut him before he could react. No one else would interrupt their fight. It was a matter of honor now. Bayan would be alone in this fight.

Hulun plunged forward. Bayan barely managed to block and sidestep. Their swords crashed together hard enough to make Bayan's arm tremble. Steel grinded against steel. Bayan shoved back, but Hulun was stronger than he had expected. Their swords slipped off each other and Hulun's blade grazed Bayan's arm, drawing blood. Bayan ground his teeth as heat radiated out from the cut, then he spun before Hulun could recover and slammed the hilt of his sword like a hammer against Hulun's skull. It cracked and began bleeding. Hulun stumbled forward and Bayan kicked his back just as Lord Bolunai used to do to him. Hulun fell to his knees with a growl of rage. Bayan seized the moment, swinging down with all his might at Hulun but the old man rolled to the side and launched back to his feet before Bayan's sword even hit the ground. *I can't beat him*, Bayan realized in a desperate moment as his sword vibrated his entire arm.

The ring of horses around them expanded as more men came to watch the fight. Bayan ignored them all as he brought his sword around to his side. Hulun's weapon sliced along his own, blade against blade, in a shower of sparks. Bayan pressed back, throwing off his balance, and Hulun's fist connected with Bayan's jaw, blindsiding him. Bayan staggered to the side as a familiar flash of blinding pain seared his jaw. He had suffered this before. He had suffered worse before.

Suddenly confident, Hulun completed a series of attacks that drove Bayan back into one of the horses. Blood rolled down Bayan's arm from the cut. Sweat dripped in his eyes despite the cold winter air. Hulun leaned in, forcing

Bayan's sword up to his own neck. He gasped as the back of the blade pressed against his windpipe. *I can't die like this*, Bayan thought desperately.

Distantly, Bayan heard Berkedai and the rest of his men cheering him on. They were watching. He couldn't lose now. There was only one game Bayan knew how to play. One Lord Bolunai had taught him well. The game of fists and feet. Without a moment of further hesitation, Bayan slammed his knee between Hulun's legs and rammed his forehead into the older man's own. Hulun fell to his knees, and Bayan struck much like Lord Bolunai had often done to him, hammering a booted foot down out at Hulun's sword arm. The weapon skittered across the ground. With renewed confidence, Bayan stalked toward Hulun, towering over him.

Hulun reached out and swept Bayan's feet out from under him, tossing Bayan onto the ground on his back with a thud. The impact made Bayan see stars for a moment as he gasped for breath. His own sword had slipped out of his hand and out of reach. Bayan attempted rolling to retrieve it, but Hulun pounced on top of him, hammering his fists into Bayan's face, his ribs. Flashbacks to Lord Bolunai's beatings caused a surge of panic to rise in Bayan's chest. He raised his arms to block the blows. Something sliced against his armguards. A knife.

Sudden rage pulsed in Bayan's ears. It quickened his pulse. All those years of abuse. All the times Lord Bolunai had beaten him. Everything poured out of Bayan on the battlefield. Bayan wrapped an arm around Hulun and rolled the old man over, pinning him to the ground as he howled and thrashed his fists into Hulun's face repeatedly. Nothing else existed. Bayan's entire body quivered violently. Spittle flew from his mouth as he screamed. His nostrils flared and he bared his teeth. Adrenaline pumped through his veins. This man was no longer Hulun, but Bolunai, Tengghar, every man who had beaten him.

"Lord Bayan." A hand fell on his shoulder. Bayan spun around, launching himself at the new attacker, throwing a fist.

Berkedai seized Bayan's trembling arm and twisted it away before Bayan's fist could connect with Berkedai's face.

Silence had settled around the fight. Mounted men all around stared, dumbstruck, at the Khan's nephew.

And then an ear shattering howl of grief shattered the silence. "No!" The guard leaped off his horse, immediately halted by a dozen arrows pointed at his chest. He tore off the helmet and mask, revealing a stunning a young woman only a few years older than Bayan with thick, full lips and black hair elaborately braided away from her round face. Grief marred her face as she cried for her father.

For the first time, Bayan gazed at Hulun—what remained of him. Bayan's stomach lurched and he gaged raising his hands to cover his mouth only to see they were slick with blood. Bayan was sure he would be sick as he stood over the corpse, and it took heroic efforts not to show it in front of these men.

A call of the Great Khan arose and Bayan's body went rigid. He did not want Manduul to see him like this, ashamed of what he had just done. Bayan never imagined himself capable of such violence.

The crowd parted as Manduul approached. Bayan kept his back to his uncle, but Manduul stepped around him, glancing down at Hulun and making a small sound of approval in his throat. The sound drew Bayan's gaze up to meet Manduul's eyes. The approving gaze Manduul bestowed upon him warmed Bayan despite the icy sensation in his soul. It chased away the churning in his gut. No one had looked at him like that before. Like a father proud of his son. And in that moment, Bayan knew what he had been missing all these years. A family. Acceptance.

And he wanted more.

Bayan needed time alone. As men moved through the Jalair camp to loot gers, Bayan sought Hulun's home. His violent display had shaken him to his core and Bayan could not dispel the image of Hulun's crushed skull from his mind. He signaled Berkedai to give him a moment on his own as he entered Hulun's ger.

The moment he stepped inside, an arrow ripped into his wrist. Another arrow followed a breath later, but Bayan had bent over and clutched his wrist to rip out the first. The second whizzed past his head and stuck in the felt.

Before Bayan could recover his wits, an elbow slammed into his back like a hammer, forcing him to the ground. Bayan scrambled away, but his attacker acted swiftly, yanking him by the injured wrist and flipping him over on his back. In a matter of seconds, he had been incapacitated and pinned to the floor of the ger.

By Hulun's daughter. Anger burned in her fierce eyes.

"I should kill you for what you have done to my people," she growled, baring her teeth. "Perhaps I can punch your skull into the ground as you did to my father."

Bayan already hated himself for what he had done. He deserved her anger. "Go for it."

She flinched, narrowing her eyes at him as if expecting some trick. "You were like a rabid dog," she finally said. "Do you know what we do with rabid dogs here?"

Despite his self-loathing, Bayan could not help the excitement rising in him as she pinned him to the floor. Bayan grinned dumbly at her, momentarily forgetting the arrow in his wrist despite the searing pain. She certainly was beautiful, with full lips smirking at him triumphantly. Despite the circumstances, he felt desire stir from deep within.

Berkedai rushed in, sword drawn, and laughed when he saw the woman holding Bayan down. "Should I give you two some privacy?"

"This won't be long," she promised.

Bayan shifted so she could feel his desire against her leg. "I think you underestimate me."

"Men," she snorted, and Berkedai left them alone, chuckling all the way.

"I'm sorry," Bayan said sincerely. "You probably don't believe that, but I am. I didn't want any of this."

She grabbed the arrow and snapped it in half, then pulled the broken end out of his wrist with a brutally expert yank. Bayan hissed through his teeth but refused to show any further weakness in front of her. The wound seared like fire in his arm.

"I am Altan," she said, digging her finger into the wound with a smirk as he squirmed. "And these Jalair men answer to me."

Bayan growled deep in his throat to keep from screaming out. The pain was blinding and hot, and he had to blink fiercely to clear his vision, sucking in quick breaths to fill his collapsing lungs.

Altan yanked a knife from her boot and thrust it toward his chest. Bayan caught her wrist with his good hand, wrestling the weapon away. Their arms quivered as they each struggled for the advantage. Her finger wiggled in the wound again, and Bayan growled aloud, writhing and mustering every ounce of strength he had to buck her off. Altan's strength belied her slight frame, and though she lost some control of her position, Bayan hadn't thrown off her grip. They rolled across the floor. Bayan pinned her down and slammed the knife hand against the floor to knock it loose. Altan used her legs to push him a few inches away. Her fist slammed into his ribs. His fist cracked her in the ear. The match became an equal bout of give and take until, at last, Bayan pinned her under him. Both of them panted, faces flushed.

"Call off your men," she said between breaths.

"Submit to me first," he said, feeling her tensing to fight back again under his crushing weight.

"No more of my people need to die," Altan said, then blew a loose hair away from her eyes.

"Berkedai!" Bayan shouted, though he didn't dare take his eyes from her for a moment. The large man's boots crunched the ground outside as he lumbered to the door. "It's over. Altan has submitted to the Borjigin."

Berkedai smirked and bowed from the doorway. "I'll send word." His shadow disappeared from the ger, leaving the two of them alone.

"Have I submitted to the Borjigin?" she asked.

"You will," he said confidently, then his lips crashed against hers.

At first, she resisted his kiss, but in just moments she returned the kiss with the force of a hundred thundering horses. Altan wrapped her limbs around him and rolled him on his back. Her hand slid between their bodies into his trousers as she shifted her own hips.

"I suppose you're right," Altan said. "Show me what it means to be a wolf."

The Jalair camp settled, though the wails of widows and children still echoed in the air. No gers burned, and they had allowed most of the families to keep their meager possessions. Manduul had seized anything worthwhile. Bayan was aware he had missed the council Manduul held as soon as they won a battle. Berkedai probably told Manduul what caused his delay, though, so Bayan didn't really concern himself with it.

He strode arrogantly along the paths between the gers beside Altan as they made their way to where Manduul had taken over a ger near the edge of camp. She would need to speak for the Jalair and offer her oath to Manduul to maintain peace.

"This meant nothing," she said, drawing Bayan from his smug revelry. "I don't want or need a husband."

Bayan shrugged. "I don't want or need a wife. Not for a few years."

Altan glanced at him from the corner of her eyes. "So we are agreed. My submission was strictly for pleasure and not any sort of arrangement between us."

Nothing else? Bayan hesitated. If she didn't surrender to Manduul's rule, she was as good as dead. He stopped, jerking her to a halt beside him.

"You will swear yourself and your people to follow Manduul Khan," he said firmly. "Or he will take your head. Or more likely, make me do it for him." Bayan didn't think he could carry out that command. Not after what she had just done to him.

Altan glanced at his hand. She had taken great care to press silver into his wounds and wrap them in a bandage for proper healing. "He is Great Khan. I shouldn't have to swear to him."

Bayan swallowed thickly. Was he afraid for her? She showed no outward signs of fear herself. "Altan ..."

"Relax." She shrugged his hand off and continued along the path. "If he needs to hear the words, I'll speak them. I just feel they are unnecessary."

Today's victory over the Jalair had been a significant one. Manduul and Bayan had worked for weeks to make this tribe fear and respect Manduul as they should. It was a small, but significant way to show Bigirsen who was truly in charge. Bayan knew to tread carefully where Bigirsen was involved with Manduul, but as they fought the Jalair, Manduul trusted Bayan even more. Loved him more. It was a strange thing to know love.

"Have you submitted to Bigirsen as you did with me?" Bayan asked, both dreading the answer and hopeful that he had taken something else from the councilor.

Altan spit at the ground. "No. He was too weak to try."

At that, Bayan knew triumph. Real, pure triumph. He had done what Bigirsen hadn't dared and reaped the rewards. And what a fantastic reward it had been.

Bayan entered Manduul's ger first. The inside was cramped with so many of Manduul's commanders within. Manduul grasped Bayan's arm with the nod and glimmer of pride Bayan so craved from his uncle. Yet the memory of Hulun's body still haunted him. How had Altan ever given herself to him after what he had done?

"You've outdone yourself this time, Bayan," Manduul said. "And I hear you won a magnificent prize."

Bayan stepped aside so Altan could slip forward. "This is Altan, daughter of Hulun."

Manduul's hungry eyes roved over her and his thick brows lifted. "A glorious prize indeed."

"I am not a prize." Altan stiffened her back, glaring at Manduul. "I came to swear the oath to the Great Khan and his family in my father's place." She glanced at Bayan. "But I have not come as a prize."

Manduul scowled. "My nephew needs a good wife. You should consider yourself honored."

"He has taken his spoils already. I have nothing else to give but my oath. Shall I give it, or will you take my head and reignite the flame of war?"

Manduul's face reddened, and Bayan felt a moment of panic, a need to protect her from Manduul's wrath. "It's okay, uncle. We've already discussed it. As a wife, she won't be much good in battle. And she can fight. It would be a substantial loss."

Manduul considered Bayan's words, then nodded. "If you call me Khan, your will is no longer yours. Kneel to me."

Altan did as instructed as the eyes of all the men present admired her supple curves and strength. Manduul placed a fat hand on her head. "I ask you for salt, milk, ponies, ger, and blood."

"They are yours, my lord Khan," Altan said without a second of hesitation.

"Then you are commander of all Jalair and kin to the Khan's." Manduul removed his hand. "We are one people."

Altan flinched in shock, nodding as she rose to her feet again. "My lord Khan."

Bayan struggled to maintain a cold warrior's face, proud of this significant achievement. It also meant that when they went to war and called on her people, she would be there to warm his bed. Assuming she wouldn't decide to hate him.

The men filtered out to seek their own spoils, leaving Bayan and Manduul alone in the ger. Manduul held out a skin of *airag* to Bayan as they settled around the stove for warmth. It was a small gesture that meant more than Bayan could have ever found words for. Sharing *airag* with the Great Khan in his ger was the highest honor a man could hope for.

As he closed his hands around the skin, Manduul's words struck hard in his heart.

"You've done well, nephew. Better than I could have expected." Manduul relaxed back in his chair, watching Bayan with glowing pride and affection. Bayan basked in it, soaking it in. "When we leave here, you and I will ride to

Khorkhonag Valley."

Bayan gulped down the *airag* in shock, lowering the skin slowly. The Khorkhonag Valley. A sacred place of brotherhood. "Uncle?"

"You are no longer the boy who came to me," Manduul said resolutely. "We are family, bound by blood and bone. And in the valley, we will bind in spirit for the nation as well."

Panic rose in Bayan's chest. Such a ceremony would be more binding than marriage. Was he worthy of such a pledge?

Yet, this announcement offered Bayan's hear that final piece he hadn't known it had been missing. Manduul no longer saw him as a threat. He did not just love Bayan. He was willing to swear his life to Bayan, to bind their lives together beyond death. At last, Bayan had someone in his life that truly cared about him.

And he had no idea how to react.

CHAPTER TWENTY-THREE

BENEATH THE LEAFY TREE

MONGKE BULAG – LATE WINTER 1465

U nebolod volunteered for watch in the middle of the night, ensuring no one raided their herds or camp cloaked in darkness. He couldn't sleep well these past days, anyway. Winter wind bit into his furs. The watch horn hung around his neck as he squinted into the northern winds. Only a handful of men kept watch at night, but in the bitter cold of winter, it was more than enough. Each man maintained his own post in various positions around camp. Unebolod took the center of the north watch, close to where Manduul and Bayan had ridden away with five thousand men nearly two months ago. Men returned once every week or so with fresh herds, food, and assorted loot seized during the raids of the Jalair.

The stories those men carried back with them hadn't worried Unebolod at first. But the more the men returned, the more reverence they carried with them for Manduul Khan and his young wolf, Bayan. The boy gathered strength while Unebolod was forced to remain behind to settle petty disputes between families. Unebolod worried Bayan would steal away too much of the respect the men had for him, even if Unebolod had taken this opportunity to establish himself as a strong ruler. It filled him with a burning desire to plunge into battle and forge his own alliances before they were lost to him for good.

Eager for a good fight, Unebolod took more frequent night watches, hoping for an excuse to use his sword or bow, but no opportunities presented themselves. He grew impatient as his future slipped out of his helpless hands.

Out of respect for his Khan, and partly out of fear that Togochi was watching, Unebolod kept his distance from Mandukhai as much as he could. She observed meetings with the council and offered her advice as she did to Manduul, but once those meetings were concluded, the two of them parted ways without comment. Outside of meetings, he hid in his ger against the bitter cold or hunted during his free time to avoid accidentally running into her around Mongke Bulag.

As word of Bayan's conquests grew, Unebolod began wondering why he restrained himself around Mandukhai. Manduul had taken everything Unebolod wanted. And now, he had brought this boy into their midst to take any chance of becoming Great Khan. The only way for Unebolod to get what he wanted, what he deserved, was to betray his oath. Yet his honor bound him to his promise so stalwartly that he couldn't even bring himself to seize power now, while Manduul and Bayan were gone, or even to plan their downfall upon their return. All he could do was hope that fate did the work for him.

The more frustrated he became with Manduul and Bayan, the more difficult Unebolod found it to resist Mandukhai. If they didn't return soon, he wouldn't be able to contain his true desires anymore.

More than once, he dreamed of their demise; of word returning to him of Manduul's death, as well as his loyal pup's, and everyone turning to Unebolod for guidance. Of finally becoming Great Khan. Of restoring the Mongols to their long-lost former glory. Of at long last submitting to deeply suppressed feelings for Mandukhai. If they didn't return, it would all be his at last.

Unebolod stood atop a hill at the edge of Mongke Bulag. The wind whipped at his deel, and he hunkered close to a tree to block the breeze. It was a frosty night for so late in the winter, but the bitter cold helped keep him alert. He tucked his hands under his arms for warmth, leaning against the tree.

Please don't return, he thought, praying to the sky father and earth mother that for just once he could step out of Manduul's shadow.

Spring came early, a sign that the sky father had blessed their tribe. Bayan reveled in the sun's warmth on his face as he walked beside Manduul into the depths of the forest valley. Only a handful of guards accompanied them to protect against unexpected attacks. The rest of the army returned to Mongke Bulag on their Khan's orders. Once the two of them reached their destination, the remaining guards would leave them alone in the forest and make camp at the mouth of the valley to wait for their Khan to return. The ceremony would be a sacred, personal exchange between the two of them and not for the eyes of others.

Their boots squelched into the wet ground as they went, and Bayan swore he could smell spring in the air. Birds darted overhead, a sign that the winter had finally come to an end, even if the snowbones of winter remained in shaded spaces.

Berkedai had been honored to lead the two mounts behind Bayan and Manduul. Each horse carried on it a bundle of items required for the ceremony. Manduul had not given Bayan much notice, so acquiring the gifts had been quick work, yet he was proud of his results.

Bayan's nerves intensified with each step. What Manduul had proposed was no paltry proposal. This ceremony would bind the two of them together for the rest of their lives as surely as any marriage. Bayan spent years avoiding such commitment, but Manduul had been so welcoming and fatherly and supportive of him that Bayan knew he could never refuse. And he trusted Manduul more than he had dared to trust anyone in his life. Manduul had offered a level of prestige with this sacred ceremony that Bayan was not sure he deserved. It also came with a burden of responsibilities he was not prepared for. His stomach tumbled, and he did his best to maintain the stony face as they continued toward the Saqlaqar Tree deep in the heart of the valley.

It took more than an hour to reach their destination, and when they approached the tree, Berkedai remained several paces back to give them privacy. Part of Bayan wanted to flee. He had spent so much time running from this level of responsibility, afraid that it would only end in death—and he certainly enjoyed living—but he also craved the status and a place to finally belong. This ceremony would make him and Manduul closer than brothers, and it would solidify Bayan's future as Great Khan after Manduul's death. Bayan spent so much time avoiding this inescapable destiny, and now he marched straight toward it. Leaving was no longer an option. If he ran, he would betray Manduul's love and trust, and he would either die alone, or ... *No, I would die. Period.* Not for the first time in his life, he was presented with an impossible choice.

Berkedai unfastened the bundle from one of the horses as Yungei did the same with Manduul's bundle. Manduul said nothing as he and Bayan waited. He placed his hand against the tree and tilted his head toward the sky as if in silent prayer. An itch grew between Bayan's shoulders. Should he join Manduul, or was this a solitary, sacred moment for him? Before he could decide, the items were laid out on their blankets and Yungei and Berkedai left Manduul and Bayan to finish the ceremony alone.

This very spot was where Genghis and Jamukha swore their vows of brotherhood. It was a sacred place. While other men swore bonds of brotherhood all over the steppe, this sacred place made the vows these two would exchange soon much deeper. Vows made beneath this tree were bound for life ... or cursed if those vows were broken. To Bayan's knowledge, no other men had made such a vow since Genghis and Jamukha in this place. It only added more pressure to his already tense shoulders.

Despite the cold air, Manduul began removing his belt and deel. Bayan followed his lead, stomach churning in uncertain knots. They would shed their former layers and accept new clothes to further solidify the oath. Bayan wanted to do this, yet he didn't. As he stood in front of Manduul under the shade of the budding Saqlaqar Tree in nothing but his trousers and boots, the cool spring air made the hairs all over his body rise to attention. He clenched his jaw to keep his teeth from chattering and did his best to maintain a stony face.

Manduul appeared unaffected by the chill. *Maybe because of all his extra natural layers*, Bayan mused, trying not to smirk.

Manduul raised his chin. "Over two hundred years ago, Genghis and Jamukha stood beneath this very tree and swore themselves as brothers. They spoke a sacred vow they could not uphold. Their broken vow brought strife and war on them and cost one of the men his life." He lifted the deel he had looted from one of their raids of the Jalair, a fine piece made from golden silk with elaborate ribbons of silver and black woven along the cuffs and edges. "We will not make their same mistakes. Men who are sworn brothers are one life, but men who make such an oath beneath this tree are bound to each other eternally. They do not abandon each other but instead become protectors of that life. They live together and die together. Now, swearing our oath of friendship, we shall love each other as we love ourselves, above all others."

Bayan stepped forward, and Manduul slipped the golden deel over Bayan's arms, then fastened it closed in front as he spoke. "With this deel, representing the light you have brought into my life, I clothe you as I would my own flesh." He picked up a golden belt of round disks, each holding a fiery painite stone, and fastened it around Bayan's waist as he continued. "With this belt, I bind my life to yours as one life. I will never, now or ever, forsake you or break my oath of brotherhood. I swear this under the Eternal Blue Sky."

All thoughts of fleeing now vanished as Manduul clothed and belted him. Instead, Bayan's face heated with a happiness he had never known or had ever imagined he would know. Manduul hadn't just accepted him as a son, but as an equal. It was more than he had ever dreamed. More than he deserved. Despite his most heroic efforts to maintain a cold warrior's face, Bayan couldn't help the way his lips curled into a smile. The world felt solid under his feet, brighter and more colorful than ever before.

As Manduul stepped back and took the reins of the chestnut mare with white spots around the hooves that Yungei had led into the valley behind them, Bayan swallowed a lump that formed in his throat. "With this mount, may we always ride together against any danger that comes our way."

Bayan took the offered reins. He loved chestnut-colored ponies—a reminder of the stallion that had raced him to freedom from Lord Bolunai's grasp—and his collection had grown from one to half a dozen during the winter raids. But this one would be the most special of all. He stroked the mare's nose. *I will call you Andayar,* he thought, marveling at the beautiful creature.

Manduul stepped back as Bayan tied the horse to the tree, then Bayan picked up a deel as white as snow with blood-red flowers embroidered around the sleeves and along the edges. Upon learning of this ceremony, Bayan knew he would have to acquire the gifts swiftly. This deel had been the only one he could find big enough to fit Manduul on such short notice that didn't look like something that came from a beggar's home, and he had to force a Jalair seamstress to make adjustments for Manduul's girth overnight.

He slipped the deel over Manduul and fastened it with only slightly quivering hands. "With this deel, representing the snows upon which our bond grew strong, I clothe you as I would my own flesh." He picked up a gold and red belt and fastened it around Manduul's substantial waist as he continued. "With this belt, I bind my life to yours as one life. I will never, now or ever, forsake you or break my oath of brotherhood. I swear this under the Eternal Blue Sky."

Pride shined in Manduul's eyes as never before, and Bayan's face felt as warm as it had under the light of the sun earlier in the day. In that moment, he knew there was nothing he wouldn't do for Manduul.

Bayan took the reins of a white and black spotted stallion, the strongest he could find from among their raids, and offered it to Manduul. "With this mount, may we always ride together against any danger that comes our way."

Manduul accepted the reins and tied it to the tree beside Bayan's horse. When he turned back to Bayan, Manduul held a jewel-hilted knife in his right hand and cut his left across the palm, then offered the knife to Bayan. The blade didn't slice deep, but it burned his skin as he opened a wound large enough to bleed. They each spit into their own hand, then clasped their hands together, clutching their free hands over the clasped ones to bind the oath.

"We are now brothers in blood," Manduul said.

"Brothers of one life," Bayan agreed.

The two set up camp together, hunted for their food, and feasted together with generous portions of *airag*. They sang and celebrated their newfound brotherhood as the guards awaited in the mouth of the valley a mile away. They would have no guards to protect them. Only their swords, knives, and each other.

And when the night came, they slept under the great sky sharing the same blanket as tradition dictated.

CHAPTER TWENTY-FOUR

More than One Elephant

Mongke Bulag – Spring 1465

Unebolod rapped his fingers against the arm of his seat out of impatient boredom as he listened to two families argue about who had particular rights over a sheep that was little more than a bag of bones. His irritated gaze fell on the bleating animal. Its skin was too thin and its bones had little meat on them. The coat was spotting, with gaps where wool should be. The animal wouldn't survive another winter. This wasn't the first family to come and argue about ownership of animals. Now that the Jalair had joined the capital and spring was in full swing, it seemed everyone had a problem with someone else allegedly stealing. For the first time, he actually wanted Manduul to return and deal with these idiots. Manduul was a Khan for the simple-minded, where Unebolod would be a Khan for the strong.

Mandukhai sat beside Yeke, watching the proceedings with wise, keen eyes. Her patience seemed endless as people continued their squabbles over petty issues. Unebolod was sure that if she hadn't been there to help, many of these disputes would have ended in bloodshed—either animals or the idiots bringing these petty issues before him.

"It would seem," said Mandukhai, reading his irritation and calling the bickering to a halt with her raised voice, "that this sheep belongs first to the Khan, not yourselves. He allows you to care for it, and who is in control of that care matters not when, in the end, the animal is his."

Unebolod sat up a little straighter as the two men looked from her to him. He nodded in agreement. "The sheep is weak. Kill it and divide the meat evenly between you. The wool will be split evenly between your wives to beat into felt."

Both men's apparent shock didn't go unnoticed. "But the Khan—"

"Put me in charge while he is away." Unebolod leaned forward, resting an arm against his knee and leveling a warning gaze at them. "Do you question my authority?"

"No, my Lord," they said in unison, bowing their heads and taking a step back.

"Good. Then go." He waved toward the door.

Both men turned to obey, each tugging at the sheep's rope for the right to lead it away. Unebolod groaned inwardly and rubbed his forehead as he sat back to avoid lunging at both of them and throttling them with his bare hands. A serving girl brought him a cup of *airag* as if reading his mind. He took a generous drink. *No wonder Manduul drinks so much.*

Manduul and Bayan had been gone nearly three months. Most of the warriors had returned to camp almost a week ago without the two of them. Was it too much to hope that they would never return? He glanced at Mandukhai from the corner of his eyes and saw her studying him with knowing eyes. *What is she thinking about?* he wondered.

Possibly, she wondered the same as he did. How much longer would they have to wait before accepting that the two of them were not returning at all? Unebolod yearned to make his move, to stake his claim on the title of Great Khan and show his true feelings for Mandukhai. But if he made a move now, without being certain of their deaths, he would lose everything when they returned. The very notion rankled him and he took another long drink.

"Bring me Toruud," he commanded.

The guard at the door slipped out. *How can a commander have no answers about his own Khan?* he thought, frustrated with not knowing the truth.

"You dig for information he doesn't have, Unebolod," Mandukhai said. How did she have so much patience?

"Do you worry so for our husband's return, Lord Unebolod?" Yeke asked tersely, hands folded in her lap. The woman had a constantly grating look on her face that Unebolod found very unappealing. It was no wonder Manduul had little interest in her.

"Someone must know something about what happened to them," he said tersely. "I intend to find out."

"Why?" Yeke pressed.

"Because he is our Khan, woman!" Unebolod hadn't meant to lose his temper with her, but everything about this situation infuriated him, and he loathed her more than anyone else in camp right now. He glared at Yeke and said, "Question me again."

Mandukhai hissed and clicked her tongue. He knew her warning and slumped a little in the seat. Regardless of how he felt about Yeke, she deserved some level of respect. "Sorry," he muttered. "This has been hard on all of us."

Yeke sniffed in disgust as Toruud entered behind the guard. He approached Unebolod, bowing deeply when he reached the head of the gathering tent. "My Lord, you called for me." He didn't say "again" but the implication was clear enough in his tone.

"Tell me again what Manduul Khan told you before sending you back," Unebolod said, sitting up straighter. They had been through this nearly every day since Toruud's return, but every time Unebolod hoped the man would remember something, that the repetition might jar some additional detail loose in Toruud's memory.

Toruud grimaced but nodded. "After we defeated the last of the Jalair, he said he and Lord Bayan had a pilgrimage to take alone. He insisted that the rest of the men weren't necessary and took only his guards along."

"Pilgrimage?" Unebolod perked up. That was new. Had he called it a pilgrimage before? "He used that word?"

Toruud nodded. "Yes, my Lord. He swore they would be safe with his guards."

Unebolod knew better than to believe that. The steppe was a dangerous place to travel with only a few men. They could have easily come under attack from another tribe. Who wouldn't love the chance to pick off a Great Khan and his heir? The glory of that alone would be worth the risk. *He's a fool.*

"And he didn't say where he was headed?" Unebolod asked for the hundredth time.

"Just east," Toruud said. "We had a full force of men loaded down with more of the Khan's loot. They had only a few horses. That would have allowed them to travel farther faster. They should be back soon, I'm sure."

Unebolod's jaw twitched. Toruud couldn't be sure of anything. They could be dead and no one would know. "I want men sent out to find them."

"But my Lord—"

"If the Khan is in danger, we need to know," Unebolod said sharply. *Or if he's dead already.* "It is our duty."

Toruud glanced at Mandukhai, and a flash of anger heated Unebolod's face. Why was he looking at her? Unebolod didn't shift his own gaze at all, glaring at Toruud and waiting for a response. Finally, Toruud agreed and bowed before heading for the exit.

Silence fell over the tent. Blissful, peaceful silence. Unebolod leaned back and closed his eyes, soaking up this moment of calm before returning to his daily duties. He heaved out a sigh.

"Should we go, Unebolod?" Yeke asked.

He waved the two women off.

Horns from the watchmen sounded, followed by another horn. Unebolod bolted upright, setting down the cup and listening as men shouted in the distance. Someone approached Mongke Bulag, and the thrill of conflict made his blood warm. *Finally, something to do.*

Unebolod surged to his feet, leaving the two women behind, and strode out of the tent to his mount. The bow and sword were attached already; he had planned on hunting as soon as duties allowed. Now he was glad for the preparedness as he leaped onto the mare and kicked her into a gallop toward the east, where the sonorous horns sounded again.

The mare darted around startled women and children who jumped out of the main paths. Before he even crested the hilltop, the sound of raised voices reached his ears. Men whooped and cheered.

Mandukhai had sensed a shift in Unebolod these past months. He wanted to be Great Khan; of this she was already certain. Yet despite this desire, every day that passed he grew increasingly tired of the daily tasks that came along with being Khan, and he grew more irritable. By the time spring had come into full bloom, it had become clear Unebolod wanted the title but none of the responsibility. He wanted the glory, but none of the tedium. He, like all men, in Mandukhai's estimation, craved the power just to prove he was better and stronger than anyone else. She found this side of him lessened his appeal but did not dispel it.

Today, Unebolod could have slept through his daily tasks without a care. If she hadn't intervened on numerous issues, he may well have dozed off. After months of observing him, she knew he simply waited to hear of Manduul's death, ready to seize control the moment he could confirm the Khan's fate.

"That one has a brilliant mind for battle, and none for governing," Yeke said irritably once they were alone in the gathering tent.

Mandukhai turned to Yeke, halfway to the exit. "You are half right. His idea of governing is broader. The subtle strokes are lost on him."

"Broader." Yeke snorted scornfully as she strode toward the door. "Yes, in battle. He would govern through blood."

"Don't they all?" Mandukhai asked as the two of them stepped out of the tent and headed toward their gers.

Yeke considered the question, then shrugged as if she couldn't care less. "Men know only one way."

"And it is our job to show them another," Mandukhai replied, glancing toward the commotion to the east. "What do you suppose is coming?"

Yeke huffed contemptuously. "Hopefully a fight so they can relieve this obnoxious bloodlust." She fidgeted with the rings on her fingers. "Do you think they are alright?"

Mandukhai found Yeke's use of they instead of he intriguing, as if she were worried about not just Manduul, but Bayan as well. Unebolod was right about Bayan. It was better if he died in battle than survived to further ruin the tribes. But they needed more royal Borjigin men first. Where Unebolod saw the tribes in broad strokes of the future, Bayan could only see the small lines of the present. A balance was necessary, but it would never come at their hands. She opened her mouth to respond to Yeke's question, but the calls of excitement from the distant east reached both women and they froze, gazing toward the horizon.

"It's them." Yeke's voice quivered with relief, and the tension that had knotted in her shoulders for months bled out. Mandukhai realized Yeke had spent the whole winter wondering if she would survive to see another. She must have known that if Manduul died, she most likely would as well when Mandukhai and Unebolod would take control of the Nation.

Mandukhai rushed to Dust. Nergui had already saddle the stallion and checked the saddle. She thanked him as she quickly mounted. If Manduul had returned, she wanted to see for herself.

Yeke must have thought the same—or she didn't want to be seen as the wife who did not appear to welcome him home—because in a matter of moments, she was on her own horse and the two of them raced away toward the eastern hill where a crowd had gathered to watch the Khan's return. Nergui rode on their heels.

By the time they crested the hill and pulled their mounts to a halt, a handful of women clustered together to watch as most of the men galloped their mounts in circles around the returning party, whooping and cheering the return of their Khan.

"It's wonderful that they have returned safely, Lady Mandukhai," Lady Satai said from among the clustered women. Mandukhai ignored the councilman's wife for now, focusing on the men.

Unebolod sat atop his own mare beside Togochi, watching with an unreadable face. Mandukhai nudged her mount closer to the two of them, and Yeke was quick to follow. A glance revealed nothing telling about Unebolod's feelings. His face formed a perfect mask of indifference. Mandukhai gazed out at the small party trotting closer to Mongke Bulag.

Manduul's deel was so white that the sun's reflection made it hard to look at. He sat his the black and white mount tall and proud, beaming almost as brightly as his deel. At his side, Bayan struck such a figure that Mandukhai gasped. He held himself straighter, stiffer, and more cold-faced than he had ever been capable of before leaving. Whatever had happened during their escapades, it changed Bayan. The golden deel he wore only enhanced the striking nature that surrounded him. Before, he was an unfletched arrow, able to strike anywhere at any time with a careless grace. It had been dangerous enough. But this new version of him was more serious. He looked more like a Khan than Manduul did.

The ring of excited tribesmen parted and rode off back into Mongke Bulag as Manduul and Bayan rode up the hill to be greeted by Mandukhai and Yeke. The guards remained vigilant, keeping their mounts a few paces away when Manduul halted his own horse in front of the line of people waiting.

Unebolod sat at Mandukhai's side. He was first to speak. "We grew concerned when you didn't return with the rest of the men."

Bayan and Manduul shared a secret smile that made Mandukhai's stomach twist.

"We are here now," Manduul said, then turned his gaze on Mandukhai and Yeke. "My beautiful wives. How I missed the two of you these past months. I look forward to getting reacquainted." The grin on his face made it clear what exactly he meant.

"Where did you go that you couldn't take your men?" Unebolod asked.

"We had our own business to attend to," Manduul said, brushing the comment off. "Let's put the worries of the past behind us! Today is a momentous day, and we have glorious cause to celebrate. See that many sheep are prepared for a feast and that we have enough *airag* to go around. Then meet me in the gathering tent just before the sun burns golden in the sky."

Manduul kicked his mount toward Mongke Bulag. Bayan followed only a breath behind him. The two rode into the camp side by side in a way that left Mandukhai certain that something critically important had happened while they were away.

Yeke and Togochi followed Manduul's guards, leaving Mandukhai and Unebolod on the hilltop alone with Nergui lingering nearby.

"You feel it, too," Unebolod said, watching the small party disappear between gers.

Mandukhai nodded. "Something has changed."

Was there now more than one elephant for the mouse to contend with?

Mandukhai admired the red posts which held up the canopy of the gathering tent: golden gilt-work of twisting birds wrapped around each, the red silks with colored embroidery which bowed out like coiled serpents from each of the birchwood lathes.

Luxury surrounded them everywhere. Beads shined in the dying light of day. Geometric rugs in dark, rich colors covered the floor. Mandukhai couldn't help but see this gathering tent as a new beast, much like Bayan. It displayed an alluring array of colors, but inside something ominous awaited.

All sides of the tent opened today so everyone could pack in to see the Khan's spectacle, even if they could not fit beneath the canopy or get an unobstructed view. Hundreds packed inside with thousands more outside the tent pressing in at the edges. All of Mongke Bulag had converged on this one spot as news of the Great Khan's big announcement spread through camp. Mandukhai had never seen so many of the Khan's people crammed into one space together. The knot of men and women was so tight she had struggled to make her way to the space where her chair would normally await.

Tonight, there were only two chairs, side by side, at the top of the dais. One Manduul used as his throne, and the other was a gilt piece with a brilliant jade cushion. Neither currently held occupants.

Manduul entered, still wearing his white deel, though it seemed cleaner now than it had been when he returned to Mongke Bulag. The white against so much red and deep colors in the tent stood out like a light in the darkness. The crowd parted for Manduul as he made his way toward the dais, climbing the steps before turning to face the large horde.

People had buzzed with excitement all day since Manduul's return. Everyone knew there would be a festival tonight, and they all wanted to know exactly what the Khan had decided they would celebrate. Victory over the Jalair, perhaps? Mandukhai had stopped by Manduul's ger once she returned to camp, asking questions about what had delayed their return, but Manduul stubbornly refused to answer. He could only promise that she would be pleased. Somehow, Mandukhai doubted that would be the case.

Manduul straightened his spine and raised his voice high above the din of the crowd. "Bayan, child of the wolf, come forward."

Mandukhai's heart jumped into her throat. No, nothing good would come of this night. She turned to the entrance along with the rest of the horde and watched as they left a narrow passage for the young man to stroll through.

Bayan made quite an appearance, too. His hair was smooth and woven back in intricate braids that fell down his back and looped over his shoulders. He approached Manduul wearing the same golden deel he'd worn upon his return, and a belt of gold disks with inlaid fiery red stones. It was colorful and brilliant. As he strolled through the tent, the colors reflected off his deel, seeming to rise on one side and set on the other like the sun. The beads that lit the area shimmered mysterious swirls of colors on the gold embroidered birds of his deel, making them look like they came to life on the cloth.

"Bayan fashions himself as a *gonji*." Esige's crescent-moon eyes sparkled as she joked quietly with Mandukhai about him being a princess.

"He is the last of the bone of Genghis Khan," Mandukhai responded in hushed, even tones. "He is more than *gonji*." Her eyes turned to Esige, the bells and jewels of her *boqta* chiming in her ears. Esige had grown a full head taller over the winter months—already nearly as tall as Mandukhai—and she resembled more of the woman she would surely become.

"Bayan," Manduul said. His voice carried across the tent so everyone could hear. "Last true son of the Great Khan, Genghis, you are honored by this court. Though by blood you are my nephew, by bone you are my son."

All of this felt far too formal. Mandukhai understood what Manduul planned. It was inevitable. *I have waited too long to stop this*, she thought as her chest tightened.

Sensing a presence looming behind her, Mandukhai glanced over her shoulder. Unebolod stood at her back, watching with a stony face, though she could see in his eyes that he worried about this gathering just as much as she did. And he should, if her guess was correct.

"Come closer, Bayan." Manduul motioned for Bayan to climb the last two steps.

Bayan obeyed. He kneeled in front of Manduul without urging, and Manduul placed a hand on his head. Unebolod's breath caught behind her. It was a subtle, small sound, easily missed by anyone else, but she understood his heart.

"One week ago, we made a sacred vow beneath the Saqlaqar Tree. We became brothers as one," Manduul said.

This time Mandukhai sucked in a breath. *That was the pilgrimage?* If they made such oaths to each other, that bond would be stronger than her own marriage. A lump swelled in Mandukhai's throat, and she glanced at Yeke across the dais. The other woman watched the two men like a proud mother. Perhaps sensing Mandukhai's eyes on her, Yeke flicked her gaze at Mandukhai, and the corner of her mouth curled up ever so slightly, as if mocking Mandukhai.

"Today," Manduul continued, "we become something more. In the blue sky above, there are the sun and the moon. And on the earth below, there are the Khan and the *Jinong*."

So this is it. Mandukhai clasped her sweating hands together inside the folds of her sleeves. Mandukhai struggled to keep her expression even as her heart hammered against her ribs. This news shouldn't have been shocking—it was inevitable—but Mandukhai had hoped to prevent it. She had hoped for more time.

Bayan was now officially the Prince of Mongols, and Manduul's heir apparent, which meant that Unebolod had just formally been replaced in the line of succession. Mandukhai felt ill and hoped it didn't show on her face. With so few words, so much had changed.

Bayan bowed his head so that Manduul could hang the *paiza* around his neck. The large gold medallion hung from a thick golden chain over Bayan's deel for all to see. "I name you from this day to the end of the Eternal Blue Sky as Bolkhu *Jinong*, the Golden Prince as radiant as the setting sun in which we stand."

The news brought a round of cheers and congratulations from the crowd. The thundering noise hammered into Mandukhai's ears. Warriors raised fists and cheered for their Golden Prince, and Bayan turned to the crowd, beaming as he soaked it all in.

Those ultimate words hammered any potential doubt away. The people would stand behind Bayan before any other. A sinking feeling dropped into the pit of her stomach. Now, Bayan had the right to claim her as his own before any other man when Manduul died.

Mandukhai turned to Unebolod, but he had already gone. Just as quietly as he had slipped in, Unebolod had slipped back out again. Mandukhai and Yeke met each other's gaze from across the dais once more. There was something in the other woman's eyes. Satisfaction. Arrogance. Taunting. Victory.

"Mandukhai…" Esige's voice was tinged with worry.

Mandukhai simply looked at the girl with a serene gaze. What could they do? Manduul had spoken. It was done.

"Rise, Bolkhu *Jinong*, so we may rule these lands together," Manduul said.

Together. Mandukhai felt everything she had worked so hard for over the last year come crashing down. *I am not yet bested.* "Stay," she whispered to Esige. "Observe. Charm him. We need Bayan on our side."

Esige nodded and Mandukhai pushed her way through the horde to where Bayan stood, surrounded by doting Mongols. They parted for the Khan's wife.

Bayan turned to face her, his back straight and proud beside Manduul. The medallion shined in the dying sunlight, catching on the eyes of the wolf at the head of the medallion. Her eyes glanced over the embossed script, but she could not read most of it. Only a few words: *power, order, Khan, Prince, offence.* Still, those few words told her more than enough. Bayan was officially protected under the Great Khan no matter where he went, and acting against him would be as if the offender acted against the Great Khan himself.

Mandukhai nodded to him, making the jewels on her crown chime. "May you rise up like the sun," Mandukhai told Bayan.

"And from the east," he said. The way his eyes sparkled with greedy pleasure was unsettling, and the manner with which they ravaged her made the hair on her skin rise. Mandukhai would either die with the changing of the Khans, or she would be brought into Bayan's ger as a wife. The very thought of his arrogant hands touching her made her skin crawl.

"My people," Manduul called out, raising a cup of *airag* high in the air. "Tonight, we feast to mark this momentous day!"

The festivities marking Bayan's new title were livelier and rowdier than Mandukhai's wedding had been. While she wanted to be upset by this, she also understood that the people had cause for celebration. For the first time in over ten years, they had an official line of succession, and a Golden Prince to thank the sky father for.

Not a single corner of Mongke Bulag was without food, drink, wrestling, games, or dancing. Celebration carried across all parts of the capital. Musicians and poets shared songs and stories, raising their voices above the din to regale the heroics of the new prince against the Jalair, and the promise of a bright future with an heir apparent. The Jalair who were sent to Mongke Bulag after each submission joined in the celebrations but kept to their own tribe outside the rings of Khorchin, Khorlod, and Borjigin tribe members.

Older boys partook in drinks with their friends and fathers. Some of them challenged each other to wrestling matches or morning hunts. Girls fawned over the boys, bringing in drinks and food and sultry words to win affections. Dancers congregated around the main gathering spaces close to the Great Khan and his Golden Prince. Such flirtatious festivity would see a boom in children a few months from now, and Mandukhai felt a surge of jealousy. Not because she wanted Manduul's child, but because she wanted an heir ... or an escape to be with the man she truly loved. Throughout the night, Mandukhai stayed close to Manduul for as long as decorum required.

When the feast began, Unebolod joined the celebration, and his expression was more unreadable than ever, as if something inside of him had died and he felt nothing at all. Her heart broke for him. But he was a Wang, a noble descendant of Khasar, not Genghis. His rule would have always been contested as long as a true heir existed. She wanted to speak to him but knew that now was not the time.

Men of every rank in the tribes came to Bayan, offering trinkets to honor his newfound power or an oath to follow him as they followed Manduul. The oaths bothered Mandukhai more than any of the other gifts. Breaking an oath was punishable by death or banishment—Bayan's choice. And every oath sworn to him stripped a little more of the power Unebolod had collected over the years. This new position left Mandukhai with only three options.

A child of her own with Manduul.

An alliance with Bayan.

Or Bayan's death and the subsequent end of the Borjigin royal line.

None of these options appealed to Mandukhai.

As the evening wore on, she observed Unebolod with Togochi and the other men, drinking and eating and appearing as if the stars had aligned. An act, and she knew it.

As the gifts and oaths dwindled, Unebolod left the cramped space. Mandukhai yearned to follow, but by the time an opportunity had presented itself, he strode back into the knotted mass of bodies. What he carried with him made her heart leap into her throat.

The black *sulde* of Genghis Khan, passed down through the generations to men of rank for stewardship. The sacred black horsehair banner ruffled in the wind. As Unebolod marched through the horde of men and women gathered, a hush fell over the crowd, and they parted as if Genghis himself passed among them. All eyes locked on the *sulde*. He stopped in front of Bayan and thrust the pole of the banner into the ground. Mandukhai heard Bayan breathe in sharply beside her, then rose to his feet.

"Bolkhu *Jinong*, I present you with the *sulde* of our people just as Manduul presented it to me. It now belongs to you," Unebolod said. "May you protect it and our people with all the fierceness of a pack of wolves, as I have done these past ten years."

Mandukhai covered her alarm by taking a slow drink of *boal*. This action could be misconstrued as a slap in Manduul's face, as if he said, *Manduul no longer sees me worthy of this, so I hope you are up to the task.*

Bayan ran a reverent hand along the pole. Firelight licked at his golden gaze as he admired the *sulde* with respectful awe. Bayan held his hand out to Unebolod. "May you ride beside me to share your knowledge and strength when we need it."

Unebolod's jaw twitched slightly, then he grasped Bayan's arm and shook. Bayan pulled him close and thumped his back, which Unebolod mimicked, and as he did, his dark eyes bore right into Mandukhai's soul. Her breath hitched at the intensity.

"I will serve the people however the Khan sees fit," Unebolod said, drawing back. It was a careful skirting of an oath of loyalty to Bayan, but no one else seemed to notice.

As the crowd closed in around Bayan and the *sulde*, Unebolod faded back into the mass until he disappeared. A moment later, lively music broke through the night. Mandukhai glanced over at Manduul and saw Yeke sitting so close she melted into his side. Mandukhai grimaced. A race for an heir would only become more fierce between the two of them now. Any son they had with Manduul could challenge Bayan's right when he came of age. Mandukhai could probably steal Manduul's attention away from Yeke easily enough—he seemed to prefer his second wife over his first—but more than anything else, Mandukhai wanted to speak to Unebolod. As the dancers came out and the space opened for them to captivate the attention of the crowd, Mandukhai slipped away.

"Enjoy yourself tonight," Mandukhai whispered to Nergui as she passed him. "No one will harm me on a night such as tonight."

Nergui looked like he wanted to protest, but he also had his fair share of *airag* already and instead belched in response as she walked away.

When she reached Unebolod's ger, even his dog was gone. No weapons hung on pegs beside the door. No fire lit the stove. Where would he go? Mandukhai passed three rings of wrestling in her search. Music played in every corner of the capital. As one song faded out, another faded in from elsewhere. Men and women had already entered their gers to warm each other's beds, and she heard the sounds from within several as she passed.

Kids ran around all over Mongke Bulag as she continued her search. They chased dogs, played knucklebones, or pretended to be warriors on the hunt, chasing each other with sticks and slings. Everyone who noticed her passing bowed respectfully and stepped aside. The attention soured her mood, and she pulled off her *boqta*, tossing it into her ger and shaking her hair loose. If anyone said anything about it, Mandukhai could easily excuse her lack of crown with a comment about the excitement of the night.

But the farther she walked, the more certain she became Unebolod was not in Mongke Bulag anymore. He wouldn't abandon his oath. He had too much honor for that. But would he consider it?

Bayan's new title meant that the Golden Prince and Yeke could align together, get rid of the Khan, and place themselves in power. Bayan was already named heir, and no one would contest his right. Aligning with Yeke would also secure him the same loyalty from Bigirsen that Manduul enjoyed. Assuming Yeke won his favor. Yeke would make certain Mandukhai disappeared forever once that happened. Hopefully Bayan took his sacred oath to Manduul seriously enough that he would not kill him now.

At the edge of Mongke Bulag, Mandukhai stopped and scanned the darkness beyond, then circled the edge of the capital to find any hint of

Unebolod's passing. She checked the ground for tracks or clues to his passage, but so many people milled around tonight that she couldn't distinguish his trail from anyone else. Eventually, she gave up and approached the river. Perhaps a dip would do her some good.

When a dog growled near the small copse of trees beside the water, she knew she'd found Unebolod. No one else would in this place, so far from the capital, with their dog when there was such jubilation in Mongke Bulag.

Unebolod stood at the edge of the river, arms crossed, gazing toward the mountains. Nearby, goats, sheep, horses, and yaks grazed freely. He loved the river, she had learned, so it should have been no surprise this was where he'd come to clear his head. Right now, Mandukhai knew his mind must be reeling. With the new official title and the responsibility for the *sulde* taken away, Unebolod was little more than an *orlok* without a war to fight. There was no title for him so long as the Golden Prince survived. There was no killing the *jinong*. Unebolod had too much honor for that.

Unebolod whistled sharply, and Kilgor stopped growling then trotted toward the river to lap up cool, fresh water.

"I still need you," she said, stopping beside him and looking out at forest across the way. This was the same place they first spoke. The same place he had given her the bow. "More than ever."

"I know." His gaze didn't shift.

Moonlight cast the landscape in an eerie, yet beautiful, glow. Mandukhai admired the beauty of the world, allowing it to wash away her own reeling thoughts.

"They will not waste much time," she said at last.

Unebolod didn't respond.

She looked at him, waiting for something, anything, to reassure her churning stomach. He offered nothing. "We will need to be prepared for your claim for the khanship. It could be necessary any day."

He let out a sigh that misted in the cool air. "There will be no claim."

"But—"

"There will be no claim, Mandukhai." Unebolod turned so he was looking squarely at her, his dark eyes mysterious pooled shadows, untouched by the moonlight, but she felt them just the same. "You know as well as I do it wouldn't work. The people are drawn to the *jinong* like a flock of sheep to a flowering field. They wouldn't follow me." Unebolod drew inward in thought for a moment, then stepped closer. "If ever there was a time for truth and trust, it's now."

Mandukhai's breath caught. "What do you mean?"

"I have spent most of my life following Manduul, watching as he grew tired and fat, as he took everything for himself. And he promised I would be his successor. It isn't the first promise he's broken. It won't be the last." His hand slid along her neck and cupped her face. Mandukhai's face heated at his touch like a fire burning into her flesh. "He has taken everything, but there is one thing I can take back."

Mandukhai had to swallow a lump of excitement that formed in her throat. "What does this have to do with trust and truth?"

"I haven't felt so strongly about anyone since Odsar died," he said, edging closer.

She could feel the heat radiating off his body, seeping into her bones. She could see his eyes burning with such intensity she feared it would consume her whole.

"I have felt nothing for any other women, if I'm being truthful. But the moment I saw you, an arrow lodged into my heart and I haven't been able to dislodge it, no matter how hard I've tried." His lips were so close. She knew she should pull away, but he trapped her under that burning gaze. "I'm done trying."

Unebolod's lips brushed against hers, as if testing whether this was what he wanted. Before she could catch her breath, he pulled her against him and pressed his lips firmly against her own with so much passion it instantly consumed them in a burst of fire. Mandukhai knew she should stop, but she didn't want to. High Heavens help her, she didn't want to. Instead of retreating, she submitted, melting into his arms, his kiss, his touch.

For a year, Mandukhai had searched for the right words to share with him at the right moment. Now all those words felt inadequate. Instead, she kissed Unebolod to show him, slow and longing and digging for more. Her fingers traced along his neck and thick braids. He moaned against her lips, running his hands along her spine and hips. It sent a thrill of heat straight through every fiber of her body. Mandukhai's lips broke away, trailing along his jaw. She relished the sound of his breath catching sharply.

"Mandukhai," he breathed out her name like a sacred thing, then pulled back sharply and took her hand, pulling her into the shadows of the trees. He sat in the leafy remnants of winter, pulling her into his lap. His hands searched along her hips and knees, where they found the edge of her silk deel, dancing along her legs underneath.

Mandukhai knew they should stop, that if anyone discovered them, they would both be dead before dawn, but she no longer cared. In this one, glorious moment, she was in control of her own fate. Instead of retreating, Mandukhai moved her hands along his chest and down to unfasten his belt, then worked the buttons on the deel until it slid from his muscular shoulders. She touched the scarred skin. Unebolod pulled back tentatively, his dark eyes pools of water in the moonlight. And for a moment she thought she saw fear in them.

"Do I frighten you?" she asked, tracing a set of scars along his chest.

"More than you could ever know." His fingers grazed the skin of her legs. "Are you sure about this?"

No one had ever asked that before. Manduul had simply assumed it, expected it. The difference was alarming. Mandukhai wasn't certain of anything. What tomorrow would bring, or if either of them would live long enough to find out, but she was certain of this. She knew she had wanted it just as long as he had. Mandukhai didn't answer. She unbuttoned her deel and let the silk slide down her body.

"I trust you," she said.

He laid her on the ground, kissing her with fierce hunger, kissing the corners of her mouth, as his hands explored every bit of her skin. His hand slid between her thighs and she gasped against his mouth, feeling a rush of excitement she had never known before and digging her nails into his back. It was exciting and dangerous.

For tonight, she succumbed to the urges she had fought so long to suppress.

CHAPTER TWENTY-FIVE

A QUESTION OF OATHS

Mandukhai had been certain someone would discover what she and Unebolod had done, and for days she lived in constant fear. Her ears were more alert than ever, listening for sounds of coming doom. She warned Nergui to remain more vigilant than ever, using the excuse that, with a new heir to the title, someone might attempt to kill her or Manduul to secure Yeke's place in the next regime—or Bigirsen's place. He accepted her excuse easily and even eyed Esige with more wariness. She had come from Yeke's court, he had said. When she and Unebolod were near each other, neither showed any outward signs that anything had changed, but deep inside, she knew everything had changed.

The first time Manduul came to her bed after returning with Bayan, Mandukhai had spent half the time afraid he would kill her the moment he finished. Yet nothing happened. Manduul seemed a changed man, revived by Bayan's presence, and his attitude was lighter and more tender than ever before, his spirit younger. Once she'd survived the first night, Mandukhai realized no one else was the wiser, and it made her wonder ... could she do it again? Would Unebolod want to?

Much to her relief, her blood came not long after her rendezvous with Unebolod. In the week that followed, Mandukhai went about her business as usual. Sitting in meetings with Manduul and Bayan. Advising them when she felt it necessary. Bayan dug his way under her skin, disagreeing with most of what she offered. In nearly every instance, Manduul sided with Bayan. This boy had taken a hold over Manduul during their time away, and she hated him for it.

During one meeting, Mandukhai grew more irritable by the moment as they spoke of other tribes, such as the Oirat, who encroached on the Khan's borders. Bayan had tasted victory, it seemed, and wanted more. He did not seem to understand that the Oirat were far different from the Jalair. They had been a burr under the Borjigin skin for centuries.

"There must be some way we can show them who their Khan is," Bayan said, his face animated as he held out his cup for a servant to refill.

Manduul had placed Bayan's seat—his throne—right beside Manduul's own as if they were equals, ruling the Nation together. Another detail that slowly drove Mandukhai to madness.

"Perhaps you might ride out against the Oirat encroaching on our borders," she said irritably, fighting off the surge of anger growing in her chest. "And kill them all instead of bartering for peace." Not that they would succeed against the Oirat without more men, or that she meant this as a serious suggestion.

Bayan threw up his hands. "At last, she speaks with wisdom."

Mandukhai flinched. *He thinks I am genuine?* "You cannot be serious."

"Very." Bayan leaned forward, resting an arm on his leg. "I'm glad to hear you come to your senses. The Oirat need to respect our boundaries, and if they can't we must show them their error."

Mandukhai's breath quickened. Her hands clenched in fists within the sleeves of her deel. Blood and death. That was all these men understood. "If you are so eager to start a war, what are you waiting for then, Bayan?"

Manduul growled low in his throat. He had renamed Bayan, as was tradition for a Khan but not a prince, when he officially named him and Manduul insisted everyone call Bayan by his new name.

"Bolkhu," Mandukhai spit the name out.

"So much tension between the two of you." Manduul sounded amused, and a vicious grin spread across his face. "Perhaps when Bolkhu returns from taming the petulant Oirat he can tame you, too."

Mandukhai balked, sitting more stiffly in her seat. Her razor-sharp eyes cut into Manduul. "I am your wife and queen, not a concubine or whore."

"We are one," Bayan said, grinning at her confidently. "Sworn beneath the sacred tree."

Mandukhai took a few deep breaths to steady her racing heart. Men did not often give their wives to other men, but the strange bond between Manduul and Bayan concerned Mandukhai. Would he truly allow Bayan to bed her? Suddenly worried, she surged to her feet and stormed toward the exit. "Send your other half against the Oirat," she snapped at Manduul. "And when he does not return, you will know your mistake."

Their laughter fueled her rage as she burst out the door into the early summer sun. A new balance of power had developed while she had been busy agonizing over her own betrayal. Manduul did not treat Bayan as a prince. He treated Bayan as an equal. She had been so overwrought with worry that she hadn't noticed the change until now. Manduul ruled those within Mongke Bulag. Bayan ruled those outside the Khan's borders.

Perhaps when Bayan rides away this time, he will not return, she thought as she returned to her ger with Nergui trailing alongside her. She and Esige had work to do.

Bayan relished his new position with Manduul. Where before Manduul had treated him like a boy who needed to learn about the Nation, since returning from the Jalair campaign Manduul instead treated Bayan like an equal. Their bond felt deeper than simple brotherhood. Manduul never questioned Bayan's decisions unless they directly affected him or Mongke Bulag. Mandukhai questioned everything, and it chaffed at Bayan's skin. Over and over, she attempted to undermine his authority with Manduul, tried to sway her husband away from the decisions that would strengthen his hold on the Nation. She didn't understand Mongol men. They needed battle. They needed blood. Without it, they grew lazy and aggressive at home.

The comment Manduul made about taming Mandukhai had taken Bayan by surprise, though he hid it very well from either of them. Sharing his duties with Bayan was one thing. Sharing his favorite wife was another.

As soon as Mandukhai left, and their laughter death died down, Bayan turned a curious eye to Manduul. "You wouldn't really have me tame your wives, would you?"

Manduul shrugged. "Yeke is so ugly I can't look at her, and so docile that when I do, she puts me to sleep. Mandukhai is a wild mare who refuses to be tamed. Maybe she needs two of us to finally break her."

Bayan shifted in his chair, staring at the closed door. She undoubtedly was beautiful—Bayan hadn't seen a woman as beautiful as her—but she would certainly put up a fierce fight. Though, if Mandukhai turned out anywhere near as vigorous as Altan had been, it might be worthwhile to try. Just thinking about the Jalair woman aroused him, and he shifted again in his chair.

"Either way, when I pass from this life, both of them will be your problem," Manduul said.

By tradition, Mandukhai and Yeke would become Bayan's wives—since they were not his blood. He would inherit them upon Manduul's death. *Yet another reason to ally with Yeke and perhaps a good reason to tame Mandukhai before that day came*, he thought, gazing into his cup.

Manduul stood and stretched his back, signaling the end of their meeting. "Take your men and ride out to meet the Oirat scum along our borders. I will join you again. It's time we remind them who rules this Nation."

Bayan stood as well, bowing ever so slightly to Manduul before marching out the door. He knew he should be thinking about the fight against the Oirat, but his mind was swirling with images of the Khan's wives. Mandukhai would sooner kill him as let him touch her, unless he could find some way to get on her good side. Yeke was not as ugly as Manduul made her out to be.

By the time he reached his ger, Bayan paused, wondering if he should visit Yeke and test the waters. Manduul gave her so little attention that Yeke would probably fall into Bayan's arms.

As if summoned by his thoughts, Yeke glided past with her servant. Yeke's brown eyes examined him sharply. Bayan didn't back down. Instead, he allowed his gaze to linger, examining her darker skin, and imagined how long those legs must be under her deel. Perhaps when he returned, he could find out. His stare must have revealed some of his thoughts, because her cheeks flushed, and she turned her attention elsewhere, clearly trying to look at anything but him.

Yes, he would find out if Manduul meant what he said. He needed Yeke on his side if he would survive her father.

Once more, Mandukhai had been left catching up as Manduul and Bayan prepared to ride out against the Oirat. Their idiocy knew no bounds, it seemed. Subjugating the Jalair was one thing. The Oirat were no small tribe. They controlled much of the west, and dozens of minor tribes followed the

Oirat and Uyghur leaders. The Oirat just might declare this an act of war.

Despite Mandukhai's furious protests, Manduul left with Bayan, taking a full *tumen* of ten thousand men along as they rode west.

Mandukhai approached the men as Manduul mounted his horse to go.

Unebolod paced alongside the Khan, his shoulders tight with fury. "Am I no longer *orlok* of your northern forces, Manduul? Am I still your brother?"

"You are," Manduul said evenly. "On both counts."

Mandukhai slowed her step, listening as she approached.

"Then why do you leave me behind like this again?"

Manduul nudged his mount closer to Unebolod and placed a hand on his shoulder. "I am honoring you, brother. I can trust no other man to watch over my Nation while I am away."

Unebolod shrugged off Manduul's hand and stepped back. "I live to serve my Lord Khan." He bowed, almost mockingly, then turned on his heel and stormed past Mandukhai. As he passed her, his gaze locked on her and a surge of heat rushed through her body. It only lasted a moment, but it proved long enough.

Mandukhai dipped her head as she approached Manduul.

He reached down as she stopped beside his horse and took her hand, pressing his dry lips against it. "Will you please talk him down, my love?" Manduul asked as he pulled his lips away. "I worry he does not understand why I must leave him, and you have such a way with words."

"I am uncertain I understand why you ride either," Mandukhai admitted. "But I will do my best to calm him."

Manduul patted her hand, then released. She stepped back, shooting a dirty look at Bayan as she caught him leering openly at her. Did he truly think Manduul's comment about taming her had been serious? *I will have to be certain he knows the truth of it, if he returns.*

The men rode away, and Mandukhai turned to seek Unebolod. Yeke stood nearby, watching Mandukhai with unbridled bitterness.

Unebolod had been easy to find. He stood on the training grounds, inspecting the equipment.

"Give us space to speak in private," Mandukhai ordered Nergui. "Manduul wants me to calm him and he won't be placated with you looming at my shoulder."

Nergui grimaced, but he stopped at the edge of the training ground and simply watched from a distance.

As Mandukhai approached, all the tension in his body was apparent by the way his deel seemed to strain over his broad shoulders. Mandukhai stepped around him, noting the way the vein in his neck throbbed.

"He sent me to talk you down," she said in amusement.

Unebolod's dark eyes flashed as he turned his attention to her. He glanced around, giving Nergui a suspicious glare, and kept his voice low as he spoke. "I always knew Manduul had a weakness for choosing his battles, but this is different."

"I understand," Mandukhai said. "But we have to trust that he will not die."

Unebolod huffed and thrust an arrow he had inspected back into the copper pot at his feet. "The issue is not whether he dies, but whether they live. Mandukhai, if they succeed again and return triumphant against the Oirat without me, it will only further solidify Bolkhu's place and further diminish my own. Manduul must know that. Yet, if they don't return this time..."

Mandukhai nodded. If Bayan and Manduul died, only Bigirsen would stand in Unebolod's way. *If they don't return this time, we can finally be together without hiding.* Yet every battle Bayan won without Unebolod in the field alongside them was also another battle Unebolod lost. And defeating the Oirat was no small feat.

The last time Manduul and Bayan rode off together had been torture for Unebolod. Mandukhai saw that tension in him increase with each passing week. Could he handle it again? *I will have to keep him distracted until we know Manduul and Bayan's fates*, she thought.

Mandukhai's hand twitched, eager to reach out and touch him, hold him, feel him, but she knew she could not. At least, not here in the open with Nergui staring at them, unblinking. She kept her voice low, though no one else was close enough to hear her. "Meet me tonight, a mile northwest. There's a bramble along a rock wall—"

"I know the place," he said. The slope of his shoulders increased as he released some of his tension.

Mandukhai nodded, and as she passed him by, offered a sympathetic pat on the arm that even Nergui could not see as anything more than innocent. Yet as her hand touched his arm, she felt his muscles relax.

The night guards Manduul posted around her ger proved predictable, allowing her to calculate the best time to leave her ger without detection. It was a skill she had learned not long after arriving in Mongke Bulag when she more seriously considered disappearing into the night.

Tonight, Mandukhai slipped out unnoticed, tiptoeing through the shadows so no one would notice the movement. She had waited for Nergui to leave his shift for the night before saddling Dust. Her guards had asked what she was doing, but Mandukhai gave them a dressing down for questioning her they would not soon forget.

Getting past the night watch was trickier. Mandukhai had to wait for the man to turn his attention away from her, then ride out quickly and quietly. Her heart hammered against her chest as she left Mongke Bulag. Would they spot her? She didn't dare glance back.

When she arrived at the bramble wall, a sense of freedom washed over Mandukhai. The surrounding briars provided enough cover to block them from sight. Mandukhai hobbled Dust around the edge of the rock wall, beside Unebolod's own mount. He had arrived before her. A surge of excitement rushed through her as Mandukhai ducked into the briars. The patch curved against a rock wall, providing thick, impenetrable cover.

Unebolod turned to her as she entered the space. His head nearly touched the rocks that curved out over their heads. Just laying eyes on him, out here, alone, caused everything inside of Mandukhai to burn with pleasure. Unebolod closed the gap between them in just a few strides, then crushed her body against him as his lips crashed into hers. The intensity of the moment made Mandukhai's head spin with delight, and she returned the kiss eagerly. Every brush of his lips against her flesh, every touch of his fingers against her body burned into Mandukhai, causing her to yearn for more.

High Heavens, please let them die and never return, she thought as Unebolod slid her deel off her shoulders, pressing his lips to her collarbone.

Unebolod waited beneath the branches of Mandukhai's favorite birch tree. After that first night in the briar patch, Mandukhai and Unebolod continued to meet under the cover of night several times a week, far enough away from Mongke Bulag that no one would stumble across them, giving in to their passion. If anyone caught the two of them, Manduul would certainly have them killed. The risk was worth the reward, though it meant they needed to exercise extra caution. Each time, they would meet in a different location, and they never left together. Unebolod had shared the best places around watch to slip away without notice. He knew the men and their routines well, and it provided them safe passage to exploit that sort of knowledge.

Around others, they gave nothing away. When they were alone, they gave away everything to each other. Each act had been deeply intimate, and he counted the moments until the next. Their time wore thin, though. To his knowledge, Manduul and Bayan had not yet died, and Unebolod began to think the High Heavens would never answer his prayers. Regardless, tonight he would enjoy his time with her again as if it were the last—as it very well could have been.

Unebolod laid out the furs in the dark, listening for her approach, and was rewarded by the familiar sound of Dust's hooves. He had grown used to the sound of her stallion's hooves against the ground, the rhythm as unique as the rider. Dust had a lighter step when he trotted, like a whisper over the grassy steppe. Unebolod checked his bow. It lay on an oiled cloth beside the furs, ready for use should they encounter trouble.

Mandukhai dismounted and tethered Dust to the tree beside his own pony. The moment she turned, she fell against him. Her lips pressed to his. They gave in to their passion swiftly, and when it was over, she rested her head against his chest, tracing a long scar along his ribs. He loved the way she touched his skin.

Mandukhai shuddered against him. Unebolod pulled up the fur to ward off the midnight chill, then pulled her closer against him, reveling in the feel of her flesh against his. He did not regret any of this. Manduul had taken everything from him. But this ... this he could seize for himself. She chose Unebolod. Even if they couldn't be together yet, they had this.

Yet something about the way Mandukhai rested against him tonight was more reserved than normal. "Something bothers you tonight," he said, his breath ruffling the hair on the top of her head. "Speak."

Mandukhai released a shaky breath. "I have missed my blood."

Unebolod's muscles tensed beneath her touch. His grip on her body tightened. For several long minutes, he couldn't draw breath. *She's with child?* he thought. There was no question who the child belonged to. Manduul had been gone since her last blood. Despite the surge of fear that rushed through him, he also felt a flash of satisfaction. He had managed what Manduul could not.

"Une. Please say something."

He swallowed so hard he was sure she could hear the lump in his throat bob. "Are you sure?"

"Fairly certain, yes. If he doesn't return soon . . ."

Unebolod nodded, understanding. She could claim it was Manduul's child if he returned soon enough. Otherwise, everyone would know it was not, and it wouldn't take long before everyone looked his way. This child put them both in perilous danger. And yet, it was everything he wanted. Another chance at having a son. If anyone threatened her or the child, he would bring down the mountains on their heads.

Mandukhai shifted, resting her chin on his chest and gazing at him. Lines of worry etched across her usually smooth face, and he tried to brush them away. "I'm scared, Une."

"Don't be." His voice took on a sharp edge. "If either of them lays a hand on you, I will kill them both."

"That's exactly what I'm afraid of." Mandukhai propped herself up on her arms as she frowned at him. Her hair cascaded around her face and he tucked it away. "Not for their sakes, but for yours. Bayan has a lot of support in the camp now."

"I haven't lost all of mine yet." He brushed a thumb over her cheek. A child. His child. It had been a long time since Unebolod knew joy quite like this.

Her lips thinned as they usually did when she turned to serious business. "We need to be smart, and careful."

"We will be."

"If Manduul doesn't return soon, I will have to abort, or he will kill us both."

Unebolod fell silent again, running a hand down her back with the other propped under his head. Abort? No. That was not an option. He would protect her and the child. *I would have to break my oath to Manduul to protect them,* Unebolod thought bitterly. Thankfully, that should not be an issue.

"He won't be long," he said at last. "I've received reports this morning they are preparing to return, and when he does—" He sighed so heavily it made the ground beneath them rumble. He couldn't put words to what they both knew she must do.

Mandukhai shook her head. "I don't want to."

"You have to," he insisted. "To save the child. He will believe it is his, and our child will take that runt's title. And when the time comes, and Manduul dies, I will challenge Bayan's claim and adopt the child as my own. No one will know."

"When the time comes." Mandukhai jerked sharply back, sitting up and yanking her deel over her shoulders.

Why is she angry with me? It left Unebolod suddenly cold.

"When the time comes," she repeated sharply. "We keep using those words, but they mean nothing." She flipped her hair out of the collar of her silk deel and began fastening the buttons. "You have said as much yourself. You will not kill them and start a war. When the time comes, if it ever comes, we will both be old, and he will raise our child as his own. It will be too late."

Mandukhai wasn't angry at him for waiting, he realized. She was upset because she was afraid that day would never arrive—a fear he shared.

"Don't." Unebolod sat up, taking one of her wrists in each of his hands to stop her. Mandukhai tugged from his grip, stubbornly resisting. She was building up that wall he had only just broken through. "Mandukhai, stop. What would you have me do? You have cautioned that we need to be patient, and you're right. This child cannot change that."

Tears rolled down Mandukhai's cheeks, making his heart ache. He loathed being the reason she cried. "I don't want him raising our child," she protested, and he could see her fight to hold herself together. "I want our child to grow as strong as steel, like his father. If left to Manduul, he will become fat and lazy." She tried to hold in a sob. "I want you."

"I know." Unebolod pulled her toward him, and Mandukhai initially strained to pull away but swiftly gave in, sagging against his chest and shaking. He stroked her hair. Somehow, he had to end this, for both of their sakes. He had to find some way to free her from this prison so they could finally be together. "Give me some time to think. I will come up with some plan."

Though he did not know what he could do short of killing both Manduul and Bayan. One he could handle. The other he had sworn to protect, and his word was iron. If he broke his vow to Manduul, Unebolod would be worthless to her.

Mandukhai eased back, and he tumbled into the shimmering dark pools of her gaze. Unebolod pressed his forehead to hers. "My heart is full," he whispered.

"As is mine," she replied.

Unebolod's heart was full and broken. He may have to choose between his oaths to his Khan and his child. It was a terrible choice to face, and he had to choose with caution.

Mandukhai and Unebolod remained under the tree together for as long as they dared, reveling in this moment of bliss before it could be ripped away. They lay until the sky promised a new day coming.

Mandukhai returned to camp first, and he watched Dust disappear into the dark toward Mongke Bulag before packing up. As he fastened the last of the furs on the back of his horse, the horn sounded to the south. Unebolod frowned. If he squinted, he could almost see far enough to watch the rider leave the capital headed south, followed swiftly by an *arban* of ten men.

Excited for a fight, eager to take his frustration out on someone, he jumped on his mount and kicked her into action. In seconds, he galloped to join the thrill of the chase.

CHAPTER TWENTY-SIX

LION IN THE WOLF S DEN

Togochi and his nine men encircled the small party that had approached Mongke Bulag. As Unebolod approached, Togochi was already deep in conversation with the newcomers. They drew none of their weapons, which disappointed Unebolod greatly. The party was small, its own *arban* of men with two familiar faces among them.

Bigirsen grimaced irritably at Togochi as Unebolod wedged his mare into a gap between two mounts. Beside Bigirsen, his young protégé, Issama, sat in the saddle with his perpetually calculating gaze. Bigirsen's sharp eyes shot at Unebolod.

"You allowed Manduul to ride into conquest without you?" Bigirsen's tone chaffed Unebolod's skin. He had no love at all for this man.

"Allowed?" Unebolod snorted. "Since when do we allow Khans permission to do things?"

Bigirsen glowered. "You are *orlok*."

"He has other men, and they have gone with him."

"Against the Oirat, no less!" Bigirsen's voice lifted into the air and carried. "Manduul's peace with them is tenuous, at best. They will not accept this insult!"

Unebolod's jaw twitched. "Do you not hold sway among them? Is it not your duty to ensure the Oirat understand why the Khan does what he does, and what is expected of them? Were they not creeping on the Khan's borders, this would not have happened. Manduul went to clarify who they answer to."

"Along with this Golden Prince I've heard about?" Bigirsen's saddle creaked as he shifted menacingly. Others might find him intimidating, but Unebolod had no fear of him. Bigirsen's power was stolen and false. Before Unebolod decided about how to handle Manduul and Bayan, he would rip Bigirsen's power away. And Bayan just might be the answer.

"He is a son of Borjigin royal blood," Unebolod said, making sure his warning came out clearly. "Do you doubt his right to be the Golden Prince?"

"Do you?" The question implied well enough that Bigirsen knew Unebolod coveted Bayan's position.

Unebolod was quite pleased not to flinch at the insinuation. Bigirsen was a menace and certainly a problem to be dealt with, but he was not an idiot. He knew Unebolod had been next in line until Bayan arrived. Unebolod did not doubt for a moment that an assassin would come for him the moment the Khan died. Bayan might be simple enough to mold, but Unebolod would never bow to Bigirsen, and Bigirsen knew that.

Bigirsen nodded to Issama, who turned his mount and rode back the way they came. "My people will set up camp here and await the Khan's return."

"We extend all Guest Rights to you, Bigirsen," Togochi said.

Unebolod wanted to punch Togochi for extending the offer. While it was formally expected, offering such protection was not required and Unebolod wished Togochi had not spoken up. Guest Rights would prevent Unebolod from threatening Bigirsen. *Unless he threatens the Khan or his family,* Unebolod thought. Perhaps he could use that to manipulate Bigirsen into making a critical mistake.

"As the Khan's Vice Regent, I expect as much," Bigirsen said, kicking his mount forward toward Mongke Bulag. "Now I will see my daughter. I hope this winter was kind to her."

Unebolod turned to ride beside Bigirsen, refusing to enter behind the Vice Regent. After all, until Manduul returned, Unebolod was acting Regent, which ranked him above Bigirsen.

Mandukhai knew Unebolod would be waiting in the gathering tent for Bigirsen to make an appearance after checking in on Yeke. Unebolod had said little about the Uyghur appearance, but with Manduul and Bayan gone it was important that Unebolod assert himself as the one in charge as Manduul had mandated. Bigirsen would surely try to seize control if Unebolod waited too long.

Mandukhai's position gave her more freedom to move around. As Unebolod waited in the gathering tent, Mandukhai sent Esige to Yeke's ger with a bucket of fuel for the stove, a task the girl sometimes assisted both women with. Esige was to listen as she delivered the fuel and report back to Mandukhai.

Meanwhile, Mandukhai changed into a fine silk deel of jade with red and gold embroidery around the collar and trim. Her hand lingered over the small chest of gifts Bigirsen had given her as a wedding gift. Inside, precious, rich jewels from the western realms were set into necklaces and bracelets. She had only opened this chest twice before—when he had given the gift and when she put away a necklace Yeke forced her to wear months ago.

With a sigh of determination, Mandukhai flipped open the lid. She would give no power to Bigirsen by wearing any of these jewels today, only the illusion of power. Mandukhai removed a jade necklace and let it hang low around her neck. The white and green smokey round disk the size of her fist dangled from a silver chain. A pure green stone the size of her thumbnail had been fitted into the center of the disk. The pendant hung precariously in the air just below her bosom. She then clipped on matching earrings a fraction of the size and adjusted her *boqta* on her head.

As Mandukhai slipped on a few carefully selected rings from the chest, Esige returned from her errand. Mandukhai simply raised a questioning brow at the girl.

"Lord Bigirsen is angry about the Golden Prince," Esige said once she was sure the door had closed securely behind her. Something about the way she shifted away from the door, glancing over her shoulder as if followed, raised Mandukhai's suspicions.

"Out with it."

Esige licked her lips and lowered her voice to a pitch Mandukhai had to edge closer to hear. "He wants her to earn Bolkhu's trust, by any means necessary."

"Did he ask her to kill Bolkhu?" Mandukhai asked. That could benefit her right now. If Bigirsen or Yeke were responsible for Bayan's death, the people would revolt against Bigirsen, and possibly Yeke as well. It also paved the way for Mandukhai's child to become Great Khan. And just what would Yeke do to befriend Bayan? Her own father was asking her to risk her life.

"No. He was very careful not to say as much." Esige glanced toward the door again. "But the hint that an heir from a Borjigin would be necessary was pretty heavy. I believe he wants her to have a child with either of them."

Mandukhai should have expected as much. Yeke had been unsuccessful with Manduul, but perhaps with Bayan things would change.

"He also asked about Unebolod," Esige reported.

Mandukhai stiffened. She did her best to act as indifferent to this news as possible. "What of him?"

"Lord Bigirsen wanted to know if Unebolod had seemed to be making any moves to remove either Manduul or Bolkhu," Esige said.

Mandukhai almost snorted in response. Unebolod may want the title, but he was infuriatingly loyal. If Mandukhai couldn't tempt him into it, nothing would. "Which only proves he doesn't understand Unebolod at all. He is as loyal as they come." *Even if he is sleeping with the Khan's wife.* Mandukhai fought to smother her smile. "Anything else?"

"He dismissed me before I could hear more, but he will be headed to meet with Unebolod soon," Esige said.

Mandukhai nodded. "Get cleaned up and changed. We are joining them."

Esige retreated a step. "Can I ask why?"

"He has taken something precious from both of us," Mandukhai said somberly. "I intend to return the favor."

Esige raised her tumultuous gaze to meet Mandukhai's and something like a steely resolve shined in Esige's eyes. Mandukhai knew that a fire burned deep within Esige to punish Bigirsen. Esige never forgave Manduul, Yeke, or Bigirsen for what they did to Borogchin.

"There is more," Esige said, chewing her bottom lip as she lowered her gaze and stepped toward Mandukhai, pulling something from within her deel. "I, um, found this." The way Esige said "found" made it clear the girl had been snooping. "It struck me as odd, because Yeke has never been one for such things. And then I remembered something I overheard her saying when you arrived in Mongke Bulag."

Mandukhai held her breath as she unfolded the white cloth to reveal a small hunting knife. She lifted it, staring at the piece with mounting anger. Her father's knife. Mandukhai's fingers traced along the horn handle carved with herons and worn down through frequent use. The blade slid easily from the narrow sheath, and Mandukhai inspected the polish of the metal in the dim light of the ger. This knife had been missing since her wedding day. Yeke stole it. She had it all along…

"What did she say that day?" Mandukhai asked sharply.

"She said, 'She has no need of the tools of men'," Esige said.

If Yeke had the knife, she had probably taken the bow as well.

"Did you see a horn bow with the Ongud mark on the limb?" she asked.
Esige shook her head.

Mandukhai's anger raged within. *No need for tools of men? I am not some soft queen*, she thought, struggling to contain her anger. When the time came, she would use this knife on Yeke and show the woman that it was no tool simply for men.

Bigirsen commanded a handful of men near Yeke's ger as Mandukhai approached. One of the men Mandukhai vaguely recalled from her wedding. Issama, Bigirsen's advisor. His beady, oily black eyes probed at her as if burrowing into her very soul. Mandukhai tried to listen to what Bigirsen said his men, but he was careful to keep his voice low enough that no one else could hear. The men noticed her and Esige approaching, offering a bow that caught Bigirsen's attention.

"Lady Mandukhai," he said, offering only a slightly deferential bow.

"Vice Regent, a surprise to see you here while Manduul is away," Mandukhai kept her tone civil.

"I expected to see you in the gathering tent," Bigirsen said, waving his men off to carry out his orders. Issama cast a glance in her direction once more, than strode away on his own errands. "I hear you've been spending a lot of time there."

"My husband trusts my judgment and has asked me to advise on all matters of State. I would be happy to walk there with you, Lord Bigirsen." Mandukhai didn't wait for an answer before turning to lead the way. Esige sauntered at her shoulder, her back straight and gaze averted from him. The girl could mask her true emotions expertly, and it made Mandukhai swell with pride.

Nergui, as always, dogged her steps like a deadly shadow.

"I would hate to trouble you with petty issues," Bigirsen said. Mandukhai could hear in his tone that he wanted her to leave the council to him, but she knew that she and Unebolod could better handle him united.

"Nonsense." She waved off the comment as he matched her stride. "There is no such thing as a petty issue when it comes to ruling an empire. Manduul knows that while he and the prince are away, it is best to have confidence in such matters with the two people he trusts most."

Oh, how she wanted to see his face in that moment, but Mandukhai kept a cool, forward face herself, showing no sign of contempt or curiosity. He needed to believe this was true.

"Perhaps I should fetch Yeke, then," he said, his words a test of the ground beneath them.

Mandukhai spared a glance at him this time, smiling sickly sweet. "I think we both know she is not the second person Manduul trusts with the Nation. Yeke is a wonderful wife, but she is not meant to lead a Nation."

A moment of triumph filled Mandukhai as she swore she could hear his teeth grinding. It had been a bold slap in his face to say as much aloud, and she reveled in his frustration.

As they rounded the corner and entered the gathering tent, Bigirsen said nothing more on the topic. Mandukhai knew she had gotten under his skin, and it felt like a good thing. He deserved far worse.

Nergui followed Mandukhai in, moving toward his position behind a column near her seat.

Unebolod perched on the top step of the dais, directly in front of the empty throne belonging to Manduul. The back of the throne fanned out behind him like a crown. The position was an obvious play on his power. He was not Khan, but he acted in Manduul's stead and Bigirsen did not. Just the sight of him there made her pulse quicken.

Unebolod never dressed in fine silks like Manduul and Bayan, but his choice of clothing that day had been as deliberate as Mandukhai's own: the padded leather vest over his red and black deel, and the shoulders of his armor lined with stunning white fur pinned in place with wide golden circles. He toed the line between a Lord of the court and a Lord of the battlefield. No matter what today brought, he was apparently prepared for Bigirsen. Mandukhai's heart soared seeing him sitting in front of the throne as if he belonged on it.

He raised his chin proudly as Bigirsen approached, not bothering to offer any form of deferential show of respect.

"Will you not show respect even in the Khan's gathering tent?" Unebolod asked, his stone-cold gaze locked on Bigirsen. Unebolod had also not missed

239

Bigirsen's lack of respect.

"I hardly owe you deference, Unebolod," Bigirsen said, though he stopped several feet short of the dais.

"The Great Khan has put me in charge until his return," Unebolod said. "And I believe that puts my position above yours. I am certain Manduul would love to hear how you disrespected his chosen Regent in his absence when he returns."

"And when will that be? When did you last hear from Manduul? I have urgent business with the Khan."

Mandukhai seated herself in her chair. Esige joined one step lower. "I thought you said your matters were petty, Vice Regent."

Bigirsen's back stiffened, and he raised his chin defiantly. "And some of them are. But other urgent matters of State are meant for a Khan, not his wife."

Unebolod scowled at Bigirsen, and there was something wolfish about him, as if he had caught Bigirsen in a trap. "You insult your queen."

Leather creaked as two royal guards shifted their position on either side of the dais, their grips on their swords tensing. Mandukhai heard Nergui shuffle closer to her back. The tension in the air was stifling. Unebolod held up a hand to signal the guards to hold their positions. Mandukhai struggled to smother a satisfied smile, realizing he had been prepared for this reaction and was ready to show his power over Bigirsen.

"I believe you owe her an apology."

Bigirsen sneered. Mandukhai knew Bigirsen would not apologize. He made himself clear already; women had a place and it was not in the gathering tent. But Manduul had put her in charge alongside Unebolod. Bigirsen had unwittingly acted against the Khan.

"Take him," Unebolod commanded.

The guards closed in around Bigirsen, whose hand twitched over his own sword. A lion had entered the wolf's den. As the story went, if the wolf wanted to survive the lion, it needed to outwit the beast at it's own game. Without Manduul present, Mandukhai would have to be the wolf and outwit Bigirsen in his own game.

Mandukhai surged to her feet. "Wait!" The guards paused, both watching Bigirsen's hand. "There is no need to resort to such aggression. He is father to a queen, after all. Vice Regent, I'm sure all will be well if you conduct your business with us until the Khan returns."

Bigirsen remained statue-still as if waiting for any of them to act against him. Mandukhai knew they had him cornered. She had shown him compassion in this dark moment, which he could not undo in the eyes of these men, who would later tell others of how the Vice Regent had bent to her will.

Bigirsen bowed to Mandukhai, knowing as well as she did she had won this battle. Yet the lion would not be so easily assuaged.

The guards backed into their corners again, but their eyes remained locked on Bigirsen.

Unebolod cast a frustrated glance at Mandukhai. *He wanted to punish Bigirsen!* she realized.

The look was fleeting, then Unebolod relaxed, leaning forward with his arms resting on his knees. "What is this urgent business for the Khan?"

Bigirsen clearly chaffed at having to stand during this meeting. He shifted from one foot to the other and folded his hands together behind his back. "The eastern and western Moghuls are falling apart. Lord Yunus has become khan of the tribe, but his alliance with the men further west causes disruption within the Khanate. I need additional men from Manduul to stamp out this rebellion and restore order before all descends into chaos."

Mandukhai found this information highly illuminating. Moghuls were part of the Uyghur alliance west of Turfan. If the Moghuls were falling into rebellion, it meant some of Bigirsen's power in the Khanate had diminished, particularly if he came asking for more men. Bigirsen was growing desperate.

"Yunus has claim to his title, yes?" Unebolod asked, his face a stony mask.

"Lord Yunus has killed the rightful heir, Kebek, and the Moghuls cannot forget." Bigirsen's voice took on a hardened edge. "The Uyghur cannot forget."

Mandukhai inclined her chin, making the *boqta* chime. "Ah. Now I understand. For you, this is personal. You wanted Kebek as a puppet of the Moghuls to strengthen your alliance with them."

Bigirsen's hand fell on his sword, but he made no move to draw it. The tension in that subtle gesture was clear enough. The guards shifted as well, and Nergui edged around the column to place himself in a defensive position between Bigirsen and Mandukhai.

Bigirsen's jaw twitched. "He would have received appropriate council until he came of age to rule."

"Your council," Mandukhai said, plainly implicating that her assumption had been correct.

"I'm afraid we can't spare the men, Vice Regent," Unebolod said. "Our Khan is working to ensure the Oirat know who they answer to. I'm sure the Golden Prince will bring the Oirat raiders to heel as he has the Jalair, but for now, he needs those men."

Bigirsen clearly worked hard to keep his expression neutral, but Mandukhai could spot that bloodlust in the eyes of men easily enough. Though whose blood he lusted after was up for debate. Perhaps Yunus. Perhaps for Unebolod or Bayan. Mandukhai took some satisfaction from seeing Bigirsen's grip on power slipping away.

She also didn't miss how Unebolod had slipped Bayan into the conversation, as if the glory belonged to this prince. She knew how he felt about Bayan's victories. Perhaps he assumed Bigirsen would be just as irritated by it and used that to pit Bigirsen against Bayan?

"I think I will wait for him to return before accepting you at your word," Bigirsen replied.

"Wait as long as you wish," Unebolod said, as if it didn't matter to him, though Mandukhai knew it had to chaff when Bigirsen refused to leave. "When Manduul returns, he can tell you what I have heard him tell others. If you cannot manage control of your own tribes, perhaps you aren't deserving of your title."

Bigirsen strode toward Unebolod. He unsheathed his sword an inch before one guard pressed a warning blade to his throat.

"You insult me here, in the Khan's court?" Bigirsen snapped. "After extending Guest Rights."

Unebolod stood, glaring down at Bigirsen. "No. You insult your Khan's Regent and wife, and expect handouts when you cannot control the men he entrusted to you. I know how Manduul handles such weakness. If you are not careful, he just might replace you with someone younger and more adept at maintaining control. You were right, Lady Mandukhai," Unebolod said, turning away from Bigirsen to take his seat again. "He brings only petty issues to the Great Khan."

"Petty!" Bigirsen's sharp eyes flashed with rage. "I'm speaking of a fracture, a break in the Moghul Khanate!" Bigirsen let go of his sword and Mandukhai nodded at the guard to step back.

"You would call such revolt petty?" Bigirsen hissed.

Unebolod shrugged. "They have not answered to the Great Khan for at least a hundred years, much like the Great Horde to the north. Their alliance is only tenuous through other men, and they lack the power to raise the black banner against the Great Khan. Manduul left the Great Horde to their own devices as punishment. I expect he will do the same to you. Wait for Manduul Khan to return, if you like. I will be certain to report your situation to him, as well as your response to my decision."

Unebolod held out his hand, and a serving girl approached with a cup of *airag*. Mandukhai noted that Unebolod did not offer one to Bigirsen, clarifying that he had dismissed Bigirsen. Unebolod walked a dangerous line, and she worried about the fallout when Manduul did return. Manduul might agree with him, or he might be furious at how Bigirsen had been treated. He could be touchy about such things.

Bigirsen glared at Unebolod in such a way that Mandukhai felt ice in her own heart. After a moment of impudence, he turned to leave.

"Vice Regent," Mandukhai called after him. "I look forward to catching up with Lady Borogchin this evening."

Esige perked up at this suggestion.

Bigirsen paused at the door and turned back to her, grinning like a lion who just devoured a feast. "Sadly, she could not make the journey in her condition. The midwife thought it best she remain in Hami."

Mandukhai flinched as if Bigirsen had slapped her face. How had she not considered this before? Bigirsen's reason for choosing Borogchin as a wife made perfect sense—dangerous sense, should Manduul and Bayan both die.

Bigirsen's sons would be the last known children born of Borjigin royal blood.

CHAPTER TWENTY-SEVEN

IN THE NAME OF THE WOLVES

Mandukhai grew increasingly worried each day that passed without
Manduul's return. Bigirsen had remained in his ger on the southern
hills of Mongke Bulag—along with his men. The looming presence of the
Uyghur clearly made Unebolod uncomfortable, and he grew more irritating
with each day that passed. Mandukhai distanced herself from all of them,
while Esige continued to nose around and keep Mandukhai informed on the
tension in Mongke Bulag. Esige took to the task with adept eagerness, and
each night at dinner they would discuss everything the girl saw: the Khorchin
grew restless with the Uyghurs so close without the Khan around, traders
were increasing but the value of the trades all over the capital increased as
well, and Issama was constantly in motion.

"What do you think he is up to?" Mandukhai asked Esige over dinner on
the third night.

The girl shrugged. "A friend told me that he has been courting one of the
Jalair girls, but I've never seen someone move around so much just to court a
girl. I think he's working on rebuilding the alliance with the Jalair for Bigirsen."

Mandukhai considered this an adept observation on Esige's part. Manduul
had stripped away some of the influence Bigirsen had among the Jalair when
he subjugated them. It made sense that Bigirsen would want some of that
power back, even if the tribe kept their oath to the Khan first. Manduul would
not live forever. If Esige was correct, and Mandukhai had no reason to believe
the girl had made a mistake in her assumption, then every day Manduul's

return delayed would only strengthen the bond between the Uyghur and Jalair.

Thankfully, it had only been three more days before Manduul and Bayan returned from their campaign against the Oirat. Esige had not managed to learn anything more of what Issama was doing for Bigirsen among the Jalair.

News spread that the Khan was returning today, and Mandukhai waited in the gathering tent for Manduul and Bayan. Unebolod and Togochi had gone out to greet them.

"I still don't understand why you think we've done anything to avenge my sister," Esige muttered, waiting beside Mandukhai with her hands folded in front of her. "That yak deserves to pay for stealing Borogchin away."

"And he will." Mandukhai knew, without a doubt, that Bigirsen was losing his power, and Bayan's new status at court would rip away even more from beneath the Khan's Vice Regent. If Unebolod had been correct, and Manduul would not support Bigirsen's request for more men, then all Mandukhai and Esige had to do was practice patience. Bigirsen would be his own undoing. "Bigirsen depends on his ability to pull more men to his aid, and with Manduul and Bayan now pursuing their own agendas, he will not get his men. He is losing his power. Soon, the lion will flee from our presence. We must be patient."

"And then what?" Esige turned her narrow eyes on Mandukhai. The beads on her headpiece clinked. "What of my sister?"

"I know it can be hard to understand, but I need you to trust me," Mandukhai said, placing a reassuring hand on Esige's shoulder. "Time is our greatest ally. Bigirsen is losing his grip, and once he does, we will send a group of men we trust to retrieve her." And should Bigirsen die, she would carve out his heart and offer it to Borogchin as a gift.

Esige nodded and lowered her chin as Bigirsen, Issama, and Yeke strode into the gathering tent. No one uttered as word as Bigirsen and Issama stood to the side to await the Khan. Yeke shot a cold face at Mandukhai as she took her seat. The air grew thick. Several times, Mandukhai felt Issama's gaze studying her, but she kept her own toward the door as she held her chin high.

At last, Manduul strode into the gathering tent, followed by Bayan, Unebolod, Togochi, and a group of guards. As the guards assumed their positions by the door and dais, Manduul's expression could hardly be called cordial. A dark cloud loomed over all of four of the men, though it seemed heaviest over Bayan and Manduul. Manduul stomped up the few steps and dropped into his throne hard enough to make the seat groan in protest. The noise sounded like thunder to accompany the story brewing around him.

A serving girl rushed to Manduul with a cup, then scurried around the room to offer drinks to everyone at a wave of Manduul's hand. His silence pressed against Mandukhai's chest.

Bayan shucked off his helmet and dropped it on the ground beside his own seat before sinking down into the chair much as Manduul had done. He slumped visibly and kept his gaze averted from everyone—and away from Manduul. *What happened while they were away?* Mandukhai wondered. Was this tension between the two of them, or a shared frustration over something else entirely? Bayan downed his *airag* and held out the cup for a refill.

As much as Mandukhai resented Bayan, she relished the apparent alarm on Bigirsen's face. A proper prince would sit on the floor at his Khan's feet. Bayan had his own chair—right beside Manduul.

"My lord Khan," Bigirsen said, edging closer to the bottom step of the dais.

Unebolod brushed past Bigirsen and perched on the second step. It placed him not as high as Bayan—nor as high as Unebolod had been during the last meeting between the two men—but certainly a step above the Khan's Vice Regent. Bigirsen bristled, then stiffened and folded his hands behind his back. Issama remained off to the side like a shadow.

"My lord Khan," he repeated, "I have waited days to speak with you, and I need to return to the city of Aksu."

"You can wait a little longer, I think," Manduul said sharply.

Mandukhai had to admit she admired the way Manduul finally seemed to have acquired a backbone in these meetings with Bigirsen. She hated that Bayan caused it.

"You have not yet greeted your Golden Prince or congratulated Bolkhu on his new title," Manduul snapped.

For just a second, Bigirsen glanced at Yeke, but her full attention was on Bayan and Manduul. Could it be too much to hope that even Bigirsen's own daughter would shut out her father in favor of these two? Mandukhai steadied her excitement and schooled her face calm, but the pulse of victory rushed through her all the same. Bigirsen was on the brink of losing everything. At long last.

Bayan shifted into a straighter position in his seat and sipped his *airag* with all the arrogance of an entitled prince. Unlike Unebolod, Bayan had no ability to conceal his true feelings behind a warrior's cold face. Despite the tension in his shoulders, Bayan smirked over the edge of his cup, his eyes shining with delight.

Bigirsen's sharp gaze bore into Bayan as he placed a hand stiffly against his heart and bowed. But it was hardly deep enough for one of the Khan's advisors, let alone a prince. He held the bowed position, waiting for Bayan to acknowledge him. To Bayan's credit, he made Bigirsen hold for several long, silent seconds.

"Rise, Vice Regent Bigirsen, so I can finally meet the man I've heard so much about," Bayan said at last. Mandukhai noted the hint of triumph in his tone.

Bigirsen straightened and once again folded his hands behind his back. Mandukhai took great pleasure in watching Bigirsen defer to those he likely considered inferiors.

"Humbled, *Jinong*, and I've heard stories about you as well," Bigirsen said. Something about his tone reminded Mandukhai of a lion on the hunt. "I have spoken with the Jalair about your campaign against them. They told me all about how you murdered their Lord."

Bayan blanched, and Mandukhai wondered what the two of them were talking about. What had Bayan done?

"My lord Khan," Bigirsen continued without missing a beat, "Why would you force subjugation of a tribe already sworn to serve the Khan? How could you allow your *jinong* to kill a Lord for refusing to swear an oath he already gave?"

Manduul leaned forward, making the seat groan beneath him. "Do not question my decisions, Vice Regent, or you risk overstepping your station. Lord Hulun forgot his place and who he served. His words made us wonder just who he truly swore his oath to."

Bigirsen only displayed a fraction of the surprise he must have felt. Mandukhai found this exchange quite curious. She knew they defeated the Jalair, but Manduul had not provided any further details. If there was a reason for dissent among the Jalair against Manduul or Bayan for their actions, that might explain what Issama had been doing these past few days.

"He seemed to believe he followed your orders, Vice Regent," Bayan added. "Even as he raided his Khan's lands. We had no choice but to remind his people who they serve."

"You go too far, boy," Bigirsen growled. "You are dangerously close to accusing me of their infractions against the Khan."

"Is he?" Manduul asked. He took a drink from his cup. "Perhaps only someone with a guilty conscience could make such an assumption."

Mandukhai hadn't realized she held her breath until she found she needed air. Something significant was happening that made her alternate between anticipation and fear. Manduul dared to stare down Bigirsen, and with the new wealth coming into the tribe from recent raids, the grip Bigirsen had on Manduul had slipped. She hated Bayan … and she loved him. He had brought about this change when she could not.

Bigirsen opened his mouth to speak, but Manduul continued as if he hadn't noticed. "I sometimes think back on what happened to my nephew, the young wolf Molon Khan, and his ill-begotten fate. I recall those events leading up to my installment as Great Khan often. I remember the butchering of the Borjigin by an Oirat usurper, how you supported those responsible for the death of the two princes, how your own blood was responsible for the trickery. Unebolod himself routed a force from your tribe when they invaded our lands. Who led them, brother?" Manduul craned his neck toward Unebolod.

Bigirsen and Unebolod glared at one another. Mandukhai knew they hated one another. Bigirsen had given him that scar on his face in the battle Manduul referred to. She watched as the two men appeared to revive that battle through their warring eyes. The tension in the room grew thick.

"I never forget a face," Unebolod said sharply. Mandukhai shivered at the coldness of his tone. "Lord Bigirsen." A hint of a smirk played across his stony face.

At her feet, Esige shivered, but not from the cold. Mandukhai placed a hand on Esige's shoulder, and the girl gazed up at her, fear shining in her brown eyes. Mandukhai suddenly understood her fear. Not for the men in this room or those in either camp, but for her sister who lived far from them now. What would happen to Borogchin if they brought Bigirsen to trial in Mongke Bulag, never to return to Turfan? What would happen if he returned to her disgraced?

"I did not come all this way to be insulted," Bigirsen said through his teeth. "We have already discussed this, Manduul. Years ago. I swore an oath to you. I hope that still means something."

Mandukhai summoned the courage to speak before things spiraled further out of control. She had to act now if she wanted to protect Borogchin.

"My Khan, my husband," Mandukhai said, shifting forward to catch their attention. "Lord Bigirsen was extended Guest Rights upon his arrival."

Manduul grimaced. Yeke gazed sidelong at Mandukhai, as if unsure why she was defending Bigirsen. Even Togochi and Unebolod had the same stunned expression on their faces. Mandukhai knew they wanted this—all of them. They wanted to avenge Molon Khan, but they had no actual proof Bigirsen had been involved, even if they all felt it deep in their bones. Mandukhai wanted more than anything for Manduul to strip Bigirsen of his title and send him back to Turfan with his tail tucked between his legs like the dog he was, but Borogchin would be waiting at the other end of that journey.

"He came to us with urgent matters regarding a looming war within the Moghul Khanate," Mandukhai said. "Perhaps we can focus on that task for today." Though she knew she would have to talk Manduul out of this righteous anger before Bigirsen left Mongke Bulag.

Bigirsen had the wherewithal to incline his head in thanks to Mandukhai, an act that warmed her far more than she would ever admit. Since his return to Mongke Bulag, she had bested him in political battle twice. And she was far from done.

For the next hour, Bigirsen laid out the grim situation among the Moghuls in stark detail. Yet when he requested the men to stamp out the rebellion, Manduul refused to answer him.

"I'm in no mood for this right now," Manduul finally declared. "We have just returned from our own campaign and I need rest. You will wait until morning, Vice Regent."

The entire conversation had Bayan's head spinning and left him utterly exhausted. Bayan wondered if Manduul would refuse because their own campaign had cost them precious men. Some losses were expected in battle, but they lost nearly a thousand men.

Bayan rubbed his forehead as Bigirsen disappeared, then huffed out a sigh and took a long drink of *airag*. Holding it together in front of Bigirsen had taken all the inner strength he could muster. It exhausted him far more than any of the battles he had taken part in over these past few months—including those brutal fights against the Oirat.

Just thinking about their most recent campaign made Bayan wince. Manduul was angry with him. While his uncle had not said as much, Bayan knew Manduul blamed him for what happened. *It seemed like a good strategy at the time*, Bayan thought miserably. Yet the Oirat had been prepared. It had taken everything the Khan's men had to pull back before suffering defeat. The strategy used against the Jalair had not been effective against the Oirat.

And then to return only to find Bigirsen waiting for them … Bayan just wanted to sleep and forget the events of the past few weeks.

Bigirsen knew how to mince and twist words around far better than he did. It was a battle of wits he'd felt quite outmatched in. Thankfully, he hadn't been in battle alone. Unebolod appeared to loathe Bigirsen more than he resented Bayan, and it had been a breath of fresh air to have the veteran warrior turn that resentment on the Vice Regent.

Mandukhai had proven herself far more capable in these matters than he'd given her credit for previously. She'd played into everything with perfect balance, tipping the conversation where it needed to go with a few simple, gentle words. Once, she had even offered Bayan praise for his work with the Jalair campaign. It warmed him to hear such kindness coming from her.

"I don't think I've ever watched that man sweat," Manduul said with a laugh.

Does this mean Manduul is no longer angry with me? Bayan wondered, casting an anxious glance at Manduul.

"Togochi, make sure there are extra men around our gers tonight. I'm not certain how much I trust Bigirsen right now."

Yeke huffed and stormed out of the gathering tent.

"I'll talk to her," Bayan said, remembering how she'd looked at him before he'd left to campaign against the Oirat—and those long legs of hers … Mandukhai still intimidated him, but Yeke intrigued him.

Manduul grimaced and waved Bayan out. He strode from the tent to catch up to Yeke.

Unebolod felt overwhelming triumph swelling in his chest as he watched Bigirsen storm out of the gathering tent. Since Bigirsen's arrival in Mongke Bulag, Unebolod had stayed a step ahead and a step above Bigirsen, but today he had soared like an eagle over the disgraced Vice Regent. Unebolod sincerely hoped Manduul would strip Bigirsen of his title and power. It would serve him right.

As he stood to leave, his gaze met Mandukhai's. So much passed in those few seconds, and all the triumph he felt before vanished as he realized what she would have to do.

"Manduul, it's good to have you back, brother," Unebolod said, taking Manduul's arm and shaking it. "If you have further need of me, I am in your service." Especially if it meant he could be there when Bigirsen was reduced to nothing.

He and Togochi said their farewells for the night and stepped outside together. "I've never seen you so happy, Unebolod," Togochi said. "Not since Odsar." He cocked his head in curious question at Unebolod.

"I've waited to see Bigirsen reduced like that for far too long," Unebolod said. "As have you."

Togochi nodded. "True. Or it could have something to do with your riding out just hours before dawn several nights a week."

Unebolod's gut churned. Did he know? "Is that a crime to enjoy riding?"

"No." Togochi shrugged. "I suppose it isn't a crime for Mandukhai to enjoy rides at the same hour either."

Unebolod shrugged in return, but he didn't dare speak.

"I would guess it also isn't a crime to take a wealth of furs with you every time." Togochi grabbed Unebolod's arm and pulled him to a stop. "Will you really make me ask again? You swore nothing happened. You gave your word."

Unebolod straightened his spine. "I don't know what you're talking about." He jerked his arm free.

"Fine. Have it your way. But if I noticed, someone else could have as well. And if Manduul finds out, he will kill one of you, if not both of you."

Unebolod's blood pumped in his ears and his heart hammered against his ribs. Fear and desperation had taken control in an instant, and he struggled to shake it off.

"You love her." Togochi shook his head. "But you know this has to stop. It doesn't matter how you feel about her. She is married to the Khan."

"I know that."

"Would you kill him?"

"Of course not!" he snapped.

"Then end it. Before he ends you." Togochi left Unebolod standing alone between their gers, contemplating whether Togochi was right. And whether he had the strength to end it.

251

Mandukhai waited for everyone else to leave the gathering tent, then dismissed Esige. Once she was alone with Manduul, Mandukhai moved around behind him and began rubbing his shoulders. He groaned, and his shoulders relaxed slightly at her touch. Mandukhai knew what needed to be done to protect her child. She had managed to avoid letting on that she was pregnant to anyone else, including Esige. Now, with Manduul back, she needed to ensure he came to her ger that night.

"You conducted yourself admirably," she said as she worked on the knots in his joints. He certainly was tense!

"As did you, as calm and level-headed as ever." Manduul lifted one of her hands to his lips and kissed it. "I missed little of this place, but I did miss you."

Mandukhai wished she could return the sentiment, but she had not missed him at all. In fact, with each passing day, she prayed he would not return. Now that he had, she knew what she had to do to protect her child.

"Perhaps we could return home and you can show me how much you missed me," she said.

Manduul chuckled, still holding her hand, and tugged her around to stand in front of him. "I don't think we need to go anywhere." With a flick of his wrist, he dismissed the guards at the door, leaving the two of them alone in the tent.

Mandukhai did not want to do this. She never wanted to be intimate with anyone but Unebolod ever again. But their child depended on this. So Mandukhai swallowed her disgust and imagined Unebolod instead of Manduul.

Bayan nodded to the guard at Yeke's door and stepped inside without a second thought. She spun around, and her big eyes widening when she noticed him standing there. He stepped deeper into the ger, careful to leave the door open. Manduul's teasing about his wives before they left Mongke Bulag still hung in the back of his mind, but Bayan wasn't really sure how serious Manduul had been. To show he meant no harm, Bayan removed his sword from the belt and placed it beside the door.

"What are you doing here?" Yeke asked, retreating a few steps into the eastern side of the ger.

Bayan held up his hands to show he meant no harm. "I told Manduul I would talk to you after you stormed out. You looked upset, and he seemed content to allow me to come and ease your tension."

Yeke jerked in shock, her beaded earrings chiming. "He threatened my father. How should I feel?"

Bayan lowered his hands and waited. For a minute, the two stood staring at the other. Yeke had removed her *boqta* before he arrived, and now her walnut hair fell in long waves around her tawny face. The nose was big, like a great hawk's beak jetting out of her face. With her hair down, she appeared years younger and less severe. Bayan didn't know her correct age, but he assumed she couldn't be much older than twenty. So young. Much closer to his age than she was to Manduul's. Perhaps she had more Muslim blood in her than Mongol, but she was still beautiful—even if she wasn't a true Mongol. How did Manduul not see that?

Yeke's thin eyebrows drew together as she shifted uncomfortably. "Why are you staring at me like that?"

"Like what?" Bayan asked.

"Like a boy assessing a horse."

"I've never seen you with your hair down," he said with a casual shrug. "That's all."

Yeke shifted again, then turned to pour him a cup of tea, offering it to him before pouring one for herself. With the tea in hand, Bayan settled on the bench along the western wall.

"You are in a curious position here at court, Yeke," Bayan said at last. "I understand that better than you may think. But are you really concerned that Manduul threatened your father?"

"He is my father," Yeke said, seating herself on her own bed. "Of course it concerns me."

Bayan sipped the salted tea. It was never much to his taste; he preferred *airag*. "A father who sold you into a loveless marriage for his own ambitions, who used your husband when he couldn't defeat him in battle. Your father is a powerful man, and smart. I don't begrudge him that. But he does what he wants no matter who it hurts."

Yeke's gaze fixed on Bayan like a deer caught in the sights of a hunter. She flushed and averted her gaze, staring instead into the depths of her teacup.

"Manduul sent you?" she asked in a timid voice. It made her seem even smaller, more child-like.

"He did." Bayan set down his teacup, and she moved to refill it. Manduul hadn't exactly sent him as much as Bayan had volunteered to come and Manduul hadn't refused him. He placed his hand over her own as she finished pouring the tea. "I'm sorry."

"For what?" Yeke asked, breathless at the touch. She couldn't look at him. He knew she was either ashamed or afraid of something.

"That you have been forced to live this life without the affection you deserve."

Yeke met his gaze at last, and he could read the fear and uncertainty in her eyes. He held her hand between both of his; her warm, soft hand trembled. Bayan rose, pulling her upright with him, and the two of them stood close enough for energy to vibrate between them. Despite that energy, Bayan did not advance or retreat. He wanted her to want this, to want him. He needed it. Either he would have Bigirsen on his side with her in Bayan's corner, or he would get Yeke to turn away from her father and reinforce his own position with her. Both options would benefit Bayan greatly.

"He did not want my company even before his second wife came," Yeke whispered, as if the words struggled to come to the surface. Bayan wondered how deep she had buried her pain.

"He's a fool to be blind to such beauty."

Yeke yanked her hand away suddenly and rushed toward the door, closing it sharply. He stalked toward her. When she turned, his face was inches from her own.

"My father hates you," she whispered. Bayan was pleased to find her breathless.

"Of course he does. He's a man of ambition alone, and I am a threat to the power he thought he had. You have more power than he does now."

"How?" Yeke asked, pressing her back to the door.

Bayan edged closer as she attempted to withdraw. "You are the Khan's wife, and you have the favor of the *jinong*."

Yeke's chest heaved. He could tell she warred with an urge to give in to hope or flee as she had always done in the past.

"You love Manduul," she said.

Bayan couldn't deny Yeke this point. He did love Manduul, and he was fiercely loyal to the Khan, but Manduul had said both women would be Bayan's problem when he died. And they had taken that vow. Manduul had little interest in Yeke, and Bayan couldn't help but feel Manduul may actually thank him for making his first wife happy.

"I do. But we are sworn brothers, and since that day we have shared all things." Bayan reached up, brushing her cheek tenderly, running his fingers along her neck. "And where he sees flaws, I see beauty."

Yeke trembled at his touch. Warmth radiated from her body. Eager to feel her give in to him, Bayan slowly closed the narrow expanse between them and brushed his lips against hers. Yeke didn't retreat. Her lips tested his delicately. He pressed more firmly. A small sound from her throat rumbled her lips against his. In moments, Yeke's kiss matched Bayan's, delicate and hungry. But his goal wasn't to take what he wanted from her. Not tonight. Bayan needed to draw her to him, build the trust and desire between them until she came to him and not the other way around. Bayan reluctantly pulled his mouth away from Yeke's and leaned his forehead against hers.

"You think I'm beautiful?" she whispered breathlessly.

"More beautiful than a sunrise." Bayan stepped back.

Yeke reached for his deel to prevent his departure.

"Stay."

"I can't. Not tonight." Bayan affectionately brushed her cheek again. "But I want you to know you aren't alone here."

Yeke dropped her hands away. Bayan retrieved his sword and slipped out the door, nodding at the guards as he passed. Now he would need to find a girl to relieve the urges mounting within him.

Unebolod couldn't sleep knowing what Mandukhai was doing to save their child alongside mounting anticipation for Manduul's confrontation with Bigirsen. His mind was spinning, so he rose early to dip into the river. Late spring was his favorite time to plunge into the waters, still chilled from the thaw but warmed by the coming summer. It created a perfect balance.

When he returned, Mandukhai and Yeke stood outside the gathering tent with Manduul and Bayan much earlier than he had expected. Unebolod joined them dressed in his best deel protected by boiled, padded leather in case Bigirsen grew too desperate and attacked. His sword hung like a familiar counterweight on his hip.

Bayan appeared far more dashing than he should have under the circumstances in his ceremonial golden deel and belt. Fiery red painite gems gleamed like small flames in the settings of the belt discs. Unebolod grimaced as the rising sun glinted off the golden opulence. The boy had no idea how to prepare for such confrontations. Instead of dressing like a warrior, prepared for a potential confrontation, Bayan looked more like a princess. The comparison amused Unebolod. With Bayan's smaller frame, he certainly could pass for a woman if he tried. Perhaps Bayan's intention was to flash his self-importance to Bigirsen and goad the man into action, though that gave Bayan more credit than he deserved. Politics didn't seem to be a game at which Bayan was terribly adept.

"There you are," Manduul said as he joined them. "We couldn't find you."

"I took a dip in the river. What is the plan, Manduul?" Unebolod asked.

Manduul glanced at the sunrise. "I intend to make it clear who is Great Khan. He can accept it and return to carry out my will, or I will remind him who he serves."

Unebolod knew this wasn't a choice Manduul offered. If Bigirsen refused, Manduul could very well strip him of his title, which would in turn disgrace Bigirsen—and also lay the groundwork for war. *There had never been another way to deal with Bigirsen*, Unebolod thought.

They waited for Togochi to join them, then left on foot to visit Bigirsen in his own camp. Unebolod could understand why Mandukhai accompanied them; she had been a steady hand last night, keeping the situation from spiraling out of control. Yeke's presence was a surprise, though. *Perhaps she worries about her father and that his choice may also disgrace her,* Unebolod thought. It seemed unlikely that she was there to support Manduul.

The Uyghur camp spread out across the southern hills. Thousands of gers with men milling about. This was an army camp, not a family camp. The very notion left Unebolod unsettled.

Two men guarded Bigirsen's door, but upon seeing Manduul, they simply bowed with their fists over their hearts.

"Tell him his Khan wishes to speak with him," Manduul commanded.

One guard ducked inside. They waited in utter silence. Unebolod tried to hear the muffled words from within, but he couldn't make out Bigirsen's words. A minute later, the guard ducked back out and held the door for them. Manduul ducked through first.

The inside of Bigirsen's ger was simple and unadorned, practical for someone accustomed to traveling swiftly. Unebolod envied that ability to move around as necessity dictated, something he had not been allowed for years. The inside of the ger shrank significantly as their party spread out in the space. Unebolod planted himself firmly beside Mandukhai, who stood at Manduul's side. Bayan positioned himself directly beside Manduul's other side, standing with a straight back and proud chin. Yeke clung close at Bayan's shoulder as if afraid of her father and actually expected Bayan, of all people, would protect her. At least Togochi was beside her, if something went awry.

Bigirsen sat in a chair on the far side of the ger with Issama. Both men rose when they spotted Manduul, but offered no deference to anyone else. "I have no tea prepared, but perhaps my Khan would like some strong black *airag*?"

Manduul waved the offer away. "We won't be long."

Bigirsen's tension visibly increased as he examined each of them, and his gaze lingered on his daughter longest of all. Unebolod gave her some credit for not wilting as she normally did under her father's withering gaze.

Issama watched everything with curious, yet impassive eyes, as if whatever happened today would have no effect on him.

Bigirsen straightened proudly and raised his chin, prepared for his punishment. "What will it be then, my lord Khan? Has my oath proven insufficient?"

"I do not question the validity of your oath," Manduul said. "Simply the means by which it came to me. If you want to prove you are still worthy of the titles and responsibilities I have given you, then you will return to Turfan and deal with this matter as a Vice Regent of the Great Khan should. I will not send men because I cannot spare them. I have already made you *orlok* of my southern forces. If you cannot handle that responsibility, I will find someone else who can."

"You expect me to end a rebellion between your tribes without your men?" Bigirsen's eyes narrowed.

"You have more than enough men, Vice Regent," Manduul said evenly. "Lord Unebolod is *orlok* of my northern *tumens*. I will not send his men to do your work. Unless you would prefer he lead."

Unebolod felt a soaring moment of victory again. If Bigirsen failed, Unebolod would be within his right to raise the black banner, destroy the Uyghur, and seize control of the southern *tumens*. He could control the full force of the Khan's army. Then Bayan would die in a hunting accident and no one would stand in Unebolod's way once Manduul passed.

"No, my lord Khan," Bigirsen said, and his tone bordered on the edge of dangerous and concerned. "I will restore order. As I have always tried to do."

"In the name of the wolves of the Borjigin, and not yourself," Bayan added.

Bigirsen bared his teeth for just a second, but it was enough to reveal his true feelings toward the Golden Prince. Unebolod wondered how long it would be before Bigirsen tried to assassinate the prince. Not that he cared if Bigirsen did. That would also work in Unebolod's favor. He could raise the black banner against Bigirsen to avenge the fallen *jinong*. *Please, do it*, Unebolod thought. *And I will finally show you just how skilled I can be in battle.*

A glance at Manduul revealed that he had not missed Bigirsen's open resentment. Manduul's face reddened in anger.

"Bring your family honor, Father," Yeke said. Though she sounded confident, she appeared on the brink of shriveling under his glare.

Manduul's head whipped in Yeke's direction, and his jaw slackened. *Do I look like that right now?* Unebolod wondered as his own alarm struck him in the chest.

Bayan smiled ever so slightly at Yeke, and Unebolod wondered what happened between them that could cause such a change. The two of them would be a dangerous alliance.

"Go to Turfan and deal with these rebels for your Khan and *Jinong*," Yeke said. She never spoke up to her father as far back and Unebolod could remember.

Bigirsen knew that as well, and seemed to be waiting for her to retreat. Bayan subtly shifted toward Yeke and Manduul nodded in approval at her statement.

While Manduul was distracted with Yeke, Unebolod glanced at Mandukhai, who clearly noticed the change between Yeke and Bayan as well judging by her brows shifted ever so slightly. Unebolod knew that look even if no one else did. She was assessing a new danger.

Bigirsen placed a fist to his heart and bowed to Manduul. "It will be as my Khan wishes."

"Good. I suggest you not waste any more time here," Manduul said, turning for the door. "Pack up and leave before sundown."

Yeke followed on Manduul's heels as if eager to leave her father's ger. Bayan glared at Bigirsen arrogantly before following her out.

Mandukhai took a step toward Bigirsen. "Please give Lady Borogchin our love and let her know we miss her."

Unebolod suddenly understood her actions last night.

CHAPTER TWENTY-EIGHT

COMPASSION, STEEL, AND ENVY

MONGKE BULAG – SUMMER 1465

Spring passed quickly into summer. Leaves bloomed early. Flowers and fresh grass for the herbs sprouted before all the snow could melt away. It offered the promise of a prosperous year for the tribe. Mandukhai had waited as long as possible before telling Manduul about the child, but as spring layers were quickly shed in favor of lighter deels, it would be hard to hide the truth much longer. Thankfully the sickness that hindered some women did not affect Mandukhai.

After Manduul's return from the Oirat campaign, Mandukhai made a point of walking around Mongke Bulag with him each evening. Nergui and Manduul's guards always lingered nearby, a silent reminder that the two of them were not alone. On these tours, Mandukhai and Manduul would observe the condition of the capital. He spoke of Bayan more than she liked, and his fondness for the prince had clearly grown stronger during their campaigns together. Manduul avoided all discussions about their Oirat campaign, and she knew that something had gone amiss. Yet neither Manduul nor Bayan would talk about it with anyone else. Mandukhai was certain Manduul adored Bayan more than either of his wives. All that could change on this night as they walked near the western edge of Mongke Bulag.

"He promises a prosperous future for our people," Manduul said. "You were right to advise me to take him in as my own. I needed him to remind me what it means to be Khan, and the people will need him to take over when I'm gone."

"He isn't the only promise for our future," Mandukhai said. He could never know the truth, that this was not his child.

Manduul cocked his head toward her curiously. "He isn't?"

Mandukhai stopped and smoothed the red silk deel over her stomach. "He isn't."

Manduul froze, his gaze locked on her belly. For a moment, he said nothing at all, but the delight in his eyes gave away his emotions even if his face remained impassive. It wasn't much of a bump, but at almost three months, she knew it could start growing quickly and then it would be impossible to hide.

Behind Manduul, Nergui stiffened in shock, then gave a nod of approval. *He has no idea, which means there could be no way anyone else suspects,* Mandukhai thought.

"Why have you waited so long to tell me?" he asked, excitement dancing in his dark eyes.

"I wanted to be sure this child stayed before telling you." Just a year ago, Mandukhai never would have imagined she would be happy to be a mother, but all of that changed once she realized it would happen. And with a man she truly held deep affection for. Even if she could not share her fondness openly, it didn't not change her heart. *No one else can ever know.*

"A son?" Manduul asked, placing his hand over her stomach.

"The midwife believes it could be," she said, putting her hand over his, reminding herself this was not his child and she was only protecting it from him.

Manduul pulled Mandukhai into a fierce hug, sweeping her off her feet and spinning her around before allowing her feet to touch the ground again. "A second heir when just a few months ago I had none." He brushed his hand over her stomach again and grinned. "You have given me a gift greater than I could ever repay."

Mandukhai stepped back, struck by what he said. "Second heir?" Her heart sunk.

Manduul frowned. "Yes."

"You would name our child second?"

Manduul may not have known the truth of this child, but he still chose to name Bayan as his heir over the child.

Mandukhai's face fell. "To Bayan, a boy you've known only a few months?"

Manduul's thick brows pulled together with concern. "Bolkhu. I have already named him."

"And you can unname him! You are Khan!"

"I swore a sacred oath with him," Manduul said, affronted. He stepped toward her and his movements were almost dangerously desperate.

Nergui tensed, glancing at Manduul's guards as if expecting a fight.

Mandukhai drew back a step.

"As brothers, not to give him what belongs to this child." Mandukhai pressed her hands to her stomach. "This child will be your blood." Saying the words felt like a betrayal to both Manduul and Unebolod, though it was a careful skirting of the truth. Technically, both men came from the same line—albeit a long time ago.

"As is Bolkhu."

"He is your nephew, and a sworn brother, not your child." Mandukhai shuddered, hoping he didn't notice how these lies were affecting her. Could she do this for the rest of Manduul's life? Could she lie to him about this child? "I thought this was what you wanted, but you are so blinded by your love for Bolkhu that it often feels like standing in the presence of the sun. No one else could ever shine as brightly."

Manduul bristled. "Don't sully this moment. I made a promise, and I am a man of my word. If I have a son and I live long enough to see him become a man, we can discuss this again. But for now, our people need an heir, and I've given that title to Bolkhu."

Mandukhai knew she shouldn't press her luck any further. Pressing too hard might make him ask questions that could reveal the truth. Instead, her shoulders sagged and she hung her head. Manduul took that as acceptance and pulled her into another hug.

"No matter what, this child will know love," he whispered against her cheek.

And that, Mandukhai knew, would be the truth. This child would know love because she would bring the world to its knees if it offered anything else. He would know love and compassion when necessary, and steel when required.

News of the Great Khan's child spread through Mongke Bulag like fire. By the end of the following day, everyone knew. Mandukhai had never known a happiness like this before. People came and offered gifts of cloth for wrappings and herbs for a healthy pregnancy. The shaman came and hung the bristly back of a hedgehog skin over the doorway to ward off bad spirits. Nergui praised Mandukhai for fulfilling her duty with so much earnest relief she had felt bad for lying to him. She had professed so many times how much she trusted him, but Mandukhai could not trust him with this most dangerous secret of all. The more people who knew the truth, the more likely it would be for the truth to come to light. She could not risk it.

Mandukhai sat in her ger, hemming together furs for a warm winter bed for the baby. He would be born during the bitter winter and she wanted to ensure he would not know cold.

Esige perched on the floor like a bird picking through sticks to make a nest as she sorted the cluster of gifts into neat piles. She worked diligently and insisted that Mandukhai rest as much as possible so no risk would come to the baby. The girl also studied everything about the way Mandukhai acted—what she ate, how she moved—as if preparing herself for the inevitability that one day she would deal with the same.

Now that she was nearly twelve and growing into a beautiful young woman, boys began taking notice of her. Esige often ignored their gazes as if they were invisible, preferring the comfort of a bow in her hand to a kiss on her cheek, but Mandukhai did not believe for a moment that the girl didn't notice everything around her. More than once, Esige had floored a boy who assumed she was just another soft girl seeking the attention of the stronger sex. She showed those ambitious boys smartly what she thought of their assumptions with a few simple wrestling moves she adopted from Mandukhai's defense lessons. Already, she was growing a reputation as the princess warrior. Mandukhai swelled with pride at this, but also suffered a pang of envy as she remembered her dream of becoming like Khutulun—strong, fierce, feared, respected.

Mandukhai sighed as she stitched more furs together. Seeing Esige flourish brought back thoughts of Borogchin. Mandukhai knew she was to have a child of her own with Bigirsen now, and perhaps she already had. How did she fare in her new life? Mandukhai wished she knew how Bigirsen treated her, especially after the way Manduul sent him away with his tail tucked between his legs. Hopefully Bigirsen never took his anger or frustration out on his new wife. The very idea of Borogchin performing her wifely duties with Bigirsen was viler than Mandukhai performing her own duties with Manduul. Mandukhai loathed Bigirsen with pure, fiery anger and swore that she would one day use that anger to burn him alive.

Esige glanced at Mandukhai as she scooped up a stack she had organized and moved it toward the baby's chest. The girl displayed far more observational skill than any other girl Mandukhai had ever known. Perhaps more than even her own. The first hints came months before, when she sent Esige into Yeke's ger to eavesdrop on a conversation with Bigirsen. The girl also had fast fingers and had swiped Mandukhai's lost knife from right under Yeke's big nose. Again, when Esige moved around Mongke Bulag, sniffing out Issama's movements, she showed her adeptness at following and moving like a shadow, almost invisible yet able to see all. Mandukhai often sent Esige on errands around camp to watch and listen. She made an exceptional spy.

Esige was not invisible to Bayan, though. She insisted he made no comments. Bayan was her cousin, after all, so he made no suggestive advances. Still, Esige insisted Bayan always noticed her, as if women were never invisible to him. Mandukhai had even tried sending in the plainest women she could find to learn more of his plans, and he often flirted even then. Mandukhai then moved on to unattractive women or young girls, but his response was still the same. While he never flirted with the old women Mandukhai sent in, he still noticed every single one of them. Spying on him would require a male, and she only trusted Nergui and Unebolod with the task. Neither would be invisible to Bayan. Most of the men were already doggedly loyal to Bayan.

Mandukhai drank the tea Tuya brought to her. It contained an herbal remedy to help with stomach sickness, according to the Khan's shaman, Khosoichi. Not that Mandukhai had need of it.

With a new heir on the horizon, Mandukhai wished more than ever that she had a reliable spy in Bayan's midst. What would Bayan do if his own position were threatened? She needed to know what he planned. Esige attempted to listen in as much as she could, but Bayan's ability to smell the presence of a female made it impossible to go undetected.

Mandukhai unwittingly pricked her finger and sighed, gazing at the red drop of blood on her fingertip a moment before popping it in her mouth. Her stomach gurgled with hunger, but before she could say a word, Esige gathered some sweet curds for Mandukhai to eat. She accepted the food with a gracious smile and popped a curd in her mouth, pressing it inside her cheek and sucking on the treat to savor the flavor as long as possible. For a moment, she considered taking a break to ride Dust. A child who could not handle riding in the womb would not be strong enough to lead.

A knock came to the door, interrupting her thoughts.

"*Sain banuul*, Mandukhai," Yeke said, ducking in without waiting for an invitation.

Nergui scowled over Yeke's shoulder, but did not stop her.

Mandukhai repeated the greeting, more out of formality than any genuine desire to defer to Yeke. Esige scooped up one of her piles and placed the items neatly in the new chest. Yeke swept inside, stepping delicately over another pile of cloths, and settled on the edge of the bed beside Mandukhai. Her thin fingers brushed over her silk deel as she arranged it around her legs. After a quick motion from Mandukhai, Tuya prepared a cup of salted tea for the two women. No one spoke until Yeke had a cup in hand. Tuya refilled Mandukhai's cup as well.

"What brings you today, Yeke?" Mandukhai asked, taking a small sip. It was too hot for her mouth, and the sweet curd in her cheek spoiled the flavor somewhat.

"I came to offer my congratulations," Yeke said after taking her own sip. "Manduul has waited a long time for an heir."

"He has one already," Mandukhai pointed out. She had a sneaking suspicion that Yeke and Bayan had some sort of friendly agreement, if not something more. Mandukhai was not about to fail acknowledging his right in front of Yeke. Especially not if she would just turn around and tell him.

"We both know there is a difference between a nephew and a son," Yeke said tartly. "Assuming it will be a boy, that is." She said the words with all the sweetness of honey laced with the bitterness of *airag*.

Mandukhai ran a hand over her belly, making sure Yeke took notice of the bump there. "The midwife is confident in this."

"The sky father and earth mother bless you, then," Yeke said, staring at the bump. Mandukhai could easily see the envy shining in Yeke's eyes. "Do you truly intend to allow Bolkhu to hold the title of Golden Prince? I would want my child to be the heir, if it were me."

Mandukhai understood this game well. Yeke goaded her to try to get her to accidentally admit she would want her child to be the heir in Bayan's place. Instead, Mandukhai smiled sweetly at Yeke. "I would love for my child to be the prince, but Manduul has already made a promise. Who am I to question that decision?"

Those were Manduul's words, not hers. Mandukhai wanted to throw Bayan off his throne by his braids, but if Yeke and Bayan were allies, she had to tread lightly. After Yeke's words to her father and the way she seemed to gather confidence around Bayan, Mandukhai would be a fool to assume otherwise.

Yeke's face remained perfectly pleasant, but a viper hid in those brown eyes. *So much for the hedgehog warding off evil,* Mandukhai thought.

"I do envy you," Yeke admitted, holding the cup delicately in her fingers. "I've longed to please Manduul with news of a child for nearly three years. I am delighted that he will have one at last, even if I could not give it to him."

"You will," Mandukhai said sweetly. Not a single bone in her body believed Yeke would ever give Manduul a child. In fact, Mandukhai sometimes wondered if Manduul was incapable of siring any children at all. Between his wives and his whores, one of them should have had a child by this time. No one else seemed to have noticed this, and pointing that out to anyone felt ill-advised under the circumstances.

Yeke took the comment graciously, but Mandukhai could tell the other woman didn't believe her for a moment. "I also wanted to offer my services, such as they are. If you need help during your pregnancy, I am at your disposal."

"That's kind, but I have Esige and she has been most helpful already. Tuya is very attentive as well."

Esige continued putting away the gifts and had thus far moved around the ger unnoticed. Mandukhai's mention of her brought the girl out of the shadows, and she straightened proudly.

"Of course, but as you progress, you may find you need more help. I am here to support you and Manduul."

Mandukhai wondered if Yeke was attempting to put herself in a position to spy. Offering the help also came across as an insult, as if Mandukhai was incapable of dealing with her own pregnancy and her own child. She struggled to keep her expression civil. Having this child proved a tremendous victory over Yeke, making her more dangerous than ever before. She would fight to get her position back.

And if Yeke uncovered the truth about this child, Mandukhai would speak to Unebolod about finding a way to dispose of the woman before she could utter a word.

"Your offer is kind, Yeke, and I thank you." Mandukhai set down her cup, indicating she was done with the conversation. "We will keep it in mind should we need help."

Yeke rose and smoothed out her silks. Something about her was different, more assured. Yeke carried herself more securely of late, wore her silks to accentuate her body as she hadn't before, and even powdered her face— something she never did in the past. This change had been gradual enough over the past few weeks that Mandukhai hadn't noticed it accumulating until now. Even the way Yeke moved exhibited more of her womanly wiles. Yeke had changed, and Mandukhai could only think of one cause for such a change.

Bayan's attention. How had Manduul not noticed this transformation but recognized early on how Mandukhai had watched Unebolod? *He is blinded by his love for the prince*, she thought bitterly. Yeke would reap the rewards of that blindness.

Mandukhai rose to walk Yeke out of the ger. She needed some fresh air as well and considered that a stroll might be in order. As the two women stepped into the sunlight, Manduul approached and pulled Mandukhai close, kissing her cheek.

"Wife, how are you feeling today?" he asked, all but ignoring Yeke's presence.

"Well," Mandukhai answered, stepping back.

Unebolod and Togochi loomed with Manduul, and Mandukhai's insides flipped at the sight of Unebolod, even if he remained as cold-faced as usual. Since Manduul's return, they had not found a way to meet without risking discovery. How she yearned to be in his arms again, to feel his warm body against her own.

Nergui noticed her gaze wandering and frowned, glancing at Unebolod from the corner of his eyes. If he put the pieces together himself ... *Don't dwell. He can't possibly know.*

"I was just thinking about taking a walk," Mandukhai said.

"Is that wise?" Manduul asked, placing his hand over her belly.

Unebolod's shoulders rose ever so slightly as Manduul touched the bump, but no one else would have noticed the subtle change if they hadn't been looking for it. Mandukhai had noticed, though, and wished she could say something to reassure him. This was his child, and nothing could change that. Nergui also noticed, and his frown deepened. *Please don't ask me later!*

"The child has taken root." Mandukhai laughed a little. "He can handle a walk."

"Perhaps someone should accompany you," Manduul said, raising worried eyes to meet hers.

"I have Esige and Nergui. I will be fine."

"I will join you in any case," Manduul said, then glanced at the two men accompanying him. "You can check the perimeter, and I will meet with you both later. Maybe by then Bolkhu will be back from his hunt."

Togochi and Unebolod voiced their assent, then Manduul turned and offered his arm to Mandukhai. "Come, wife. We can visit that curd-maker you enjoy so much."

Mandukhai knew there was no escaping it, so she slipped her arm through Manduul's and they started up the path with Nergui and Esige close behind. Mandukhai swore she could feel Yeke's glare burn into her back, but she didn't give the other woman the satisfaction of looking back.

Unebolod and Togochi had taken their time riding around the perimeter of Mongke Bulag, checking in on watch stations and testing for potential points of weakness. This may be the land of the Great Khan, but a careless or ambitious man may still take the risk of raiding or stealing. One could never be too careful.

As they reached the final watch station on the western edge of Mongke Bulag, Togochi dismounted and allowed his mare to graze and drink from the river. Unebolod followed his lead and dismounted as well.

"I have not told Manduul," Togochi said.

The confession surprised Unebolod, though it was unnecessary. If Manduul knew what Togochi suspected, Unebolod had no doubt he would have been called in front of the Khan to answer the accusation long ago.

"I know."

Togochi crossed his arms, gazing across the river. "I've only held my tongue because I haven't noticed you sneaking off since his return." He turned his dark eyes to Unebolod, and his gaze reeked of suspicion. "Unless I've missed some detail."

Unebolod assumed a similar stance beside Togochi, shaking his head. "No." But how he missed those stolen moments with Mandukhai. The smoothness of her body. The feel of her silky hair against his chest. He ached to hold her again.

The corner of Togochi's mouth curled up in a bitter smirk. "It drives you crazy, doesn't it? Watching her with him and not being able to touch her."

Unebolod's chest tightened, and he turned his gaze to the endless blue sky. The colors had just begun to shift toward sunset, painting the sky with a hint of pink. He could think of no appropriate answer to the question. Yes, it made him angry. Furious. At times he wanted to kill Manduul just for touching her, but he couldn't. He wouldn't. Manduul was his brother. He made a vow, and his word was iron. Speaking feelings aloud with any of his brothers made him appear weak. He rarely spoke them even with Mandukhai, but she often found fresh ways to lower his guard.

"Do you remember when you chose Odsar?" Togochi asked.

The question jolted Unebolod, and he glanced sidelong at Togochi. "I do. I had never been so sure of anything in my life." He also remembered how Odsar made him feel as if he hadn't failed his father and true brothers. She understood the pain of his failure, at the time still fresh, that burned him from the inside out.

"I remember, as well," Togochi said. "But my perspective is not the same as yours. Manduul and I had been walking the perimeter of the Borjigin camp beside the Khorlod, just as you and I walk today. We stumbled across the two of you outside her father's ger. You handed him the white handkerchief. We watched her father unfold it. We didn't have to be close to know it contained sugar, tea leaves, and pastern."

Unebolod allowed himself a small smile, remembering the way Odsar's face lit up like the sun. Though she smiled brightly, he recalled how hard she had struggled to hold her excitement at bay, nearly bouncing on her toes as she waited for her father to pass the gift to her—one of the few fond memories Unebolod held from those dark days. All of his fond memories from those days were tethered to her.

"She was so pleased," Unebolod recalled. "But why do you bring this up?"

Togochi had never been good at hiding his feelings. Unebolod recognized the deep sadness in his brother, even if it only appeared to be a ghost of its true form on the surface.

"Manduul broke in that moment," Togochi said. "He spent weeks summoning the courage to approach her. That day, he told me he had prepared himself. And that night, he had planned on offering her the white handkerchief."

Unebolod started. "To Odsar?"

"It broke him watching you do it first. Brother, he wept."

Wept? Manduul never wept. Unebolod could only think of another time Manduul had even appeared on the brink of tears. *When she died,* he realized. At the time, Unebolod assumed he just felt grief for his brother's loss. Now, he understood. "He loved her." Unebolod couldn't wrap his mind around it. "Why did he never speak of it?"

"What would he tell you? That he saw her first? That he loved her more?" Togochi scoffed and shook his head. "He knew he could never compare to you in her eyes. And you loved her. We could all see that plainly."

One of the horses snorted nearby, and they both accepted the distraction to check for danger.

"He never considered sabotaging courtship," Togochi continued. "As much as he loved her, he wanted her to be happy, and he knew she would be happier with you."

Guilt wrenched Unebolod's gut. Manduul had stepped aside when he could not. And now Manduul believed this child was his own.

"I was barely sixteen when I joined you two," Togochi said, turning to face him. "But even I knew you wanted to be the next Khan, so Manduul must have known it as well. I believe Manduul accepted Bigirsen's support as a sort of justice for stealing Odsar. He knew you had the respect and admiration of several of the tribal Lords. Enough for a respectable bid at *kurultai.*"

"Would you have supported me?" Unebolod asked.

"Maybe."

Togochi's admission struck Unebolod. He could have been Khan if he had hadn't been overcome with his own grief for Odsar.

"You stole Odsar. He stole the khanship." Togochi shook his head. "The two of you have been shrouded in envy for what the other has for as long as I have known you. Yet neither of you have been able to appreciate what you have for yourself. It started with her, and I don't think it will end until one or either of you is dead. I would prefer the two of you find a more peaceful resolution."

Unebolod had nothing. Manduul had everything. How could Togochi not see that? What did he have to be thankful for? Perhaps he had won Odsar, but she had died only a year later. Unebolod had won Odsar, then had lost everything in exchange. *Am I being punished by the sky father for loving Odsar?* he wondered. It hardly seemed fair or just to be punished for such a thing.

"Manduul never once considered stealing your wife," Togochi said. "He buried his feelings as deeply as he could. Now you want his wife, and you cannot return the favor." He stepped away, gathering the reins of his mount. "I don't understand how the two of you have not killed each other yet. Honor, maybe. Bonds of brotherhood, perhaps. But make no mistake. If Manduul uncovers any scraps of evidence that you are stealing his wife away when he didn't steal yours, he will destroy you tooth and foot."

The threat sank deep into Unebolod's bones as Togochi mounted his mare in a smooth motion, then turned it to face Unebolod. "And if I find out this child isn't his, I will tell him everything." He kicked the mount and lurched toward Mongke Bulag.

The weight of Togochi's threat pressed down on Unebolod's shoulders, straining them painfully beneath the burden. To protect Mandukhai and his child, he would have to ensure no scraps of evidence remained. But could he kill Togochi to shield them? No. Togochi was his brother. Unebolod would have to bury his own feelings, just as Manduul had done, for his own safety as well as Mandukhai's ... and their child.

The nightmares he'd had a year ago, right before he caught Mandukhai preparing to run away, surfaced. He had gone to the river to wash away the sweat coating his skin and experienced pain in his feet and chest that he could not explain. Now, those forgotten nightmares that drove such odd sensations rose to the surface.

Manduul strapping him to horses by each limb then cutting all the skin from his feet for trespassing where he did not belong. Manduul using the horses to tear his limbs from the sockets for agony repaid. Manduul driving a stake down his throat for the lies, through his heart for the theft of his love, through his lungs for breathing the words of brotherhood and breaking them, and into the ground so his body could not touch the earth mother. Unebolod's mangled carcass hung from the stake, where carrion birds could pick apart his flesh until nothing remained but bone and sinew.

Guilt twisted in Unebolod's stomach. He loved Manduul, and had sworn an oath to protect him. Yet his love for Mandukhai was so much deeper, especially now that she carried his child. How had he let it come to this?

Bayan heard the news that spread through camp. Manduul and Mandukhai were having a child. He knew he should be worried about what this meant to his position as prince. An heir could supplant him, but it would take time. Manduul had called him to meet, but it had been brief placating reassurances he would remain the Golden Prince, and that Manduul's word was iron.

The truth remained hidden beneath the surface, though. Bayan had never wanted to rule. He had run from it for years. It wasn't until Manduul had taken him in and he could see the benefits of being Khan that Bayan wondered if he *did* want to rule, if for no other reason than it allowed him to send others to fight while he reaped the rewards. And women. So many women.

Returning to his ger from the meeting with Manduul, Bayan wondered if he could take this child in as Manduul had taken him in. One day, they could rule together. Bayan could attain more wealth, and this child could do the actual fighting. Bayan would be in his mid-thirties by then. Who wanted to fight in battle at that age? However, to do that he would need Mandukhai's support, and he had put in great effort to gather Yeke's thus far. What would she say if he struck a deal with Mandukhai? She could keep her position, become his first wife, and her child would be his first heir. *Yeke would never agree*, he thought bitterly. The two women harbored a strange bitterness toward each other.

For a fleeting moment, Bayan thought of Batu, a misshapen and weak child destined to die. He had no interest in the child himself. No one did. *He is long since dead*, Bayan thought as he reached the door.

Berkedai took up his post near the door as Bayan stepped inside. He would be sure to sit outside and drink with his guard tonight. Berkedai was one of the few friends Bayan had in this place, aside from Manduul.

A cloaked figure on his bed drew Bayan up short, and he pulled his sword from his belt. A closer examination revealed a feminine form, though women could be just as dangerous as men. Sometimes more so.

"Close the door," she whispered.

Bayan immediately recognized Yeke's voice and did as she commanded, then he slid the sword back into its place. Yeke lowered the hood of the simple cloak. Her braided hair hung over her shoulder.

"What are you doing here?" he asked quietly, glancing over his shoulder at the closed door.

Yeke rose, her hands fidgeting in the sleeves of her cloak. Her shoulders drooped, and her eyes appeared reddened as they darted around him toward the door. It didn't take a smart man to see that something was terribly wrong. Bayan inched closer. Yeke dropped her trembling chin to her chest.

"What's wrong?" he asked, tilting her chin up. "Did someone hurt you?"

"In a manner of speaking," Yeke said, and Bayan noticed that her voice was worn and weak.

Bayan tried to catch her eyes with his own, but she looked everywhere but at him. His voice adopted a dangerous edge. "Who?"

Yeke's brown eyes finally locked on his, burning with fire and despair. "Mandukhai."

Bayan flinched, jerking his hands away from her face. "Yeke—"

"I was little more than a womb for his heir before," she said. "What does that make me now? Less than nothing." Yeke snatched his retreating hand, pressing it to her cheek. "You told me I was beautiful. Did you mean it?"

Excitement pulsed through Bayan. The seed he'd planted weeks ago began to grow. She had taken longer than he had expected to finally reach this moment.

"Yes." His thumb stroked her cheek. Yeke, like all women, was beautiful in her own way. Manduul couldn't see it. He couldn't look past the plainness of her or the beak of her nose on that long, angular face or the flatness of her chest.

"And you are brothers, as one, sharing everything," she said, quivering as he stroked her cheek.

"Yes." Bayan had not confirmed as much with Manduul, but the comment still resonated. Manduul had no interest in Yeke. *I would be doing him a favor,* Bayan thought. And there would be no child to risk their relationship. Bayan had learned ways to ensure that would not happen.

"I want to feel beautiful." Yeke unfastened her cloak and dropped it on the floor. Beneath it, she wore nothing at all. "If you can give me that, I will give you anything."

And she was beautiful. The tint of her tawny skin. The smooth lines of her hips and neck. She was thinner than most women, but taller and more majestic, like a foreign bird.

"I can do so much more than that." Bayan's hand slid down along her shoulder, chest, hip.

Yeke bit her bottom lip as his hand traced over her body. A tear rolled down her cheek. He pulled her against him, kissing the tear. His mouth moved along her sharp, pointed jaw. Yeke melted against him as he pressed a slow, passionate kiss to her lips.

CHAPTER TWENTY-NINE

FURY OF THE DRAGON AND THE WOLF

Nergui paced the inside of Mandukhai's ger. She found his incessant motion irritating. Tuya had left only a few minutes ago to retrieve fuel for the evening stove. Nergui entered as soon as Tuya had gone, and he cast a suspicious glance at Esige. He said nothing as Esige finished putting away dishes they had used for dinner, but Mandukhai could see how he wanted her to leave. The moment Esige finished, Mandukhai smiled sweetly at her.

"Could you be a dear and give us a few minutes to talk?" Mandukhai asked.

Esige eyed Nergui with just as much suspicion as he eyed her with, but she nodded. "I will go brush down Dust and see that he is fed."

"Thank you, Esige." Mandukhai followed her to the door, then closed it gently behind the girl and turned to Nergui. "Stop! You are pacing like a caged animal and it is driving me crazy. What is your problem?"

Nergui halted and turned, rising to his full height as he stared at her. Mandukhai watched as he clenched his hands together behind his back. His jaw twitched.

"Should I whip it out of you?" Mandukhai snapped.

"I warned you," Nergui hissed, glancing at the closed door as if he expected someone to be standing there.

"I'm afraid you will have to be more specific," Mandukhai said tersely.

Nergui's gaze flicked to her slightly swelling stomach. She was hardly three months, and only a small bump showed. Yet Mandukhai had no doubt what he meant.

"I will not ask, my Lady," Nergui said sharply. "But I need to know. Does anyone else know?"

Mandukhai swallowed. She could not admit the truth, or he would realize for certain she had been unfaithful to Manduul. Yet if he was to protect her, he needed to be aware of who he could and could not trust.

"Do I strike you as a fool?" she answered carefully, skirting around the truth.

Nergui grimaced. "Should I be concerned that someone specific may come for you?"

Mandukhai knew full well what he meant. Nergui suspected that perhaps this was not Manduul's child, yet he would not insult her with accusations. Nergui had one job. To protect her. His reference clearly indicated Manduul.

"I am carrying an heir to the Nation," Mandukhai said assertively. "You would be unwise not to be concerned that *anyone* might come for me."

Nergui's shoulders tightened. "Very well. Tonight, I will stand guard. I doubt I will sleep anyway. Tomorrow, I will enlist men I trust to watch over you while I am unable." Nergui bowed formally to Mandukhai, but before he opened the door, he turned to her once more. "It would certainly make my job easier if you keep your distance and your eyes to yourself, my Lady, or it's only a matter of time before someone else notices as well."

"I'm afraid I have no notion what you refer to, Nergui," Mandukhai said flatly as he pulled open the door.

Before he ducked outside, Nergui cast a disapproving frown in her direction and grunted.

Mongke Bulag was silent so late in the night. Bayan pulled on his trousers and glanced at the opening at the top of the ger. He could almost see the moon through the gap. Yeke sat up on the bed, allowing the furs to fall off her bare chest as she ran her fingers over her still-braided hair. The braid was quite a rumpled mess, but who would notice before she returned to her ger? For a moment, Bayan's gaze lingered on her chest, and her fingers traced down his spine as he sat on the edge of the bed.

"It's time to go," he said, tearing his gaze away from her. Bayan stood and slipped on his deel, then tossed her cloak on the bed beside her. "The guards are usually easy to slip past at this time."

"Manduul won't care," Yeke pouted, pulling the cloak tight around her as she slid off the bed.

"Maybe not, but rumors will affect him all the same." Bayan stomped into his boots and stood, then held a hand to her. "Come on. Let's get you back to your ger."

Yeke pulled the hood of her cloak up around her head to mask her face before slipping her hand into his. When Bayan reached for the door, she pulled him back, pressing close.

"I am a queen, Bolkhu," she whispered. "Don't discard me like you do with all the other girls."

"I wouldn't dream of it." The corner of his mouth tipped up into a grin. He had her.

Yeke pressed another kiss to his lips, which he eagerly returned. Manduul had called her boring in bed, but that had not been Bayan's experience. Perhaps she just needed the right guidance or attention to bring her to life.

They slipped out of his ger and past his guard, sticking to the shadows as they moved along the edges of his ger. Yeke's ger was a short walk behind his own. He had considered having her go alone, but worried about her alone in the middle of the night. If something happened to her, someone might trace her movements back to him. It wasn't worth the risk.

Yeke clung to his hand, and he wondered if she believed him when he told her this would happen again. Because it would. He was quite certain of that.

"*Jinong*," a male voice called to him in hushed tones.

Bayan jumped, nudging Yeke behind him more out of fear that someone would see him with her than any genuine concern for her. He needed Yeke, but that didn't mean he wanted others to know he spent time with her; especially if he would need to earn Mandukhai's trust.

Then his heart sank.

Mandukhai's guard, Nergui, closed the distance between her ger and where Bayan and Yeke stood. Nergui grinned dumbly at Yeke and for a moment Bayan held his breath, afraid Nergui recognized her, but he didn't seem to realize who it was. Yeke's face hid within the darkness of her hood.

"Keeping warm tonight?" Nergui asked with that dumb grin on his face.

Bayan glanced around, looking for the guards usually on duty around Manduul and Mandukhai at night. They likely were on a different path around the central ger. Nergui was constantly in Mandukhai's shadow, but at night other men guarded her door. Panic gripped Bayan's chest. *Why is he here tonight?*

"You know me," Bayan joked. His anxiety bled into his voice and he silently cursed himself.

Nergui's grin slipped ever so slightly as he glanced past Bayan. The corners of his mouth turned downward and his shoulders tensed.

Bayan's heart leaped into his throat. Manduul may or may not care if he slept with Yeke—that decision had been unclear—but Mandukhai would. *I need her, and if she hears what he saw I will never be able to earn her trust.* Nergui seemed to understand his life was in danger. The fear shined in his eyes as his hand casually rested on the hilt of his sword.

Yeke sensed the tension and released Bayan's hand. She held her cloak tight around her body and hustled away.

Why did I leave my sword behind? Bayan thought bitterly. At least he still had his knife tucked in his belt. He waited, not touching his knife, afraid of what would happen if he did.

The moment her door closed, he played the part everyone expected of him—the swaggering and confident *jinong*. "I believe we can discuss this like adults," he said with a cocky smirk on his face.

Sleep had been difficult in the night as Mandukhai's stomach roiled and threatened to spill her dinner. It seemed that all her luck avoiding the stomach sickness that came with pregnancy would hit her all at once. Eventually, she rose to chew on ginger root until her stomach finally settled. After sinking back on the bed, her chest was so tender she couldn't find a comfortable position. It took far too long to fall asleep despite the overwhelming exhaustion.

Barking dogs and shouting men woke her at the wolf dawn—far too early after a restless night—followed only a moment later by the door to her ger flying open. Manduul stormed through, sword in hand, with Unebolod close on his heels. She yelped and pressed her back to the wall beside the bed, clutching her furs.

"Are you hurt?" Manduul asked, lowering his sword and striding toward her in just a few steps.

Mandukhai frowned. "I'm fine. A bit tired."

As he if didn't believe her, Manduul set his sword on the bed and ran worried hands over her shoulders as she hugged the fur blanket tighter against her body. "Are you certain?"

"Yes!" Mandukhai glanced over his shoulder at Unebolod and saw relief soften his usually stony face. Unebolod drew in a slow breath through his nostrils and let it out just as slowly as he tucked his sword away. "What is going on?" she asked.

Outside, the dogs continued barking, moving away from the ger. Such commotion was uncommon in Mongke Bulag, as was the way the two of them rushed into her home with swords drawn. *They thought something happened to me,* Mandukhai realized, reaching for a deel beside the bed and slipping it over her shoulders.

Manduul turned to Unebolod. "I want every tracker and dog out there searching for the killer. Whoever it was couldn't have gone far. Slit the throats of any man who refuses to help."

Unebolod's relief washed away into a hardness Mandukhai had never witnessed before, like a warrior's mask of death. He marched out the door without a word. Her stomach began turning again, and she grasped Manduul's arm.

"Esige. Where is Esige?" Panic raised her voice to a higher pitch.

Manduul patted her hand. "She's with Yeke. She's fine. Bolkhu is watching over them in the gathering tent."

Mandukhai let out a breath of relief, releasing her grip. But someone was killed. "Then who?" She pushed off the furs and adjusted her deel on the way to the door when Manduul pulled her back.

"Don't."

Mandukhai frowned at his hand on her arm. Manduul hadn't grabbed her like that since she had stormed his council meeting and humiliated herself at his feet. His grip was firm, and her heart plummeted into her already churning stomach. There could be only one reason he didn't want her going outside.

"No." She shook her head, feebly jerking toward the door.

Manduul didn't want her to step outside. If Esige was safe, as were Unebolod and Manduul, that only left one victim. Nergui. Who else? Mandukhai squeezed her eyes shut as the room spun and tilted around her. Nergui was the last piece of her previous life, her link to her Ongud clan. *He did nothing to deserve this fate. Nothing except guard me,* she thought bitterly as her limbs became heavier.

Large arms wrapped around her and Manduul held her close. Part of her wanted to crumble apart in his arms, but doing so would make her appear fragile. Mandukhai was not weak. She was a queen, and a queen would fight for justice.

Mandukhai extracted herself from Manduul's grip, her jaw clenching with stubborn resolve. Before he could stop her again, Mandukhai thrust the door open and stepped over the threshold. She would see this for herself.

"Mandukhai, stop," Manduul called after her, but it was too late.

The sun did not yet chase away night, but the lighter blue sky of the wolf dawn seemed to make the trail of blood stand out. Mandukhai followed it around her ger to a ring of men nearby urine ditch. Togochi attempted blocking Mandukhai's path, but she pushed past him until she could see Nergui's body for herself.

The overwhelming stench of blood, urine, and excrement wafted up her nose, and the child inside her protested. She swallowed repeatedly to hold down the vomit lodged in her throat. Nergui laid at an odd angle in the ditch. His sword was missing. Who would kill him and throw his body in the ditch like this? Mandukhai's heart broke. Surely he deserved more respect than this.

Mandukhai tried to study the scene, but as her eyes moved the world tilted again. Her legs shook beneath her and Togochi wrapped his arms around her to hold her upright as she leaned over, retching. Even after everything came up, Mandukhai fought to control her stomach, afraid it would attempt to dig up more. This child attempted preventing her from investigating, and she wished she had more control over her own body.

"You need to rest," Manduul insisted, easing her away from Togochi. "I'll have someone make you some tea, and then you can lie down in my ger, where my men will guard you."

Mandukhai shrugged him off and straightened. "I don't need rest. I need answers." She forced herself to look at Nergui again, seeking any clues.

Manduul's voice firmed. "Mandukhai!"

He reached for her, but she swatted him away. "I said I'm fine!"

Bayan and Yeke joined the ring of onlookers. Mandukhai hardly spared them more than a glance, consumed by grief.

Heedless of the blood near the ditch staining her silk deel, Mandukhai knelt beside Nergui. His arms reached up the sides of the ditch at an odd angle, and she could easily see that whoever killed him tried rolling his body into the ditch. Did they not expect anyone to find the body? Bile rose up her throat again and Mandukhai battled to keep it down. His empty gaze seemed to fixate on her, and it chilled Mandukhai to the bone. The cause of death was without question the deep, clean slice across his throat. Mandukhai couldn't understand why. She brushed his braided hair away from his face, leaving a streak of blood across the bald top of his head.

"I have everyone out in search of the killer," Manduul reassured her, hovering at her back. "And all the dogs are trying to track the scent."

Mandukhai rose and her eyes watered. She blinked furiously. Crying was not an option. The harder she fought to hold down the grief and revulsion within her, the more detached from the situation she felt. Colder and more calculating.

Her gaze swept everyone present, seeking out signs of guilt. Was the killer someone she knew? Was it someone Nergui trusted? Her gaze fell on Yeke, who had turned an ugly shade of green and averted her gaze from Nergui's body. Bayan stood statue still, his face pale and his gaze locked on Nergui. The lump in his throat bobbed repeatedly. Togochi's jaw was locked tight, his eyes angry as he examined the scene. None of the guards gave any indication they knew any more than she did.

"We will find whoever did this to him," Manduul said. "I swear it."

"I want the killer brought to me," Mandukhai said, surprised by how frosty her voice sounded.

"I will feed this killer's heart to the dogs, if that would please you," Manduul said.

Her sharp gaze struck him like a well-aimed arrow. "I reserve the right to decide if he lives or dies, and how. He will be brought to me alive, even if it means cutting off his feet to keep him from fleeing. I want him to know that his life is at my mercy. I want him to feel the full fury of the Dragon and the Wolf. I want my smiling face to be the last thing he sees before I rip out his heart."

Manduul, to Mandukhai's surprise, bowed in agreement. Bayan's startled gaze flicked to Manduul. Did he doubt her right? Or was that look about something more?

Yeke slapped a hand over her mouth and hustled away as if she would be sick herself.

Nergui had known or seen something he shouldn't have. Any other explanation did not account for her survival. If this was an attack against her, surely the killer could have finished her before alarms were raised. Mandukhai would find the truth. Whoever had done this, they would learn the truth of her heart—that Mandukhai was a warrior and not a helpless woman.

As search parties moved further from Mongke Bulag, Mandukhai had Nergui's body cleaned and taken to the hill near her favorite birch tree. There, his body would feed the earth and wildlife as his spirit rose into the Eternal Blue Sky. The shaman Khosoichi accompanied her, as did Manduul.

As Khosoichi gave the final rites to the sky father and earth mother, Mandukhai stared at the scarred tree, remembering her first meeting with Unebolod so long ago, and Nergui finding them there together. From the moment Nergui was chosen to guard her to the instant he died, he had been unfailingly loyal to her. Mandukhai would not find another guard she could trust so absolutely.

The wind made her fresh yellow deel flutter around her ankles as she watched Khosoichi place stones around the body to keep away evil spirits. Stray hairs blew across her face and she swiped them away.

Togochi uncovered a rumor that Nergui owed a gambling debt to another man. Now that man and his wife were missing, perhaps having fled before his body could be discovered. That did not settle well with Mandukhai. If Nergui owed such a debt, he knew he could come to her for help. It felt like a cover for something far more sinister. If he saw or knew something he shouldn't have, then that would explain the need to get rid of him. Or perhaps the killer wanted to remove her loyal guard from her service to get closer to her. Removing him now put Mandukhai in greater danger.

The most likely suspects were Yeke and Bayan. The two of them had the most to gain from her downfall. Yet she could not be certain either of them was involved. If this was a ploy to remove her guard and make her more vulnerable, the cleverness of the plan was beyond the skills either of those two possessed. Bigirsen, on the other hand, had a lot to gain if she were to fall. Was his influence far reaching enough to touch her in Mongke Bulag?

Of one thing, Mandukhai was certain. It was not a random act of violence. It was a necessary risk.

Mandukhai strode into the gathering tent where Bayan, Yeke, and Esige waited during Nergui's ceremony. Esige had wanted to join Mandukhai, but she convinced the girl to monitor Bayan and Yeke for her. Now, as she crossed the threshold, Esige rose from where she sat on the dais, watching Mandukhai with those soulful young eyes.

In the corner near Bayan's throne, he and Yeke huddled together, whispering to each other. Mandukhai approached and dipped her chin low.

Yeke came forward first, offering Mandukhai a hug that gave no real comfort. "I am so relieved you were unharmed," Yeke said as she stepped back. "Manduul would be devastated if he lost you and his child."

Mandukhai squeezed out a few tears. She opened her mouth as if to speak, then shuddered as if no words would surface.

Bayan inched closer, remaining behind Yeke's shoulder as he watched Mandukhai. *Is he shielding himself with her?* Mandukhai wondered. His countenance certainly appeared aggitated.

"Come." Yeke turned Mandukhai toward a pillowed chair. Mandukhai didn't resist as Yeke guided her. "You!" Yeke snapped her fingers at a serving girl, whose eyes widened in alarm. "Bring the Khan's wife tea."

The servant hesitated a moment, glancing from Yeke to Bayan to Mandukhai.

"Is there a problem?" Bayan asked the girl, placing his hand on his sword. An odd reaction. "Do as you were commanded. Now."

The girl dipped her head in shame and rushed off to obey. Mandukhai felt bad for her.

"I just don't understand," Mandukhai said, sniffling as she brushed a tear away with the heel of her palm. "Who would kill him?"

Bayan shifted his feet, glancing toward the door as if he expected someone to enter. "I've heard the rumors that he owed a gambling debt."

Mandukhai didn't buy into the story. It did not ring true for Nergui. "He didn't gamble."

Bayan shrugged her comment off with ease. "That you know of. He did something with his time off, though. How would you know?"

"I know him," Mandukhai snapped. "That is how!"

Bayan and Yeke exchanged uneasy glances at her outburst. What did that look mean?

The serving girl returned with tea, offering first to Mandukhai, then Yeke and Bayan. Mandukhai hesitated to drink it. If Yeke was responsible for Nergui, would she go so far as to attempt poisoning her? Yeke took a drink first, showing no indication that she worried over possible toxins.

Bayan took a drink and coughed, slapping the cup back down on the tray.

"Where's the *airag?*" he asked.

The serving girl flushed and bowed away from them, reappearing only a moment later with a cup of *airag* for Bayan.

Mandukhai sighed softly and took a careful sip. The tea was more bitter than usual. *No wonder Bayan gagged on it.* But the churning in her gut lessened after taking that first sip. Mandukhai waited a moment for something else to happen, but when she felt fine, she took another drink. It helped calm her nerves and her stomach.

"I am sorry for your loss, Mandukhai," Bayan said, choking out the words.

He actually sounds like he is grieving, too, she thought. Perhaps she was wrong to question his motives.

"Unebolod and the trackers are out there hunting this mysterious gambler down as we speak," he said.

What would they find? Another body in a ditch? Mandukhai wondered if this mysterious man would ever be tracked down at all. Somehow, deep down, she knew she would never see this man alive.

Yeke placed a reassuring hand on her shoulder. "They will find him, Mandukhai." Yeke had never been great at lying, but this time her eyes did not give her away.

"Good." Mandukhai sat up straighter and took a longer drink of her tea. "Manduul has promised that his men will return the killer to me alive. They would not dare disobey his command."

Yeke's hand slipped away as she took a sip of her own tea, obscuring her face so Mandukhai couldn't read the response.

Mandukhai finished her tea and set the cup aside. "I only hope Nergui did not suffer much before his death. He was a good, loyal man. He deserved better. Tossing him in a urine ditch like that..." Mandukhai blanched and her stomach twisted in grief. "It's the act of a coward."

Bayan snorted at that, then downed the rest of his *airag* and held out the cup. Another serving girl rushed over to refill it. "More of a coward than running away?" he asked.

"Does the difference matter?" Mandukhai asked. "Either way, this killer's act was a disgrace." Again, her stomach twisted in cramps caused by her grief.

"Did the killer take Nergui's coin pouch?" Yeke asked, setting her own empty cup aside.

"Yes." Mandukhai eyed Yeke. *What a strange question...* "Why do you ask?"

"It just seems that if this was a cover for something else, then the coins would have been left behind, perhaps forgotten. The fact that this killer took them must mean he meant to settle the debt." Yeke shrugged, straightening her back.

While Mandukhai could understand the logic, the fact that Yeke brought it up so casually seemed suspicious on its own. The grief and anger churned her stomach again, then an intense pain grasped her insides as if someone had reached inside and twisted her innards into a fist. More tea. She needed more tea to calm her stomach. Mandukhai motioned for a serving girl, but a pain stabbed in her gut. Mandukhai doubled over and gasped.

"Mandukhai?" Bayan crouched in front of her, his brows creasing together in genuine alarm.

"Esige, get the midwife!" Yeke hollered as she eased Mandukhai onto her back on the floor and propped pillows beneath her.

Esige rushed out the door as Mandukhai's eyes flooded with tears. In seconds, the pain overwhelmed Mandukhai, and she cradled her stomach against the grasp of the earth mother, who reached inside her to rip her baby away. And she recognized that familiar taste in the tea as heat flooded her face. Mugwort, mixed with something far more sinister.

"The tea…" Mandukhai sucked in a sharp breath as pain twisted her insides in a knot.

"Where is the girl who brough Lady Mandukhai's tea?" Bayan demanded, surging to his feet.

Mandukhai's vision blurred until she couldn't distinguish one form from another. Sounds of leather, boots, and steel pierced the air.

CHAPTER THIRTY

BLOOD SACRIFICE

Men bustled around Unebolod in a flurry of activity as they organized the spread of their search party. Nergui's killer was out there, and Unebolod would find him. The man would not escape. A rider raced to the outpost southeast of the capital, where Unebolod had busied himself all day. Unebolod straightened as the rider dismounted and rushed over.

"Do you have news of the search?" Unebolod asked.

The rider bowed. "No, my Lord. It is Lady Mandukhai. Manduul Khan sends word that she is in labor."

Unebolod's heart dropped to his stomach. The air grew thick. *Labor? It's too soon!*

"Soke!" Unebolod shouted, spinning to find his second in command.

Soke rushed to catch up to Unebolod as who strode toward his mount. "Yes, *Orlok?*"

"You are in charge until I return," Unebolod said as he gathered his reins. He jumped into the saddle.

Unebolod turned his mare and galloped out of the command center toward Mongke Bulag. He raced his mount back to the center of Mongke Bulag, heedless of who stepped in his way. People scattered away like birds, squawking their offense in his wake. None of that mattered. Panic consumed Unebolod, pressing on his chest, heightening his senses while narrowing his focus. *Not again...*

When he arrived at the gathering tent, Mandukhai's screams split the sky. Mandukhai never screamed. She shouted in anger, but never screamed. The sound shot down Unebolod's spine like bolts of lightning. Terror gripped him. He jumped off his mare deftly and tossed the reins to the nearest guard, but before he could step inside, one of the men blocked his path.

"Khan's orders. No one goes in without his command," the guard said.

"But he sent word to me," Unebolod protested, attempting to edge past.

Again, the guards barred his entrance. Unebolod growled and clenched his fists. He tried to peer past the man, but the door had been closed so tight that he couldn't even hope to see through a crack along the edge. He stepped back and began pacing. Every one of her cries slammed into his chest like a thousand arrows lodged in his heart. He couldn't breathe. The only image that came to his mind was Odsar, crying and weak, unable to meet his gaze, blaming herself for birthing a dead child. The memory of the coldness of her hand in his resurfaced, and he stopped pacing. This couldn't be happening again. He stared at his hand. Was he cursed?

Mandukhai lay on a bed of pillows as intense pain contracted her entire abdomen. Esige pressed damp, cool cloths to her forehead as the midwife monitored the situation. Manduul paced in the background of the gathering tent, but Mandukhai hardly registered his presence. Mandukhai did not know how long she had lain there in pain. Her back ached. Her head hurt. Sweat flowed out of every pore of her skin. She hadn't considered sending Yeke away or blaming the other woman. Mandukhai couldn't even think clearly. She whimpered as the contractions passed like a great fist releasing her body.

"Don't take my baby. Don't take my baby." The plea echoed through her head, chasing away all other worries.

Manduul nudged the midwife aside, which earned him a thump against the head.

"You are in the way. Get out of mine so I can do my job," the midwife snapped, then pushed her fraying gray braid over her shoulder for the hundredth time.

"Don't take my…" The great fist of pain once more seized Mandukhai, squeezing her body. She cried out.

Someone had poisoned her. They wanted her dead, or only the child.

Regardless, Mandukhai could not help the deep sorrow of her own failure, as if this was her punishment for lying to the Khan. Exhaustion seeped into every bone in her body, and she couldn't fight this any longer. This loss seized her as surely as the great fists of pain. It was a warning. This happened for a reason.

The High Heavens had spoken. Unebolod's children were unfit to be princes.

Mandukhai whimpered again and closed her eyes.

"No!" The midwife shouted, slapping Mandukhai alert. "Stay awake!"

Mandukhai's eyes snapped open, but she quickly gave in to the exhaustion again. The agony collapsed against her broken heart.

And she dreamed of the sacred Mother Tree.

Fear consumed Bayan as he paced his ger. First Nergui, now the child. Someone would think him responsible for both. *I should run now, before it's too late*, he thought. Trembling, he took another swig of *airag*. Manduul wouldn't really believe him responsible, though ... would he?

Bayan stumbled against the edge of his bed, catching himself before he fell over. No. Manduul wouldn't blame him. Manduul adored him and trusted him. Losing a child wouldn't change that. *It might change that if he thinks I caused the loss.* Bayan tipped back the skin of *airag* again only to come up empty. With a growl, he threw it on the ground and staggered to the shelf for more.

He and Manduul swore a sacred vow. It was a deep promise. Deeper than anything else. Deeper than his marriage to Mandukhai. *Not deeper than his love for his own child.* Bayan couldn't compare to Manduul's own child, no matter what vows they made. *He will kill me. I need to run.*

After another swig to help wash away his own fear and steel himself for the attempt to escape, Bayan staggered toward the door. After three steps, he tumbled onto the bed. He would never escape Mongke Bulag in this condition. His fate, it seemed, was sealed.

Bayan pushed himself upright on the bed, bracing his back against the wall, and heaved out a shuddering sigh. His blurry gaze fixed on the door and he patted his sword. At least he could protect himself.

The shaman Khosoichi joined Unebolod's vigil outside the gathering tent. The guards had barred his entrance as well, despite his protests. Instead, Khosoichi sprinkled mare's milk around the doorway and chanted to the High Heavens for protection. The old man's face sagged, and the layers of his ceremonial garb chimed with each movement. Unebolod had little faith in shamans since Odsar's death, but he didn't interrupt.

Manduul stumbled outside, shouting profanities at the midwife as Yeke closed the door in his face. At the moment, Unebolod didn't care if Manduul knew the truth or if he accidentally condemned himself. All he could think of was Mandukhai and the baby and how he couldn't handle losing her. Not like he lost Odsar.

"Manduul, brother, how is she?" Unebolod said, rushing toward him.

Manduul swiped his sleeve across the sweat coating his forehead. He opened his mouth, but only a croak escaped. He shook his head, face crumbling. The utter hopelessness in his posture crushed the last of Unebolod's hope. Both men stood frozen.

"She lost consciousness," Manduul said at last, his voice little more than a hoarse whisper. "The midwife said it may be all she can do to save Mandukhai."

The two men fell into silence. What could be said? No words would make up for the loss or reduce the danger.

Khosoichi edged closer. "My lord Khan, if she is so dire, we should perform a sacrifice immediately. Let us appease the High Heavens and show the importance of the queen and the child."

"It didn't save Odsar," Unebolod said sharply, glaring at the shaman.

"She was not a queen chosen by the High Heavens," Khosoichi said. "Mandukhai is both, but she will be lost if we don't do this at once."

Before Manduul could respond, Togochi marched over with a serving girl tied and thrown over his shoulder. She cried through the gag stuffed in her mouth and squirmed, but it did her no good.

"That's her?" Manduul asked, his voice darkening to match his expression.

Togochi tossed her on the ground like a sack of loot and grunted in agreement.

Unebolod frowned at the frightened girl. She couldn't be much older than fourteen or fifteen, and her gaze was wild with fear as she took in each of them. A gag had been stuffed and tied into her mouth, but it didn't stop her cries. Was this her fault? The girl attempted squirming away as they spoke, but her eyes fell on Unebolod's hand clenching the sword and she froze.

"She insisted she didn't poison the queen," Togochi said. "That it was an herbal tea to help calm her nerves. But she chucked this as she tried to flee." He tossed a small leather pouch through the air.

Manduul caught it, yanking it open and dumping ground herbs in the dirt. "What is this?"

The shaman crouched beside the herbs and tested it before making a sour face and spitting on the ground. "Mugwort laced with pennywort. In a high enough dose, this is more than enough to force the child out and poison your wife."

Unebolod's chest heaved with angry breaths. *Poison.* He lumbered toward the girl, eager to thrust his sword through her chest, to torture her until she screamed as Mandukhai had screamed, until her throat bled and her voice gave out.

"Let me question her," he said through his teeth.

Tears rolled down her cheeks. She scooted away from him as quickly as she could only to bump into Togochi's legs. Around her gag, she attempted pleading.

Manduul's body quivered with rage as he nodded.

Unebolod's lips peeled back in a snarl as he stalked toward her, pulling out his knife instead of the sword. She squeezed her eyes closed as he crouched in front of her. The knife sliced through the gag and her cheek. She cried as the cloth fell away.

"My lord Khan, we are losing time," Khosoichi said.

"It can wait a little longer," Manduul snapped.

"I swear to you, I thought it was just tea!" the girl said as Unebolod seized her bound hands and wrenched one of her fingers free of her fist. "Please. He said it would help with her stomach!"

Unebolod pinched her finger in his hand, holding the knife between them. "Who?"

"Altan! His name is Altan!"

Togochi chortled. "Right. The most common of names."

Unebolod tried to conjure anyone of importance with that name, but came up empty. "Where can we find him?"

"I don't know," she whimpered miserably.

Unebolod slid the knife under her nail as she screamed, prying it off. Sweat beaded on her forehead and her face turned a brilliant share of red. Blood coated his hand and she pulled away from him. Unebolod growled and grabbed her hands again, yanking them closer and pulling out another finger. "Try again," he said. Her scream was not nearly satisfying enough.

She whimpered, snot bubbling from her nose. "I swear. He comes and goes. I haven't seen him in weeks."

"What tribe is he in?" Manduul snarled, looming behind Unebolod.

The pitiful whimper she released, followed by the sobs, told Unebolod enough. She did not know where this Altan came from.

"She's useless," Manduul growled, his patience run dry.

Her crimes had been committed. Manduul nudged Unebolod out of the way and drew his sword, gripping her hair at her scalp tight and yanking the girl to her feet. Tears streamed down her face. Unebolod tightened his grip on his own sword, wishing he could be the one to kill her. He felt the passionate fury of bloodlust pulsing through him. She had not suffered nearly enough.

"Manduul, wait," Togochi said.

The girl's raised her bound, bleeding hands up as she pleaded with Manduul. Unebolod knew there was no point in begging. There would be no sympathy, no mercy.

Manduul didn't make it quick. He yanked her head back by the hair as she screamed, then pushed his sword into her gut inch by painful inch as slowly as he could. His face was a mask of pure rage and loathing as he watched the light slowly leave her eyes. Before the last moment, as the sword exited through her back, he sharply twisted the blade with a snarl. As he yanked it out, she slumped, held up only by the strength of his grip in her hair. Her lifeless body crumpled in a heap at Manduul's feet.

"We need to perform a sacrifice now," Khosoichi said. "Before it's too late for either of them."

Manduul cleaned off his sword on the girl's deel, straightened, and nodded. They headed away from the tent, following the shaman. Unebolod hesitated, staring at the door.

"We just leave?" he asked.

Manduul placed a bloody hand on Unebolod's shoulder. "The women do their job. This is ours. And once the sacrifice is done, we will tear Mongke Bulag apart to find Altan. You don't have to join us. This is my responsibility." Manduul wiped the blood from his hand on the front of his deel and turned to a few of the warriors lingering nearby. "Bring her family to the training grounds. I will get answers from them next."

Manduul, Togochi, and Khosoichi strode away with a few of Manduul's guards trailing behind them. The warriors darted off to find the girl's family. Unebolod watched them go. No. This was not Manduul's responsibility. The child was his. It was his burden to bear. But if he admitted as much, Manduul would know the truth.

Togochi glanced at Unebolod as the Khan's party rounded the corner. Unebolod knew Togochi waited for him to speak up, to admit the truth.

If I tell him the truth, I'm dead, Unebolod thought, frozen in uncertainty. *If I don't take part in this sacrifice, it could be for nothing.* As much as he lost faith in the shamans, he was still not willing to risk Mandukhai's life or his child. They had failed Odsar, but perhaps Khosoichi was right. Mandukhai was different.

He glanced once more at the closed door of the gathering tent and knew what he had to do. He owed it to Mandukhai. He owed it to Manduul.

Perhaps there was one way he could participate in the sacrifice to help save her. But he would need Bayan's help.

The prince proved easy to find. As Unebolod entered Bayan's ger, he inhaled the stench of *airag*. Bayan sat on the bed with his back to the wall, holding the half-empty skin in his hand. Unebolod expected to see a girl lounging around the ger somewhere. Bayan was alone. Was this guilt gnawing away at the prince?

"You're drunk," Unebolod said flatly.

Bayan belched. "Been a rough day."

Unebolod winced as the sour smell washed over him. He waved a hand in front of his face to push the fumes away. "Mandukhai needs our help."

Bayan snorted and raised the skin to take another drink. Unebolod closed the gap between them, knocking aside Bayan's sword as the prince feebly raised it in defense. Unebolod threw the weapon aside and pressed his own bloody knife to Bayan's throat. The two froze. Bayan stared at Unebolod with wide eyes. How he would have loved to kill the prince right then. The boy had no respect for anyone but himself or Manduul. He deserved death.

"Did Manduul send you?" Bayan asked, his words slurring together.

Unebolod's eyes narrowed. "Why should he?"

"'Cause he thinks I poisoned her," Bayan said. "Baby was a threat to my position. Who else would it be?"

Did he just confess? But the girl said it was Altan. Unebolod frowned. Surely the girl would have known who Bayan was if he had given her the herbs. Unless he hired someone else to do it for him.

"Altan," Unebolod said.

Bayan's face screwed up in confusion. "What?"

Now was not the time. Unebolod shook his head and put the knife back in his belt. Bayan raised the skin of *airag*, and Unebolod snatched it away. Then he smacked Bayan in the side of the head.

"If you care about Manduul at all, you will get up. Now. Before it's too late."

Bayan scowled and stumbled to his feet. In his condition, Bayan could hardly stand on his own, leaning most of his weight against Unebolod as they made their way to the Khan's herd.

Manduul held Dust's reins as they arrived. Unebolod's heart leaped into his throat as he realized Manduul intended to use Mandukhai's stallion as a sacrifice.

"Wait, what are you doing, Manduul?" Unebolod asked, releasing Bayan so quickly the prince nearly tumbled to the ground. Unebolod strode toward Dust, stroking the stallion's nose. "You can't use her horse."

"What better white mount to sacrifice in exchange for her life?" Manduul asked, tugging on the reins as he attempted lowering Dust to the ground.

"First of all, shouldn't we be using mares and not stallions?" Unebolod asked.

Manduul glanced at Khosoichi, who nodded in agreement.

"White for the purity of her soul, and female for the purity of her body," Khosoichi agreed. "Using a stallion might send the wrong message."

Manduul hesitated, then nodded as he handed over Dust's reins to Unebolod.

"I have a white mare you can have," Unebolod offered.

"It needs to be from the Khan's herd," Khosoichi said.

Manduul sent a man to retrieve a white mare from his herd, then turned to Bayan. "Where have you been all day?" Manduul snapped. "I could have used you sooner."

Bayan worked his jaw, but no words came out. Manduul edged toward the prince, and Bayan flinched back.

"Grief is no excuse for abandoning me," Manduul said. He waved a hand and his nose curled in disgust.

Togochi busied himself lowering the new mare to the ground. He hobbled it with a horsehair rope, glancing occasionally at Unebolod. Something about the way Togochi stared at him raised Unebolod's worry. What did he know? Did he know anything? Togochi had suspected him and Mandukhai for some time. Would he speak up now?

"Manduul, I was thinking ..." Unebolod said. "if we want our sacrifice to truly reach the High Heavens so the sky father hears us and the earth mother accepts our offering, we should raise our voices as one. Let's show Lord Tengri that we are loyal brothers of the Mongol Nation. The last of the Borjigin wolves making this sacrifice to save our queen. The sky father could not ignore us united, as Genghis and his brothers were. Let us make Genghis proud."

Manduul considered this. Togochi didn't appear fooled, folding his arms over his chest as he stood, but he said nothing. This was not the time to point fingers and cause more trouble. Time was of the essence. Manduul nodded and waved Unebolod and Bayan forward to join him, then motioned for Togochi to join as well.

"You are our sworn brother as well, Togochi," Manduul said. "Let's do this right."

Bayan belched loudly enough to startle the first mare. Manduul grabbed his collar and slapped him. "Drink when you want, but if your knife doesn't strike true, you'll meet the end of mine next."

Bayan blinked in alarm and sobered, nodding.

Khosoichi sprinkled milk over the mare's mouth, then waved jasmine toward the sky as he sang to the sky father his prayer for the blessing. As he fanned the jasmine at the ground, he motioned them forward. The four stepped toward the struggling, prone mare, each holding a knife in hand. As the prayers finished, Khosoichi kneeled beside the mare's head and held a bowl steady. Several warriors labored to hold the animal down.

Unebolod, Togochi, Manduul, and Bayan each kneeled around the horse. Bayan raised his knife, swaying slightly, and Unebolod worried Bayan would miss his aim and screw everything up.

A small crowd gathered, watching the last of the wolves as they struck in unison, slicing the mare's neck and belly open. Thankfully, Bayan hit the horse with his knife, even if the cut was not as clean as the others. Khosoichi held the bowl to the neck where Unebolod had sliced across the throat with Manduul. Gathering the blood was an important part of the ceremony representing honor for the noble sacrifice. Once the bowl was full and the mare stopped moving, the shaman raised the bowl to the sky as proof of the sacrifice, and sprinkled drops onto the earth for rebirth.

Unlike Odsar's sacrifice—the white sheep—this noble mount provided a more valuable offering to the Heavens. Would Odsar have survived if Unebolod had sacrificed a white mare instead?

Manduul was the first to drink the blood from the bowl as a show of the noble sacrifice and acceptance of the will of the Heavens. They accepted the purity of the mare and the rebirth of Mandukhai's wellbeing through their own bodies in this way. Manduul held out the bowl, and before Bayan could accept it, Unebolod grabbed the bowl and took a generous drink. He wouldn't have anyone else doing this before him. Not when it was his child and Mandukhai at risk. The liquid was warm, thick, and had the metallic tang he came to associate with blood. Swallowing it down took some effort, and he had to open the back of his throat and let it slide down before the acrid taste lingered too long in his mouth.

As Bayan and Togochi drank from the bowl, Khosoichi inspected the innards of the horse and raised a blue-red length of innards in the air for everyone to see—blue for the sky father, red for the earth mother. "They approve!"

Unebolod breathed out in relief. Bayan's face turned green as he pressed the back of his hand to his mouth. Manduul snatched the prince's collar and pulled him close until they stood toe-to-toe.

"If you don't hold it down, I will make you drink the whole damn bowl," Manduul growled under his breath. "Go sober up. Not another drop. Do you understand me, boy?"

Bayan heaved, holding both hands over his mouth to keep from vomiting on the ground. Unebolod wasn't certain if the sudden change in Bayan's pallor was from the blood, or Manduul's anger. He sneered at the weak prince, using a cloth to wipe the blood from his hands. *Please let that work,* he thought. *Please let that be enough.* But it didn't feel like enough. It hadn't been enough to save Odsar.

CHAPTER THIRTY-ONE

SMOKE IN THE WIND

After the sacrifice, Bayan had returned to his ger and tumbled on the bed, immediately passing out. Nightmares plagued him. Unebolod had taken his head, blaming him for Mandukhai's death. Manduul had carved out Bayan's heart and eaten it as he was forced to watch. Yeke had pointed the finger at Bayan, accusing him of poisoning Mandukhai and the baby even though it had been Yeke's doing. Through all of it, Lord Bolunai's disembodied, oversized head watched from above, chortling at Bayan's demise and reminding him that he had been warned.

Bayan woke in the middle of the night dripping in sweat. He shed the soaked deel and his steps quivered as he ambled toward his stash of *airag*. Manduul had ordered him to sober up, but after that nightmare, Bayan needed a drink to take the edge off.

"He told you not a drop."

Bayan jumped out of his skin, spinning around to see Yeke closing the door behind her.

"You shouldn't be here," Bayan said, ashamed of the tremble in his voice.

"Manduul will never notice me missing," Yeke said briskly, waving off his protest. She perched on the edge of his bed.

"They are watching everything!" Bayan began pacing the floor.

Did she not understand what was happening in the capital? With Mandukhai losing this child, Manduul would tear everything apart looking for clues. If he found them together right now, it would be worse than damning.

Yeke did not seem to care about any of this. A sudden, horrible thought pulled him up short and he froze, staring at her. *She doesn't care because she is responsible. Did she hire Altan?* Perhaps she assumed she was doing them both a favor. Without a male heir, Bayan was the only choice, thus solidifying their relationship and their future. But was Yeke capable of that sort of cruelty? She had been so desperate for affection the night before, but killing a child...

He growled low in his throat and strode toward Yeke so abruptly she flinched and sank back against the wall of the ger. "If Manduul discovers what we were doing last night ..."

He did not know how to finish that sentence. Would his uncle be disappointed in him, angry with him, or call for his head? Under the circumstances, Manduul being thankful that Bayan had found a way to keep Yeke happy seemed unlikely. Sure, they had sworn their lives together and shared just about everything, but this was Manduul's wife. He could still hold it against Bayan. He could still exact vengeance. He might even be more likely to do so after what happened to Mandukhai today.

Yeke's chin trembled. "You said—"

"I know what I said," he snapped, then pulled back suddenly as she shrank away from him. Tears brimmed her eyes. "I'm sorry. I just don't know how he will actually take this news now."

Yeke licked her lips anxiously and turned watery eyes on him. "Was anything you said true?"

Bayan's heart hammered against his ribs, and that utter devastation in her eyes was enough to break through the fear pumping through his veins. He sank to his knees and took her hands in his own. Hers were like ice where his were coated in a sheen of sweat.

"Yes." His gaze tethered her so she could not look away. "I swear it to you. My desires for you have not changed."

"Did you kill Nergui for me?" she asked timidly.

Bayan had not wanted to kill anyone. But Nergui would have told Mandukhai what he had seen. While Manduul might not condemn him, Mandukhai would, and Bayan was acutely aware of how he needed to keep her trust. Killing Nergui had covered his own tracks, but Yeke did not need to know that.

He didn't even flinch as he lied to her. "Yes."

"I won't be used again, Bolkhu *Jinong*," she said with a soft fury that he admired. "Do you understand me?"

295

"I do." He reached up and brushed tears from her cheek. "But I need to know … did you poison Mandukhai?"

Yeke swatted him away. "I could ask you the same question!"

"Yeke, please." Bayan shifted his feet, sitting on his legs before her. "I told you, we are in this together to the end. But if I am to protect you and our interests, I need to know the truth. Was it you?"

"No. I may be envious, but I would not kill his child." Yeke slipped her hand over Bayan's and he took pleasure from the small touch. "Then you did not either?"

Bayan shook his head. "I'm worried that if Manduul finds out about Nergui, he will assume it was me. Unless we can find this Altan they were talking about."

Yeke lifted his sweaty hand and pressed it to her cheek. "They will suspect my father as well."

"Do you think it was him?" Bayan certainly wouldn't put anything past Bigirsen. The man had a firm grip on Manduul and the fate of the Mongol nation. The child could ruin that.

Yeke chewed her lip, but she didn't answer. Bayan supposed that, in the end, she didn't really need to answer. They both already knew it could very well have been her father. Or someone her father had hired.

Bayan leaned forward and kissed her cheek. "Let's worry about us first. We can worry about him later."

Yeke turned her head so their lips met, burning with hunger and desperation. Bayan slid his arms around her and pulled Yeke toward him as her hands brushed over his bare chest.

With any luck, the search for Mandukhai's assassin would distract the men from tracking Nergui back to him. And if they took long enough to investigate, the animals would get to the bodies before the search parties.

By nightfall, Mongke Bulag was ablaze with torchlight. Not a corner had been left in shadow. Unebolod took great pleasure in overseeing the interrogations of the serving girl's family. Yet no matter how many of them he question himself—or how brutally he questioned them—their screams and cries and confessions had not been nearly enough to satiate the beast within him struggling to break free.

The training grounds was covered in blood. Unebolod could not help but think of the days he had spent here with Mandukhai, when everything had still been fresh and clean. It felt like a fitting homage to that time to have blood on the ground now as they sought clues regarding Altan.

Once they had finished with the family, the Khan's men scoured the capital for any man named Altan, or anyone who knew someone by that name. Unebolod had burned with a desire to torture every last man until one confessed. When the first few man arrived on the training grounds and saw what remained of the family, their cold warrior faces shattered as terror took hold.

"Question every last one of them until you uncover some truth leading to this man," Manduul commanded in a loud, hard voice.

Togochi glanced at the men, then edged toward Manduul and lowered his voice. "Manduul, brother, we are seeking someone with one of the most common names. If you are not careful, people may compare this to the Borjigin Butchering and you will have a revolt on your hands. Allow me to take charge of this endeavor and protect your interests."

Manduul huffed in frustration and tugged at one of his looped braids. "Fine. You are in charge, Togochi. We will show any man who comes willingly leniency as long as he answers our questions. But any man who skirts the truth will be flayed and boiled. And any who hides or runs will be dragged here behind a horse and questioned without mercy."

Togochi nodded. "Go see to your wife. I will take care of this. If we uncover any news, I will report it immediately."

Manduul grunted and lumbered away, rubbing the back of his neck.

Togochi turned to Unebolod. "You should go as well, brother. I can handle this. We have one lead right now. Why don't you go see to this serving girl's friend and find out what she knows."

The last thing Unebolod wanted was to leave the interrogation to hunt down some girl. He needed to take out his anger on these men until one of them gave answers.

"We cannot both be here and there," Togochi pointed out. "And someone needs to find this other girl before she disappears."

Unebolod grimaced. Togochi had a point. Nergui's killer was still missing, and if this girl was the final link to Altan, they needed to get to her before Altan did.

Unebolod left the interrogations to Togochi. On the way to find this new

297

girl, he wandered to where the servant had been captured, asking questions of everyone nearby, waking any who had the audacity to sleep while their queen's life hung in the balance. One glance at his blood-stained hands and clothing loosened tongues quickly.

Yungei had joined him in the middle of the night. Their search brought Unebolod to the friend's family ger. If the servant's family knew nothing, her friend most likely did. Women talked about everything.

As Unebolod stalked toward the door, Yungei drew his own sword, giving him a nod of encouragement. This time, Unebolod did not bother knocking. He kicked in the ger's door and stormed in with Yungei. As the parents protested and cried out for him to stop, Unebolod grabbed the girl he sought by the arm and dragged her outside to the thoroughfare, throwing her down on the ground. Yungei covered his back as the girl's father followed on their heels, protesting the entire way.

"Sarnia is a good girl!" her father insisted. "She's done nothing wrong!"

"Who is Altan?" Unebolod demanded, looming over Sarnia with his sword in his hand. He ignored her father. Yungei would deal with him, if necessary.

Sarnia held up her hands as if they could stop the swing of his sword should he strike. "I don't know. You—you are talking about Chimeg, yes? And her suitor?"

Unebolod's shoulders tensed and Sarnia seemed to take that as a threat against her life. Perhaps it was. "That's not what her family called him." Her family had known nothing about the man.

"Chimeg told me only a little," she blurted, glancing at Yungei, then past them both toward her parents. Shame flushed her face, and she turned her gaze at the ground. "Please, my Lord, I will tell you everything I know. Just spare my family."

"Then talk," Unebolod snarled. "Now."

"Chimeg met Altan several times over the last year, but I never met him myself," Sarnia said quickly. "She was ... she was smitten with him. She said he promised to free her from the Khan's service, and—" She bit her lip.

"And what?" Could Sarnia know more of what happened? Unebolod did not dare to hope.

"And from—from their beds." Her face burned crimson.

Unebolod did not need to ask to know whom she meant. Manduul and Bayan had bedded the girl, Chimeg. The news was hardly shocking. Could this have been Chimeg's act of revenge for what they did to her? If so, that would eliminate Bayan as a suspect. Unless Bayan seduced her into doing this for him. But she would not have given another man's name. *Unless that was also part of the plan. If she was caught, Bayan would insist that she give a false name, maybe on the assumption that he could save her life if no one learned the truth.* Unebolod's chest heaved with wild breaths. He would wring that boy's neck himself! At some point, all this anger would boil over.

"Have you ever seen this Altan yourself?"

"Sort of, but I never got a good look at him," Sarnia said, trembling in the dirt. "She only ever met him alone. I saw them walking together once at night, but all I saw were his eyes." She shivered. "It was as if he could see straight through me. He was—he was not as large as yourself. Smaller, thin-framed."

Bayan. Unebolod's nostrils flared. Would Manduul kill him for this? Unebolod could only hope so, or he would do it himself.

"Would you recognize his eyes if you saw them in the dark again?" Unebolod asked.

Sarnia appeared ready to faint in fear, looking at her parents for support. Then she dipped her chin against her chest. "Maybe. I will help however I can. Please. Just don't hurt my family."

"That will depend on you," Unebolod said. "Stand up, girl. My patience only lasts so long." He held a hand out to her.

She gazed at the blood dried on his hands, hesitating.

Impatient to get moving, Unebolod seized her arm and hurled her to her feet. "She's coming with me."

Her mother darted toward her. "Sarnia! No!"

Yungei grabbed the woman's arm and thrust her toward her husband. "Control her. We are on business of the Great Khan, and we are authorized to punish any who interfere."

Sarnia's parents cowered back at the obvious threat. Unebolod did not bother looking back as he marched Sarnia across Mongke Bulag. If Bayan cost him the khanship, Mandukhai, and his child, Unebolod was not certain he would be able to wait for the Khan's justice. He was likely to carry it out himself.

Unebolod released Sarnia's arm only after she offered reassurances she would not run.

"Where are we going?" Sarnia asked timidly.

Unebolod ignored her question. The more he considered this mysterious man, the more certain he became that Altan was not Altan. What sort of idiot would give his true name if he had grand designs against the Khan or his wives? Could it have been Bigirsen? He had been in camp a few weeks before, though at the time Unebolod had been the only to know about the child.

"Did you get enough of a look to see if he had any gray hair?" Unebolod asked.

With the investigation in full swing, many of the citizens were still awake at this late hour. Those who were out and about hurried out of Unebolod's path, dipping their heads and staring at the ground.

"I couldn't tell, but I don't think so," Sarnia said. The way she drew out each word sounded uncertain.

Unebolod frowned. "Anything besides his eyes. Did he wear rich furs or have a large nose? Did he seem imposing or intimidating?"

Again she shook her head, and her steps slowed. Unebolod took her arm and pulled her along again.

"I know who you speak of," she mumbled, unable to meet his gaze. "It was definitely not the Vice Regent. He was too small to be him. I'm sorry, my Lord. I wish I had more useful information for you. I just don't see why she would do something like this."

If not Bigirsen, it must have been Bayan. Who else could it be? Yet if Sarnia knew who Bigirsen was, she likely would have identified the Golden Prince already as well. *Unless she is afraid to confess.* Implicating the prince would require secrecy, and Unebolod could not afford witnesses.

"Yungei," Unebolod called over his shoulder. "Go relieve Soke. I have not checked in with him since this began."

"Your will, my Lord," Yungei said, then slipped away.

Unebolod could allow no one else know what he was up to. If he was wrong and Yungei told Manduul, it could end in catastrophe. Unless he had obvious proof against the prince, he could not hint at misgivings.

Bayan stood outside his ger with Berkedai. While neither man smiled, they both appeared relaxed. How could Bayan be relaxed at a time like this?

Sarnia froze, then retreated a step, her big eyes gazing at Unebolod. "No. You don't—"

"Do you recognize either?" Unebolod asked, keeping his voice low and sticking close to the wall of a nearby ger.

"Yes, but not from what you speak of," Sarnia said. She retreated another step. "Can I go home now? I don't want to be involved in this further."

"You're certain it isn't either of them?"

Sarnia appeared like a rabbit ready to run from a hunter. "Yes. I would have recognized him. And the other is too big. My Lord, please. Can I go now? I've told you all I know."

Unebolod grimaced and gave a tight nod. Sarnia darted away between gers, clearly eager to get away from this situation.

The trail had gone cold. It was not Bayan or Bigirsen, and if it was a man, it most likely wasn't Yeke. He found it unlikely she had a man she trusted enough to do this work for her.

Unebolod lumbered past Bayan and Berkedai, hardly even acknowledging them as he headed toward the gathering tent. The door stood open. Heart in his throat, he rushed into the tent.

A host of servants scoured the wood covering the ground. Scrubbing away blood. Unebolod's gaze swept the tent, but Mandukhai was not there. He rushed to her ger, gripping his sword to keep it from tangling his legs in his haste.

Manduul and Bayan stood outside her closed door, along with Togochi.

"There you are," Togochi said. "Any luck?"

Unebolod shook his head and glanced once more at her door.

Manduul's shoulders were sloped downward. Unebolod couldn't tell if Manduul was more concerned for his wife or the child. It hardly mattered. Unebolod already knew they lost the child. No one had confirmed it, but complications that lasted so long could not end with the child surviving. Not this early in the pregnancy. He fought to hold back tears. It would help no one to show his own grief.

"She rests in her ger now," Manduul said. The exhaustion and strain in his voice mirrored what Unebolod felt inside. Manduul did love Mandukhai. "The midwife has given Esige and Tuya instructions on how to care for her, but she lost a lot of blood. Recovery will take time."

"And the child?" Unebolod asked, knowing full well what the answer would be. His throat constricted.

Manduul shook his head. "Nothing could be done. The shaman is performing healing rights."

"What more can I do?" Unebolod asked. He knew there was no chance he could sit still and wait for her to recover. "What do we know of Altan at this point?"

"Nothing," Togochi said. "Little more than we knew from the start. No one else in Mongke Bulag seems to know who this Altan is, and none of the

Altan's here will confess. We were told that he came and went. Perhaps he isn't here now."

"Then how would the girl have gotten the herbs and known to administer it today, while Mandukhai was distracted?" Bayan asked.

Unebolod raised a brow at the prince. That question was a bit on the nose.

"She could have had it for some time," Togochi said with a shrug. "Usually it is Tuya or Esige who serves Mandukhai. It may have been her first opportunity. It's late and we are all too exhausted to think through this clearly. I suggested we all get a few hours of much needed rest."

Manduul glanced at Mandukhai's door and nodded soberly. "Do you have men you trust heading the investigation?"

"I do." Togochi nodded.

"A few hours will do us some good." Manduul lumbered toward his own ger next door. "That's an order, in case that wasn't clear enough." He waved a dismissive hand as he opened his door.

Unebolod lingered outside Mandukhai's ger, but he knew he could not go in. Not with all the guards and the suspicion in the air. Togochi frowned at him, and Unebolod spun and trudged away.

Unebolod retreated to his ger. Kilgor nosed his hand, and he scratched behind her ears as he sank down on the bed. He tried to focus his energy on the problem at hand—Altan and the poison and Nergui's murder—but his thoughts continued to drift back to the loss of the child. Another child. He was being punished by the gods despite his best efforts to keep his oaths and honor his word and his tribe. Two children lost, both from different mothers. It couldn't be a coincidence.

The investigations had served as enough of a distraction for Unebolod not to dwell on the child. Now, alone in his ger, despair gripped his chest. The wall he built around his sorrow for the last day broke down. Unebolod leaned forward on the edge of his bed and buried his face in his hands, unable to stop the tears now that no one was around to see him break down. His spine bowed, and he rested his arms on his legs as everything trembled. Heaviness in his chest and limbs weight him down as if trying to drown him.

Kilgor whined, pawing at his leg. Unebolod turned his gaze to the dog only to discover his vision had blurred. And once the tears started, he couldn't stop them. Unebolod pulled Kilgor's fluffy head toward him and buried his face in her fur as he wept. No matter how hard he tried, Unebolod could not fill his lungs with enough air.

The grief ripped at Unebolod until his lungs burned. Kilgor pulled away and growled. Unebolod had no time to collect himself as the door opened.

Togochi stepped in and closed the door behind him, then crossed his arms over his chest. Those thick eyebrows of his pulled together. Togochi shook his head. "I knew it."

Unebolod straightened his back and sniffled, brushing the sleeve of his deel over his face in a lame attempt at recovery. He knew his face would be a mess either way, and he struggled to control his breathing.

"Would you have ever told him the truth?" Togochi asked. Though his expression was sympathetic, his voice took on a hard edge.

Unebolod hung his head, brushing his hands over his hair. Nothing he had to say would redeem him any longer. *My honor is broken.* He closed his eyes, afraid that realization would bring on a fresh wave of grief.

"He will kill you, brother," Togochi said.

It took an immense effort to swallow the lump that had lodged in his throat, then gather the courage to meet Togochi's gaze.

"Do what you must," Unebolod said, his voice strained with grief. "It was worth it. I only ask that you consider this. If you denounce me, I will accept the punishment, but you will also condemn her and break him."

Togochi did not blink as he stared Unebolod down, weighing him. The silence was deep, ominous. With just a few words, Togochi could bring about Unebolod's doom. But he had already lost the child. He would likely lose Mandukhai regardless of what happened. Death would be preferable to watching her live with Manduul and being unable to touch her again.

Togochi raised his chin. "Manduul has lost enough for one day. I won't take his brother from him as well. Tomorrow is a new day. At some point, Unebolod, you will have to accept that you cannot keep your oath to Manduul as his brother and keep her. You need to choose. Is your she more important to you than your honor?"

The question was as good as a knife in his heart.

"I actually came here to tell you I investigated the gambler's ger," Togochi said. "The man and his wife have disappeared. The men tore apart the ger for clues regarding Nergui, but they came up with nothing helpful. More troublesome, though, is that nothing about their home indicated they had known this danger was looming on their doorstep. If a man knows he might commit murder and be hunted, he would have been better packed for the trip, or at least taken everything of value. But they left behind everything. We know nothing new about Altan. He is smoke in the wind. But I suspect that whoever is behind Nergui's death did not act alone."

With that said, Togochi jerked open the door and left Unebolod alone once more.

Is she more important than your honor? The question echoed in Unebolod's mind. Without his honor, what did he have?

Worse, the truth of that question was clear to him. If he wanted to repair the honor he had broken and the trust Manduul had given him, he needed to distance himself from Mandukhai. At least until Manduul died. That could be days ... or years. *Or he could outlive me,* Unebolod realized. In which case, he could never touch her again.

CHAPTER THIRTY-TWO

THE WOLF OF THE PLAINS

Mandukhai stood beneath an expanse of stars as far as she could see in the wide blue sky. Beneath her, the cold stone of the Khangai Mountains pressed into her bare feet, though the icy cold did not seep into her skin. A breeze ruffled her white silky deel around her legs. Moonlight made the cloth glow. Her hair whipped around her head as if trying to turn her body north.

Far below, the fires of Mongke Bulag scattered across the plain like a hundred flickering fireflies. Mandukhai raised her foot to step toward the camp, but a jagged peak shot up to block her path. The wind once more pulled at her hair, and the deel around her legs spun so sharply that it forced her to turn and follow.

A path opened before her as trees pulled their roots to step aside for her, and uneven rocks smoothed into a level path. She glanced over her shoulder and as the landscape shifted back to normal, leaving her only one direction to explore … North and up the mountain pass.

She walked until her feet bled, yet she felt no pain, until her legs quivered from the climb, though she felt no ache. She carried on until she reached a copse of trees near the top. For a moment, she waited for a path to open before her, but none appeared.

Mandukhai bit her lip and stepped into the trees. The world plunged into darkness. Smoke swirled around her. A sense of peace washed over her as the ground beneath her feet pitched forward, forcing her steps. Mandukhai did not resist. A spirit guided her, and she would know its purpose.

Unebolod had been awake nearly a full day. The exhaustion wore down on him. Everything ached. Yet no matter how much he tried to sleep, all he could do was toss and turn in his bed. Togochi had been right. Unebolod could not continue as he had done for the past year. He loved Mandukhai more than he had loved anyone in his life. Sharing himself with her had been amazing and deeply personal.

I cannot carry on with this, he thought as he sat up on the bed and rubbed the exhaustion from his eyes. Without his honor, he was worthless to her. She deserved better. *I have to be better.*

The search for Altan had come to a dead end. Manduul would not risk a revolt to find the assassin, nor would Mandukhai want him to. Unebolod knew her well. Mandukhai had the patience of a falcon on the hunt. She would want the assassin found, but not at the expense of Manduul's position. *I cannot find the assassin, but maybe I can still track Nergui's killer*, Unebolod thought as he surged to his feet.

Kilgor stood, raising her hackles and growling at the door.

"*Orlok!*" A call came from outside, followed immediately by a pounding on the wooden door. "Hold your dog."

Kilgor barked, and Unebolod gave a sharp whistle. Her ears wilted, then she slowly sank back on her haunches, still alert.

Unebolod opened the door. The wolf dawn approached.

Yungei waited on the other side. "Soke found the gambler."

Eager for something to help pass the time, Unebolod strapped on his sword and strode out into the night.

"Is he alive?" Unebolod asked as he retrieved his mount.

"No, *orlok*." Yungei scowled as if he found this fact deeply insulting on a personal level. He swung onto his own horse.

Unebolod sagged slightly in his saddle. "Show me."

Yungei led them out of Mongke Bulag. The two of them raced across the southwestern steppe, away from the capital. Yungei leaned close to his own mount for increased speed. A hundred questions ran through Unebolod's mind as they galloped at neck-break speed. If the gambler was already dead, what killed him? How far had he gotten? What made him flee before gathering his valuables?

Their horses splashed across the river. Unebolod's trousers soaked with water and it sloshed in his boots. Unphased, Unebolod had a singular purpose: a vision of blood and justice and death that would take more than a little muddy water to extinguish.

Unebolod didn't slow. At least, not until he and Yungei reached deep into the Black Forest. From there, Yungei guided Unebolod along the path through the trees toward a mountain pass. Miles passed before Unebolod spotted an *arban* of men holding up torches in a circle. Soke stood among them. Unebolod dismounted even as his mare skidded to a halt. In just a few steps, he stood over the gambler. Or what remained of him.

Animals had already gotten to him. Chunks of flesh had been torn out with teeth, leaving jagged gashes in the skin and rough gaps where the predators had consumed him. His sword lay on the ground at his hand. All of the excitement and bloodlust slipped away as Unebolod's disappointment settled in.

"Has anyone touched him?" he asked, crouching near the body to inspect for clues.

"No," Soke said, handing his torch to Unebolod. "He is as we found him."

Unebolod grimaced, accepting the light. The canopy from the trees blocked out the early light of the wolf dawn as it came into full effect. "And the wife?"

"Here, *orlok*." Another warrior motioned behind a tree. "It appears she attempted to flee and was taken down from behind."

Unebolod inspected the dead man's body for a suspicious cause of death, but the animals had done their work. If anyone else had been behind this, no traces of a struggle remained. To be sure, Unebolod checked the man's belt. Nothing. Someone had mentioned Nergui's coin pouch was missing. Where could it have gone?

Unebolod moved on to the wife. Perhaps she had a story to tell. Her body lay facing the forest canopy, eyes wide in fear. An animal had ripped out her throat. An echo of Mandukhai's scream rose in his ears, and he glanced around before realizing that it was only in his memory. He brushed his wrist across his sweaty forehead.

"So, animals killed them." Unebolod rose, scowling at the bodies. "The Khan will not be pleased." And the animals had found them quickly to do such damage in a day. Or even just this night. Either the animals had grown bolder, or these two were killed and left for the animals to destroy the evidence. He glanced at the leaves above, watching the waning wolf dawn stream through the gaps onto the forest floor.

"Bring their bodies back to Mongke Bulag," Unebolod said. "He will want to see this for himself."

Not only could Unebolod not exact justice on this man, but he couldn't even question him. Still, if this had been set up, some evidence must still linger. As Soke and Yungei organized the handful of men to wrap what remained of the bodies and take them to the capital for Manduul, Unebolod expanded his search.

Soke's men had ridden their mounts over the area enough times to cover any other tracks that could've been left. If someone had wanted to keep these deaths a secret, he would have taken a more covert path back to the capital. Was it possible that Altan could have been responsible for both? Perhaps he had followed these two, killed them, then fled the area before anyone could find him. Unebolod could not rule out the coincidence.

Unebolod walked in slow circles, examining the ground, the shrubs, trees, and the canopy above. Soke offered to stay behind with him, but Unebolod ordered Soke and Yungei to make sure the bodies were delivered to Manduul. They rode off as the sun broke through the trees.

At long last, near the northern edge of the space, Unebolod spotted a potential clue. He edged toward the shrub and noticed a broken branch on one side. Unebolod crouched to investigate and discovered a leather pouch in the dirt. He unfastened the string tying the pouch closed and peered at the pile of silver coins within. Without comment, he tucked it in his own belt. Either the debt was paid or someone had paid him off because that was too much silver for a man of simple means.

The branch alone could have been nothing, but the coins were hard to ignore. Unebolod put out the torch in the dirt, then peered closer at the ground as sunlight caught something on the ground. He picked it up, holding it between his fingers toward the rays of dawn.

A single painite stone flickered with light like a small flame in his fingers. *Bayan.*

The world sped away, as if Mandukhai's body were being swept down a rushing river. She twisted around and reached for something solid to control the flow, but met nothing. Water filled her lungs, and Mandukhai struggled for every breath. A voice in her mind echoed the same rhythmic chant. *Free your mind to the spirits.* She held her breath and opened her mind, but still the current swept her away.

When at last she grasped ahold of a branch and pulled herself ashore, Mandukhai's hands were coated in blood. She yelped and scrubbed the blood on her clothes, but it soaked them through as if the river made were of blood. The sticky, sour stench seeped into her skin.

There, on the banks of the blood-red river, lay the body of a baby. Mandukhai's breath caught and for a moment she froze, yet she knew it could not be her child. This baby was fully formed, and hers had hardly had a chance to grow. As it stared at her with dead black eyes, the accusation of her sins pierced her heart. She stumbled back and fell over the edge of a cliff, tumbling through the air. She screamed, but no sound came from her lips. *Free your mind to the spirits,* the chanting voice commanded.

Mandukhai fell into a bed of furs. As her fingers brushed across the soft fur, a tall, broad-shouldered figure loomed over her. She recognized him instantly, despite the shadows that masked his body. Unebolod leaned closer, and firelight flickered across his face, revealing the anger in his eyes and the fury marring his normally stoic expression. For the first time, she feared him. Mandukhai shuffled backward, trying to escape as he raised a wolf-head sword over her heart. *Free your mind to the spirits.*

Mandukhai tried. Her chin trembled as she whimpered. Her legs grew weak as she scrambled away from him. Mandukhai squeezed her eyes closed and attempted to block him out, but the fear of Unebolod's anger and the sword poised to strike made it impossible to clear her mind. Mandukhai prayed to the High Heavens to rid her of this terrible vision.

After a few hammering heartbeats, no deadly stroke fell from Unebolod's sword. Mandukhai opened one eye, holding her breath. But instead of the bed of furs, she now stood in the Gobi. In the distance, a lone figure lay face down in the sands. Her steps were slowed, absorbed by the deep sands, as she approached the familiar figure in a golden silk deel.

The imprint of hooves and boots remained pressed into the ground behind the shrub. Unebolod tucked the painite stone into the pouch of silver. Anger pulsed through him. Bayan did this. Such a stone was rare, and only the Golden Prince had a belt full of them. Would this be enough to condemn him? Manduul certainly had a blind spot where the prince was involved. Unebolod needed more than just a stone found on the ground. He needed solid, undisputable evidence if he wanted to turn Manduul against Bayan.

Mandukhai was right, he thought as he stood and follow the tracks north, guiding his mount by the reins. *The boy will be his own undoing.* Once more, his admiration for her swelled. Somehow, he would have to block her from his heart.

The tracks met with the river and disappeared into the current. Unebolod mounted his mare and rode along the rocky riverbank, observant for any sign of passing. After nearly a mile, he met with his reward. Tracks emerged on the near side of the river, headed toward Mongke Bulag. Bayan was smarter than Unebolod had given him credit for. He had crisscrossed the river to try covering his tracks. A clever move. Had Unebolod not been so determined, he might have given up searching long ago.

Unebolod urged his mount into a canter, first watching the tracks in the dirt, then the bent, trampled grass. He followed them all the way to Mongke Bulag, where the tracks were harder to discern among more recent hooves or boots. A few times, he lost the trail and had to backtrack. Eventually, the tracks crisscrossed themselves near a herd of six horses. Unebolod sat straighter in his saddle and glanced around him. This family lived on the western edge of the capital.

The woman caring for the mounts bobbed her head in respect as he stopped beside her.

"Whose herd is this?" he asked.

"My husband's," she said, keeping her eyes lowered toward the ground.

"I must speak with him," Unebolod said. "Fetch him now."

She bobbed her head again and rushed to the nearby ger.

Unebolod dismounted, inspecting the six horses. Two stallions and four mares. He lifted their hooves, hoping to find a match to the one he had tracked here. None were obviously discernable as the horse he sought. Unebolod stood, rubbing at a knot in the small of his back as he looked over each of the mounts again.

The chestnut stallion whinnied. Bayan had a strange preference to chestnut mounts. He traded off his own ponies if they did not have the chestnut coloring. Nearly all of the prince's herd had been either bred or traded to accommodate his taste. If Bayan was to take any of these horses, it would most likely be the stallion.

"My Lord Unebolod," the woman's husband said as he joined Unebolod among the mounts. "My wife and I are honored by your visit. Please, come in for some tea. You are welcome in our home."

Unebolod nodded, casting one more glance at the chestnut stallion as he followed the couple inside. Out of sight was probably best for this investigation.

Their ger was modest but comfortable. They introduced themselves as Gergen and Sortokhanai. She busied herself preparing tea for their guest as Gergen motioned toward the bed for Unebolod to take first choice of seats. Once all three were settled with their tea, Unebolod chose a more abrupt approach to the conversation.

"Where were you two nights ago, Gergen?" Unebolod asked. He didn't bother touching the tea.

"Here, my Lord," Gergen replied quickly. Unebolod would have been inclined to disbelieve him were it not for the absolute innocence on his face. "With my wife."

Sortokhanai nodded but said nothing to interrupt their conversation.

"Did anyone come visit that night?" he asked.

Gergen paused this time. His face scrunched together as he thought through the events of the night. "My brother stopped over to borrow some of our felts for his wife. She is having a child soon and has had a hard time with her back. The extra felts help."

"How late was that?"

"I don't know exactly, my Lord." Gergen rubbed his head and glanced at his wife for help. "Shortly before dusk, yes?"

Sortokhanai nodded again.

"And what time did you go to bed?"

"I'm sorry, my Lord." Gergen shifted, clearly uncomfortable with the conversation. "Have we done something wrong? I don't know anyone named Altan."

Unebolod scowled. By now, no one in Mongke Bulag would not have heard about the Khan's investigation.

"Just answer the question." Unebolod could not tell if the man was trying to hide anything, but so far his responses seemed sincere.

"It was just past full dark," Sortokhanai said at last. "I remember because I pulled the flap closed and could see the stars just appearing." She motioned toward the flap in the center of the roof, which was now open.

"Did any unusual sounds or commotion from the horses wake you in the night?"

"Not to my recollection," Gergen replied.

"And neither of you took a midnight ride?"

Sortokhanai smirked as if his question amused her, then placed a playful hand on her husband's arm. "That depends on how you define a ride."

Gergen's face reddened. "Sortokhanai, this is not the time for your jokes. No. Though I woke her for—"

"I get it," Unebolod said, holding up a hand. They knew nothing. Or if they did, the two of them were very good at covering it up. Neither seemed to understand what he was digging for, which meant they could not have been the ones who rode out in the night. "How early did you wake the next morning?"

"Late," Sortokhanai said with a grin.

Unebolod rubbed at his forehead. No, they were not involved, but their stallion certainly was. He had no doubt about that, which meant whoever borrowed the mount wanted to cover their tracks. *Not whoever. Bayan.* Once more, the boy's cleverness impressed Unebolod. Borrowing a different mount to ride out after the gambler and his wife, then returning it before anyone knew better. Had Unebolod not found that stone, he would not have known Bayan had been involved at all.

"My Lord, I assure you, we had nothing to do with what happened to the Khan's wife," Gergen said swiftly, pleadingly. "And I do not know any man named Altan personally. If there was anything we could offer…"

Unebolod nodded earnestly and stood. "Thank you for your time. If you learn anything, please come directly to me. No one else. And speak of this to no one. If they want to know why I came, just tell them I was admiring your herd."

"Of course, my Lord."

Though they had no information to share with him, Unebolod knew as he stepped into the morning sun that he had uncovered the truth. Bayan's own mounts were watched over and protected. If Bayan had wanted to cover his tracks when he followed the gambler out of Mongke Bulag, he could not have taken his horse. Instead, he had walked to the edge of the encampment and had taken a mount from someone else—and what better than his characteristic chestnut horse? It still was not enough evidence to present to Manduul. If this couple had seen anything, perhaps he could have used them as witnesses. Deep down, Unebolod knew he still needed more proof. He would not let this go unpunished. Even if he had to do it himself.

A strong male voice carried on the air, sending a chill down Mandukhai's spine. "Only the one who carries the spirit can reunite the One Nation. Only he of my bone will have the might to hold it."

Mandukhai spun around, but only the man in sand lay before her. She knelt beside him and was about to roll him over when she recognized the belt of golden discs, each of which held a gleaming painite gemstone. Mandukhai pressed a hand to his back, but she knew he was dead. She closed her eyes and said a prayer for him, but when she opened her eyes, she knelt beside the sacred Mother Tree, and her hand now rested against the bark of the tree.

Smoke swirled around her, drawing Mandukhai to her feet. She felt a moment of panic, turning to find a source or a fire. Then the smoke cleared to reveal a tall, burly man in rich, thick furs standing before the Mother Tree. His looped braids hung long and low over his shoulders, covered only by his fur hat, perfectly matched to the rest of his clothes. His back remained to her, and Mandukhai hesitated, uncertain what his intentions would be if he discovered her there. He pressed a hand to the tree and bowed his head. Mandukhai held her breath. Who was this broad-shouldered mystery man praying at the Mother Tree? She waited for some sort of revelation to hit her. What was the significance of all of this?

When at long last he straightened and turned toward her, the smoke twisted around him, lit only by the moonlight filtering through the leaves. Only his eyes were visible, the golden eyes of a Wolf.

"I brought to kneel all colors of the tribes," he said. His voice carried on the smoke, rolling out in waves in every direction. The voice was deep, commanding, and sent a tremor of awe through Mandukhai's very soul. "I bleached them white and bound them as one."

The man stepped forward, and the smoke rolled away as if bowing at his feet. His massive hand rested on the handle of his sword with all the casual ease of a viper always at the ready, prepared to strike. The hilt of the sword bore the head of a golden wolf with jade eyes. Hanging from that golden hilt, thick black horsehairs swayed with each of his steps. Mandukhai knew he could kill her in an instant, and she had no way to defend herself. He both terrified and mesmerized her. *Should I run?*

"I am the wolf of the plains. The bones of the hills. There are no tribes under the Eternal Blue Sky," he said. He stood a full head taller than Mandukhai. Everything about him was massive, but not in the way Manduul was. Mandukhai didn't doubt for a moment that he was more muscle than anything else.

Mandukhai gasped and dropped to her knees, trembling before the spirit of Genghis Khan. If this was a vision, she would be certain to honor the spirit of the first Great Khan, the man who had united the Mongols under one banner.

Genghis passed her as if she were nothing more than the smoke that bowed at his feet. "This is not One Nation," he said. "They forget where their lands come from and who gave it to them."

Mandukhai circled the tree, searching for Genghis. What did he mean by this? Was he angry with his descendants? When she circled back to the front of the tree, a great red eagle stared at her from one of the branches. It cocked its head as it observed her, then its beady eyes twitched downward. Mandukhai followed the gaze, stumbling back when she saw Esen's body dangling from the tree, just as he had been hung by the men who revolted against him.

The eagle spread its wings and launched off the branch. It transformed into Genghis Khan; tall, imposing, and wolf-like. He landed on his feet as if he had jumped to the ground himself then turned to face Esen. "I am the flail of God. Had you not created great sins, God would not have sent a punishment like me upon you."

In one smooth, expert motion, Genghis drew his sword and cut the rope that hung Esen. The dead man hit the ground with a thump, then sucked in a breath as would a drowning man breaking the surface of a river. Esen's dark eyes fell on Mandukhai first. He snarled in recognition. Genghis stepped closer, drawing Esen's attention, whose eyes widened in terror.

"You are a mutt who pretended at being a wolf," Genghis said. His voice took on an edge as sharp and dangerous as his sword. Genghis roared, striking his sword across Esen's legs, forcing him to his knees.

The rage startled Mandukhai and she staggered a few steps away from Genghis, hugging her arms over her chest. Why was he showing her this?

Terrified of staying, terrified of running, Mandukhai quivered in uncertainty until her knees gave out.

"You are not of the bone or blood," Genghis said to Esen. "You are nothing more than greed, dust, and earth." As he spoke the final words, Esen's body turned to dirt and fell to the earth beneath the tree.

"Rise, daughter of the dragon, queen of the wolves," Genghis said as he swung his sword through the air. Blood flew off the blade in an arcing spray. As he slid the clean blade into its place on his belt, he took her arm and pulled her to her feet.

CHAPTER THIRTY-THREE

FATE OF THE WOLF

Bayan returned to his ger with Berkedai. The two had spent the morning improving Bayan's sword fighting skills. Bayan had convinced Berkedai to teach him everything he knew. He had a lot to learn if he ever hoped to best Unebolod—a fight he knew deep down would come one day. Manduul would not live forever to protect Bayan from anyone ambitious enough to usurp his claim to the title. A few months ago, he would have given away the title freely. Now that Bayan had a taste of the Khan's power, he wanted more.

Unebolod also had no love for Bayan. His constant terse remarks and sharp glares told Bayan all he needed to know. Unebolod was also Lord Bolunai's brother, which meant he likely had the same disposition for violence as his older brother.

"You've done well today," Berkedai said, seizing Bayan's shoulder affectionately. "Same time tomorrow?"

Bayan nodded as his gaze fell on the Khorchin mark on the collar of Berkedai's deel. When the day came, would Berkedai be loyal to him or to his Khorchin lord, Unebolod? *I can't doubt him now*, he thought as he ducked into his ger. Berkedai strode away. Since retrieving Bayan from among the Chakhar tribe, Berkedai had proven his loyalty to Bayan repeatedly. But tribe ties could run deeper.

Bayan set his sword on the table beside the door, then stripped off the padded leather armor he had used for sparring. Berkedai certainly hadn't taken it easy on him. Bayan thumbed a nick in the leather he would have to get patched as he laid the armor on the table beside the sword. Once freed from the extra weight, Bayan rolled his shoulders and neck to stretch them out. He preferred the comfort of silk to the confinement of armor. One day, when Manduul passed on and he became Great Khan, he would make others fight for him.

The one weight Bayan could not remove was that of Nergui's death. It had been little more than a day, and much had happened since. Still, Bayan had waited for Manduul to storm his ger, turn out his things, and accuse him of killing Nergui. He hadn't wanted to do it. Bayan hated killing on such a personal level. But if Nergui had spread word of what he saw—particularly to Mandukhai or Unebolod—Bayan would have been in danger, as would Yeke. The danger Mandukhai posed was not one Bayan could fight with a sword or bow. He knew her well enough now to know she would outmaneuver him before he ever saw it coming.

Using the gambling debt excuse had worked in Bayan's favor, and he'd been careful to cover his tracks. He had given the man and his wife more silver than they would ever need and promised that they would be safe among the tribes in the far north until he became Great Khan. Then he would welcome them back. It had also helped that they were terrified he would kill them if they hadn't obeyed. Bayan thought his plan clever, even if it had involved more killing.

As ill-fated as the loss of the child had been, it served as enough of a distraction to keep Manduul's men from investigating Nergui's death. No one seemed to suspect Bayan.

"Enkh!" Bayan called as his stomach grumbled. He hadn't been able to eat much for the last day.

But his servant did not come. Grumbling to himself, he went to the shelf and rummaged for something to eat. Curds and *airag*. Bayan reached for the cup sitting on the butcher's block, uncorked the jug of *airag* with his teeth, and was about to pour when he spotted something in the bottom of his cup.

A single painite stone.

He spit the cork on the block, set down the jug, and reached into the cup to pull out the stone. The sunlight streamed through the open door and caught the stone in such a way it burned with a fiery light. Someone had placed it there. They wanted him to find it.

Panic seized Bayan and, forgetting his food, he rushed to the chest to retrieve his golden belt. After he had returned and burned the bloodied clothes yesterday, Bayan had put the belt away until he would have more time to clean it. It had been in his chest since he returned from the woods. Bayan extracted the belt and examined it one golden disc at a time until he found one missing a stone. He strapped it on experimentally and noticed the stone was missing from his left hip. The memory of his fight against the man in the woods rushed back, and Bayan sucked in quick, uneven breaths.

The gambler had been too startled at first to realize what Bayan was there for. Bayan had swung his sword; they had struggled as the wife attempted to flee. Bayan had wrestled his sword free from the man's grasp just long enough to thrust the blade deep into his gut. For good measure, Bayan had twisted the blade. The man had grappled at Bayan desperately as he slumped, tearing at his belt to keep from falling to the ground.

But the man had ripped at his belt. How had the stone ended up here, in the cup in Bayan's ger?

Noises from Mongke Bulag became more acute as Bayan glanced toward the door. No one loomed in the doorway. No shadowy figure caused the pressing weight on Bayan's shoulders or the feel of someone watching him. He was utterly alone. His gaze darted around the ger for any other signs or warnings, but he spotted none. The air seemed too thin, and Bayan struggled to keep control of his breathing. He closed his eyes as everything tilted slightly, but it did little for the churning anxiety in his gut.

The belt had to go until he could fix it. Bayan rushed back to the chest, tucking away the belt and the stone and slamming lid closed. He stumbled back, watching the chest like a wolf. His legs hit the bed and he flopped back and laid his head back to attempt calming himself.

A lump beneath his feather-stuffed pillow made Bayan wince. He reached under the pillow and pulled out a small pouch. *No. It can't be.* Bayan launched upright on the bed and tore open the pouch to reveal the silver coins he had given to the couple. As if it burned his fingers to touch, he thrust the pouch away from him. The contents spilled across the floor.

Bayan's mouth dried. He swallowed repeatedly, unable to dislodge the forming lump. *Airag. I need a drink.*

He surged to his feet, moving with stiff limbs to the block and pouring a generous cup of *airag*. He downed it and refilled the cup. After the second cup, he pressed his palms to the block and leaned against it. *Someone knows what I've done, but why haven't they taken this to Manduul? Why play these games with me?*

318

Bayan's mind reeled.

"Are you feeling ill, Bolkhu *Jinong*?" Unebolod said from behind him.

Bayan opened his mouth to respond, his back to Unebolod, but nothing would rise past the lump in his throat.

"I can fetch a healer," Unebolod offered, and in his anxious state, Bayan could not discern Unebolod's tone. Nor could he move. "Or perhaps a midwife."

Midwife. Did he think Bayan was behind the miscarriage? Bayan found his voice at last, able to move enough to pour another cup of *airag.* "I had nothing to do with that."

"Did I say you did?"

Bayan straightened, sweeping up his cup as he spun around to face Unebolod. The other man stood casually near the door, blocking Bayan's escape. Unebolod's hand rested seemingly harmless on his sword. But Bayan would be a fool to underestimate him.

"You had your fun with that serving girl in the past, though, didn't you?" Unebolod asked. Even his tone was casual, but there was an edge in it just as dangerous as his stance. "Her friend seemed to think so."

"So did Manduul," Bayan retorted. "Yet you are here accusing me."

"I haven't accused you of anything." Unebolod glanced at the silver spilled out on the floor.

He knows. Bayan raised his chin stubbornly, doing his best to mask the fear pulsing through his veins.

"I will not tell Manduul what you did to Nergui," Unebolod said, his voice taking on that dangerous edge. "There would be no point. But I will tell her. And she will never forget. She has the patience to wait for her vengeance. Manduul cannot protect you forever."

Bayan drank the *airag* greedily, then set the cup down with a thump against the butcher's block and strode toward Unebolod. "When he dies, she will either submit to me or suffer the consequences. Not even you can protect her from her fate."

"If you think she needs my protection, you have grossly underestimated her." Unebolod snorted in disgust, and his fingers tightened coolly on his sword hilt. "And if you think you can force her to submit to any man, you have learned nothing from Manduul." He stalked slowly closer. "A dragon hoards its treasures and only reveals them when the time to pay has come. You are out of your depth, pup. A wolf cannot conquer a dragon." Unebolod turned to duck out of the ger.

"If you are so confident I had anything to do with what happened, why will you not go to Manduul?" Bayan blurted before Unebolod could escape.

Unebolod paused in the doorway, turning back to him with a perilous grin. "Have you not been paying attention? Manduul cannot protect you forever. The fate of the wolf is out of your hands. And when Manduul dies, you will have a dragon to contend with." He did not linger long enough for Bayan to press for more information. Unebolod slid out the door and disappeared from sight.

Bayan stared after Unebolod, dumbstruck. Mandukhai could not be so powerful, could she? Once Manduul did die, whenever that day came, she would lose the power she held. It was directly linked to Manduul. If she wanted to hold that power and position, she would have no choice but to submit to Bayan ... wouldn't she?

Mandukhai quivered at Genghis' touch on her arms. "What shall my purpose be? Just tell me and I will serve," she said resolutely.

"Purpose." Genghis snorted and turned his wolfish gaze to the Mother Tree. His shoulders sagged ever so slightly in a way that reminded Mandukhai of Unebolod. Both were men of great intelligence and power. "I dedicated my life to uniting my people under one banner and punishing those who would tear us apart. That was my purpose. I gave my empire to my sons and daughters, and their sons and daughters. I taught them to heed the call of the wolf. How quickly they have gone deaf."

The smoke swirled around them, and when it cleared, Mandukhai stood beside Genghis on an open plain overlooking the remains of a battle. Dead bodies littered the ground. Moghul. Uyghur. Her gaze swept the dead for Bigirsen but found nothing.

"I gave them an empire, and they have forgotten their unity and purpose. They have abandoned my vision, that one arrow alone can be easily broken, but many arrows are indestructible."

He grimaced, suddenly holding up a cup in his right hand. "The land remembers, though. The earth mother remembers. I left the greatest empire in the world, but my heirs have failed at remaining united to preserve it. They have fallen into discord. They have forgotten the One Nation."

Mandukhai bowed her head in shame. "I offer my deepest regret at our failure, Great Khan."

Genghis shook his head, and the world beneath them shifted until they stood outside a small nomad's ger in the shadows of a mountain not far from Hami. "Not all have forgotten."

A small child with a hunched back and twisted limbs limped out of the ger. He couldn't have been older than two or three. Mandukhai watched as he cried while feeding the two chickens outside. The pain in his broken body must have been overwhelming. Mandukhai frowned and stepped toward him, but Genghis grabbed her shoulder and held her back.

"Not yet," he said. "The people need a strong leader to follow if they are to save the fractured empire."

"Manduul? Is he not adequate?"

Genghis snorted. "He is not much longer. And he will not affect change."

Mandukhai's heart hammered in her chest. Not much longer? Would Manduul die soon?

The boy screamed as one of the chickens pecked at his leg. Mandukhai did not understand why she had been given this particular vision. Who was this child? And why wouldn't Genghis allow her to approach him?

Genghis shook his head at the boy in disgust, then offered Mandukhai the cup. "The strength of a man comes from the strength of the woman who guides him through life. Come and sip from the cup of destruction."

Mandukhai accepted the cup with a deep bow. As she raised it to her lips, she noticed the cup contained blood, not milk or tea or *airag* as she had expected. Not wanting to insult the spirit of Genghis Khan, she took a generous drink, then held the cup out to him. Genghis accepted, smiling at the blood on her lips. He brushed it away with his thumb, and she flinched at the touch despite how gentle it had been.

"I have seen the strength of women," Genghis said. "I have underestimated their value and learned to listen when they offered their advice." He turned his wolf-like eyes to the boy. "You will give your heart twice. Once to passion. Once to compassion. Yet they are not equally powerful."

A newfound strength pulsed through Mandukhai as she bowed to Genghis Khan. Her skin glowed as if the sun were within her. As she rose, he plunged a horn-handled knife into her chest and cut over her heart. Mandukhai gasped but was surprised to feel no pain. Shock ripped through her as he shoved his hand into the wound and ripped out her beating heart, clutching it in his iron grip.

"Remember, always, who your heart belongs to, daughter of the dragon, queen of the wolves," Genghis said as he squeezed.

Mandukhai raised her chin, standing tall and proud with a righteous purpose that radiated from her. She knew power as she'd never known before. Power and purpose.

She felt the fate of the wolf pulsing through her veins.

HISTORICAL NOTES

Lineage gets a bit tricky with some of the Borjigin royals. Instead of wasting space to explain. I included a graphic on the first pages of the book. Manduul's claim was tenuous, at best, and it could have been because his mother was not a wife, but a concubine. No evidence supports this issue either way, but it makes his hold on the title weak compared to someone like Bayan.

Believe it or not, the trick with baby Bayan in the basket was recorded in historical record as the man attempted to rescue baby Bayan from the anger and hate of his grandfather, according to the *History of the Mongols from 9th to the 19th Century*. Bayan's first years are actually quite fascinating. His grandfather was obsessed with destroying anyone who could supplant him, and that included the infant boy. Bayan's mother and great-great-grandmother managed to disguise him as a girl for the first few years of his life when they heard the command to kill the baby if it was a boy. I wrote a separate short story, *Prosperous Eternity*, that goes into more detail on Bayan's early years because his backstory is fascinating.

Bigirsen did, in fact, suggest installing Manduul as Great Khan because the Mongol tribes were fractured and needed a royal leader. Manduul's weak position beneath Bigirsen (also called Beg-Arslan) was a fairly well-known fact. Manduul had no real understanding of just how powerless he truly was, and Bigirsen did everything he could to maintain the illusion that Manduul was the one in charge of the Nation.

No significant evidence remains that Mandukhai and Unebolod (also called Une-Bolod) had an intimate relationship, but it is widely believed that the two were very close. Taking the step from them being close to having deeper feelings seems logical, especially considering the sexual politics that were rampant in Manduul Khan's court.

Unebolod's actual age is unknown. One historical record indicates that he "retired" to his homeland when Bayan was made the Golden Prince, but I do not feel this accurately indicates his age. Considering the potential relationship he had with Mandukhai, as well as his presence in a few of the later battles, it is safe to assume he was probably in his twenties at this point in time. If he did "retire" to his homeland, it was most likely because he felt displaced by the arrival of the prince.

Manduul was notoriously blind to any of Bayan's wrongs—to a deep fault. The relationship the two had was strong and binding beyond anyone else. Even if Manduul might have doubted Bayan's abilities, he never doubted his motives or his right to be the heir.

Bayan and Manduul did, in fact, visit the Khorkhonag Valley to make a sacred vow of brotherhood to one another. While other men considered themselves "brothers" and may have even sworn oaths to one another, none of those brothers were considered as close as this ceremony made Bayan and Manduul. In fact, even Manduul's relationship and commitment to his wives came second to his commitment to Bayan. That's how close they were. "They declared themselves sworn friends and loved each other," according to the *Mongol Secret History*.

When Manduul installed Bayan as the Golden Prince, he did rename him to Bolkhu so that Bayan's name would more closely resemble his own in meaning: Rising (Manduul) and Rising Up (Bolkhu). The quote, "In the blue sky above, there are the sun and the moon. And on the earth below, the Khan and the Jinong" was an actual quote according to the translation from *The Mongolian Titles Jinong and Sigejin*.

Not a lot was written about Yeke Qabar-tu. She was Bigirsen's daughter and married to Manduul in an attempt at what we can only assume was an offer of peace between the two men. Many considered her ugly and unworthy of being a queen. There is no evidence that she and Manduul ever had an intimate relationship. In fact, some histories question whether or not the marriage was consummated at all, and that he "stayed absent from her" according to the *Mongol Chronicle Altan Tobci*. Given the intensity of sexual politics at the time, and the fact that she was a woman, I find it hard to believe they never shared a bed. However, it is easy to believe that she was unappealing to him and Manduul spent little time with her at all.

During this period, only Bigirsen's Mongol army had any activity. Manduul had not fought in battle since the death of Taisun's sons. The battles of

Manduul and Bayan were only considered small "skirmishes" and very little was written about them. Some historians and chronicles believe that Bayan's goal was to remove some of Bigirsen's power from Manduul's court. Given Bayan's track record and age, I believe this might give him a bit more credit than he deserved. Perhaps he wanted to strip away some of that power, but I don't believe he had any grand designs against Bigirsen aside from what anyone could see on the surface.

Several of the lines Genghis delivers to Mandukhai in this book are quotes from other historical texts from Genghis Khan himself. I did my best to meld them into a cohesive conversation for their spirit walk together. However, evidence of Mandukhai's miscarriage and this spirit walk with Genghis are entirely for entertainment purposes. Up to this point in the story, Mandukhai had no children according to historical records.

A note on pronunciations: Many of the name pronunciations in this novel have been simplified to make it easier for American readers. For example, Genghis is actually pronounced Chinggis. There are also many more tribes and characters in the true story than I have included in the book. To make it easier for readers to digest without being overwhelmed by hundreds of names and dozens of tribes, I compressed some characters/tribes into only a few key figures throughout the epic tale.

TERMS

airag (eye-rahg) – alcoholic drink made from fermented mare's milk, typically milky in color

arban (ahr-bahn) – unit of ten Mongol warriors

Bankhar (bahn-khahr) – traditional sheepherding dog of the Mongolian steppe; 24-31 inches tall at the shoulder with typically dark brown hair

Biyelgee (bey-eel-geeh) – traditional dance of celebration and community

black airag – stronger version of regular airag with a longer fermentation process, typically clear in color

boal (boh-ahl) – honey wine

boqta (bohk-tah) – column-like headdress decorated with beads and silver; the taller the boqta, the more prominent the woman wearing it

buuz (boos) – meat stuffed dumplings

deel (deal) – robe-like wrap worn by the Mongol people, traditionally made of silk, velvet, or woolen felt with ties or silver buttons and belted at the waist with a belt; lined with sheep's wool or fur in the winter

ger (grr) – round, dome-like house made of Birchwood lattice and lathes, then covered in wool felt; known in America as a yurt

gonji (goonj) – a princess

jagan (jah-gahn) – unit of 100 Mongol warriors (or 10 arban)

jinong (gee-nong) – a prince

kurultai (kuh-ruhl-tai) – a gathering of tribal lords where they elected the next Great Khan

mingghan (min-ghahn) – unit of 1000 Mongol warriors (or 10 jagan)

orlok (oor-lahk) – field commander of multiple tumens

paiza (pahee-zah) – a golden medallion of safe passage, given only to high-ranking officials as a means of protection under the Great Khan

shanaavch (shah-navsh) – headdress made of long strings of beads and bells, typically silver, coral, or turquoise

sulde (sool-duh) – a banner made of colored horse-hair, typically arranged in a circle

toortsog (toort-sogh) – hat made of silk, sometimes with fur or felt lining and a knot of colored tails or feathers at the top; typically worn by noble men

tumen (tyoo-mehn) – regiment of 10,000 Mongol warriors

uni (oo-nee) – a pole made of birth; used as a support beam for the ceiling of a ger

CHARACTERS

Altan (ahl-tahn) – Lady and commander of the Jalair; Hulun's daughter

Bayan Bolkhu Mongke (bay-yahn bohl-koo mohng-kay) – Borjigin prince; last true descendant of Genghis Khan

Berkedai (buhr-ke-daee) – Khorchin commander; Bayan's guard

Bigirsen (big-er-sehn) – Uyghur warlord; Manduul Khan's Vice Regent; orlok of the southern tumens of the Great Khan

Bolunai (boh-loo-nahee) – Khorchin khan; older brother of Unebolod; descendant of Khasar

Borogchin (boh-rohg-chin) – Borjigin princess; niece of Manduul Khan

Degghar (dehg-har) – Chakhar man; Siker's father

Esen (eh-sehn) – Oirat Lord and leader; Borjigin Butcher

Esige (eh-seeg-ay) – Borjigin princess; niece of Manduul Khan

Genghis Khan (jehn-giss) – First Great Khan of the Mongol Nation; died 1227

Getei (jet-ee) – Ongud soothsayer

Guden (goo-dehn) – Chakhar khan; leader and lord of the clan

Hulun (huh-loon) – Lord of the Jalair

Issama (ee-sah-mah) – Bigirsen's Uyghur advisor

Khasar (kah-sahr) – brother of Genghis; son of Hoelun

Khosoichi (ko-soy-chi) – Borjigin shaman

Khutulun (koo-too-loon) – daughter of Kaidu; warrior princess

Korgiz (koor-gis) – Lord of the Ongud

Mahmed (mahk-mehd) – Lord of the Great Horde

Mandukhai (mahn-doo-kaee) – Ongud daughter of a lord; Manduul Khan's second wife

Manduul Khan (mahn-dool) – Oirat-Borjigin ruler of Mongolia; descendent of Genghis Khan

Molon Khan (moh-lohn) – 17-year-old Great Khan before Manduul; Manduul's nephew; killed in battle

Nergui (nehr-gooee) – Mandukhai's loyal Ongud guard

Odsar (ohd-sahr) – Unebolod's dead wife

Samur (sah-moor) – great-great-grandmother of Bayan

Siker (see-kur) – daughter of Degghar; Chakhar girl; Bayan's lover

Soke (soh-kay) – Khorchin commander

Taisun Khan (taee-soon) – Manduul's older half-brother; killed by Esen

Tengghar (tayng-har) – Khorchin lord; Bolunai's son; Unebolod's nephew

Tsetseg (zeht-sehg) – Esen's daughter; Bayan's mother

Togochi (toh-goh-chee) – lord and General of the Khorlod; Manduul's loyal sworn brother (no blood)

Tuya (too-eeah) – Mandukhai's Ongud servant

Unebolod (oo-nuh-boh-lohd) – lord of the Khorchin; Manduul's loyal sword brother (no blood); Orlok of the northern tumens of the Great Khan

Unige (oo-nee-kay) – Alyghuchid Lord/leader; Borjigin loyalist; a member of Manduul Khan's council

Yeke (yeh-keh) – Uyghur daughter of Bigirsen; Manduul Khan's first wife

Yungei (yoon-geh-hee) – Khorchin commander; Bayan's guard

TRIBES AND LOCATIONS

Borjigin (bohr-eh-jin) – tribe of the Great Khan Genghis

Chakhar (shah-kahr) – tribe of the southern steppe; Siker's tribe

Gansu (gahn-soo) – corridor between the mountains and rivers leading into China.

Great Horde – tribe of the far norther steppe (Russian territory); formerly the Golden Horde

Hami (ha-mee) – oasis city in the Gobi connecting the far east to the far west

Jalair (jah-laeer) – tribe of the northernmost steppe

Karakorum (kah-rah-koh-rum) – Mongolian sacred capital city

Kherlen (curl-ehn) – river of the Mongol steppe

Khorchin (koor-chin) – tribe of Genghis Khan's younger brother Khasar; Yuan Dynasty ally

Khorkhanag Valley (kohr-kin-ahg) – sacred valley location where Genghis and Jamuka swore sacred vows of brotherhood

Khorlod (koor-lahd) – tribe of the eastern steppe; Togochi's clan

Mongke Bulag (mohng-kay boo-lahg) – Manduul Khan's capital in the Orkhon Valley

Oirat (oee-rot) – collective of four major western tribes who oppose Borjigin rule; commonly called "Four Oirat"

Ongud (ahn-goot) – tribe of the southern steppe; Mandukhai's birth tribe

Orkhon Valley (ohrk-hohn) – lush river valley of the Mongole steppe

Turfan (tur-fahn) – city in the former Chagatai khanate

Urainkhai (oo-ree-ahng-high) – southern tribe of the steppe

Uyghur (wee-ger) – tribe of the southwestern step; formerly Chagatai Khanate

MILITARY STRUCTURE

Arban = 10 men

Jagan = 100 men (10 arban)

Mingghan = 1000 men (10 jagan)

Tumen = 10000 men (10 mingghan)

Officer - man in command of a single jagan or arban

Commander - officer in charge of a single mingghan

General - commander in charge of a tumen

Orlok - field marshal in charge of multiple tumens; military strategist

AUTHOR ACKNOWLEDGMENTS

The Fractured Empire Saga has been years in the making. I first discovered the amazing true story of Mandukhai back in 2012 when I had to write a research paper on a historical figure. Her story fell into my lap, and I knew she was one of the most underappreciated women in history. I took years digging up research and forming a story that I feel represents the tale in an honest and engaging way.

I owe a massive thank you to my professor from that history class, Kyle Fingerson, for assigning the paper that led me to Mandukhai. None of this would have happened had it not been for you. I also want to thank Lori Lindeman Sciame, the advisor who read the paper and called the tale "epic," stating it "read like a movie." Your reaction to Mandukhai's story has stuck with me all these years and encourages me even now to continue writing it.

To Jack Weatherford, I owe you my deepest gratitude as well. Your research inspired me. The information you shared with me and the music dedicated to Mandukhai's life is a fantastic inspiration to keep me going even after you could no longer help me with the project. The early support you gave me truly motivated me when I hit a massive bump in the road. Your encouragement kept me going when I was beyond frustrated.

To the SPWG—Dennis, Mike I, Mike P, Gail, Jennifer, Danielle, and Kyle. Your enthusiasm for this book and constructive advice helped transform the early draft into something much more poignant and epic. I couldn't have given this book the justice it deserved without all of you.

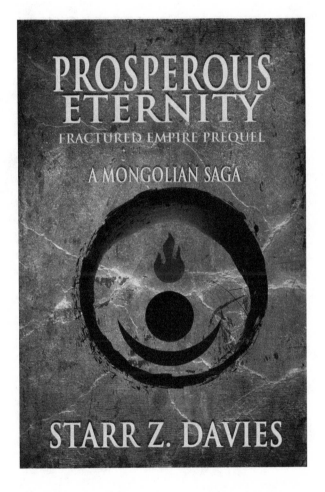

IN A NATION TORN APART BY POWERFUL
MEN, ONE WOMAN RISES.

LORDS OF THE BLACK BANNER

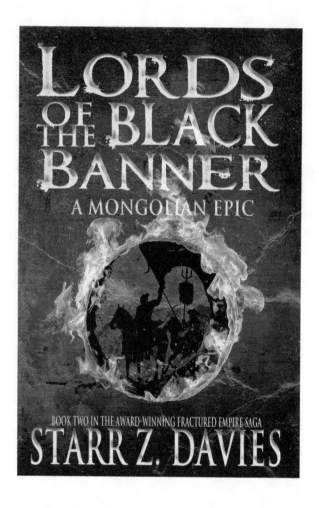

Read the full Fractured Empire Saga

About the Author

STARR Z. DAVIES is a Midwesterner at heart. While pursuing a degree at the University of Wisconsin, Starr gained a reputation as the "Character Assassin" because she had a habit of utterly destroying her characters emotionally and physically – a habit she steadfastly maintains. During her undergraduate work, Starr uncovered the true story of the powerful Mongolian queen Mandukhai. From that moment, she knew one day the tale would need to be told.

Follow Starr on Social Media:
Facebook: @SZDavies
Twitter: @SZDavies
Instagram: S.Z.Davies

Sign up for her newsletter on Starr's website.
www.StarrZDavies.com

MORE FROM STARR Z. DAVIES:

Stones: A Steampunk Mystery

Powers Series:
Superior (Powers Prequel)
Ordinary (Powers Book 1)
Unique (Powers Book 2)
(extra)Ordinary (Powers Book 3)

Fractured Empire Saga:
Daughter of the Yellow Dragon (Book 1)
Lords of the Black Banner (Book 2)
Mother of the Blue Wolf (Book 3)
Empress of the Jade Realm (Book 4)

CPSIA information can be obtained
at www.ICGtesting.com
Printed in the USA
BVHW082006030921
615989BV00007B/185